THE

GUARDIAN ANGEL

OLIVER   WENDELL   HOLMES

LITERATURE HOUSE / GREGG PRESS
Upper Saddle River, N. J.

Republished in 1970 by
LITERATURE HOUSE
an imprint of The Gregg Press
121 Pleasant Avenue
Upper Saddle River, N. J. 07458

Standard Book Number—8398-0787-2
Library of Congress Card—70-104486

Printed in United States of America

OLIVER WENDELL HOLMES

Holmes opened an office as general practitioner in Cambridge in 1836, and although he was evidently an extremely good doctor, he was not successful—perhaps because of his reputation as a literary man and a wit. He turned more and more to the academic side of medicine, and began to write papers on a variety of subjects. Some of them were collected and published in book form: *Boylston Prize Dissertations, Homeopathy and its Kindred Delusions,* and *Medical Essays* were the most important. Holmes worked for three years in the Massachusetts General Hospital, one of the finest in the country, and for two years was Professor of Anatomy at Dartmouth. He became an expert on fevers, and during the forties, his controversial papers on this subject were as famous in medical circles as his poems were among the literary public. In 1847 he was appointed Parkman Professor of Anatomy at the Harvard Medical School, and eventually became Dean of that Institution. He was extremely popular with his students, and seasoned his lectures with witty asides and pathetic anecdotes. It is said that his classes were scheduled late in the day because he was the only professor who could keep his students awake at that time. Holmes took an aesthetic joy in the structures of the vertebrates which he studied, and the intricacies of the human organism were his special delight. One of his best poems, "The Living Temple," is a paean to the wonders he saw there.

He was equally fascinated by the human nervous system, a phenomenon which was only beginning to be investigated by science. He speaks with awe of the experiments of Galvani, who discovered animal electricity. In a naive, deterministic way, Holmes attempts to formulate a theory of personality based on scientific cause and effect; a mechanistic theory which shows how close he always was to the Calvinism which he hated so.

Holmes wrote three "psychiatric" novels, the first of which appeared more than thirty years before Freud's *Studien über Hysterie, Elsie Venner,* according to C. P. Oberndorf, Professor of Psychiatry at Columbia, is a brilliant study of a schizophrenic girl. *The Guardian Angel* is a literary presentation of a case of multiple personality, and *A Mortal Antipathy* portrays a young man suffering from a severe phobia. Professor Oberndorf's conclusions probably represent one of the rare instances in which a man in his profession has been justified in labeling fiction with categories of this sort, for these books are closer to essays or case histories than they are to literary art.

Though they lack imaginative power, Holmes's are nevertheless landmarks in American literature, for they show the breakdown of the Puritan ethic, and the first hesitant steps toward a civilized attitude concerning sexual and nervous disturbances.

Upper Saddle River, N. J.
December, 1969

F. C. S.

THE

GUARDIAN ANGEL

BY

OLIVER WENDELL HOLMES

TWENTY-FOURTH EDITION

BOSTON AND NEW YORK
HOUGHTON, MIFFLIN AND COMPANY
The Riverside Press, Cambridge
1888

To

JAMES T. FIELDS,

A TOKEN OF KIND REGARD

FROM ONE OF MANY WRITERS

WHO HAVE FOUND HIM

A WISE, FAITHFUL, AND GENEROUS

FRIEND.

TO MY READERS.

"A NEW PREFACE" is, I find, promised
with my story. If there are any among
my readers who loved Æsop's Fables chiefly on
account of the *Moral* appended, they will perhaps
be pleased to turn backward and learn what I
have to say here.

This tale forms a natural sequence to a former
one, which some may remember, entitled "Elsie
Verner." Like that, it is intended for two classes
of readers, of which the smaller one includes the
readers of the "Morals" in Æsop and of this
Preface.

The first of the two stories based itself upon an
experiment which some thought cruel, even on paper. It imagined an alien element introduced into
the blood of a human being before that being saw
the light. It showed a human nature developing
itself in conflict with the ophidian characteristics
and instincts impressed upon it during the pre-natal
period. Whether anything like this ever happened,

or was possible, mattered little : it enabled me, at any rate, to suggest the limitations of human responsibility in a simple and effective way.

The story which follows comes more nearly within the range of common experience. The successive development of inherited bodily aspects and habitudes is well known to all who have lived long enough to see families grow up under their own eyes. The same thing happens, but less obviously to common observation, in the mental and moral nature. There is something frightful in the way in which not only characteristic qualities, but particular manifestations of them, are repeated from generation to generation. Jonathan Edwards the younger tells the story of a brutal wretch in New Haven who was abusing his father, when the old man cried out, "Don't drag me any further, for I did n't drag my father beyond this tree."[1] I have attempted to show the successive evolution of some inherited qualities in the character of Myrtle Hazard, not so obtrusively as to disturb the narrative, but plainly enough to be kept in sight by the small class of preface-readers.

If I called these two stories Studies of the Reflex

[1] The original version of this often-repeated story may be found in Aristotle's Ethics, Book 7th, Chapter 7th.

Function in its higher sphere, I should frighten away all but the professors and the learned ladies. If I should proclaim that they were protests against the scholastic tendency to shift the total responsibility of all human action from the Infinite to the finite, I might alarm the jealousy of the cabinet-keepers of our doctrinal museums. By saying nothing about it, the large majority of those whom my book reaches, not being preface-readers, will never suspect anything to harm them beyond the simple facts of the narrative.

Should any professional alarmist choose to confound the doctrine of limited responsibility with that which denies the existence of any self-determining power, he may be presumed to belong to the class of intellectual half-breeds, of which we have many representatives in our new country, wearing the garb of civilization, and even the gown of scholarship. If we cannot follow the automatic machinery of nature into the mental and moral world, where it plays its part as much as in the bodily functions, without being accused of laying "all that we are evil in to a divine thrusting on," we had better return at once to our old demonology, and reinstate the Leader of the Lower House in his time-honored prerogatives.

As fiction sometimes *seems* stranger than truth, a few words may be needed here to make some of my characters and statements appear probable. The long-pending question involving a property which had become in the mean time of immense value finds its parallel in the great De Haro land-case, decided in the Supreme Court while this story was in progress (May 14th, 1867). The experiment of breaking the child's will by imprisonment and fasting is borrowed from a famous incident, happening long before the case lately before one of the courts of a neighboring Commonwealth, where a little girl was beaten to death because she would not say her prayers. The mental state involving utter confusion of different generations in a person yet capable of forming a correct judgment on other matters, is almost a direct transcript from nature. I should not have ventured to repeat the questions of the daughters of the millionnaires to Myrtle Hazard about her family conditions, and their comments, had not a lady of fortune and position mentioned to me a similar circumstance in the school history of one of her own children. Perhaps I should have hesitated in reproducing Myrtle Hazard's " Vision," but for a singular experience

of his own related to me by the late Mr. Forceythe
Willson.

Gifted Hopkins (under various aliases) has been
a frequent correspondent of mine. I have also
received a good many communications, signed with
various names, which must have been from near
female relatives of that young gentleman. I once
sent a kind of encyclical letter to the whole family connection; but as the delusion under which
they labor is still common, and often leads to the
wasting of time, the contempt of honest study or
humble labor, and the misapplication of intelligence
not so far below mediocrity as to be incapable of
affording a respectable return when employed in
the proper direction, I thought this picture from
life might also be of service. When I say that
no genuine young poet will apply it to himself,
I think I have so far removed the sting that few
or none will complain of being wounded.

It is lamentable to be forced to add that the
Reverend Joseph Bellamy Stoker is only a softened
copy of too many originals to whom, as a regular
attendant upon divine worship from my childhood
to the present time, I have respectfully listened
while they dealt with me and mine and the bulk

of their fellow-creatures after the manner of their sect. If, in the interval between his first showing himself in my story and its publication in a separate volume, anything had occurred to make me question the justice or expediency of drawing and exhibiting such a portrait, I should have reconsidered it, with the view of retouching its sharper features. But its essential truthfulness has been illustrated every month or two, since my story has been in the course of publication, by a fresh example from real life, stamped in darker colors than any with which I should have thought of staining my pages.

There are a great many good clergymen to one bad one, but a writer finds it hard to keep to the true proportion of good and bad persons in telling a story. The three or four good ministers I have introduced in this narrative must stand for many whom I have known and loved, and some of whom I count to-day among my most valued friends. I hope the best and wisest of them will like this story and approve it. If they cannot all do this, I know they will recognize it as having been written with a right and nonest purpose

CONTENTS.

———◆———

THE GUARDIAN ANGEL.

CHAPTER I.

AN ADVERTISEMENT.

ON Saturday, the 18th day of June, 1859, the "State Banner and Delphian Oracle," published weekly at Oxbow Village, one of the principal centres in a thriving river-town of New England, contained an advertisement which involved the story of a young life, and startled the emotions of a small community. Such faces of dismay, such shaking of heads, such gatherings at corners, such halts of complaining, rheumatic wagons, and dried-up, chirruping chaises, for colloquy of their still-faced tenants, had not been known since the rainy November Friday, when old Malachi Withers was found hanging in his garret up there at the lonely house behind the poplars.

The number of the "Banner and Oracle" which contained this advertisement was a fair specimen enough of the kind of newspaper to which it belonged. Some extracts from a stray copy of the issue of the date referred to will show the reader what kind of entertainment the paper was accustomed to furnish its patrons, and also serve some incidental purposes of the writer in bringing into notice a few personages who are to figure in this narrative.

The copy in question was addressed to one of its regular

subscribers, — " B. Gridley, Esq." The sarcastic annota-
tions at various points, enclosed in brackets *and italicised*
that they may be distinguished from any other comments,
were taken from the pencilled remarks of that gentleman,
intended for the improvement of a member of the family
in which he resided, and are by no means to be attributed
to the harmless pen which reproduces them.

Byles Gridley, A. M., as he would have been styled by
persons acquainted with scholarly dignities, was a bachelor,
who had been a schoolmaster, a college tutor, and afterwards for many years professor, — a man of learning, of
habits, of whims and crotchets, such as are hardly to be
found, except in old, unmarried students, — the double
flowers of college culture, their stamina all turned to petals,
their stock in the life of the race all funded in the individual. Being a man of letters, Byles Gridley naturally rather
undervalued the literary acquirements of the good people
of the rural district where he resided, and, having known
much of college and something of city life, was apt to
smile at the importance they attached to their little local
concerns. He was, of course, quite as much an object of
rough satire to the natural observers and humorists, who
are never wanting in a New England village, — perhaps
not in any village where a score or two of families are
brought together, — enough of them, at any rate, to furnish the ordinary characters of a real-life stock company.

The old Master of Arts was a permanent boarder in the
house of a very worthy woman, relict of the late Ammi
Hopkins, by courtesy Esquire, whose handsome monument
— in a finished and carefully colored lithograph, repre-
senting a finely shaped urn under a very nicely groomed

willow — hung in her small, well-darkened, and, as it were, monumental parlor. Her household consisted of herself, her son, nineteen years of age, of whom more hereafter, and of two small children, twins, left upon her doorstep when little more than mere marsupial possibilities, taken in for the night, kept for a week, and always thereafter cherished by the good soul as her own; also of Miss Susan Posey, aged eighteen, at school at the "Academy" in another part of the same town, a distant relative, boarding with her.

What the old scholar took the village paper for it would be hard to guess, unless for a reason like that which carried him very regularly to hear the preaching of the Rev. Joseph Bellamy Stoker, colleague of the old minister of the village parish; namely, because he did not believe a word of his favorite doctrines, and liked to go there so as to growl to himself through the sermon, and go home scolding all the way about it.

The leading article of the "Banner and Oracle" for June 18th must have been of superior excellence, for as Mr. Gridley remarked, several of the "metropolitan" journals of the date of June 15th and thereabout had evidently conversed with the writer and borrowed some of his ideas before he gave them to the public. The Foreign News by the Europa at Halifax, 15th, was spread out in the amplest dimensions the type of the office could supply. More battles! The Allies victorious! The King and General Cialdini beat the Austrians at Palestro! 400 Austrians drowned in a canal! Anti-French feeling in Germany! Allgermine Zeiturg talks of conquest of Allsatia and Loraine and the occupation of Paris! [Vicious digs with a pencil through the above proper names.] Race for the

Derby won by Sir Joseph Hawley's Musjid! [*That's what England cares for! Hooray for the Darby! Italy be deedeed!*] Visit of Prince Alfred to the Holy Land. Letter from our own Correspondent. [*Oh! Oh! A West Minkville?*] Cotton advanced. Breadstuffs declining. — Deacon Rumrill's barn burned down on Saturday night. A pig missing; supposed to have "fallen a prey to the devouring element." [*Got roasted.*] A yellow mineral had been discovered on the Doolittle farm, which, by the report of those who had seen it, bore a strong resemblance to California gold ore. Much excitement in the neighborhood in consequence. [*Idiots! Iron pyrites!*] A hen at Four Corners had just laid an egg measuring 7 by 8 inches. Fetch on your biddies! [*Editorial wit!*] A man had shot an eagle measuring six feet and a half from tip to tip of his wings. — Crops suffering for want of rain. [*Always just so. "Dry times, Father Noah!"*] The editors had received a liberal portion of cake from the happy couple whose matrimonial union was recorded in the column dedicated to Hymen. Also a superior article of [*article of! bah!*] steel pen from the enterprising merchant [*shopkeeper*] whose advertisement was to be found on the third page of this paper. — An interesting Surprise Party [*cheap theatricals*] had transpired [*bah!*] on Thursday evening last at the house of the Rev. Mr. Stoker. The parishioners had donated [*donated!* GIVE *is a good word enough for the Lord's Prayer.* DONATE *our daily bread!*] a bag of meal, a bushel of beans, a keg of pickles, and a quintal of salt-fish. The worthy pastor was much affected, etc., etc. [*Of course. Call 'em* SENSATION *parties and done with it!*] The Rev. Dr. Pemberton and the venerable Dr. Hurlbut honored the occasion with their presence

— We learn that the Rev. Ambrose Eveleth, rector of St. Bartholomew's Chapel, has returned from his journey, and will officiate to-morrow.

Then came strings of advertisements, with a luxuriant vegetation of capitals and notes of admiration. More of those PRIME GOODS! Full Assortments of every Article in our line! [*Except the one thing you want!*] Auction Sale. Old furniture, feather-beds, bed-spreads [*spreads! ugh!*], setts [*setts!*] crockery-ware, odd vols., ullage bbls. of this and that, with other household goods, etc., etc., etc., — the etceteras meaning all sorts of insane movables, such as come out of their bedlam-holes when an antiquated domestic establishment disintegrates itself at a country "vandoo." — Several announcements of "Feed," whatever that may be, — not restaurant dinners, anyhow, — also of "Shorts," — terms mysterious to city ears as *jute* and *cudbear* and *gunnybags* to such as drive oxen in the remote interior districts. — Then the marriage column above alluded to, by the fortunate recipients of the cake. — Right opposite, as if for matrimonial ground-bait, a Notice that Whereas my wife, Lucretia Babb, has left my bed and board, I will not be responsible, etc., etc., from this date. — Jacob Penhallow (of the late firm Wibird and Penhallow) had taken Mr. William Murray Bradshaw into partnership, and the business of the office would be carried on as usual under the title Penhallow and Bradshaw, Attorneys at Law. — Then came the standing professional card of Dr. Lemuel Hurlbut and Dr. Fordyce Hurlbut, the medical patriarch of the town and his son. Following this, hideous quack advertisements, some of them with the certificates of Honorables, Esquires, and Clergymen — Then a cow, strayed or stolen from the subscriber. — Then the advertisement referred to in our first paragraph : —

MYRTLE HAZARD has been missing from her home in this place since Thursday morning, June 16th. She is fifteen years old, tall and womanly for her age, has dark hair and eyes, fresh complexion, regular features, pleasant smile and voice, but shy with strangers. Her common dress was a black and white gingham check, straw hat, trimmed with green ribbon. It is feared she may have come to harm in some way, or be wandering at large in a state of temporary mental alienation. Any information relating to the missing child will be gratefully received and properly rewarded by her afflicted aunt,

MISS SILENCE WITHERS,
Residing at the Withers Homestead, otherwise known as " The Poplars," in this village je 18 i s It

CHAPTER II.

GREAT EXCITEMENT.

THE publication of the advertisement in the paper brought the village fever of the last two days to its height. Myrtle Hazard's disappearance had been pretty well talked round through the immediate neighborhood, but now that forty-eight hours of search and inquiry had not found her, and the alarm was so great that the young girl's friends were willing to advertise her in a public journal, it was clear that the gravest apprehensions were felt and justified. The paper carried the tidings to many who had not heard it. Some of the farmers who had been busy all the week with their fields came into the village in their wagons on Saturday, and there first learned the news, and saw the paper, and the placards which were posted up, and listened, open-mouthed, to the whole story.

Saturday was therefore a day of much agitation in Oxbow Village, and some stir in the neighboring settlements. Of course there was a great variety of comment, its character depending very much on the sense, knowledge, and disposition of the citizens, gossips, and young people who alked over the painful and mysterious occurrence.

The Withers Homestead was naturally the chief centre of interest. Nurse Byloe, an ancient and voluminous woman, who had known the girl when she was a little bright-eyed child, handed over "the baby" she was holding to another attendant, and got on her things to go straight up to The Poplars. She had been holding "the baby" these forty years and more, but somehow it never got to be more than a month or six weeks old. She reached The Poplars after much toil and travail. Mistress Fagan, Irish, house-servant, opened the door, at which Nurse Byloe knocked softly, as she was in the habit of doing at the doors of those who sent for her.

"Have you heerd anything yet, Kitty Fagan?" asked Nurse Byloe.

"Niver a blissed word," said she. "Miss Withers is up stairs with Miss Bathsheby, a cryin' and a lam-entin'. Miss Badlam's in the parlor. The men has been draggin' the pond. They have n't found not one thing, but only jest two, and that was the old coffee-pot and the gray cat, — it's them nigger boys hanged her with a string they tied round her neck and then drownded her." [P. Fagan, Jr Æt. 14, had a snarl of similar string in his pocket.]

Mistress Fagan opened the door of the best parlor. A woman was sitting there alone, rocking back and forward, and fanning herself with the blackest of black fans.

"Nuss Byloe, i. that you? Well, to be sure, I'm glad to see you, though we're all in trouble. Set right down, Nuss, do. O, its dreadful times!"

A handkerchief which was in readiness for any emotional overflow was here called on for its function.

Nurse Byloe let herself drop into a flaccid squab chair with one of those soft cushions, filled with slippery feath-ers, which feel so fearfully like a very young infant, or a nest of little kittens, as they flatten under the subsiding person.

The woman in the rocking-chair was Miss Cynthia Bad lam, second-cousin of Miss Silence Withers, with whom she had been living as a companion at intervals for some years

She appeared to be thirty-five years old, more or less, and looked not badly for that stage of youth, though of course she might have been handsomer at twenty, as is often the case with women. She wore a not unbecoming cap; frequent headaches had thinned her locks somewhat of late years. Features a little too sharp, a keen, gray eye, a quick and restless glance, which rather avoided being met, gave the impression that she was a wide-awake, cautious, suspicious, and, very possibly, crafty person.

"I could n't help comin'," said Nurse Byloe, "we do so love our babies, — how can we help it, Miss Badlam?"

The spinster colored up at the nurse's odd way of using the possessive pronoun, and dropped her eyes, as was natural on hearing such a speech.

"I never tended children as you have, Nuss," she said. "But I 've known Myrtle Hazard ever since she was three years old, and to think she should have come to such an end, — 'The heart is deceitful above all things and desperately wicked,' " — and she wept.

"Why, Cynthy Badlam, what *do* y' mean?" said Nurse Byloe. "Y' don't think anything dreadful has come o' that child's wild nater, do ye?"

"Child!" said Cynthia Badlam, — "child enough to wear this very gown I have got on and not find it too big for her neither." [It would have pinched Myrtle here and there pretty shrewdly.]

The two women looked each other in the eyes with subtle interchange of intelligence, such as belongs to their sex in virtue of its specialty. Talk without words is half their conversation, just as it is all the conversation of the lower animals. Only the dull senses of men are dead to it as to the music of the spheres.

1 *

Their minds travelled along, as if they had been yoked together, through whole fields of suggestive speculation, until the dumb growths of thought ripened in both their souls into articulate speech, — consentingly, as the movement comes after the long stillness of a Quaker meeting.

Their lips opened at the same moment. "You don't mean" — began Nurse Byloe, but stopped as she heard Miss Badlam also speaking.

"They need n't drag the pond," she said. "They need n't go beating the woods as if they were hunting a patridge, — though for that matter Myrtle Hazard was always more like a patridge than she was like a pullet. Nothing ever took hold of that girl, — not catechising, nor advising, nor punishing. It 's that dreadful will of hers never was broke. I 've always been afraid that she would turn out a child of wrath. Did y' ever watch her at meetin' playing with posies and looking round all the time of the long prayer? That 's what I 've seen her do many and many a time. I 'm afraid — O dear! Miss Byloe, I 'm afraid to say what I 'm afraid of. Men are so wicked, and young girls are full of deceit and so ready to listen to all sorts of artful creturs that take advantage of their ignorance and tender years." She wept once more, this time with sobs that seemed irrepressible.

"Dear suz!" said the nurse, "I won't believe no sech thing as wickedness about Myrtle Hazard. You mean she 's gone an' run off with some good-for-nothin' man or other? If that ain't what y' mean, what do y' mean? It can't be so, Miss Badlam: she 's one o' my babies. At any rate, I handled her when she fust come to this village, — and none o' my babies never did sech a thing. Fifteen year old, and be bringin' a whole family into disgrace

If she was thirty year old, or five-an'-thirty or more, and never 'd had a chance to be married, and if one o' them artful creturs you was talkin' of got hold of her, — then, to be sure, — why, —— dear me! — law! I nevei thought, Miss Badlam! — but then of course you could have had your pickin' and choosin' in the time of it; and I don't mean to say it's too late now if you felt called that way, for you 're better lookin' now than some that 's younger, and there 's no accountin' for tastes."

A sort of hysteric twitching that went through the frame of Cynthia Badlam dimly suggested to the old nurse that she was not making her slightly indiscreet personality much better by her explanations. She stopped short, and surveyed the not uncomely person of the maiden lady sitting before her with her handkerchief pressed to her eyes, and one hand clenching the arm of the rocking-chair, as if some spasm had clamped it there. The nurse looked at her with a certain growing interest she had never felt before. It was the first time for some years that she had had such a chance, partly because Miss Cynthia had often been away for long periods, — partly because she herself had been busy professionally. There was no occasion for her services, of course, in the family at The Poplars; and she was always following round from place to place after that everlasting migratory six-weeks or less old baby.

There was not a more knowing pair of eyes, in their way, in a circle of fifty miles, than those kindly tranquil orbs that Nurse Byloe fixed on Cynthia Badlam. The silver threads in the side fold of hair, the delicate lines at the corner of the eye, the slight drawing down at the angle of the mouth, — almost imperceptible, but the nurse dwelt upon it, — a certain moulding of the features as of

an artist's clay model worked by delicate touches with the
fingers, showing that time or pain or grief had had a hand
in shaping them, the contours, the adjustment of every fold
of the dress, the attitude, the very way of breathing, were
all passed through the searching inspection of the ancient
expert, trained to know all the changes wrought by time
and circumstance. It took not so long as it takes to describe it, but it was an analysis of imponderables, equal to
any of Bunsen's with the spectroscope.

Miss Badlam removed her handkerchief and looked in
a furtive, questioning way, in her turn, upon the nurse.

"It's dreadful close here,—I'm 'most smothered,"
Nurse Byloe said; and, putting her hand to her throat,
unclasped the catch of the necklace of gold beads she had
worn since she was a baby,—a bead having been added
from time to time as she thickened. It lay in a deep
groove of her large neck, and had not troubled her in
breathing before, since the day when her husband was run
over by an ox-team.

At this moment Miss Silence Withers entered, followed
by Bathsheba Stoker, daughter of Rev. Joseph Bellamy
Stoker.

She was the friend of Myrtle, and had come to comfort
Miss Silence, and consult with her as to what further
search they should institute. The two, Myrtle's aunt and
her friend, were as unlike as they could well be. Silence
Withers was something more than forty years old, a
shadowy, pinched, sallow, dispirited, bloodless woman,
with the habitual look of the people in the funeral carriage which follows next to the hearse, and the tone in
speaking that may be noticed in a household where one of its
members is lying white and still in a cool, darkened cham

ber overhead. Bathsheba Stoker was not called hand-some; but she had her mother's youthful smile, which was as fresh and full of sweetness that she seemed like a beau-ty while she was speaking or listening; and she could never be plain so long as any expression gave life to her features. In perfect repose, her face, a little prematurely touched by sad experiences, — for she was but seventeen years old, — had the character and decision stamped in its outlines which any young man who wanted a companion to warn, to comfort, and command him, might have de-pended on as warranting the courage, the sympathy, and the sense demanded for such a responsibility. She had been trying her powers of consolation on Miss Silence. It was a sudden freak of Myrtle's. She had gone off on some foolish but innocent excursion. Besides, she was a girl that would take care of herself; for she was afraid of nothing, and nimbler than any boy of her age, and almost as strong as any. As for thinking any bad thoughts about her, that was a shame; she cared for none of the young fellows that were round her. Cyprian Eveleth was the one she thought most of; but Cyprian was as true as his sister Olive, — and who else was there?

To all this Miss Silence answered only by sighing and moaning. For two whole days she had been kept in constant fear and worry, afraid every minute of some tragical message, perplexed by the conflicting advice of all manner of officious friends, sleepless of course through the two nights, and now utterly broken down and col-lapsed.

Bathsheba had said all she could in the way of consola-tion, and hastened back to her mother's bedside, which she hardly left, except for the briefest of visits.

"It's a great trial, Miss Withers, that's laid on you," said Nurse Byloe.

"If I only knew that she was dead, and had died in the Lord," Miss Silence answered, — "if I only knew that; but if she is living in sin, or dead in wrong-doing, what is to become of me? — O, what is to become of me when 'He maketh inquisition for blood'?"

"Cousin Silence," said Miss Cynthia, "it isn't your fault, if that young girl has taken to evil ways. If going to meeting three times every Sabbath day, and knowing the catechism by heart, and reading of good books, and the best of daily advice, and all needful discipline, could have corrected her sinful nature, she would never have run away from a home where she enjoyed all these privileges. It's that Indian blood, Cousin Silence. It's a great mercy you and I have n't got any of it in our veins! What can you expect of children that come from heathens and savages? You can't lay it to yourself, Cousin Silence, if Myrtle Hazard goes wrong — "

"The Lord will lay it to me, — the Lord will lay it to me," she moaned. "Did n't he say to Cain, 'Where is Abel, thy brother?'"

Nurse Byloe was getting very red in the face. She had had about enough of this talk between the two women. "I hope the Lord 'll take care of Myrtle Hazard fust, if she's in trouble, 'n' wants help," she said; "'n' *then* look out for them that comes next. Y' 're too suspicious, Miss Badlam; y' 're too easy to believe stories. Myrtle Hazard was as pretty a child and as good a child as ever I see, if you did n't rile her; 'n' d'd y' ever see one o' them hearty lively children, that had n't a sperrit of its own? For my part, I 'd rather handle one of 'em than a dozen o' them

.ittle waxy, weak-eyed, slim-necked creturs that always do what they tell 'em to, and die afore they're a dozen year old; and never was the time when I've seen Myrtle Hazard, sence she was my baby, but what it's always been, 'Good mornin', Miss Byloe,' and 'How do you do, Miss Byloe? I'm so glad to see you.' The handsomest young woman, too, as all the old folks will agree in tellin' you, sence the time o' Judith Pride that was, — the Pride of the County they used to call her, for her beauty. Her great-grandma, y' know, Miss Cynthy, married old King David Withers. What I want to know is, whether anything has been heerd, and jest what's been done about findin' the poor thing. How d' ye know she has n't fell into the river? Have they fired cannon? They say that busts the gall of drownded folks, and makes the corpse rise. Have they looked in the woods everywhere? Don't believe no wrong of nobody, not till y' *must*, — least of all of them that come o' the same folks, partly, and has lived with ye all their days. I tell y', Myrtle Hazard's jest as innocent of all what y' 've been thinkin' about, — bless the poor child; she 's got a soul that 's as clean and sweet — well, as a pond-lily when it fust opens of a mornin', without a speck on it no more than on the fust pond-lily God Almighty ever made!"

That gave a turn to the two women's thoughts, and their handkerchiefs went up to their faces. Nurse Byloe turned her eyes quickly on Cynthia Badlam, and repeated her close inspection of every outline and every light and shadow in her figure. She did not announce any opinion as to the age or good looks or general aspect or special points of Miss Cynthia; but she made a sound which the books write *humph!* but which real folks make with closed lips, thus: *m' !* — a sort of half-suppressed labio-palato-nasal utterance, implying that there is a good deal which might be said, and all the vocal organs want to have a chance a it, if there is to be any talking.

Friends and neighbors were coming in and out; and the next person that came was the old minister, of whom, an of his colleague, the Rev. Joseph Bellamy Stoker, some account may here be introduced.

The Rev. Eliphalet Pemberton — Father Pemberton as brother ministers called him, Priest Pemberton as he was commonly styled by the country people — would have seemed very old, if the medical patriarch of the village had not been so much older. A man over ninety is a great comfort to all his elderly neighbors: he is a picket-guard at the extreme outpost; and the young folks of sixty and seventy feel that the enemy must get by him before he can come near their camp. Dr. Hurlbut, at ninety-two, made Priest Pemberton seem comparatively little advanced; but the college catalogue showed that he must be seventy-five years old, if, as we may suppose, he was twenty at the time of his graduation.

He was a man of noble presence always, and now, in the grandeur of his flowing silver hair and with the gray shaggy brows overhanging his serene and solemn eyes, with the slow gravity of motion and the measured dignity of speech which gave him the air of an old pontiff, he was an imposing personage to look upon, and could be awful, if the occasion demanded it. His creed was of the sternest: he was looked up to as a bulwark against all the laxities which threatened New England theology. But it was a creed rather of the study and of the pulpit than of every-day application among his neighbors. He dealt too much m the lofty abstractions which had always such fascinations for the higher class of New England divines, to busy himself as much as he might have done with the spiritual condition of individuals. He had also a good deal in him of what he used to call the Old Man, which, as he confessed, he had never succeeded in putting off, — meaning thereby certain qualities belonging to humanity, as much as the natural gifts of the dumb creatures belong to them, and tending to make a man beloved by his weak and erring fellow-mortals.

In the olden time he would have lived and died king of his parish, monarch, by Divine right, as the noblest, grandest, wisest of all that made up the little nation within hearing of his meeting-house bell. But Young Calvinism has less reverence and more love of novelty than its forefathers. It wants change, and it loves young blood. Polyandry is getting to be the normal condition of the Church; and about the time a man is becoming a little over-ripe for the livelier human sentiments, he may be pretty sure the women are looking round to find him a colleague. In this way it was that the Rev. Joseph Bellamy Stoker became the colleague of the Rev. Eliphalet Pemberton.

If one could have dived deep below all the Christian graces — the charity, the sweetness of disposition, the humility — of Father Pemberton, he would have found a small remnant of the " Old Man," as the good clergyman would have called it, which was never in harmony with the Rev. Mr. Stoker. The younger divine felt his importance, and made his venerable colleague feel that he felt it. Father Pemberton had a fair chance at rainy Sundays and hot summer-afternoon services; but the junior pushed him aside without ceremony whenever he thought there was like to be a good show in the pews. As for those courtesies which the old need, to soften the sense of declining faculties and failing attractions, the younger pastor bestowed them in public, but was negligent of them, to say the least, when not on exhibition.

Good old Father Pemberton could not love this man but he would not hate him, and he never complained to him or of him. It would have been of no use if he had: the women of the parish had taken up the Rev. Mr. Stoker; and when the women run after a minister or a doctor, what do the men signify?

Why the women ran after him, some thought it was not hard to guess. He was not ill-looking, according to the village standard, parted his hair smoothly, tied his white cravat carefully, was fluent, plausible, had a gift in prayer, was considered eloquent, was fond of listening to their spiritual experiences, and had a sickly wife. This is what Byles Gridley said; but he was apt to be caustic at times.

Father Pemberton visited his people but rarely. Like Jonathan Edwards, like David Osgood, he felt his call to be to study-work, and was impatient of the egotisms and spiritual megrims, in listening to which, especially from the younger females of his flock, his colleague had won the hearts of so many of his parishioners. His presence had a wonderful effect in restoring the despondent Miss Silence to her equanimity; for not all the hard divinity he had preached for half a century had spoiled his kindly nature; and not the gentle Melanchthon himself, ready to welcome death as a refuge from the rage and bitterness of theologians, was more in contrast with the disputants with whom he mingled, than the old minister, in the hour of trial, with the stern dogmatist in his study, forging thunderbolts to smite down sinners.

It was well that there were no tithingmen about on that next day, Sunday; for it shone no Sabbath day for the young men within half a dozen miles of the village. They were out on Bear Hill the whole day, beating up the bushes as if for game, scaring old crows out of their ragged nests, and in one dark glen startling a fierce-eyed, growling, bob-tailed catamount, who sat spitting and looking all ready to spring at them, on the tall tree where he clung with his claws unsheathed, until a young fellow came up with a gun and shot him dead. They went through and through the swamp at Musquash Hollow; but found nothing better than a wicked old snapping-turtle, evil to behold, with his snaky head and alligator tail, but worse to meddle with, if his horny jaws were near enough to spring their man-trap on the curious experimenter. At Wood-End there were some Indians, ill-conditioned savages in a dirty tent, making baskets, the miracle of which was that they were so clean. They had seen a young lady answering the description, about a week ago. She had bought a basket. — Asked them if they had a canoe they wanted to sell. — Eyes like hers (pointing to a squaw with a man's hat on).

At Pocasset the young men explored all the thick woods, — some who ought to have known better taking their guns, which made a talk, as one might well suppose it would. Hunting on a Sabbath day! They did n't mean to *shoot* Myrtle Hazard, did they? it was keenly asked. A good many said it was all nonsense, and a mere excuse to get away from meeting and have a sort of frolic on pretence that it was a work of necessity and mercy, one or both.

While they were scattering themselves about in this way, some in earnest, some rejoicing in the unwonted license, lifting off for a little while that enormous Sabbath-day pressure which weighs like forty atmospheres on every true-born Puritan, two young men had been since Friday in search of the lost girl, each following a clew of his own, and determined to find her if she was among the living.

Cyprian Eveleth made for the village of Mapleton, where his sister Olive was staying, trusting that, with her aid, he might get a clew to the mystery of Myrtle's disappearance.

William Murray Bradshaw struck for a railroad train going to the great seaport, at a station where it stops for wood and water.

In the mean time, a third young man, Gifted Hopkins by name, son of the good woman already mentioned, sat down, with tears in his eyes, and wrote those touching stanzas, "The Lost Myrtle," which were printed in the next "Banner and Oracle," and much admired by many who read them.

CHAPTER III.

ANTECEDENTS.

THE Withers Homestead was the oldest mansion in town. It was built on the east bank of the river, a little above the curve which gave the name to Oxbow Village. It stood on an elevation, its west gable close to the river's edge, an old orchard and a small pond at the foot of the slope behind it, woods at the east, open to the south, with a great row of Lombardy poplars standing guard in front of the house. The Hon. Selah Withers, Esq., a descendant of one of the first colonists, built it for his own residence, in the early part of the last century. Deeply impressed with his importance in the order of things, he had chosen to place it a little removed from the cluster of smaller dwellings about the Oxbow; and with some vague fancy in his mind of the castles that overlook the Rhine and the Danube, he had selected this eminence on which to place his substantial gambrel-roofed dwelling-house. Long afterwards a bay-window, almost a little room of itself, had been thrown out of the second story on the west side, so that it looked directly down on the river running beneath it. The chamber, thus half suspended in the air, had been for years the special apartment of Myrtle Hazard; and as the boys paddling about on the river would often catch glimpses, through the window, of the little girl dressed in the scarlet jacket she fancied in those days, one of them, Cyprian Eveleth had given it a name which became current among the young people, and indeed furnished to Gifted Hopkins the subject of one of his earliest poems, to wit, " The Fire-hang-bird's Nest."

If we would know anything about the persons now living at the Withers Homestead, or The Poplars, as it was more commonly called of late years, we must take a brief inventory of some of their vital antecedents. It is by no means certain that our individual personality is the single inhabitant of these our corporeal frames. Nay, there is recorded an experience of one of the living persons mentioned in this narrative, — to be given in full in its proper place, — which, so far as it is received in evidence, tends to show that some, at least, who have long been dead, may enjoy a kind of secondary and imperfect, yet self-conscious life, in these bodily tenements which we are in the habit of considering exclusively our own. There are many circumstances, familiar to common observers, which favor this belief to a certain extent. Thus, at one moment we detect the look, at another the tone of voice, at another some characteristic movement of this or that ancestor, in our relations or others. There are times when our friends do not act like themselves, but apparently in obedience to some other law than that of their own proper nature. We all do things both awake and asleep which surprise us. Perhaps we have cotenants in this house we live in. No less than eight distinct personalities are said to have coexisted in a single female mentioned by an ancient physician of unimpeachable authority. In this light we may perhaps see the meaning of a sentence, from a work which will be repeatedly referred to in this narrative, viz.: " *This body in which we journey across the isthmus between the two oceans is not a private carriage, but an omnibus.*"

The ancestry of the Withers family had counted a mar

tyr to their faith before they were known as Puritans. The record was obscure in some points; but the portrait, marked "Ann Holyoake, burned by yᵉ bloudy Papists, año 15 .." (figures illegible), was still hanging against the panel over the fireplace in the west parlor at The Poplars. The following words were yet legible on the canvas:—

"Thov hast made a couenant O Lord with mee and my children forever."

The story had come down, that Ann Holyoake spoke these words in a prayer she offered up at the stake, after the fagots were kindled. There had always been a secret feeling in the family, that none of her descendants could finally fall from grace, in virtue of this solemn "covenant."

There had been also a legend in the family, that the martyred woman's spirit exercised a kind of supervision over her descendants; that she either manifested herself to them, or in some way impressed them, from time to time; as in the case of the first pilgrim before he cast his lot with the emigrants, — of one Mrs. Winslow, a descendant in the third generation, when the Indians were about to attack the settlement where she lived, — and of another, just before he was killed at Quebec.

There was a remarkable resemblance between the features of Ann Holyoake, as shown in the portrait, and the miniature likeness of Myrtle's mother. Myrtle adopted the nearly obsolete superstition more readily on this account, and loved to cherish the fancy that the guardian spirit which had watched over her ancestors was often near her, and would be with her in her time of need.

The wife of Selah Withers was accused of sorcery in the evil days of that delusion. A careless expression in one of her letters, that "yᵉ Parson was as lyke to bee in league with yᵉ Divell as anie of em," had got abroad, and given great offence to godly people. There was no doubt that some odd "manifestations," as they would be called now-a-days, had taken place in the household when she was a girl, and that she presented many of the conditions belonging to what are at the present day called mediums.

Major Gideon Withers, her son, was of the very common type of hearty, loud, portly men, who like to show themselves at militia trainings, and to hear themselves shout orders at musters, or declaim patriotic sentiments at town-meetings and in the General Court. He loved to wear a crimson sash and a military cap with a large red feather, in which the village folk used to say he looked as "hahnsome as a piny," — meaning a favorite flower of his, which is better spelt peony, and to which it was not unnatural that his admirers should compare him.

If he had married a wife like himself, there might probably enough have sprung from the alliance a family of moon-faced children, who would have dropped into their places like posts into their holes, asking no questions of life, contented, like so many other honest folks, with the part of supernumeraries in the drama of being, their wardrobe of flesh and bones being furnished them *gratis*, and nothing to do but to walk across the stage wearing it. But Major Gideon Withers, for some reason or other, married a slender, sensitive, nervous, romantic woman, which accounted for the fact that his son David, "King David," as he was called in his time, had a very different set of tastes from his father, showing a turn for literature and sentiment in his youth, reading Young's "Night Thoughts," and Thomson's "Seasons," and sometimes in those early days writing verses himself to Celia or to Chloe, which sounded just as fine to him as Effie and Minnie sound to young people now, as Musidora, as Saccharissa, as Lesbia, as Helena, as Adah and Zillah, have all sounded to young people in their time, — ashes of roses as they are to us now, and as our endearing Scotch diminutives will be to others by and by.

King David Withers, who got his royal prefix partly because he was rich, and partly because he wrote hymns occasionally, when he grew too old to write love-poems, married the famous beauty before mentioned, Miss Judith Pride, and the race came up again in vigor. Their son, Jeremy, took for his first wife a delicate, melancholic girl, who matured into a sad-eyed woman, and bore him two children, Malachi and Silence, both of whom inherited her temperament. When she died, he mourned for her bitterly almost a year, and then put on a ruffled shirt and went across the river to tell his grief to Miss Virginia Wild, there residing. This lady was said to have a few drops of genuine aboriginal blood in her veins; and it is certain that her cheek had a little of the russet tinge which a Seckel pear shows on its warmest cheek when it blushes. — Love shuts itself up in sympathy like a knife-blade in its handle, and opens as easily. — All the rest followed in due order according to Nature's kindly programme.

Captain Charles Hazard, of the ship Orient Pearl, fell desperately in love with their daughter Candace, married her, and carried her with him to India, where their first and only child was born, and received the name of Myrtle, as fitting her cradle in the tropics. So her earliest impressions, — it would not be exact to call them recollections, — besides the smiles of her father and mother, were of dusky faces, of loose white raiment, of waving fans, of

2

breezes perfumed with the sweet exhalations of sandal-
wood, of gorgeous flowers and glowing fruit, of shady veran-
das, of gliding palanquins, and all the languid luxury of
the South. The pestilence which has its natural home in
India, but has journeyed so far from its birthplace in these
later years, took her father and mother away, suddenly, in
the very freshness of their early maturity. A relation of
Myrtle's father, wife of another captain, was returning to
America on a visit, and the child was sent back, under her
care, while still a mere infant, to her relatives at the old
homestead. During the long voyage, the strange mystery
of the ocean was wrought into her consciousness so deeply,
that it seemed to belong to her being. The waves rocked
her, as if the sea had been her mother; and, looking over
the vessel's side from the arms that held her with tender
care, she used to watch the play of the waters, until the
rhythm of their movement became a part of her, almost
as much as her own pulse and breath.

The instincts and qualities belonging to the ancestral
traits which predominated in the conflict of mingled lives
lay in this child in embryo, waiting to come to maturity.
It was as when several grafts, bearing fruit that ripens at
different times, are growing upon the same stock. Her
earlier impulses may have been derived directly from her
father and mother, but all the ancestors who have been
mentioned, and more or less obscurely many others, came
uppermost in their time, before the absolute and total result
of their several forces had found its equilibrium in the
character by which she was to be known as an individual.
These inherited impulses were therefore many, conflicting,
ome of them dangerous. The World, the Flesh, and the
Devil held mortgages on her life before its deed was pu ·

in her hands; but sweet and gracious influences were also born with her; and the battle of life was to be fought between them, God helping her in her need, and her own free choice siding with one or the other. The formal statement of this succession of ripening characteristics need not be repeated, but the fact must be borne in mind.

This was the child who was delivered into the hands of Miss Silence Withers, her aunt on the father's side, keeping house with her brother Malachi, a bachelor, already called Old Malachi, though hardly entitled by his years to such a venerable prefix. Both these persons had inherited the predominant traits of their sad-eyed mother. Malachi, the chief heir of the family property, was rich, but felt very poor. He owned this fine old estate of some hundreds of acres. He had moneys in the bank, shares in various companies, wood-lots in the town, and a large tract of Western land, the subject of a lawsuit which seemed as if it would never be settled, and kept him always uneasy.

Some said he hoarded gold somewhere about the old house, but nobody knew this for a certainty. In spite of his abundant means, he talked much of poverty, and kept the household on the narrowest footing of economy. One Irishwoman, with a little aid from her husband now and then, did all their work; and the only company they saw was Miss Cynthia Badlam, who, as a relative, claimed a home with them whenever she was so disposed.

The "little Indian," as Malachi called her, was an awkward accession to the family. Silence Withers knew no more about children and their ways and wants than if she had been a female ostrich. Thus it was that she found it necessary to send for a woman well known in the place as the first friend whose acquaintance many of the little people of the town had made in this vale of tears.

Thirty years of practice had taught Nurse Byloe the art of handling the young of her species with the soft firmness which one may notice in cats with their kittens, — more grandly in a tawny lioness mouthing her cubs. Myrtle did not know she was held; she only felt she was lifted, and borne up, as a cherub may feel upon a white-woolly cloud, and smiled accordingly at the nurse, as if quite at home in her arms.

"As fine a child as ever breathed the breath of life. But where did them black eyes come from? Born in Injy, — that's it, ain't it? No, it's her poor mother's eyes to be sure. Does n't it seem as if there was a kind of Injin look to 'em? She 'll be a lively one to manage, if I know anything about childun. See her clinchin' them little fists!"

This was when Miss Silence came near her and brought her rather severe countenance close to the child for inspection of its features. The ungracious aspect of the woman and the defiant attitude of the child prefigured in one brief instant the history of many long coming years.

It was not a great while before the two parties in that wearing conflict of alien lives, which is often called education, began to measure their strength against each other. The child was bright, observing, of restless activity, inquisitively curious, very hard to frighten, and with a will which seemed made for mastery, not submission.

The stern spinster to whose care this vigorous life was committed was disposed to discharge her duty to the girl faithfully and conscientiously; but there were two points in her character and belief which had a most important bearing on the manner in which she carried out her laudable intentions. First, she was one of that class of human beings whose one single engrossing thought is their own welfare, — in the next world, it is true, but still their own personal welfare. The Roman Church recognizes this class, and provides every form of specific to meet their spiritual condition. But in so far as Protestantism has thrown out works as a means of insuring future safety, these unfortunates are as badly off as nervous patients who have no drops, pills, potions, no doctors' rules, to follow. Only tell a poor creature what to *do*, and he or she will do it, and be made easy, were it a pilgrimage of a thousand miles, with shoes full of split peas instead of boiled ones; but if once assured that *doing* does no good, the drooping Littlefaiths are left at leisure to worry about their souls, as the other class of weaklings worry about their bodies. The effect on character does not seem to be very different in the two classes. Metaphysicians may discuss the nature of selfishness at their leisure ; if to have all her thoughts centring on the one point of her own well-being by and by was selfishness, then Silence Withers was supremely selfish ; and if we are offended with that form of egotism, it is no more than ten of the twelve Apostles were, as the reader may see by turning to the Gospel of St. Matthew, the twentieth chapter and the twenty-fourth verse.

The next practical difficulty was, that she attempted to carry out a theory which, whatever might be its success in other cases, did not work kindly in the case of Myrtle Hazard, but, on the contrary, developed a mighty spirit of antagonism in her nature, which threatened to end in utter lawlessness. Miss Silence started from the approved doctrine, that all children are radically and utterly wrong in all their motives, feelings, thoughts, and deeds, so long as they remain subject to their natural instincts. It was by the eradication, and not the education, of these instincts, that the character of the human being she was moulding was to be determined. The first great preliminary process, so soon as the child manifested any evidence of intelligent and persistent self-determination, was *to break her will*.

There is no doubt that this was a legitimate conclusion from the teaching of Priest Pemberton, but it required a colder and harder nature than his own to carry out many of his dogmas to their practical application. He wrought in the pure mathematics, so to speak, of theology, and left the working rules to the good sense and good feeling of his people.

Miss Silence had been waiting for her opportunity to apply the great doctrine, and it came at last in a very trivial way.

" Myrtle does n't want brown bread. Myrtle won't have brown bread. Myrtle will have white bread."

" Myrtle is a wicked child. She will have what Aunt Silence says she shall have. She won't have anything but brown bread."

Thereupon the bright red lip protruded, the hot blood mounted to her face, the child untied her little " tire," got down from the table, took up her one forlorn, featureless doll, and went to bed without her supper. The next morning the worthy woman thought that hunger and reflection would have subdued the rebellious spirit. So there stood yesterday's untouched supper waiting for her breakfast. She would not taste it, and it became necessary to enforce that extreme penalty of the law which had been threatened, but never yet put in execution. Miss Silence, in obedience to what she felt to be a painful duty, without any

passion, but filled with high, inexorable purpose, carried
the child up to the garret, and, fastening her so that she
could not wander about and hurt herself, left her to her
repentant thoughts, awaiting the moment when a plaintive
entreaty for liberty and food should announce that the evil
nature had yielded and the obdurate will was broken.

The garret was an awful place. All the skeleton-like
ribs of the roof showed in the dim light, naked overhead,
and the only floor to be trusted consisted of the few boards
which bridged the lath and plaster. A great, mysterious
brick tower climbed up through it, — it was the chimney,
but it looked like a horrible cell to put criminals into.
The whole place was festooned with cobwebs, — not light
films, such as the housewife's broom sweeps away before
they have become a permanent residence, but vast gray
draperies, loaded with dust, sprinkled with yellow powder
from the beams where the worms were gnawing day and
night, the home of old, hairy spiders who had lived there
since they were eggs and would leave it for unborn spiders who would grow old and huge like themselves in it,
long after the human tenants had left the mansion for a
narrower home. Here this little criminal was imprisoned,
six, twelve, — tell it not to mothers, — eighteen dreadful
hours, hungry until she was ready to gnaw her hands, a
prey to all childish imaginations ; and here at her stern
guardian's last visit she sat, pallid, chilled, almost fainting,
but sullen and unsubdued. The Irishwoman, poor stupid
Kitty Fagan, who had no theory of human nature, saw her
over the lean shoulders of the spinster, and, forgetting all
differences of condition and questions of authority, rushed
to her with a cry of maternal tenderness, and, with a tempest of passionate tears and kisses bore her off to her own

humble realm, where the little victorious martyr was fed from her best stores, until there was as much danger from repletion as there had been from famine. How the experiment might have ended but for this empirical and most unphilosophical interference, there is no saying; but it settled the point that the rebellious nature was not to be subjugated in a brief conflict.

The untamed disposition manifested itself in greater enormities as she grew older. At the age of four years she was detected in making a cat's-cradle at meeting, during sermon-time, and, on being reprimanded for so doing, laughed out loud, so as to be heard by Father Pemberton, who thereupon bent his threatening, shaggy brows upon the child, and, to his shame be it spoken, had such a sudden uprising of weak, foolish, grandfatherly feelings, that a mist came over his eyes, and he left out his "ninthly" altogether, thereby spoiling the logical sequence of propositions which had kept his large forehead knotty for a week.

At eight years old she fell in love with the high-colored picture of Major Gideon Withers in the red sash and the red feather of his exalted military office. It was then for the first time that her Aunt Silence remarked a shade of resemblance between the child and the portrait. She had always, up to this time, been dressed in sad colors, as was fitting, doubtless, for a forlorn orphan; but happening one day to see a small negro girl peacocking round in a flaming scarlet petticoat, she struck for bright colors in her own apparel, and carried her point at last. It was as if a ground-sparrow had changed her gray feathers for the burning plumage of some tropical wanderer; and it was natural enough that Cyprian Eveleth should have called her he fire-hang-bird, and her little chamber the fire-hang bird's nest, — using the country boy's synonyme for the Baltimore oriole.

At ten years old she had one of those great experiences which give new meaning to the life of a child.

Her Uncle Malachi had seemed to have a strong liking for her at one time, but of late years his delusions had gained upon him, and under their influence he seemed to regard her as an encumbrance and an extravagance. He was growing more and more solitary in his habits, more and more negligent of his appearance. He was up late at night, wandering about the house from the cellar to the garret, so that, his light being seen flitting from window to window, the story got about that the old house was haunted.

One dreary, rainy Friday in November, Myrtle was left alone in the house. Her uncle had been gone since the day before. The two women were both away at the village. At such times the child took a strange delight in exploring all the hiding-places of the old mansion. She had the mysterious dwelling-place of so many of the dead and the living all to herself. What a fearful kind of pleasure in its silence and loneliness! The old clock that Marmaduke Storr made in London more than a hundred years ago was clicking the steady pulse-beats of its second century. The featured moon on its dial had lifted one eye, as if to watch the child, as it had watched so many generations of children, while the swinging pendulum ticked them along into youth, maturity, gray hairs, death-beds, — ticking through the prayer at the funeral, — ticking without grief through all the still or noisy woe of mourning, — ticking without joy when the smiles and gayety of comforted heirs had come back again. She looked at herself

2 *   c

in the tall, bevelled mirror in the best chamber. She
pulled aside the curtains of the stately bedstead whereon
the heads of the house had slept until they died and were
stretched out upon it, and the sheet shaped itself to them
in vague, awful breadth of outline, like a block of monumental marble the sculptor leaves just hinted by the chisel.

She groped her way up to the dim garret, the scene of
her memorable punishment. A rusty hook projected from
one of the joists a little higher than a man's head. Something was hanging from it, — an old garment, was it? She
went bravely up and touched — a cold hand. She did what
most children of that age would do, — uttered a cry and
ran down stairs with all her might. She rushed out of the
door and called to the man Patrick, who was doing some
work about the place. What could be done was done, but
it was too late.

Uncle Malachi had made away with himself. That was
plain on the face of things. In due time the coroner's verdict settled it. It was not so strange as it seemed; but it
made a great talk in the village and all the country round
about. Everybody knew he had money enough, and yet
he had hanged himself for fear of starving to death.

For all that, he was found to have left a will, dated some
years before, leaving his property to his sister Silence, with
the exception of a certain moderate legacy to be paid in
money to Myrtle Hazard when she should arrive at the
age of twenty years.

The household seemed more chilly than ever after this
tragical event. Its depressing influence followed the child
to school, where she learned the common branches of knowledge. It followed her to the Sabbath-day catechisings,
where she repeated the answers about the federal headship

of Adam, and her consequent personal responsibilities, and other technicalities which are hardly milk for babes, perhaps as well as other children, but without any very profound remorse for what she could not help, so far as she understood the matter, any more than her sex or stature, and with no very clear comprehension of the phrases which the New England followers of the Westminster divines made a part of the elementary instruction of young people.

At twelve years old she had grown tall and womanly enough to attract the eyes of the youth and older boys, several of whom made advances towards her acquaintance. But the dreary discipline of the household had sunk into her soul, and she had been shaping an internal life for herself which it was hard for friendship to penetrate. Bathsheba Stoker was chained to the bedside of an invalid mother. Olive Eveleth, a kind, true-hearted girl, belonged to another religious communion; and this tended to render their meetings less frequent, though Olive was still her nearest friend. Cyprian was himself a little shy, and rather held to Myrtle through his sister than by any true intimacy directly with herself. Of the other young men of the village Gifted Hopkins was perhaps the most fervent of her admirers, as he had repeatedly shown by effusions in verse, of which, under the thinnest of disguises, she was the object.

Murray Bradshaw, ten years older than herself, a young man of striking aspect and claims to exceptional ability, had kept his eye on her of late; but it was generally supposed that he would find a wife in the city, where he was in the habit of going to visit a fashionable relative, Mrs. Clymer Ketchum, of 24 Carat Place. *She*, at any rate, understood very well that he meant, to use his own phrase, " to go in for a corner lot," — understanding thereby a young lady with possessions and without encumbrances. If the old man had only given his money to Myrtle, Murray Bradshaw would have made sure of her; but she was not likely ever to get much of it. Miss Silence Withers, it was understood, would probably leave her money as the Rev. Mr. Stoker, her spiritual director, should indicate, and it seemed likely that most of it would go to a rising educational institution where certain given doctrines were to be taught through all time, whether disproved or not, and whether those who taught them believed them or not, provided only they would say they believed them.

Nobody had promised to say masses for her soul if she made this disposition of her property, or pledged the word of the Church that she should have plenary absolution. But she felt that she would be making friends in Influential Quarters by thus laying up her treasure, and that she would be safe if she had the good-will of the ministers of her sect.

Myrtle Hazard had nearly reached the age of fourteen and, though not like to inherit much of the family property was fast growing into a large dower of hereditary beauty. Always handsome, her features shaped themselves in a finer symmetry, her color grew richer, her figure promised a perfect womanly development, and her movements had the grace which high-breeding gives the daughter of a queen, and which Nature now and then teaches the humblest of village maidens. She could not long escape the notice of the lovers and flatterers of beauty, and the time of danger was drawing near.

At this period of her life she made two discoveries which changed the whole course of her thoughts, and opened for her a new world of ideas and possibilities.

Ever since the dreadful event of November, 1854, the garret had been a fearful place to think of, and still more to visit. The stories that the house was haunted gained in frequency of repetition and detail of circumstance. But Myrtle was bold and inquisitive, and explored its recesses at such times as she could creep among them undisturbed. Hid away close under the eaves she found an old trunk covered with dust and cobwebs. The mice had gnawed through its leather hinges, and, as it had been hastily stuffed full, the cover had risen, and two or three volumes had fallen to the floor. This trunk held the papers and books which her great-grandmother, the famous beauty, had left behind her, records of the romantic days when she was the belle of the county, — story-books, memoirs, novels, and poems, and not a few love-letters, — a strange collection, which, as so often happens with such deposits in old families, nobody had cared to meddle with, and nobody had been willing to destroy, until at last they had passed out of mind, and waited for a new generation to bring them into light again.

The other discovery was of a small hoard of coin. Under one of the boards which formed the imperfect flooring of the garret was hidden an old leather mitten. Instead of a hand, it had a fat fist of silver dollars, and a thumb of gold half-eagles.

Thus knowledge and power found their way to the simple and secluded maiden. The books were hers to read as much as any other's; the gold and silver were only a part of that small provision which would be hers by and by, and if she borrowed it, it was borrowing of herself. The tree of the knowledge of good and evil had shaken its fruit into her lap, and, without any serpent to tempt her, she took thereof and did eat.

CHAPTER IV.

BYLES GRIDLEY, A. M.

THE old Master of Arts was as notable a man in his outside presentment as one will find among five hundred college alumni as they file in procession. His strong, squared features, his formidable scowl, his solid-looking head, his iron-gray hair, his positive and as it were categorical stride, his slow, precise way of putting a statement, the strange union of trampling radicalism in some directions and high-stepping conservatism in others, which made it impossible to calculate on his unexpressed opinions, his testy ways and his generous impulses, his hard judgments and kindly actions, were characteristics that gave him a very decided individuality.

He had all the aspects of a man of books. His study, which was the best room in Mrs. Hopkins's house, was filled with a miscellaneous-looking collection of volumes, which his curious literary taste had got together from the shelves of all the libraries that had been broken up during his long life as a scholar. Classics, theology, especially of the controversial sort, statistics, politics, law, medicine, science, occult and overt, general literature, — almost every branch of knowledge was represented. His learning was very various, and of course mixed up, useful and useless, new and ancient, dogmatic and rational, — like his library, in short; for a library gathered like his is a looking-glass in which the owner's mind is reflected.

The common people about the village did not know

what to make of such a phenomenon. He did not preach, marry, christen, or bury, like the ministers, nor jog around with medicines for sick folks, nor carry cases into court for quarrelsome neighbors. What *was* he good for? Not a great deal, some of the wiseacres thought, — had " all sorts of sense but common sense,"—"smart mahn, but not prahc-tical." There were others who read him more shrewdly. He knowed more, they said, than all the ministers put to-gether, and if he 'd stan' for Ripresentative they 'd like to vote for him, — they hed n't hed a smart mahn in the Gin-eral Court sence Squire Wibird was thar.

They may have overdone the matter in comparing his knowledge with that of all the ministers together, for Priest Pemberton was a real scholar in his special line of study, — as all D. D.s are supposed to be, or they would not have been honored with that distinguished title. But Mr. Byles Gridley not only had more learning than the deep-sea line of the bucolic intelligence could fathom; he had more wis-dom also than they gave him credit for, even those among them who thought most of his abilities.

In his capacity of schoolmaster he had sharpened his wits against those of the lively city boys he had in charge, and made such a reputation as " Master" Gridley, that he kept that title even after he had become a college tutor and professor. As a tutor he had to deal with many of these same boys, and others like them, in the still more vivacious period of their early college life. He got rid of his police duties when he became a professor, but he still studied the pupils as carefully as he used once to watch them and learned to read character with a skill which might have fitted him for governing men instead of adolescents. But he loved quiet and he dreaded mingling with the brawlers of the market-place, whose stock in trade is a voice and a vocabulary. So it was that he had passed his life in the patient mechanical labor of instruction, leaving too many of his instincts and faculties in abeyance.

The alluvium of all this experience bore a nearer resemblance to worldly wisdom than might have been conjectured much nearer, indeed, than it does in many old instructors, whose eyes get fish-like as their blood grows cold, and who are not fit to be trusted with anything more practical than a gerund or a cosine. Master Gridley not only knew a good deal of human nature, but he knew how to keep his knowledge to himself upon occasion. He understood singularly well the ways and tendencies of young people. He was shrewd in the detection of trickery, and very confident in those who had once passed the ordeal of his well-schooled observing powers. He had no particular tendency to meddle with the personal relations of those about him; but if they were forced upon him in any way, he was like to see into them at least as quickly as any of his neighbors who thought themselves most endowed with practical skill.

In leaving the duties of his office he considered himself, as he said a little despondently, like an old horse unharnessed and turned out to pasture. He felt that he had separated himself from human interests, and was henceforth to live in his books with the dead, until he should be numbered with them himself. He had chosen this quiet village as a place where he might pass his days undisturbed, and find a peaceful resting-place in its churchyard, where the gravel was dry, and the sun lay warm, and the glowing woods of autumn would spread their many-colored counterpane over the bed where he would be taking his rest. It som-

times came over him painfully that he was never more to
be of any importance to his fellow-creatures. There was
nobody living to whom he was connected by any very near
ties. He felt kindly enough to the good woman in whose
house he lived; he sometimes gave a few words of counsel
to her son; he was not unamiable with the few people he
met; he bowed with great consideration to the Rev. Dr.
Pemberton; and he studied with no small interest the
physiognomy of the Rev. Joseph Bellamy Stoker, to whose
sermons he listened, with a black scowl now and then, and
a nostril dilating with ominous intensity of meaning. But
he said sadly to himself, that his life had been a failure, —
that he had nothing to show for it, and his one talent was
ready in its napkin to give back to his Lord.

He owed something of this sadness, perhaps, to a cause
which many would hold of small significance. Though he
had mourned for no lost love, at least so far as was known,
though he had never suffered the pang of parting with a
child, though he seemed isolated from those joys and griefs
which come with the ties of family, he too had his private
urn filled with the ashes of extinguished hopes. He was
the father of a dead book.

Why "Thoughts on the Universe, by Byles Gridley,
A. M.," had not met with an eager welcome and a permanent demand from the discriminating public, it would take
is too long to inquire in detail. Indeed, he himself was
never able to account satisfactorily for the state of things
which his bookseller's account made evident to him. He
had read and re-read his work; and the more familiar ne
became with it, the less was he able to understand the
singular want of popular appreciation of what he could
not help recognizing as its excellences. He had a special

copy of his work, printed on large paper and sumptuously
bound. He loved to read in this, as people read over the
letters of friends who have long been dead; and it might
have awakened a feeling of something far removed from
the ludicrous, if his comments on his own production could
have been heard. "That's a thought, now, for you!—
See Mr. Thomas Babington Macaulay's Essay *printed six
years after this book*." "A felicitous image!—and so
everybody would have said if only Mr. Thomas Carlyle
had hit upon it." "If this is not genuine pathos, where
will you find it, I should like to know? And nobody to
open the book where it stands written but one poor old
man—in this generation, at least—in this generation!"
It may be doubted whether he would ever have loved his
book with such jealous fondness if it had gone through a
dozen editions, and everybody was quoting it to his face.
But now it lived only for him; and to him it was wife and
child, parent, friend, all in one, as Hector was all in all to
his spouse. He never tired of it, and in his more sanguine moods he looked forward to the time when the world
would acknowledge its merits, and his genius would find
full recognition. Perhaps he was right: more than one
book which seemed dead and was dead for contemporary
readers has had a resurrection when the rivals who tri-
umphed over it lived only in the tombstone memory of an-
tiquaries. Comfort for some of us, dear fellow-writer!

It followed from the way in which he lived that he must
have some means of support upon which he could depend.
He was economical, if not over frugal in some of his habits; but he bought books, and took newspapers and re-
views, and had money when money was needed; the fac'
being, though it was not generally known, that a distar

relative had not long before died, leaving him a very comfortable property.

His money matters had led him to have occasional dealings with the late legal firm of Wibird and Penhallow, which had naturally passed into the hands of the new partnership, Penhallow and Bradshaw. He had entire confidence in the senior partner, but not so much in the young man who had been recently associated in the business.

Mr. William Murray Bradshaw, commonly called by his last two names, was the son of a lawyer of some note for his acuteness, who marked out his calling for him in having him named after the great Lord Mansfield. Murray Bradshaw was about twenty-five years old, by common consent good-looking, with a finely formed head, a searching eye, and a sharp-cut mouth, which smiled at his bidding without the slightest reference to the real condition of his feeling at the moment. This was a great convenience; for it gave him an appearance of good-nature at the small expense of a slight muscular movement which was as easy as winking, and deceived everybody but those who had studied him long and carefully enough to find that this play of his features was what a watchmaker would call a detached movement.

He had been a good scholar in college, not so much by hard study as by skilful veneering, and had taken great pains to stand well with the Faculty, at least one of whom, Byles Gridley, A. M., had watched him with no little interest as a man with a promising future, provided he were not so astute as to outwit and overreach himself in his excess of contrivance. His classmates could not help liking him; as to loving him, none of them would have thought

of that. He was so shrewd, so keen, so full of practical
sense, and so good-humored as long as things went on to
his liking, that few could resist his fascination. He had a
way of talking with people about what they were interested in, as if it were the one matter in the world nearest to
his heart. But he was commonly trying to find out something, or to produce some impression, as a juggler is working at his miracle while he keeps people's attention by his
voluble discourse and make-believe movements. In his
lightest talk he was almost always edging towards a practical object, and it was an interesting and instructive
amusement to watch for the moment at which he would
ship the belt of his colloquial machinery on to the tight
pulley. It was done so easily and naturally that there
was hardly a sign of it. Master Gridley could usually
detect the shifting action, but the young man's features
and voice never betrayed him.

He was a favorite with the other sex, who love poetry
and romance, as he well knew, for which reason he often
used the phrases of both, and in such a way as to answer
his purpose with most of those whom he wished to please.
He had one great advantage in the sweepstakes of life:
he was not handicapped with any burdensome ideals. He
took everything at its market-value. He accepted the
standard of the street as a final fact *for to-day*, like the
broker's list of prices.

His whole plan of life was laid out. He knew that law
was the best introduction to political life, and he meant to
use it for this end. He chose to begin his career in the
country, so as to feel his way more surely and gradually to
its ultimate aim ; but he had no intention of burying his
shining talents in a grazing district, however tall its grass

might grow. His business was not with these stiff-jointed, slow-witted graziers, but with the supple, dangerous, far-seeing men who sit scheming by the gas-light in the great cities, after all the lamps and candles are out from the Merrimac to the Housatonic. Every strong and every weak point of those who might probably be his rivals were laid down on his charts, as winds and currents and rocks are marked on those of a navigator. All the young girls in the country, and not a few in the city, with which, as mentioned, he had frequent relations, were on his list of possible availabilities in the matrimonial line of speculation, provided always that their position and prospects were such as would make them proper matches for so considerable a person as the future Hon. William Murray Bradshaw.

Master Gridley had made a careful study of his old pupil since they had resided in the same village. The old professor could not help admiring him, notwithstanding certain suspicious elements in his character; for after muddy village talk, a clear stream of intelligent conversation was a great luxury to the hard-headed scholar. The more he saw of him, the more he learned to watch his movements, and to be on his guard in talking with him. The old man could be crafty, with all his simplicity, and he had found out that under his good-natured manner here often lurked some design more or less worth noting, and which might involve other interests deserving pro-ection.

For some reason or other the old Master of Arts had of late experienced a certain degree of relenting with regard to himself, probably brought about by the expressions of gratitude from worthy Mrs. Hopkins for acts of kind-ness to which he himself attached no great value. He

had been kind to her son Gifted ; he had been fatherly
with Susan Posey, her relative and boarder ; and he had
shown himself singularly and unexpectedly amiable with
the little twins who had been adopted by the good woman
into her household. In fact, ever since these little creatures had begun to toddle about and explode their first
consonants, he had looked through his great round spectacles upon them with a decided interest ; and from that
time it seemed as if some of the human and social sentiments which had never leafed or flowered in him, for want
of their natural sunshine, had begun growing up from
roots which had never lost their life. His liking for the
twins may have been an illustration of that singular law
which old Dr. Hurlbut used to lay down, namely, that at
a certain period of life, say from fifty to sixty and upward, the *grand*-paternal instinct awakens in bachelors, the
rhythms of Nature reaching them in spite of her defeated
intentions; so that when men marry late they love their
autumn child with a twofold affection, — father's and
grandfather's both in one.

However this may be, there is no doubt that Mr. Byles
Gridley was beginning to take a part in his neighbors'
welfare and misfortunes, such as could hardly have been
expected of a man so long lost in his books and his scholastic duties. And among others, Myrtle Hazard had
come in for a share of his interest. He had met her now
and then in her walks to and from school and meeting,
and had been taken with her beauty and her apparent un-
consciousness of it, which he attributed to the forlorn kind
of household in which she had grown up. He had got so
far as to talk with her now and then, and found himself
puzzled, as well he might be, in talking with a girl who

had been growing into her early maturity in antagonism with every influence that surrounded her.

"Love will reach her by and by," he said, "in spite of the dragons up at the den yonder.

' Centum fronte oculos, centum cervice gerebat
Argus, et hos unus sæpe fefellit amor.' "

But there was something about Myrtle,—he hardly knew whether to call it dignity, or pride, or reserve, or the mere habit of holding back brought about by the system of repression under which she had been educated,— which kept even the old Master of Arts at his distance. Yet he was strongly drawn to her, and had a sort of presentiment that he might be able to help her some day, and that very probably she would want his help; for she was alone in the world, except for the dragons, and sure to be assailed by foes from without and from within.

He noticed that her name was apt to come up in his conversations with Murray Bradshaw; and, as he himself never introduced it, of course the young man must have forced it, as conjurers force a card, and with some special object. This set him thinking hard; and, as a result of it, he determined the next time Mr. Bradshaw brought her name up to set him talking. So he talked, not suspecting how carefully the old man listened.

"It was a demonish hard case," he said, "that old Malachi had left his money as he did. Myrtle Hazard was going to be the handsomest girl about, when she came to her beauty, and she was coming to it mighty fast. If they could only break that will,—but it was no use trying. The doctors said he was of sound mind for at least two years after making it. If Silence Withers got the land claim, there 'd be a pile, sure enough. Myrtle Hazard ought to have it. If the girl had only inherited that property — whew! She 'd have been a match for any fellow. That old Silence Withers would do just as her minister told her, — even chance whether she gives it to the Parson-factory, or marries Bellamy Stoker, and gives it to him — after his wife's dead. He 'd take it if he had to take her with it. Earn his money, — hey, Master Gridley ? "

"Why, you don't seem to think very well of the Rev. Joseph Bellamy Stoker ? " said Mr. Gridley, smiling.

"Think well of him ? Too fond of using the Devil's pitchfork for my fancy ! Forks over pretty much all the world but himself and his lot into — the bad place, you know ; and toasts his own cheese with it with very much the same kind of comfort that other folks seem to take in that business. Besides, he has a weakness for pretty saints — and sinners. That 's an odd name he has. More *belle amie* than *Joseph* about him, I rather guess ! "

The old professor smiled again. "So you don't think he believes all the mediæval doctrines he is in the habit of preaching, Mr. Bradshaw ? "

"No, sir ; I think he belongs to the class I have seen described somewhere. 'There are those who hold the opinion that truth is only safe when diluted, — about one fifth to four fifths lies, — as the oxygen of the air is with its nitrogen. Else it would burn us all up.' "

Byles Gridley colored and started a little. This was one of his own sayings in "Thoughts on the Universe." But the young man quoted it without seeming to suspect ts authorship.

"Where did you pick up that saying, Mr. Bradshaw ? "

" I don't remember. Some paper, I rather think. It 's one of those good things that get about without anybody's knowing who says 'em. Sounds like Coleridge."

" That 's what I call a compliment worth having," said Byles Gridley to himself, when he got home. " Let me look at that passage."

He took down " Thoughts on the Universe," and got so much interested, reading on page after page, that he did not hear the little tea-bell, and Susan Posey volun- teered to run up to his study and call him down to tea.

CHAPTER V.

THE TWINS.

MISS SUSAN POSEY knocked timidly at his door and informed him that tea was waiting. He rather liked Susan Posey. She was a pretty creature, slight blonde, a little too light, a village beauty of the second or third grade, effective at picnics and by moonlight,—the kind of girl that very young men are apt to remember as their first love. She had a taste for poetry, and an admiration of poets; but, what was better, she was modest and simple, and a perfect sister and mother and grandmother to the two little forlorn twins who had been stranded on the Widow Hopkins's door-step.

These little twins, a boy and girl, were now between two and three years old. A few words will make us acquainted with them. Nothing had ever been known of their origin. The sharp eyes of all the spinsters had been through every household in the village and neighborhood, and not a suspicion fixed itself on any one. It was a dark night when they were left; and it was probable that they had been brought from another town, as the sound of wheels had been heard close to the door where they were found, had stopped for a moment, then been heard again, and lost in the distance.

How the good woman of the house took them in and kept them has been briefly mentioned. At first nobody thought they would live a day, such little absurd attempts at humanity did they seem. But the young doctor came and the old doctor came, and the infants were laid in cotton-wool, and the room heated up to keep them warm, and baby-teaspoonfuls of milk given them, and after being kept alive in this way, like the young of opossums and kangaroos, they came to a conclusion about which they did not seem to have made up their thinking-pulps for some weeks, namely, to go on trying to cross the sea of life by tugging at the four-and-twenty oars which must be pulled day and night until the unknown shore is reached, and the oars lie at rest under the folded hands.

As it was not very likely that the parents who left their offspring round on door-steps were of saintly life, they were not presented for baptism like the children of church-members. Still, they must have names to be known by, and Mrs. Hopkins was much exercised in the matter. Like many New England parents, she had a decided taste for names that were significant and sonorous. That which she had chosen for her oldest child, the young poet, was either a remarkable prophecy, or it had brought with it the endowments it promised. She had lost, or, in her own more pictorial language, she had buried, a daughter to whom she had given the names, at once of cheerful omen and melodious effect, Wealthy Amadora.

As for them poor little creturs, she said, she believed they was rained down out o' the skies, jest as they say toads and tadpoles come. She meant to be a mother to 'em for all that, and give 'em jest as good names as if they was the governor's children, or the minister's. If Mr. Gridley would be so good as to find her some kind of a real handsome Chris'n name for 'em, she 'd provide 'em with the other one. Hopkinses they shall be bred and taught, and Hopkinses they shall be called. Ef their fa-

ther and mother was ashamed to own 'em, she was n't.
Could n't Mr. Gridley pick out some pooty-sounding names
from some of them great books of his. It 's jest as well to
have 'em pooty as long as they don't cost any more than if
they was Tom and Sally.

A grim smile passed over the rugged features of Byles
Gridley. "Nothing is easier than that, Mrs. Hopkins,"
he said. "I will give you two very pretty names that I
think will please you and other folks. They 're new names,
too. If they should n't like to keep them, they can change
them before they 're christened, if they ever are. *Isosceles*
will be just the name for the boy, and I 'm sure you won't
find a prettier name for the girl in a hurry than *Helminthia.*

Mrs. Hopkins was delighted with the dignity and novelty
of these two names, which were forthwith adopted. As
they were rather long for common use in the family, they
were shortened into the easier forms of Sossy and Minthy,
under which designation the babes began very soon to
thrive mightily, turning bread and milk into the substance
of little sinners at a great rate, and growing as if they were
put out at compound interest.

This short episode shows us the family conditions sur-
rounding Byles Gridley, who, as we were saying, had just
been called down to tea by Miss Susan Posey.

"I am coming, my dear," he said, — which expression
quite touched Miss Susan, who did not know that it was a
kind of transferred caress from the delicious page he was
reading. It was not the living child that was kissed, but
the dead one lying under the snow, if we may make a
trivial use of a very sweet and tender thought we all remember.

Not long after this, happening to call in at the lawyer's office, his eye was caught by the corner of a book lying covered up by a pile of papers. Somehow or other it seemed to look very natural to him. Could that be a copy of " Thoughts on the Universe " ? He watched his opportunity, and got a hurried sight of the volume. His own treatise, sure enough ! *Leaves uncut.* Opened of itself to the one hundred and twentieth page. The axiom Murray Bradshaw had quoted — he did not remember from what, — " sounded like Coleridge " — was staring him in the face from that very page. When he remembered how he had pleased himself with that compliment the other day, he blushed like a school-girl ; and then, thinking out the whole trick, — to hunt up his forgotten book, pick out a phrase or two from it, and play on his weakness with it, to win his good opinion, — for what purpose he did not know, but doubtless to use him in some way, — he grinned with a contempt about equally divided between himself and the young schemer.

" Ah ha " ! he muttered scornfully. " Sounds like Coleridge, hey ? Niccolo Macchiavelli Bradshaw ! "

From this day forward he looked on all the young lawyer's doings with even more suspicion than before. Yet he would not forego his company and conversation ; for he was very agreeable and amusing to study ; and this trick he had played him was, after all, only a diplomatist's way of flattering his brother plenipotentiary. Who could say ? Some time or other he might cajole England or France or Russia into a treaty with just such a trick. Shallower men than he had gone out as ministers of the great Republic. At any rate the fellow was worth watching.

CHAPTER VI.

THE USE OF SPECTACLES.

THE old Master of Arts had a great reputation in the house where he lived for knowing everything that was going on. He rather enjoyed it; and sometimes amused himself with surprising his simple-hearted landlady and her boarders with the unaccountable results of his sagacity. One thing was quite beyond her comprehension. She was perfectly sure that Mr. Gridley could *see out of the back of his head,* just as other people see with their natural organs. Time and again he had told her what she was doing when his back was turned to her, just as if he had been sitting squarely in front of her. Some laughed at this foolish notion; but others, who knew more of the nebulous sciences, told her it was like 's not jes' so. Folks had read letters laid ag'in' the pits o' their stomachs, 'n' why should n't they see out o' the backs o' their heads?

Now there was a certain fact at the bottom of this belief of Mrs. Hopkins; and as it would be a very small thing to make a mystery of so simple a matter, the reader shall have the whole benefit of knowing all there is in it, — not quite yet, however, of knowing all that came of it. It was not the mirror trick, of course, which Mrs. Felix Lorraine and other dangerous historical personages have so long made use of. It was nothing but this. Mr. Byles Gridley wore a pair of formidable spectacles with large round glasses. He had often noticed the reflection of objects behind him when they caught their images at certain angles, and had got the habit of very often looking at the reflecting surface of one or the other of the glasses, when he seemed to be looking through them. It put a singular power into his possession, which might possibly hereafter lead to something more significant than the mystification of the Widow Hopkins.

A short time before Myrtle Hazard's disappearance, Mr. Byles Gridley had occasion to call again at the office of Penhallow and Bradshaw on some small matter of business of his own. There were papers to look over, and he put on his great round-glassed spectacles. He and Mr. Penhallow sat down at the table, and Mr. Bradshaw was at a desk behind them. After sitting for a while, Mr. Penhallow seemed to remember something he had meant to attend to, for he said all at once: "Excuse me, Mr. Gridley. Mr. Bradshaw, if you are not busy, I wish you would look over this bundle of papers. They look like old receipted bills and memoranda of no particular use; but they came from the garret of the Withers place, and might possibly have something that would be of value. Look them over, will you, and see whether there is anything there worth saving."

The young man took the papers, and Mr. Penhallow sat down again at the table with Mr. Byles Gridley.

This last-named gentleman felt just then a strong impulse to observe the operations of Murray Bradshaw. He could not have given any very good reason for it, any more than any of us can for half of what we do.

"I should like to examine that conveyance we were speaking of once more," said he. "Please to look at this one in the mean time, will you, Mr. Penhallow?"

Master Gridley held the document up before him. He

did not seem to find it quite legible, and adjusted his spec‐
tacles carefully, until they were just as he wanted them.
When he had got them to suit himself, sitting there with
his back to Murray Bradshaw, he could see him and all
his movements, the desk at which he was standing, and
the books in the shelves before him, — all this time ap‐
pearing as if he were intent upon his own reading.

The young man began in a rather indifferent way to
look over the papers. He loosened the band round them,
and took them up one by one, gave a careless glance at
them, and laid them together to tie up again when he had
gone through them. Master Gridley saw all this process,
thinking what a fool he was all the time to be watching such a
simple proceeding. Presently he noticed a more sudden
movement : the young man had found something which
arrested his attention, and turned his head to see if he was
observed. The senior partner and his client were both
apparently deep in their own affairs. In his hand Mr.
Bradshaw held a paper folded like the others, the back of
which he read, holding it in such a way that Master Grid‐
ley saw very distinctly three large spots of ink upon it,
and noticed their position. Murray Bradshaw took an‐
other hurried glance at the two gentlemen, and then quick‐
ly opened the paper. He ran it over with a flash of his
eye, folded it again, and laid it by itself. With another
quick turn of his head, as if to see whether he were observed
or like to be, he reached his hand out and took a volume
down from the shelves. In this volume he shut the docu‐
ment, whatever it was, which he had just taken out of the
bundle, and placed the book in a very silent and as it were
stealthy way back in its place. He then gave a look at
each of the other papers, and said to his partner : " Old

bills, old leases, and insurance policies that have run out. Malachi seems to have kept every scrap of paper that had a signature to it."

"That's the way with the old misers, always," said Mr. Penhallow.

Byles Gridley had got through reading the document he held, — or pretending to read it. He took off his spectacles.

"We all grow timid and cautious as we get old, Mr. Penhallow." Then turning round to the young man, he slowly repeated the lines, —

> "' Multa senem circumveniunt incommoda, vel quod
> Quœrit et inventis miser abstinet, ac timet uti ;
> Vel quod res omnes timide, gelideque ministrat — '

You remember the passage, Mr. Bradshaw?"

While he was reciting these words from Horace, which he spoke slowly as if he relished every syllable, he kept his eyes on the young man steadily, but without betraying any suspicion. His old habits as a teacher made that easy.

Murray Bradshaw's face was calm as usual, but there was a flush on his cheek, and Master Gridley saw the slight but unequivocal signs of excitement.

"Something is going on inside there," the old man said to himself. He waited patiently, on the pretext of business, until Mr. Bradshaw got up and left the office. As soon as he and the senior partner were alone, Master Gridley took a lazy look at some of the books in his library. There stood in the book-shelves a copy of the *Corpus Juris Civilis*, — the fine Elzevir edition of 1664. It was bound in parchment, and thus readily distinguishable at a glance from all the books round it. Now Mr. Penhallow was not

3 *

much of a Latin scholar, and knew and cared very little
about the civil law. He had fallen in with this book at an
auction, and bought it to place in his shelves with the other
"properties" of the office, because it would look respectable. Anything shut up in one of those two octavos might
stay there a lifetime without Mr. Penhallow's disturbing
it; that Master Gridley knew, and of course the young
man knew it too.

We often move to the objects of supreme curiosity or
desire, not in the lines of castle or bishop on the chess-
board, but with the knight's zigzag, at first in the wrong
direction, making believe to ourselves we are not after the
thing coveted. Put a lump of sugar in a canary-bird's
cage, and the small creature will illustrate the instinct for
the benefit of inquirers or sceptics. Byles Gridley went
to the other side of the room and took a volume of Reports
from the shelves. He put it back and took a copy of
" Fearne on Contingent Remainders," and looked at that
for a moment in an idling way, as if from a sense of having
nothing to do. Then he drew the back of his forefinger
along the books on the shelf, as if nothing interested him in
them, and strolled to the shelf in front of the desk at which
Murray Bradshaw had stood. He took down the *second*
volume of the *Corpus Juris Civilis*, turned the leaves over
mechanically, as if in search of some title, and replaced it.

He looked round for a moment. Mr. Penhallow was
writing hard at his table, not thinking of him, it was plain
enough. He laid his hand on the FIRST volume of the
Corpus Juris Civilis. There was a document shut up in
it. His hand was on the book, whether taking it out or
putting it back was not evident, when the door opened and
Mr. William Murray Bradshaw entered.

"Ah, Mr. Gridley," he said, "you are not studying the civil law, are you?" He strode towards him as he spoke, his face white, his eyes fixed fiercely on him.

"It always interests me, Mr. Bradshaw," he answered, "and this is a fine edition of it. One may find a great many valuable things in the *Corpus Juris Civilis.*"

He looked impenetrable, and whether or not he had seen more than Mr. Bradshaw wished him to see, that gentleman could not tell. But there stood the two books in their place, and when, after Master Gridley had gone, he looked in the first volume, there was the document he had shut up .n it.

CHAPTER VII.

MYRTLE'S LETTER. — THE YOUNG MEN'S PURSUIT.

"YOU know all about it, Olive?" Cyprian Eveleth said to his sister, after a brief word of greeting.

"Know of what, Cyprian?"

"Why, sister, don't you know that Myrtle Hazard is missing, — gone! — gone nobody knows where, and that we are looking in all directions to find her?"

Olive turned very pale and was silent for a moment At the end of that moment the story seemed almost old to her. It was a natural ending of the prison-life which had been round Myrtle since her earliest years. When she got large and strong enough, she broke out of jail, — that was all. The nursery-bar is always climbed sooner or later, whether it is a wooden or an iron one. Olive felt as if she had dimly foreseen just such a finishing to the tragedy of the poor girl's home bringing-up. Why could not she have done something to prevent it? Well, — what shall we do now, and as it is? — that is the question.

"Has she left no letter, — no explanation of her leaving in this way?"

"Not a word, so far as anybody in the village knows."

"Come over to the post-office with me; perhaps we may find a letter. I think we shall."

Olive's sagacity and knowledge of her friend's character had not misled her. She found a letter from Myrtle to herself, which she opened and read as here follows: —

"MY DEAREST OLIVE: — Think no evil of me for what

I have done. The fire-hang-bird's nest, as Cyprian called it, is empty, and the poor bird is flown.

"I can live as I have lived no longer. This place is chilling all the life out of me, and I must find another home. It is far, far away, and you will not hear from me again until I am there. Then I will write to you.

"You know where I was born, — under a hot sun and in the midst of strange, lovely scenes that I seem still to remember. I must visit them again: my heart always yearns for them. And I must cross the sea to get there, — the beautiful great sea that I have always longed for and that my river has been whispering about to me ever so many years. My life is pinched and starved here. I feel as old as Aunt Silence, and I am only fifteen, — a child she has called me within a few days. If this is to be a child, what is it to be a woman?

"I love you dearly, — and your brother is almost to me as if he were mine. I love our sweet, patient Bathsheba, — yes, and the old man that has spoken so kindly with me, good Master Gridley; I hate to give you pain, — to leave you all, — but my way of life is killing me, and I am too young to die. I cannot take the comfort with you, my dear friends, that I would; for it seems as if I carried a lump of ice in my heart, and all the warmth I find in you cannot thaw it out.

"I have had a strange warning to leave this place, Olive. Do you remember how the angel of the Lord appeared to Joseph and told him to flee into Egypt? I have had a dream like that, Olive. There is an old belief in our family that the spirit of one who died many generations ago watches over some of her descendants. They say it led our first ancestor to come over here when

It was a wilderness. I believe it has appeared to others of the family in times of trouble. I have had a strange dream at any rate, and the one I saw, or thought I saw told me to leave this place. Perhaps I should have stayed if it had not been for that, but it seemed like an angel's warning.

"Nobody will know how I have gone, or which way I have taken. On Monday, you may show this letter to my friends, not before. I do not think they will be in danger of breaking their hearts for me at our house. Aunt Silence cares for nothing but her own soul, and the other woman hates me, I always thought. Kitty Fagan will cry hard. Tell her perhaps I shall come back by and by. There is a little box in my room, with some keepsakes marked, — one is for poor Kitty. You can give them to the right ones. Yours is with them.

"Good by, dearest. Keep my secret, as I told you, till Monday. And if you never see me again, remember how much I loved you. Never think hardly of me, for you have grown up in a happy home, and do not know how much misery can be crowded into fifteen years of a young girl's life. God be with you!

"MYRTLE HAZARD."

Olive could not restrain her tears, as she handed the letter to Cyprian. "Her secret is as safe with you as with me," she said. "But this is madness, Cyprian, and we must keep her from doing herself a wrong. What she means to do, is to get to Boston, in some way or other, and sail for India. It is strange that they have not tracked her. There is no time to be lost. She shall not go out into the world in this way, child that she is. No; she

shall come back, and make her home with us, if she cannot be happy with these people. Ours *is* a happy and a
cheerful home, and she shall be to me as a younger sister, — and your sister too, Cyprian. But you must see
her; you must leave this very hour; and you may find
her. Go to your cousin Edward, in Boston, at once; tell
him your errand, and get him to help you find our poor dear
sister. Then give her the note I will write, and say — I
know your heart, Cyprian, and I can trust that to tell you
what to say."

In a very short time Cyprian Eveleth was on his way
to Boston. But another, keener even in pursuit than he,
was there before him.

Ever since the day when Master Gridley had made that
over-curious observation of the young lawyer's proceedings
at the office, Murray Bradshaw had shown a far livelier
interest than before in the conditions and feelings of Myrtle Hazard. He had called frequently at The Poplars to
talk over business matters, which seemed of late to require a deal of talking. He had been very deferential to
Miss Silence, and had wound himself into the confidence
of Miss Badlam. He found it harder to establish any
very near relations with Myrtle, who had never seemed to
care much for any young man but Cyprian Eveleth, and
to care for him quite as much as Olive's brother as for any
personal reason. But he carefully studied Myrtle's tastes
and ways of thinking and of life, so that, by and by, when
she should look upon herself as a young woman, and not as
a girl, he would have a great advantage in making her more
intimate acquaintance.

Thus, she corresponded with a friend of her mother's in
India. She talked at times as if it were her ideal home,

and showed many tastes which might well be vestiges of early Oriental impressions. She made herself a rude hammock, — such as are often used in hot climates, — and swung it between two elms. Here she would lie in the hot summer days, and fan herself with the sandal-wood fan her friend in India had sent her, — the perfume of which, the women said, seemed to throw her into day-dreams, which were almost like trances.

These circumstances gave a general direction to his ideas, which were presently fixed more exactly by two circumstances which he learned for himself and kept to himself; for he had no idea of making a hue and cry, and yet he did not mean that Myrtle Hazard should get away if he could help it.

The first fact was this. He found among the copies of the city newspaper they took at The Poplars a recent number from which a square had been cut out. He procured another copy of this paper of the same date, and found that the piece cut out was an advertisement to the effect that the A 1 Ship Swordfish, Captain Hawkins, was to sail from Boston for Calcutta, on the 20th of June.

The second fact was the following. On the window-sill of her little hanging chamber, which the women allowed him to inspect, he found some threads of long, black, glossy hair caught by a splinter in the wood. They were Myrtle's of course. A simpleton might have constructed a tragedy out of this trivial circumstance, — how she had cast herself from the window into the waters beneath it, — how she had been thrust out after a struggle, of which this shred from her tresses was the dreadful witness, — and so on. Murray Bradshaw did not stop to guess and wonder. He said nothing about it, but wound the shining threads on his finger, and, as soon as he got home, examined them with a magnifier. They had been cut off smoothly, as with a pair of scissors. This was part of a mass of hair, then, which had been shorn and thrown from the window. Nobody would do that but she herself. What would *she* do it for? To disguise her sex of course. The other inferences were plain enough.

The wily young man put all these facts and hints together, and concluded that he would let the rustics drag the ponds and the river, and scour the woods and swamps, while he himself went to the seaport town from which she would without doubt sail if she had formed the project he thought on the whole most probable.

Thus it was that we found him hurrying to the nearest station to catch the train to Boston, while they were all looking for traces of the missing girl nearer home. In the cars he made the most suggestive inquiries he could frame, to stir up the gentlemanly conductor's memory. Had any young fellow been on the train within a day or two, who had attracted his notice? Smooth, handsome face, black eyes, short black hair, new clothes, not fitting very well, looked away when he paid his fare, had a soft voice like a woman's, — had he seen anybody answering to some such description as this? The gentlemanly conductor had not noticed, — was always taking up and setting down way-passengers, — might have had such a young man aboard, — there was two or three students one day in the car singing college songs, — he did n't care how folks looked if they had their tickets ready, — and minded their own business, — and, so saying, he poked a young man upon whose shoulder a ringleted head was reclining with that delightful *abandon* which the railroad train eems to provoke in lovely woman, — " Fare ! "

It is a fine thing to be set down in a great, over-crowded
hotel, where they do not know you, looking dusty, and for
the moment shabby, with nothing but a carpet-bag in your
hand, feeling tired, and anything but clean, and hungry,
and worried, and every way miserable and mean, and to
undergo the appraising process of the gentleman in the
office, who, while he shoves the book round to you for
your name, is making a hasty calculation as to how high
up he can venture to doom you. But Murray Bradshaw's
plain dress and carpet-bag were more than made up for by
the air and tone which imply the habit of being attended
to. The clerk saw that in a glance, and, as he looked at
the name and address in the book, spoke sharply in the
explosive dialect of his tribe, —

"Jun! ta'tha'genlm'n'scarpetbag'n'showhimupt'thirtyone!"

When Cyprian Eveleth reached the same hotel late at
night, he appeared in his best clothes and with a new
valise ; but his amiable countenance and gentle voice and
modest manner sent him up two stories higher, where he
found himself in a room not much better than a garret,
feeling lonely enough, for he did not know he had an
acquaintance in the same house. The two young men
were in and out so irregularly that it was not very strange
that they did not happen to meet each other.

The young lawyer was far more likely to find Myrtle if
she were in the city than the other, even with the help of
his cousin Edward. He was not only older, but sharper,
better acquainted with the city and its ways, and, whatever
might be the strength of Cyprian's motives, his own were
of such intensity that he thought of nothing else by day
and dreamed of nothing else by night. He went to work,
therefore, in the most systematic manner. He first visited

the ship Swordfish, lying at her wharf, saw her captain,
and satisfied himself that as yet nobody at all corresponding to the description of Myrtle Hazard had been seen
by any person on board.   He visited all the wharves,
inquiring on every vessel where it seemed possible she
might have been looking about.   Hotels, thoroughfares,
every place where he might hear of her or meet her, were
all searched.   He took some of the police into his confidence, and had half a dozen pairs of eyes besides his own
opened pretty widely, to discover the lost girl.

On Sunday, the 19th, he got the first hint which encouraged him to think he was on the trail of his fugitive.   He
had gone down again to the wharf where the Swordfish,
advertised to sail the next day, was lying.   The captain
was not on board, but one of the mates was there, and he
addressed his questions to him, not with any great hope of
hearing anything important, but determined to lose no
chance, however small.   He was startled with a piece of
information which gave him such an exquisite pang of
delight that he could hardly keep the usual quiet of his
demeanor.   A youth corresponding to his description of
Myrtle Hazard in her probable disguise had been that
morning on board the Swordfish, making many inquiries as
to the hour at which she was to sail, and who were to be
the passengers, and remained some time on board, going all
over the vessel, examining her cabin accommodations, and
saying he should return to-morrow before she sailed, —
doubtless intending to take passage in her, as there was
plenty of room on board.   There could be little question,
from the description, who this young person was.   It was
a rather delicate-looking, dark-haired youth, smooth-faced,
somewhat shy and bashful in his ways, and evidently ex-

cited and nervous. He had apparently been to look about him, and would come back at the last moment, just as the vessel was ready to sail, and in an hour or two be beyond the reach of inquiry.

Murray Bradshaw returned to his hotel, and, going to his chamber, summoned all his faculties in state council to determine what course he should follow, now that he had the object of his search certainly within reaching distance. There was no danger now of her eluding him; but the grave question arose, what was he to do when he stood face to face with her. She must not go, — that was fixed. If she once got off in that ship, she might be safe enough; but what would become of certain projects in which *he* was interested, — that was the question. But again, she was no child, to be turned away from her adventure by cajolery, or by any such threats as common truants would find sufficient to scare them back to their duty. He could tell the facts of her disguise and the manner of her leaving home to the captain of the vessel, and induce him to send her ashore as a stray girl, to be returned to her relatives. But this would only make her furious with him; and he must not alienate her from himself at any rate. He might plead with her in the name of duty, for the sake of her friends, for the good name of the family. She had thought all these things over before she ran away. What if he should address her as a lover, throw himself at her feet, implore her to pity him and give up her rash scheme, and, if things came to the very worst, offer to follow her wherever she went, if she would accept him in the only relation that would render it possible. Fifteen years old, — he nearly ten years older, — but such things had happened before, and this was no time to stand on trifles.

He worked out the hypothesis of the matrimonial offer as he would have reasoned out the probabilities in a law case he was undertaking.

1. He would rather risk that than lose all hold upon her. The girl was handsome enough for his ambitious future, wherever it might carry him. She came of an honorable family, and had the great advantage of being free from a tribe of disagreeable relatives, which is such a drawback on many otherwise eligible parties. To these considerations were to be joined other circumstances which we need not here mention, of a nature to add greatly to their force, and which would go far of themselves to determine his action.

2. How was it likely she would look on such an extraordinary proposition? At first, no doubt, as Lady Anne looked upon the advances of Richard. She would be startled, perhaps shocked. What then? She could not help feeling flattered at such an offer from him, — him, William Murray Bradshaw, the rising young man of his county, at her feet, his eyes melting with the love he would throw into them, his tones subdued to their most sympathetic quality, and all those phrases on his lips which every day beguile women older and more discreet than this romantic, long-imprisoned girl, whose rash and adventurous enterprise was an assertion of her womanhood and her right to dispose of herself as she chose. He had not lived to be twenty-five years old without knowing his power with women. He believed in himself so thoroughly, that his very confidence was a strong promise of success.

3. In case all his entreaties, arguments, and offers made no impression, should he make use of that supreme resource, not to be employed save in extreme need, but

which was of a nature, in his opinion, to shake a resolution stronger than this young girl was like to oppose to it? That would be like Christian's coming to his weapon called All-prayer, he said to himself, with a smile that his early readings of Bunyan should have furnished him an image for so different an occasion. The question was one he could not settle till the time came, — he must leave it to the instinct of the moment.

The next morning found him early waking after a night of feverish dreams. He dressed himself with more than usual care, and walked down to the wharf where the Swordfish was moored. The ship had left the wharf, and was lying out in the stream. A small boat had just reached her, and a slender youth, as he appeared at that distance, climbed, not over-adroitly, up the vessel's side.

Murray Bradshaw called to a boatman near by and ordered the man to row him over as fast as he could to the vessel lying in the stream. He had no sooner reached the deck of the Swordfish than he asked for the young person who had just been put on board.

"He is in the cabin, sir, just gone down with the captain," was the reply.

His heart beat, in spite of his cool temperament, as he went down the steps leading to the cabin. The young person was talking earnestly with the captain, and, on his turning round, Mr. William Murray Bradshaw had the pleasure of recognizing his young friend, Mr. Cyprian Eveleth.

CHAPTER VIII.

DOWN THE RIVER.

LOOK at the flower of a morning-glory the evening before the dawn which is to see it unfold. The delicate petals are twisted into a spiral, which at the appointed
hour, when the sunlight touches the hidden springs of its
life, will uncoil itself and let the day into the chamber of
its virgin heart. But the spiral must unwind by its own
law, and the hand that shall try to hasten the process will
only spoil the blossom which would have expanded in
symmetrical beauty under the rosy fingers of morning.

We may take a hint from Nature's handling of the
flower in dealing with young souls, and especially with
the souls of young girls, which, from their organization
and conditions, require more careful treatment than those
of their tougher-fibred brothers. Many parents reproach
themselves for not having enforced their own convictions
on their children in the face of every inborn antagonism
they encountered. Let them not be too severe in their
self-condemnation. A want of judgment in this matter
has sent many a young person to Bedlam, whose nature
would have opened kindly enough if it had only been trusted to the sweet influences of morning sunshine. In such
cases it may be that the state we call insanity is not always an unalloyed evil. It may take the place of something worse, — the wretchedness of a mind not yet dethroned, but subject to the perpetual interferences of
another mind governed by laws alien and hostile to its

own. Insanity may perhaps be the only palliative left
to Nature in this extremity. But before she comes
to that, she has many expedients. The mind does
not know what diet it can feed on until it has been
brought to the starvation point. Its experience is like
that of those who have been long drifting about on rafts
or in long-boats. There is nothing out of which it will not
contrive to get some sustenance. A person of note, long
held captive for a political offence, is said to have owed
the preservation of his reason to a *pin*, out of which he
contrived to get exercise and excitement by throwing it
down carelessly on the dark floor of his dungeon, and then
hunting for it in a series of systematic explorations until
he had found it.

Perhaps the most natural thing Myrtle Hazard could
have done would have been to go crazy, and be sent to
the nearest asylum, if Providence. which in its wisdom
makes use of the most unexpected agencies, had not made
a special provision for her mental welfare. She was in
that arid household as the prophet in the land where there
was no dew nor rain for these long years. But as he had
the brook Cherith, and the bread and flesh in the morning
and the bread and flesh in the evening which the ravens
brought him, so she had the river and her secret store of
books.

The river was light and life and music and companionship to her. She learned to row herself about upon it,
to swim boldly in it, for it had sheltered nooks but a little
way above The Poplars. But there was more than that
in it, — it was infinitely sympathetic. A river is strangely like a human soul. It has its dark and bright days, its
troubles from within, and its disturbances from without

It often runs over ragged rocks with a smooth surface,
and is vexed with ripples as it slides over sands that are
level as a floor. It betrays its various moods by aspects
which are the commonplaces of poetry, as smiles and dim-
ples and wrinkles and frowns. Its face is full of winking
eyes, when the scattering rain-drops first fall upon it, and
it scowls back at the storm-cloud, as with knitted brows,
when the winds are let loose. It talks, too, in its own
simple dialect, murmuring, as it were, with busy lips all
the way to the ocean, as children seeking the mother's
breast and impatient of delay. Prisoners who know what
a flower or an insect has been to them in their solitary
cell, invalids who have employed their vacant minds in
studying the patterns of paper-hangings on the walls of
their sick-chambers, can tell what the river was to the
lonely, imaginative creature who used to sit looking into
its depths, hour after hour, from the airy height of the
Fire-hang-bird's Nest.

Of late a thought had mingled with her fancies which
had given to the river the aspect of something more than
a friend and a companion. It appeared all at once as a
Deliverer. Did not its waters lead, after long wanderings,
to the great highway of the world, and open to her the
gates of those cities from which she could take her departure unchallenged towards the lands of the morning or of
the sunset? Often, after a freshet, she had seen a child's
miniature boat floating down on its side past her window,
and traced it in imagination back to some crystal brook
flowing by the door of a cottage far up a blue moun-
tain in the distance. So she now began to follow down
the stream the airy shallop that held her bright fancies.
These dreams of hers were colored by the rainbows of an

enchanted fountain, — the books of adventure, the romances, the stories which fortune had placed in her hands,
— the same over which the heart of the Pride of the
County had throbbed in the last century, and on the
pages of some of which the traces of her tears might still
be seen.

The literature which was furnished for Myrtle's improvement was chiefly of a religious character, and, however interesting and valuable to those to whom it was
adapted, had not been chosen with any wise regard to its
fitness for her special conditions. Of what use was it to
offer books like the " Saint's Rest " to a child whose idea
of happiness was in perpetual activity? She read " Pilgrim's Progress," it is true, with great delight. She liked
the idea of travelling with a pack on one's back, the odd
shows at the House of the Interpreter, the fighting, the
adventures, the pleasing young ladies at the palace the
name of which was Beautiful, and their very interesting
museum of curiosities. As for the allegorical meaning, it
went through her consciousness like a peck of wheat
through a bushel measure with the bottom out, — without
touching.

But the very first book she got hold of out of the hidden treasury threw the " Pilgrim's Progress " quite into
the shade. It was the story of a youth who ran away
and lived on an island, — one Crusoe, — a homely narrative, but evidently true, though full of remarkable adventures. There too was the history, coming much
nearer home, of Deborah Sampson, the young woman who
served as a soldier in the Revolutionary War, with a portrait of her in man's attire, looking intrepid rather than
lovely. A virtuous young female she was, and married

well, as she deserved to, and raised a family with as good a name as wife and mother as the best of them. But perhaps not one of these books and stories took such hold of her imagination as the tale of Rasselas, which most young persons find less entertaining than the Vicar of Wakefield, with which it is now-a-days so commonly bound up. It was the prince's discontent in the Happy Valley, the iron gate opening to the sound of music, and closing forever on those it admitted, the rocky boundaries of the imprisoning valley, the visions of the world beyond, the projects of escape, and the long toil which ended in their accomplishment, which haunted her sleeping and waking. She too was a prisoner, but it was not in the Happy Valley. Of the romances and the love-letters we must take it for granted that she selected wisely, and read discreetly; at least we know nothing to the contrary.

There were mysterious reminiscences and hints of her past coming over her constantly. It was in the course of the long, weary spring before her disappearance, that a dangerous chord was struck which added to her growing restlessness. In an old closet were some sea-shells and coral-fans, and dried star-fishes and sea-horses, and a natural mummy of a rough-skinned dog-fish. She had not thought of them for years, but now she felt impelled to look after them. The dim sea odors which still clung to them penetrated to the very inmost haunts of memory, and called up that longing for the ocean breeze which those who have once breathed and salted their blood with it never get over, and which makes the sweetest inland airs seem to them at last tame and tasteless. She held a tiger-shell to her ear, and listened to that low, sleepy murmur, whether in the ense or in the soul we hardly know, like that which had

so often been her lullaby, — a memory of the sea, as Lan
dor and Wordsworth have sung.

"You are getting to look like your father," Aunt Silence
said one day; "I never saw it before. I always though:
you took after old Major Gideon Withers. Well, I hope
you won't come to an early grave like poor Charles, — or
at any rate, that you may be prepared."

It did not seem very likely that the girl was going out
of the world at present, but she looked Miss Silence in the
face very seriously, and said, "Why not an early grave,
aunt, if this world is such a bad place as you say it is?"

"I'm afraid you are not fit for a better."

She wondered if Silence Withers and Cynthia Badlam
were just ripe for heaven.

For some months Miss Cynthia Badlam, who, as was
said, had been an habitual visitor at The Poplars, had
lived there as a permanent resident. Between her and
Silence Withers, Myrtle Hazard found no rest for her
soul. Each of them was for untwisting the morning-glory
without waiting for the sunshine to do it. Each had her
own wrenches and pincers to use for that purpose. All
this promised little for the nurture and admonition of the
young girl, who, if her will could not be broken by imprisonment and starvation at three years old, was not likely
to be over-tractable to any but gentle and reasonable
treatment at fifteen.

Aunt Silence's engine was *responsibility*, — her own responsibility, and the dreadful consequences which would
follow to her, Silence, if Myrtle should in any way go
wrong. Ever since her failure in that moral *coup d'état*
:y which the sinful dynasty of the natural self-determining
power was to be dethroned, her attempts in the way of

education had been a series of feeble efforts followed by plaintive wails over their utter want of success. The face she turned upon the young girl in her solemn expostulations looked as if it were inscribed with the epitaphs of hope and virtue. Her utterances were pitched in such a forlorn tone, that the little bird in his cage, who always began twittering at the sound of Myrtle's voice, would stop in his song, and cock his head with a look of inquiry full of pathos, as if he wanted to know what was the matter, and whether he could do anything to help.

The specialty of Cynthia Badlam was to point out all the dangerous and unpardonable transgressions into which young people generally, and this young person in particular, were likely to run, to hold up examples of those who had fallen into evil ways and come to an evil end, to present the most exalted standard of ascetic virtue to the lively girl's apprehension, leading her naturally to the conclusion that a bright example of excellence stood before her in the irreproachable relative who addressed her. Especially with regard to the allurements which the world offers to the young and inexperienced female, Miss Cynthia Badlam was severe and eloquent. Sometimes poor Myrtle would stare, not seeing the meaning of her wise caution, sometimes look at Miss Cynthia with a feeling that there was something about her that was false and forced, that she had nothing in common with young people, that she had no pity for them, only hatred of their sins, whatever these might be, — a hatred which seemed to extend to those sources of frequent temptation. youth and beauty, as if they were in themselves objectionable.

Both the lone women at The Poplars were gifted with a thin vein of music. They gave it expression in psalmody of course, in which Myrtle, who was a natural singer, was expected to bear her part. This would have been pleasanter if the airs most frequently selected had been cheerful or soothing, and if the favorite hymns had been of a sort to inspire a love for what was lovely in this life, and to give some faint foretaste of the harmonies of a better world to come. But there is a fondness for minor keys and wailing cadences common to the monotonous chants of cannibals and savages generally, to such war-songs as the wild, implacable " Marseillaise," and to the favorite tunes of low-spirited Christian pessimists. That mournful " China,' which one of our most agreeable story-tellers has justly singled out as the cry of despair itself, was often sung at The Poplars, sending such a sense of utter misery through the house, that poor Kitty Fagan would cross herself, and wring her hands, and think of funerals, and wonder who was going to die, — for she fancied she heard the *Banshee's* warning in those most dismal ululations.

On the first Saturday of June, a fortnight before her disappearance, Myrtle strolled off by the river-shore, along its lonely banks, and came home with her hands full of leaves and blossoms. Silence Withers looked at them as if they were a kind of melancholy manifestation of frivolity on the part of the wicked old earth. Not that she did not inhale their faint fragrance with a certain pleasure, and feel their beauty as none whose souls are not wholly shrivelled and hardened can help doing, but the world was, in her estimate, a vale of tears, and it was only by a momentary forgetfulness that she could be moved to smile at anything.

Miss Cynthia, a sharper-edged woman, had formed the habit of crushing everything for its moral, until it lost its sweetness and grew almost odious, as flower-de-luces do when handled roughly. "There's a worm in that leaf, Myrtle. He has rolled it all round him, and hidden himself from sight; but there is a horrid worm in it, for all it is so young and fresh. There is a worm in every young soul, Myrtle."

"But there is not a worm in *every* leaf, Miss Cynthia. Look," she said, "all these are open, and you can see all over and under them, and there is nothing there. Are there never any worms in the leaves after they get old and yellow, Miss Cynthia?"

That was a pretty fair hit for a simple creature of fifteen, — but perhaps she was not so absolutely simple as one might have thought.

It was on the evening of this same day that they were sitting together. The sweet season was opening, and it seemed as if the whispering of the leaves, the voices of the birds, the softness of the air, the young life stirring in everything, called on all creatures to join the universal chorus of praise that was going up around them.

"What shall we sing this evening?" said Miss Silence.

"Give me one of the books, if you please, Cousin Silence," said Miss Cynthia. "It is Saturday evening, Holy time has begun. Let us prepare our minds for the solemnities of the Sabbath."

She took the book, one well known to the schools and churches of this nineteenth century.

"Book Second. Hymn 44. Long metre. I guess Putney' will be as good a tune as any to sing it to."

The trio began, —

> "With holy fear, and humble song," —

and got through the first verse together pretty well.

Then came the second verse: —

> " Far in the deep where darkness dwells,
> The land of horror and despair,
> Justice has built a dismal hell,
> And laid her stores of vengeance there.'

Myrtle's voice trembled a little in singing this verse, and she hardly kept up her part with proper spirit.

" Sing out, Myrtle," said Miss Cynthia, and she struck up the third verse: —

> " Eternal plagues and heavy chains,
> Tormenting racks and fiery coals,
> And darts t' inflict immortal pains,
> Dyed in the blood of damnéd souls."

This last verse was a duet, and not a trio. Myrtle closed her lips while it was singing, and when it was done threw down the book with a look of anger and disgust. The hunted soul was at bay.

" I won't sing such words," she said, " and I won't stay here to hear them sung. The boys in the streets say just such words as that, and I am not going to sing them. You can't scare me into being good with your cruel hymn-book !"

She could not swear: she was not a boy. She would not cry: she felt proud, obdurate, scornful, outraged. All these images, borrowed from the Holy Inquisition, were meant to frighten her, and had simply irritated her. The blow of a weapon that glances off, stinging, but not penetrating, only enrages. It was a moment of fearful danger to her character, to her life itself.

Without heeding the cries of the two women, she sprang up stairs to her hanging chamber. She threw open the window and looked down into the stream. For one mo-

ment her head swam with the sudden, overwhelming,
almost maddening thought that came over her, — the impulse to fling herself headlong into those running waters
and dare the worst these dreadful women had threatened
her with. Something — she often thought afterwards it
was an invisible hand — held her back during that brief
moment, and the paroxysm — just such a paroxysm as
throws many a young girl into the Thames or the Seine —
passed away. She remained looking, in a misty dream,
into the water far below. Its murmur recalled the whisper of the ocean waves. And through the depths it seemed
as if she saw into that strange, half-remembered world of
palm-trees and white robes and dusky faces, and amidst
them, looking upon her with ineffable love and tenderness, until all else faded from her sight, the face of a fair
woman, — was it *hers*, so long, long dead, or that dear
young mother's who was to her less a recollection than
a dream?

Could it have been this vision that soothed her, so that
she unclasped her hands and lifted her bowed head as if
she had heard a voice whispering to her from that unknown
world where she felt there was a spirit watching over her?
At any rate, her face was never more serene than when
she went to meeting with the two maiden ladies on the fol
lowing day, Sunday, and heard the Rev. Mr. Stoker preach
a sermon from Luke vii. 48, which made both the women
shed tears, but especially so excited Miss Cynthia that she
was in a kind of half-hysteric condition all the rest of the
day.

After that Myrtle was quieter and more docile than
ever before. Could it be, Miss Silence thought, that the
Rev. Mr. Stoker's sermon had touched her hard heart

4 *   F

However that was, she did not once wear the stormy look
with which she had often met the complaining remon-
strances Miss Silence constantly directed against all the
spontaneous movements of the youthful and naturally vivacious subject of her discipline.

June is an uncertain month, as everybody knows, and
there were frosts in many parts of New England in the
June of 1859. But there were also beautiful days and
nights, and the sun was warm enough to be fast ripening
the strawberries, — also certain plans which had been in
flower some little time.   Some preparations had been going
on in a quiet way, so that at the right moment a decisive
movement could be made.   Myrtle knew how to use her
needle, and always had a dexterous way of shaping any
article of dress or ornament, — a natural gift not very rare,
but sometimes very needful, as it was now.

On the morning of the 15th of June she was wandering
by the shores of the river, some distance above The Poplars, when a boat came drifting along by her, evidently
broken loose from its fastenings farther up the stream.   It
was common for such waifs to show themselves after heavy
rains had swollen the river.   They might have run the
gauntlet of nobody could tell how many farms, and perhaps
passed by half a dozen towns and villages in the night, so
that, if of common, cheap make, they were retained without
scruple, by any who might find them, until the owner called
for them, if he cared to take the trouble.

Myrtle took a knife from her pocket, cut down a long,
slender sapling, and coaxed the boat to the side of the bank.
A pair of old oars lay in the bottom of the boat; she took
one of these and paddled it into a little cove, where it could
lie hid among the thick alders.   Then she went home and

busied herself about various little matters more interesting to her than to us.

She was never more amiable and gracious than on this day. But she looked often at the clock, as they remembered afterwards, and studied over a copy of the Farmer's Almanac which was lying in the kitchen, with a somewhat singular interest. The days were nearly at their longest, the weather was mild, the night promised to be clear and bright.

The household was, to all appearance, asleep at the usual early hour. When all seemed quiet, Myrtle lighted her lamp, stood before her mirror, and untied the string that bound her long and beautiful dark hair, which fell in its abundance over her shoulders and below her girdle.

She lifted its heavy masses with one hand, and severed it with a strong pair of scissors, with remorseless exaction of every wandering curl, until she stood so changed by the loss of that outward glory of her womanhood, that she felt as if she had lost herself and found a brother she had never seen before.

" Good by, Myrtle!" she said, and, opening her window very gently, she flung the shining tresses upon the running water, and watched them for a few moments as they floated down the stream. Then she dressed herself in the character of her imaginary brother, took up the carpet-bag in which she had placed what she chose to carry with her, stole softly down stairs, and let herself out of a window on the lower floor, shutting it very carefully so as to be sure that nobody should be disturbed.

She glided along, looking all about her, fearing she might be seen by some curious wanderer, and reached the cove where the boat she had concealed was lying. She got into it, and, taking the rude oars, pulled herself into the middle of the swollen stream. Her heart beat so that it seemed to her as if she could hear it between the strokes of the oar. The lights were not all out in the village, and she trembled lest she should see the figure of some watcher looking from the windows in sight of which she would have to pass, and that a glimpse of this boat stealing along at so late an hour might give the clew to the secret of her disappearance, with which the whole region was to be busied in the course of the next day.

Presently she came abreast of The Poplars. The house lay so still, so peaceful, — it would wake to such dismay! The boat slid along beneath her own overhanging chamber.

"No song to-morrow from the Fire-hang-bird's Nest!" she said. So she floated by the slumbering village, the flow of the river carrying her steadily on, and the careful strokes of the oars adding swiftness to her flight.

At last she came to the "Broad Meadows," and knew that she was alone, and felt confident that she had got away unseen. There was nothing, absolutely nothing, to point out which way she had gone. Her boat came from nobody knew where, her disguise had been got together at different times in such a manner as to lead to no suspicion, and not a human being ever had the slightest hint that she had planned and meant to carry out the enterprise which she had now so fortunately begun.

Not till the last straggling house had been long past, not till the meadows were stretched out behind her as well as before her, spreading far off into the distance on each side, did she give way to the sense of wild exultation which was coming fast over her. But then, at last, she drew a long, long breath, and, standing up in the boat looked all around her. The stars were shining over her head and deep down beneath her. The cool wind came fresh upon her cheek over the long grassy reaches. No living thing moved in all the wide level circle which lay about her. She had passed the Red Sea, and was alone in the Desert.

She threw down her oars, lifted her hands like a priestess, and her strong, sweet voice burst into song, — the song of the Jewish maiden when she went out before the chorus of women and sang that grand solo, which we all remember in its ancient words, and in their modern paraphrase, —

> " Sound the loud timbrel o'er Egypt's dark sea!
> Jehovah hath triumphed, his people are free ! "

The poor child's repertory was limited to songs of the religious sort mainly, but there was a choice among these. Her aunt's favorites, beside " China," already mentioned, were " Bangor," which the worthy old New England clergyman so admired that he actually had the down-east city called after it, and " Windsor," and " Funeral Hymn." But Myrtle was in no mood for these. She let off her ecstasy in " Ballerma," and " Arlington," and " Silver Street," and at last in that most riotous of devotional hymns, which sounds as if it had been composed by a saint who had a cellar under his chapel, — " Jordan." So she let her wild spirits run loose ; and then a tenderer feeling stole over her, and she sang herself into a more tranquil mood with the gentle music of " Dundee." And again she pulled quietly and steadily at her oars, until she reached the wooded region through which the river winds after leaving the " Broad Meadows. '

The tumult in her blood was calmed yet every sense

and faculty was awake to the manifold delicious, mysterious impressions of that wonderful June night. The stars were shining between the tall trees, as if all the jewels of heaven had been set in one belt of midnight sky. The voices of the wind, as they sighed through the pines, seemed like the breath of a sleeping child, and then, as they lisped from the soft, tender leaves of beeches and maples, like the half-articulate whisper of the mother hushing all the intrusive sounds that might awaken it. Then came the pulsating monotone of the frogs from a far-off pool, the harsh cry of an owl from an old tree that overhung it, the splash of a mink or musquash, and nearer by, the light step of a woodchuck, as he cantered off in his quiet way to his hole in the nearest bank. The laurels were just coming into bloom, — the yellow lilies, earlier than their fairer sisters, pushing their golden cups through the water, not content, like those, to float on the surface of the stream that fed them, — emblems of showy wealth, and, like that, drawing all manner of insects to feed upon them. The miniature forests of ferns came down to the edge of the stream, their tall, bending plumes swaying in the night breeze. Sweet odors from oozing pines, from dewy flowers, from spicy leaves, stole out of the tangled thickets, and made the whole scene more dream-like with their faint, mingled suggestions.

By and by the banks of the river grew lower and marshy, and in place of the larger forest-trees which had covered them stood slender tamaracks, sickly, mossy looking as if they had been moon-struck and were out of their wits, their tufts of leaves staring off every way from their spindling branches. The winds came cool and damp out of the hiding-places among their dark recesses. The country people about here called this region the "Witches Hollow," and had many stories about the strange things that happened there. The Indians used to hold their "powwows," or magical incantations, upon a broad mound which rose out of the common level, and where some old hemlocks and beeches formed a dark grove, which served them as a temple for their demon-worship. There were many legends of more recent date connected with this spot, some of them hard to account for, and no superstitious or highly imaginative person would have cared to pass through it alone in the dead of the night, as this young girl was doing.

She knew nothing of all these fables and fancies. Her own singular experiences in this enchanted region were certainly not suggested by anything she had heard, and may be considered psychologically curious by those who would not think of attributing any mystical meaning to them. We are at liberty to report many things without attempting to explain them, or committing ourselves to anything beyond the fact that so they were told us. [The reader will find Myrtle's "Vision," as written out at a later period from her recollections, at the end of this chapter.]

The night was passing, and she meant to be as far away as possible from the village she had left, before morning. But the boat, like all craft on country rivers, was leaky, and she had to work until tired, bailing it out, before she was ready for another long effort. The old tin measure, which was all she had to bail with, leaked as badly as the boat, and her task was a tedious one. At last she got it in good trim, and sat down to her oars with the determination to pull steadily as long as her strength would hold out.

Hour after hour she kept at her work, sweeping round

the long bends where the river was hollowing out one bank and building new shore on the opposite one, so as gradually to shift its channel; by clipper-shaped islands, sharp at the bows looking up stream, sharp too at the stern, looking down, — their shape solving the navigator's problem of least resistance, as a certain young artist had pointed out; by slumbering villages; by outlying farm-houses; between cornfields where the young plants were springing up in little thready fountains; in the midst of stumps where the forest had just been felled; through patches where the fire of the last great autumnal drought had turned all the green beauty of the woods into brown desolation; and again amidst broad expanses of open meadow stretching as far as the eye could reach in the uncertain light. A faint yellow tinge was beginning to stain the eastern horizon. Her boat was floating quietly along, for she had at last taken in her oars, and she was now almost tired out with toil and excitement. She rested her head upon her hands, and felt her eyelids closing in spite of herself. And now there stole upon her ear a low, gentle, distant murmur, so soft that it seemed almost to mingle with the sound of her own breathing, but so steady, so uniform, that it soothed her to sleep, as if it were the old cradle-song the ocean used to sing to her, or the lulla-by of her fair young mother.

So she glided along, slowly, slowly, down the course of the winding river, and the flushing dawn kindled around her as she slumbered, and the low, gentle murmur grew louder and louder, but still she slept, dreaming of the murmuring ocean.

APPENDIX TO CHAPTER VIII.

MYRTLE HAZARD'S STATEMENT.

"A Vision seen by me, Myrtle Hazard, aged fifteen, on the night of June 15, 1859. Written out at the request of a friend from my recollections.

"The place where I saw these sights is called, as I have been told since, Witches' Hollow. I had never been there before, and did not know that it was called so, or anything about it.

"The first strange thing that I noticed was on coming near a kind of hill or mound that rose out of the low meadows. I saw a *burning cross* lying on the slope of that mound. It burned with a pale greenish light, and did not waste, though I watched it for a long time, as the boat I was in moved slowly with the current and I had stopped rowing.

"I know that my eyes were open, and I was awake while I was looking at this cross. I think my eyes were open when I saw these other appearances, but I felt just as if I were dreaming while awake.

"I heard a faint rustling sound, and on looking up I saw many figures moving around me, and I seemed to see myself among them as if I were outside of myself.

"The figures did not walk, but slid or glided with an even movement, as if without any effort. They made many gestures, and seemed to speak, but I cannot tell whether I *heard* what they said, or knew its meaning in some other way.

"I knew the faces of some of these figures. They were the same I have seen in portraits, as long as I can re

member, at the old house where I was brought up, called
The Poplars. I saw my father and my mother as they look
in the two small pictures ; also my grandmother, and her
father and mother and grandfather, and one other person,
who lived a great while ago. All of these have been long
dead, and the longer they had been dead the less like substance they looked and the more like shadows, so that the
oldest was like one's breath of a frosty morning, but
shaped like the living figure.

"There was no motion of their breasts, and their lips
seemed to be moving as if they were saying, Breath!
Breath! Breath! I thought they wanted to breathe the
air of this world again in my shape, which I seemed to see
as it were empty of myself and of these other selves, like
a sponge that has water pressed out of it.

"Presently it seemed to me that I returned to myself,
and then those others became part of me by being taken
up, one by one, and so lost in my own life.

"My father and mother came up, hand in hand, looking
more real than any of the rest. Their figures vanished,
and they seemed to have become a part of me ; for I felt
all at once the longing to live over the life they had led, on
the sea and in strange countries.

"Another figure was just like the one we called the
Major, who was a very strong, hearty-looking man, and
who is said to have drank hard sometimes, though there
is nothing about it on his tombstone, which I used to read
in the graveyard. It seemed to me that there was something about his life that I did not want to make a part of
mine, but that there was some right he had in me through
my being of his blood, and so his health and his strength
went all through me, and I was always to have what

was left of his life in that shadow-like shape, forming a portion of mine.

" So in the same way with the shape answering to the portrait of that famous beauty who was the wife of my great-grandfather, and used to be called the Pride of the County.

" And so too with another figure which had the face of that portrait marked on the back, *Ruth Bradford,* who married one of my ancestors, and was before the court, as I have heard, in the time of the witchcraft trials.

" There was with the rest a dark, wild-looking woman, with a head-dress of feathers. She kept as it were in shadow, but I saw something of my own features in her face.

" It was on my mind very strongly that the shape of that woman of our blood who was burned long ago by the Papists came very close to me, and was in some way made one with mine, and that I feel her presence with me since, as if she lived again in me; but not always, — only at times, — and then I feel borne up as if I could do anything in the world. I had a feeling as if she were my guardian and protector.

" It seems to me that these, and more, whom I have not mentioned, do really live over some part of their past lives in my life. I do not understand it all, and perhaps it can be accounted for in some way I have not thought of. I write it down as nearly as I can give it from memory, by request, and if it is printed at this time had rather have all the real names withheld.

" MYRTLE HAZARD."

NOTE BY THE FRIEND.

" This statement must be accounted for in some way, or

pass into the category of the supernatural. Probably it was one of those intuitions, with *objective projection*, which sometimes come to imaginative young persons, especially girls, in certain exalted nervous conditions. The study of the portraits, with the knowledge of some parts of the history of the persons they represented, and the consciousness of instincts inherited in all probability from these same ancestors, formed the basis of Myrtle's ' Vision.' The lives of our progenitors are, as we know, reproduced in different proportions in ourselves. *Whether they as individuals have any consciousness of it*, is another matter. It is possible that they do get a second as it were fractional life in us. It might seem that many of those whose blood flows in our veins struggle for the mastery, and by and by one or more get the predominance, so that we grow to be like father, or mother, or remoter ancestor, or two or more are blended in us, not to the exclusion, however, it must be understood, of a special personality of our own, about which these others are grouped. Independently of any possible scientific value, this ' Vision ' serves to illustrate the above-mentioned fact of common experience, which is not sufficiently weighed by most moralists.

" How much it may be granted to certain young persons to see, not in virtue of their intellectual gifts, but through those direct channels which worldly wisdom may possibly close to the luminous influx, each reader must determine for himself by his own standards of faith and evidence.

" One statement of the narrative admits of a simple natural explanation, which does not allow the lovers of the marvellous to class it with the *quasi* miraculous appearance seen by Colonel Gardiner, and given in full by Dr Doddridge in his Life of that remarkable Christian soldier

Decaying wood is often phosphorescent, as many readers must have seen for themselves. The country people are familiar with the sight of it in wild timber-land, and have given it the name of ' Fox-fire.' Two trunks of trees in this state, lying across each other, will account for the fact observed, and vindicate the truth of the young girl's story without requiring us to suppose any exceptional occurrence outside of natural laws.'

CHAPTER IX.

MR. CLEMENT LINDSAY RECEIVES A LETTER, AND BEGINS HIS ANSWER.

IT was already morning when a young man living in the town of Alderbank, after lying awake for an hour thinking the unutterable thoughts that nineteen years of life bring to the sleeping and waking dreams of young people, rose from his bed, and, half dressing himself, sat down at his desk, from which he took a letter, which he opened and read. It was written in a delicate, though hardly formed female hand, and crossed like a checker-board, as is usual with these redundant manuscripts. The letter was as follows : —

                         " OXBOW VILLAGE, June 13, 1859.

"MY DEAREST CLEMENT, — You was *so* good to write me such a sweet little bit of a letter, — only, dear, you never seem to be in quite so good spirits as you used to be. I wish your Susie was with you to cheer you up ; but no, she must be patient, and you must be patient too, for you are so ambitious ! I have heard you say so many times that nobody could be a great artist without passing years and years at work, and growing pale and lean with thinking so hard. *You* won't grow pale and lean, I hope ; for I do so love to see that pretty color in your cheeks you have always had ever since I have known you ; and besides, I do not believe you will have to work so *very* hard to do something great, — you have so much *genius,* and people of genius do such beautiful things with so little trouble. You remember those beautiful lines out of our newspaper I sent you? Well, Mr. Hopkins told me he wrote those lines *in one evening* without stopping! I wish you could see Mr. Hopkins, — he is a very talented person. I cut out this little piece about him from the paper on purpose to show you, — for genius loves genius, — and you would like to hear him read his own poetry, — he reads it beautifully. Please send this piece from the paper back, as I want to put it in my scrap-book, under his autograph : —

" ' Our young townsman, Mr. Gifted Hopkins, has proved himself worthy of the name he bears. His poetical effusions are equally creditable to his head and his heart, displaying the highest order of genius and powers of imagination and fancy hardly second to any writer of the age. He is destined to make a great sensation in the world of letters.'

" Mrs. Hopkins is the same good soul she always was. She is very proud of her son, as is natural, and keeps a copy of everything he writes. I believe she cries over them every time she reads them. You don't know how I take to little Sossy and Minthy, those two twins I have written to you about before. Poor little creatures, — what a cruel thing it was in their father and mother not to take care of them! What do you think? Old bachelor Gridley lets them come up into his room, and builds forts and castles for them with his big books! ' The world 's coming to an end,' Mrs. Hopkins said the first time he did so. He looks so savage with that scowl of his, and talks so gruff when he is scolding at things in general, that nobody would have believed he would have let such little things come anywhere near him. But he seems to be growing kind to all of us and everybody. I saw him talking to the Fire-hang-bird the other day. You know who the Fire-hang-bird is, don't you? Myrtle Hazard her name is. I wish you could see her. I don't know as I do, though. You would want to make a statue of her, or a painting, I know. She is so handsome that all the young men stand round to see her come out of meeting. Some say that Lawyer Bradshaw is after her; but my! he is ten years older than she is. She is nothing but a girl, though she looks as if she was eighteen. She lives up at a place called The Poplars, with an old woman that is her aunt or something, and nobody seems to be much acquainted with her except Olive Eveleth, who is the minister's daughter at Saint Bartholomew's Church. She never has *beauxs* round her, as some young girls do — they say that she is not happy with her aunt and another woman that stays with her, and that is the reason she keeps so much to herself. The minister came to see me the other day, — Mr. Stoker his name is. I was all alone, and it frightened me, for he looks, O, so solemn on Sundays! But he called me ' My dear,' and did n't say anything horrid, you know, about my being such a dreadful, dreadful sinner, as I have heard of his saying to some people, — but he looked very kindly at me, and took my hand, and laid his hand on my shoulder like a brother, and hoped I would come and see him in his study. I suppose I must go, but I don't want to. I don't seem to like him exactly.

" I hope you love me as well as ever you did. I can't help feeling sometimes as if you was growing away from me, — you know what I mean, — getting to be too great a person for such a small person as I am. I know I can't always understand you when you talk about *art*, and that you know a great deal too much for such a simple girl as I am. O, if I thought I could never make you happy! . . . . There, now! I am almost ashamed to send this paper so spotted. — Gifted Hopkins wrote some beautiful verses one day on ' A Maiden Weeping.' He compared the tears fall-

ing from her eyes to the drops of dew which one often sees
upon the flowers in the morning. Is n't it a pretty thought?

"I wish I loved *art* as well as I do poetry; but I am
afraid I have not so much taste as some girls have. You
remember how I liked that picture in the illustrated maga-
zine, and you said it was *horrid.* I have been afraid since
to like almost anything, for fear you should tell me some
time or other it was *horrid.* Don't you think I shall ever
learn to know what is nice from what is n't?

"O, dear Clement, I wish you would do one thing to
please me. Don't say no, for you can do everything you
try to, — I am sure you can. I want you to write me
some *poetry,* — just three or four little verses To SUSIE.
O, I should feel so proud to have some lines written all on
purpose for me. Mr Hopkins wrote some the other day,
and printed them in the paper, 'To M——e.' I believe
he meant them for Myrtle, — the first and last letter of
her name, you see, 'M' and 'e.'

"Your letter was a *dear* one, only *so* short! I wish you
would tell me all about what you are doing at Alderbank.
Have you made that model of Innocence that is to have
my forehead, and hair parted like mine! Make it pretty,
do, that is a darling.

"Now don't make a face at my letter. It is n't a very
good one, I know; but your poor little Susie does the best
she can, and she loves you *so* much!

"Now do be nice and write me one little bit of a mite of
a poem, — it will make me just as happy!

"I am very well, and as happy as I can be when you are
away.

"Your affectionate SUSIE."

(Directed to Mr. Clement Lindsay, Alderbank.)

The envelope of this letter was unbroken, as was before said, when the young man took it from his desk. He did not tear it with the hot impatience of some lovers, but cut it open neatly, slowly, one would say sadly. He read it with an air of singular effort, and yet with a certain tenderness. When he had finished it, the drops were thick on his forehead; he groaned and put his hands to his face, which was burning red.

This was what the impulse of boyhood, years ago, had brought him to! He was a stately youth, of noble bearing, of high purpose, of fastidious taste; and, if his broad forehead, his clear, large blue eyes, his commanding features, his lips, firm, yet plastic to every change of thought and feeling, were not an empty mask, might not improbably claim that Promethean quality of which the girl's letter had spoken, — the strange, divine, dread gift of genius.

This poor, simple, innocent, trusting creature, so utterly incapable of coming into any true relation with his aspiring mind, his large and strong emotions, — this mere child, all simplicity and goodness, but trivial and shallow as the little babbling brooklet that ran by his window to the river, to lose its insignificant being in the swift torrent he heard rushing over the rocks, — this pretty idol for a weak and kindly and easily satisfied worshipper, was to be enthroned as the queen of his affections, to be adopted as the companion of his labors! The boy, led by the commonest instinct, the mere attraction of biped to its female, which accident had favored, had thrown away the dearest possession of manhood, — liberty, — and this bawble was to be his life-long reward! And yet not a bawble either, for a pleasing person and a gentle and sweet nature, which had once made her seem to him the very paragon of loveliness, were still hers. Alas. her simple words were true, — he had grown away from her. Her only fault was that she had not grown with him, and surely he could not reproach her with that.

"No," he said to himself, "I will never leave her so long as her heart clings to me. I have been rash, but she shall not pay the forfeit. And if I may think of myself, my life need not be wretched because she cannot share all my being with me. The common human qualities are more than all exceptional gifts. She has a woman's heart; and what talent of mine is to be named by the love a true woman can offer in exchange for these divided and cold affections? If it had pleased God to mate me with one more equal in other ways, who could share my thoughts, who could kindle my inspiration, who had wings to rise into the air with me as well as feet to creep by my side upon the earth, — what cannot such a woman do for a man!

"What! cast away the flower I took in the bud because it does not show as I hoped it would when it opened? I will stand by my word; I will be all as a man that I promised as a boy. Thank God, she is true and pure and sweet. My nest will be a peaceful one; but I must take wing alone, — alone."

He drew one long sigh, and the cloud passed from his countenance. He must answer that letter now, — at once. There were reasons, he thought, which made it important. And so, with the cheerfulness which it was kind and becoming to show, so far as possible, and yet with a little excitement on one particular point, which was the cause of his writing so promptly, he began his answer.

ALDERBANK, Thursday morning, June 16, 1859.

" MY DEAR SUSIE, — I have just been reading your pleasant letter ; and if I do not send you the poem you ask for so eloquently, I will give you a little bit of advice, which will do just as well, — won't it, my dear? I was interested in your account of various things going on at Oxbow Village. I am very glad you find young Mr. Hopkins so agreeable a friend. His poetry is better than some which I see printed in the village papers, and seems generally unexceptionable in its subjects and tone. I do not believe he is a dangerous companion, though the habit of writing verse does not always improve the character. I think I have seen it make more than one of my acquaintances idle, conceited, sentimental, and frivolous, — perhaps it found them so already. Don't make too much of his talent, and particularly don't let him think that because he can write verses he has nothing else to do in this world. That is for his benefit, dear, and you must skilfully apply it.

" Now about yourself. My dear Susie, there was something in your letter that did not please me. You speak of a visit from the Rev. Mr. Stoker, and of his kind, brotherly treatment, his cordiality of behavior, and his asking you to visit him in his study. I am very glad to hear you say that you ' don't seem to like him.' He is very familiar, it seems to me, for so new an acquaintance. What business had he to be laying his hand on your shoulder? I should like to see him try these free-and-easy ways in my presence! He would not have taken that liberty, my dear! No, he was alone with you, and thought it safe to be disrespectfully familiar. I want you to maintain your dignity always with such persons, and I beg you not to go to the study of this clergyman, unless some older friend goes with you on every occasion, and sits through the visit. I must speak plainly to you, my dear, as I have a right to. If the minister has anything of importance to say, let it come through the lips of some mature person. It may lose something of the fervor with which it would have been delivered at first hand, but the great rules of Christian life are not so dependent on the particular individual who speaks them, that you must go to this or that young man to find out what they are. If to any *man*, I should prefer the old gentleman whom you have mentioned in your letters, Father Pemberton. You understand me, my dear girl, and the subject is not grateful. You know how truly I am interested in all that relates to you, — that I regard you with an affection which — "

HELP! HELP! HELP!

A cry as of a young person's voice was heard faintly, coming from the direction of the river. Something in the tone of it struck to his heart, and he sprang as if he had been stabbed. He flung open his chamber window and leaped from it to the ground. He ran straight to the bank of the river by the side of which the village of Alderbank was built, a little farther down the stream than the house in which he was living.

Everybody that travels in that region knows the beautiful falls which break the course of the river just above the village; narrow and swift, and surrounded by rocks of such picturesque forms that they are sought and admired by tourists. The stream was now swollen, and rushed in a deep and rapid current over the ledges, through the rocky straits, plunging at last in tumult and foam, with loud, continuous roar, into the depths below the cliff from which it tumbled.

A short distance above the fall there projected from the water a rock which had, by parsimonious saving during a long course of years, hoarded a little soil, out of which a small tuft of bushes struggled to support a decent vegetable existence. The high waters had nearly submerged it, but a few slender twigs were seen above their surface.

A skiff was lying close to this rock, between it and the brink of the fall, which was but a few rods farther down. In the skiff was a youth of fourteen or fifteen years, holding by the slender twigs, the boat dragging at them all the time, and threatening to tear them away and go over the fall. It was not likely that the boy would come to shore alive if it did. There were stories, it is true, that the Indians used to shoot the fall in their canoes with safety; but everybody knew that at least three persons had been lost by going over it since the town was settled; and more than one dead body had been found floating far down the river, with bruises and fractured bones, as if it had taken the same fatal plunge.

There was no time to lose. Clement ran a little way up the river-bank, flung off his shoes, and sprang from the bank as far as he could leap into the water. The current swept him toward the fall, but he worked nearer and nearer the middle of the stream. He was making for the rock, thinking he could plant his feet upon it and at the worst hold the boat until he could summon other help by shouting. He had barely got his feet upon the rock, when the twigs by which the boy was holding gave way. He seized the boat, but it dragged him from his uncertain footing, and with a desperate effort he clambered over its side and found himself its second doomed passenger.

There was but an instant for thought.

" Sit still," he said, " and, just as we go over, put your arms round me under mine, and don't let go for your life ! "

He caught up the single oar, and with a few sharp paddle-strokes brought the skiff into the blackest centre of the current, where it was deepest, and would plunge them into the deepest pool.

" Hold your breath ! God save us ! Now ! "

They rose, as if with one will, and stood for an instant, the arms of the younger closely embracing the other as he had directed.

A sliding away from beneath them of the floor on which they stood, as the drop fails under the feet of a felon. A great rush of air, and a mighty, awful, stunning roar, — an involuntary gasp, a choking flood of water that came bellowing after them, and hammered them down into the black depths so far that the young man, though used to diving and swimming long distances under water, had well-nigh yielded to the fearful need of air, and sucked in his death in so doing.

The boat came up to the surface, broken in twain, splintered, a load of firewood for those who raked the river lower down. It had turned crosswise, and struck the rocks. A cap rose to the surface, such a one as boys wear, — the same that boy had on. And then — after how many seconds by the watch cannot be known, but after a time long enough, as the young man remembered it, to live his whole life over in memory — Clement Lindsay felt the blessed air against his face, and, taking a great breath, came to his full consciousness. The arms of the boy were still locked around him as in the embrace of death. A few strokes brought him to the shore, dragging his senseless burden with him.

He unclasped the arms that held him so closely encircled, and laid the slender form of the youth he had almost died to save gently upon the grass. It was as if dead. He loosed the ribbon that was round the neck, he tore open the checked shirt —

The story of Myrtle Hazard's sex was told; but she was deaf to his cry of surprise, and no blush came to her cold cheek. Not too late, perhaps, to save her, — not too late to try to save her, at least!

He placed his lips to hers, and filled her breast with the air from his own panting chest. Again and again he renewed these efforts, hoping, doubting, despairing, — once more hoping, and at last, when he had almost ceased to hope, she gasped, she breathed, she moaned, and rolled her eyes wildly round her, — she was born again into this mortal life.

He caught her up in his arms, bore her to the house, laid her on a sofa, and, having spent his strength in this last effort, reeled and fell, and lay as one over whom have just been whispered the words, " He is gone."

CHAPTER X.

MR. CLEMENT LINDSAY FINISHES HIS LETTER. — WHAT
CAME OF IT.

THE first thing Clement Lindsay did, when he was
fairly himself again, was to finish his letter to Susan
Posey. He took it up where it left off, " with an affection
which " ——— and drew a long dash, as above. It was with
great effort he wrote the lines which follow, for he had got
an ugly blow on the forehead, and his eyes were "in
mourning," as the gentlemen of the ring say, with unbecoming levity.

" An adventure! Just as I was writing these last words,
I heard the cry of a young person, as it sounded, for help.
I ran to the river and jumped in, and had the pleasure of
saving a life. I got some bruises which have laid me up
for a day or two; but I am getting over them very well
now, and you need not worry about me at all. I will
write again soon ; so pray do not fret yourself, for I have
had no hurt that will trouble me for any time."

Of course, poor Susan Posey burst out crying, and cried
as if her heart would break. O dear! O dear! what
should she do! He was almost killed, she knew he was,
or he had broken some of his bones. O dear! O dear!
She would go and see him, there ! — she must and would.
He would die, she knew he would, — and so on.

It was a singular testimony to the evident presence of a
human element in Mr. Byles Gridley that the poor girl,
on her extreme trouble, should think of him as a counsel-
5 *

lor. But the wonderful relenting kind of look on his grave
features as he watched the little twins tumbling about his
great books, and certain marks of real sympathy he had
sometimes shown for her in her lesser woes, encouraged
her, and she went straight to his study, letter in hand. She
gave a timid knock at the door of that awful sanctuary.

"Come in, Susan Posey," was its answer, in a pleasant
tone. The old master knew her light step and the maid-
enly touch of her small hand on the panel.

What a sight! There were Sossy and Minthy intrenched in a Sebastopol which must have cost a good
half-hour's engineering, and the terrible Byles Gridley
besieging the fortress with hostile manifestations of the
most singular character. He was actually discharging a
large sugar-plum at the postern gate, which having been
left unclosed, the missile would certainly have reached one
of the garrison, when he paused as the door opened, and
the great round spectacles and four wide, staring infants'
eyes were levelled at Miss Susan Posey.

She almost forgot her errand, grave as it was, in astonishment at this manifestation. The old man had emptied
his shelves of half their folios to build up the fort, in the
midst of which he had seated the two delighted and up-
roarious babes. There was his Cave's "Historia Liter-
aria," and Sir Walter Raleigh's "History of the World,"
and a whole array of Christian Fathers, and Plato, and
Aristotle, and Stanley's book of Philosophers, with Effi-
gies, and the Junta Galen, and the Hippocrates of Foesius,
and Walton's Polyglot, supported by Father Sanchez on
one side and Fox's "Acts and Monuments" on the other
— an odd collection, as folios from lower shelves are apt
to be.

The besieger discharged his sugar-plum, which was so well aimed that it fell directly into the lap of Minthy, who acted with it as if the garrison had been on short rations for some time.

He saw at once, on looking up, that there was trouble " What now, Susan Posey, my dear ? "

" O Mr. Gridley, I am in such trouble ! What shall I do ? What shall I do ? "

She turned back the name and the bottom of the letter in such a way that Mr. Gridley could read nothing but the few lines relating their adventure.

" So Mr. Clement Lindsay has been saving a life, has he, and got some hard knocks doing it, hey, Susan Posey? Well, well, Clement Lindsay is a brave fellow, and there is need of hiding his name, my child. Let me take the letter again a moment, Susan Posey. What is the date of it ? June 16th. Yes, — yes, — yes ! "

He read the paragraph over again, and the signature too, if he wanted to ; for poor Susan had found that her secret was hardly opaque to those round spectacles and the eyes behind them, and, with a not unbecoming blush, opened the fold of the letter before she handed it back.

" No, no, Susan Posey. He will come all right. His writing is steady, and if he had broken any bones he would have mentioned it. It 's a thing his wife will be proud of, if he is ever married, Susan Posey," (blushes,) " and his children too," (more blushes running up to her back hair,) " and there 's nothing to be worried about. But I 'll tell you what my dear, I 've got a little business that calls me down the river to-morrow, and I should n't mind stopping an hour at Alderbank and seeing how our young friend Clement Lindsay is ; and then, if he was

going to have a long time of it, why we could manage it
somehow that any friend who had any special interest in
him could visit him, just to while away the tiresomeness
of being sick. That's it, exactly. I'll stop at Alderbank, Susan Posey. Just clear up these two children for
me, will you, my dear? Isosceles, come now, — that's a
good child. Helminthia, carry these sugar-plums down
stairs for me, and take good care of them, mind!"

It was a case of gross bribery and corruption, for the
fortress was immediately evacuated on the receipt of a
large paper of red and white comfits, and the garrison
marched down stairs much like conquerors, under the
lead of the young lady, who was greatly eased in mind by
the kind words and the promise of Mr. Byles Gridley.

But he, in the mean time, was busy with thoughts she
did not suspect. "A young *person*," he said to himself,
— "why a young *person*? Why not say a *boy*, if it was
a boy? What if this should be our handsome truant? —
'*June* 16*th, Thursday morning!*' — About time to get to
Alderbank by the river, I should think. None of the
boats missing? What then? She may have made a raft,
or picked up some stray skiff. Who knows? And then
got shipwrecked, very likely. There are rapids and falls
farther along the river. It will do no harm to go down
there and look about, at any rate."

On Saturday morning, therefore, Mr. Byles Gridley set
forth to procure a conveyance to make a visit, as he said,
down the river, and perhaps be gone a day or two. He
went to a stable in the village, and asked if they could let
him have a horse.

The man looked at him with that air of native superi
ority which the companionship of the generous steed con

fers on all his associates, down to the lightest weight among the jockeys.

"Wal, I hain't got nothin' in the shape of a *hoss*, Mr Gridley. I 've got a *mare* I s'pose I could let y' have."

"O, very well," said the old master, with a twinkle in his eye as sly as the other's wink, — he had parried a few jokes in his time, — "they charge half-price for mares always, I believe."

That was a new view of the subject. It rather took the wind out of the stable-keeper, and set a most ammoniacal fellow, who stood playing with a currycomb, grinning at his expense. But he rallied presently.

"Wal, I b'lieve they do for *some* mares, when they let 'em to *some* folks; but this here ain't one o' them mares, and you ain't one o' them folks. All my cattle 's out but this critter, 'n' I don't jestly want to have nobody drive her that ain't pretty car'ful, — she 's faäst, I tell ye, — don't want no whip. — How fur d'd y' want t' go ? "

Mr. Gridley was quite serious now, and let the man know that he wanted the mare and a light covered wagon, at once, to be gone for one or two days, and would waive the question of sex in the matter of payment.

Alderbank was about twenty miles down the river by the road. On arriving there, he inquired for the house where a Mr. Lindsay lived. There was only one Lindsay family in town, — he must mean Dr. William Lindsay. His house was up there a little way above the village, lying a few rods back from the river

He found the house without difficulty, and knocked at the door. A motherly-looking woman opened it immediately, and held her hand up as if to ask him to speak and move softly.

" Does Mr. Clement Lindsay live here ? "

" He is staying here for the present. He is a nephew
of ours. He is in his bed from an injury."

" Nothing very serious, I hope ? "

" A bruise on his head, — not very bad, but the doctor
was afraid of erysipelas. Seems to be doing well enough
now."

" Is there a young person here, a stranger ? "

" There is such a young person here. Do you come
with any authority to make inquiries ? "

" I do. A young friend of mine is missing, and I
thought it possible I might learn something here about it.
Can I see this young person ? "

The matron came nearer to Byles Gridley, and said :
" This person is a young woman disguised as a boy. She
was rescued by my nephew at the risk of his life, and she
has been delirious ever since she has recovered her consciousness. She was almost too far gone to be resuscitated,
but Clement put his mouth to hers and kept her breathing
until her own breath returned and she gradually came to."

" Is she violent in her delirium ? "

" Not now. No ; she is quiet enough, but wandering,
— wants to know where she is, and whose the strange
faces are, — mine and my husband's, — that 's Dr. Lindsay, — and one of my daughters, who has watched with
her."

" If that is so, I think I had better see her. If she is
the person I suspect her to be, she will know me ; and a
familiar face may bring back her recollections and put a
stop to her wanderings. If she does not know me, I will
not stay talking with her. I think she will, if she is the
one I am seeking after. There is no harm in trying."

Mrs. Lindsay took a good long look at the old man. There was no mistaking his grave, honest, sturdy, wrinkled, scholarly face. His voice was assured and sincere in its tones. His decent black coat was just what a scholar's should be, — old, not untidy, a little shiny at the elbows with much leaning on his study-table, but neatly bound at the cuffs, where worthy Mrs. Hopkins had detected signs of fatigue and come to the rescue. His very hat looked honest as it lay on the table. It had moulded itself to a broad, noble head, that held nothing but what was true and fair, with a few harmless crotchets just to fill in with, and it seemed to know it.

The good woman gave him her confidence at once. "Is the person you are seeking a niece or other relative of yours ?"

(Why did not she ask if the girl was *his daughter?* What is that look of paternity and of maternity which observing and experienced mothers and old nurses know so well in men and in women?)

"No, she is not a relative. But I am acting for those who are."

"Wait a moment and I will go and see that the room is all right."

She returned presently. "Follow me softly, if you please. She is asleep, — so beautiful, — so innocent!"

Byles Gridley, Master of Arts, retired professor, more than sixty years old, childless, loveless, stranded in a lonely study strewed with wrecks of the world's thought, his work in life finished, his one literary venture gone down with all it held, with nobody to care for him but accidental acquaintances, moved gently to the side of the bed and looked upon the pallid, still features of Myrtle Hazard

He strove hard against a strange feeling that was taking hold of him, that was making his face act rebelliously, and troubling his eyes with sudden films. He made a brief stand against this invasion. "A weakness, — a weakness!" he said to himself. "What does all this mean? Never such a thing for these twenty years! Poor child! poor child! — Excuse me, madam," he said, after a little interval, but for what offence he did not mention. A great deal might be forgiven, even to a man as old as Byles Gridley, looking upon such a face, — so lovely, yet so marked with the traces of recent suffering, and even now showing by its changes that she was struggling in some fearful dream. Her forehead contracted, she started with a slight convulsive movement, and then her lips parted, and the cry escaped from them, — how heart-breaking when there is none to answer it, — " Mother !"

Gone back again through all the weary, chilling years of her girlhood to that hardly remembered morning of her life when the cry she uttered was answered by the light of loving eyes, the kiss of clinging lips, the embrace of caressing arms !

"It is better to wake her," Mrs. Lindsay said; "she is having a troubled dream. Wake up, my child, here is a friend waiting to see you."

She laid her hand very gently on Myrtle's forehead. Myrtle opened her eyes, but they were vacant as yet.

"Are we dead?" she said. "Where am I? This is n't heaven — there are no angels — O, no, no, no! don't send me to the other place — fifteen years, — only fifteen years old — no father, no mother — nobody loved me. *Was it wicked in me to live?*" Her whole theologica training was condensed in that last brief question.

The old man took her hand and looked her in the face, with a wonderful tenderness in his squared features. " Wicked to live, my dear? No indeed! Here! look at me, my child; don't you know your old friend Byles Gridley ? "

She was awake now. The sight of a familiar countenance brought back a natural train of thought. But her recollection passed over everything that had happened since Thursday morning.

" Where is the boat I was in ? " she said. " I have just been in the water, and I was dreaming that I was drowned. O Mr. Gridley, is that you ? Did you pull me out of the water ? "

" No, my dear, but you are out of it, and safe and sound: that is the main point. How do you feel now you are awake ? "

She yawned, and stretched her arms and looked round, but did not answer at first. This was all natural, and a sign that she was coming right. She looked down at her dress. It was not inappropriate to her sex, being a loose gown that belonged to one of the girls in the house.

" I feel pretty well," she answered, " but a little confused. My boat will be gone, if you don't run and stop it now. How did you get me into dry clothes so quick ? "

Master Byles Gridley found himself suddenly possessed by a large and luminous idea of the state of things, and made up his mind in a moment as to what he must do. There was no time to be lost. Every day, every hour, of Myrtle's absence was not only a source of anxiety and a cause of useless searching, but it gave room for inventive fancies to imagine evil. It was better to run some risk of injury to health, than to have her absence prolonged another day.

H

" Has this adventure been told about in the village, Mrs. Lindsay ? "

" No, we thought it best to wait until she could tell her own story, expecting her return to consciousness every hour, and thinking there might be some reason for her disguise which it would be kinder to keep quiet about. "

" You know nothing about her, then ? "

" Not a word. It was a great question whether to tell the story and make inquiries ; but she was safe, and could hardly bear disturbance, and, my dear sir, it seemed too probable that there was some sad story behind this escape in disguise, and that the poor child might need shelter and retirement. We meant to do as well as we could for her."

" All right, Mrs. Lindsay. You do not know who she is, then ? "

" No, sir, and perhaps it is as well that I should not know. Then I shall not have to answer any questions about it."

" Very good, madam, — just as it should be. And your family, are they as discreet as yourself ? "

" Not one word of the whole story has been or will be told by any one of us. That was agreed upon among us."

" Now then, madam. My name, as you heard me say, is Byles Gridley. Your husband will know it, perhaps ; at any rate I will wait until he comes back. This child is of good family and of good name. I know her well, and mean, with your kind help, to save her from the consequences which her foolish adventure might have brought upon her. Before the bells ring for meeting to-morrow morning this girl must be in her bed at her home, at Ox bow Village, and we must keep her story to ourselves as

far as may be. It will all blow over, if we do. The gossips will only know that she was upset in the river and
cared for by some good people, — good people and sensible
people too, Mrs. Lindsay. And now I want to see the
young man that rescued my friend here, — Clement Lindsay, — I have heard his name before.

Clement was not a beauty for the moment, but Master Grid-
lay saw well enough that he was a young man of the right
kind. He knew them at sight, — fellows with lime enough
in their bones and iron enough in their blood to begin with,
— shapely, large-nerved, firm-fibred and fine-fibred, with
well-spread bases to their heads for the ground-floor of the
facúlties, and well-vaulted arches for the upper range of
apprehensions and combinations. " Plenty of basements,"
he used to say, " without attics and skylights. Plenty of
skylights without rooms enough and space enough below."
But here was " a three-story brain," he said to himself as
he looked at it, and this was the youth who was to find his
complement in our pretty little Susan Posey ! His judgment may seem to have been hasty, but he took the measure of young men of twenty at sight from long and saga-
cious observation, as Nurse Byloe knew the " heft " of a
baby the moment she fixed her old eyes on it.

Clement was well acquainted with Byles Gridley, though
he had never seen him, for Susan's letters had had a good
deal to say about him of late. It was agreed between them
that the story should be kept as quiet as possible, and that
the young girl should not know the name of her deliverer,
— it might save awkward complications. It was not likely
that she would be disposed to talk of her adventure, which
had ended so disastrously, and thus the whole story would
soon die out.

The effect of the violent shock she had experienced was to change the whole nature of Myrtle for the time. Her mind was unsettled: she could hardly recall anything except the plunge over the fall. She was perfectly docile and plastic, — was ready to go anywhere Mr. Gridley wanted her to go, without any sign of reluctance. And so it was agreed that he should carry her back in his covered wagon that very night. All possible arrangements were made to render her journey comfortable. The fast mare had to trot very gently, and the old master would stop and adjust the pillows from time to time, and administer the restoratives which the physician had got ready, all as naturally and easily as if he had been bred a nurse, vastly to his own surprise, and with not a little gain to his self-appreciation. He was a serviceable kind of body on occasion, after all, was he not, hey, Mr. Byles Gridley? he said to himself.

At half past four o'clock on Sunday morning the shepherd brought the stray lamb into the paved yard at The Poplars, and roused the slumbering household to receive back the wanderer.

It was the Irishwoman, Kitty Fagan, huddled together in such amorphous guise, that she looked as if she had been fitted in a tempest of petticoats and a whirlwind of old shawls, who presented herself at the door.

But there was a very warm heart somewhere in that queer-looking bundle of clothes, and it was not one of those that can throb or break in silence. When she saw the long covered wagon, and the grave face of the old master she thought it was all over with the poor girl she loved, and that this was the undertaker's wagon bringing back only what had once been Myrtle Hazard. She screamed aloud, — so wildly that Myrtle lifted her head from the pillow against which she had rested it, and started forward.

The Irishwoman looked at her for a moment to assure herself that it was the girl she loved, and not her ghost. Then it all came over her, — she had been stolen by thieves, who had carried her off by night, and been rescued by the brave old man who had brought her back What crying and kisses and prayers and blessings were poured forth, in a confusion of which her bodily costume was a fitting type, those who know the vocabulary and the enthusiasm of her eloquent race may imagine better than we could describe it.

The welcome of the two other women was far less demonstrative. There were awful questions to be answered before the kind of reception she was to have could be settled. What they were, it is needless to suggest; but while Miss Silence was weeping, first with joy that her " responsibility " was removed, then with a fair share of pity and kindness, and other lukewarm emotions, — while Miss Badlam waited for an explanation before giving way to her feelings, — Mr. Gridley put the essential facts before them in a few words. She had gone down the river some miles in her boat, which was upset by a rush of the current, and she had come very near being drowned. She was got out, however, by a person living near by, and cared for by some kind women in a house near the river, where he had been fortunate enough to discover her. — Who cut her hair off? Perhaps those good people, — she had been out of her head. She was alive and unharmed, at any rate, wanting only a few days' rest. They might be very thankful to get her back, and leave her to tell the rest of her story when she had got her strength and memory, for she was not quite herself yet, and might not be for some days.

And so there she was at last laid in her own bed, listening again to the ripple of the waters beneath her, Miss Silence sitting on one side looking as sympathetic as her insufficient nature allowed her to look ; the Irishwoman uncertain between delight at Myrtle's return, and sorrow for her condition ; and Miss Cynthia Badlam occupying herself about house-matters, not unwilling to avoid the necessity of displaying her conflicting emotions.

Before he left the house, Mr. Gridley repeated the statement in the most precise manner, — some miles down the river — upset and nearly drowned — rescued almost dead — brought to and cared for by kind women in the house where he, Byles Gridley, found her. These were the facts, and nothing more than this was to be told at present They had better be made known at once, and the shortest and best way would be to have it announced by the minister at meeting that forenoon. With their permission, he would himself write the note for Mr. Stoker to read, and tell the other ministers that they might announce it to their people.

The bells rang for meeting, but the little household at The Poplars did not add to the congregation that day. In the mean time Kitty Fagan had gone down with Mr. Byles Gridley's note, to carry it to the Rev. Mr. Stoker. But, on her way, she stopped at the house of one Mrs. Finnegan, a particular friend of hers ; and the great event of the morning furnishing matter for large discourse, and various social allurements adding to the fascination of having a story to tell, Kitty Fagan forgot her note until meeting had begun and the minister had read the text of his sermon. " Bless my soul ! and sure I 've forgot ahl about the letter ! " she cried all at once, and away she tramped for the meeting-house. The sexton took the note, which was folded, and said he would hand it up to the pulpit after the sermon, — it would not do to interrupt the preacher.

The Rev. Mr. Stoker had, as was said, a somewhat re-markable gift in prayer, — an endowment by no means confined to profoundly spiritual persons, — in fact, not rarely owing much of its force to a strong animal nature underlying the higher attributes. The sweet singer of Israel would never have written such petitions and such hymns if his manhood had been less complete ; the flavor of remembered frailties could not help giving a character to his most devout exercises, or they would not have come quite home to our common humanity. But there is no gift more dangerous to the humility and sincerity of a minister. While his spirit ought to be on its knees before the throne of grace, it is too apt to be on tiptoe, following with ad miring look the flight of its own rhetoric. The essentially intellectual character of an extemporaneous composition spoken to the Creator with the consciousness that many of his creatures are listening to criticise or to admire, is the great argument for set forms of prayer.

The congregation on this particular Sunday was made ip chiefly of women and old men. The young men were :unting after Myrtle Hazard. Mr. Byles Gridley was in his place, wondering why the minister did not read his notice before the prayer. This prayer was never reported, as is the questionable custom with regard to some of these performances, but it was wrought up with a good deal of rasping force and broad pathos. When he came to pray for "our youthful sister, missing from her pious home, perhaps nevermore to return to her afflicted relatives," and the women and old men began crying, Byles Gridley was on the very point of getting up and cutting short the whole matter by stating the simple fact that she had got back, all right, and suggesting that he had better pray for some of the older and tougher sinners before him. But on the whole it would be more decorous to wait, and perhaps he was willing to hear what the object of his favorite antipathy had to say about it. So he waited through the prayer. He waited through the hymn, "Life is the time — " He waited to hear the sermon.

The minister gave out his text from the Book of Esther, second chapter, seventh verse : "*For she had neither father nor mother, and the maid was fair and beautiful.*" It was to be expected that the reverend gentleman, who loved to produce a sensation, would avail himself of the excitable state of his audience to sweep the key-board of their emotions, while, as we may say, all the stops were drawn out. His sermon was from notes ; for, though absolutely extemporaneous composition may be acceptable to one's Maker, it is not considered quite the thing in speaking to one's fellow-mortals. He discoursed for a time on the loss of parents, and on the dangers to which the unfortunate orphan is exposed. Then he spoke of the peculiar risks of the tender female child, left without its natural guardians. Warming with his subject, he dilated with wonderful unction on the temptations springing from personal attractions He pictured the " fair and beautiful " women of Holy Writ, lingering over their names with lover-like devotion. He brought Esther before his audience, bathed and perfumed for the royal presence of Ahasuerus. He showed them the sweet young Ruth, lying down in her innocence at the feet of the lord of the manor. He dwelt with special luxury on the charms which seduced the royal psalmist, — the soldier's wife for whom he broke the commands of the decalogue, and the maiden for whose attentions, in his cooler years, he violated the dictates of prudence and propriety. All this time Byles Gridley had his stern eyes on him. And while he kindled into passionate eloquence on these inspiring themes, poor Bathsheba, whom her mother had sent to church that she might get a little respite from her home duties, felt her blood growing cold in her veins, as the pallid image of the invalid wife, lying on her bed of suffering, rose in the midst of the glowing pictures which borrowed such warmth from her husband's imagination.

The sermon, with its hinted application to the event of the past week, was over at last. The shoulders of the nervous women were twitching with sobs. The old men were crying in their vacant way. But all the while the face of Byles Gridley, firm as a rock in the midst of this lachrymal inundation, was kept steadily on the preacher, who had often felt the look that came through the two round glasses searching into the very marrow of his bones.

As the sermon was finished, the sexton marched up through the broad aisle and handed the note over the door of the pulpit to the clergyman, who was wiping his face after the exertion of delivering his discourse. Mr. Stoker looked at it, started, changed color, — his vision of " The Dangers of Beauty, a Sermon printed by Request," had vanished, — and passed the note to Father Pemberton, who sat by him in the pulpit. With much pains he deciphered its contents, for his eyes were dim with years, and, having

6

read it, bowed his head upon his hands in silent thanks-giving. Then he rose in the beauty of his tranquil and noble old age, so touched with the message he had to proclaim to his people, that the three deep furrows on his forehead, which some said he owed to the three dogmas of original sin, predestination, and endless torment, seemed smoothed for the moment, and his face was as that of an angel while he spoke.

"Sisters and Brethren, — Rejoice with us, for we have found our lamb which had strayed from the fold. This our daughter was dead and is alive again; she was lost and is found. Myrtle Hazard, rescued from great peril of the waters, and cared for by good Samaritans, is now in her home. Thou, O Lord, who didst let the water-flood overflow her, didst not let the deep swallow her up, nor the pit shut its mouth upon her. Let us return our thanks to the God of Abraham, the God of Isaac, the God of Jacob, who is our God and Father, and who hath wrought this great deliverance."

After his prayer, which it tried him sorely to utter in unbroken tones, he gave out the hymn,

> "Lord, thou hast heard thy servant cry,
> And rescued from the grave";

but it was hardly begun when the leading female voice trembled and stopped, — and another, — and then a third, — and Father Pemberton, seeing that they were all overcome, arose and stretched out his arms, and breathed over them his holy benediction.

The village was soon alive with the news. The sexton forgot the solemnity of the Sabbath, and the bell acted as if it was crazy, tumbling heels over head at such a rate and with such a clamor, that a good many thought there was a fire, and, rushing out from every quarter, instantly caught the great news with which the air was ablaze.

A few of the young men who had come back went even further in their demonstrations. They got a small cannon in readiness, and without waiting for the going down of the sun, began firing rapidly, upon which the Rev. Mr. Stoker sallied forth to put a stop to this violation of the Sabbath. But in the mean time it was heard on all the hills, far and near. Some said they were firing in the hope of raising the corpse; but many who heard the bells ringing their crazy peals guessed what had happened. Before night the parties were all in, one detachment bearing the body of the bob-tailed catamount swung over a pole, like the mighty cluster of grapes from Eshcol, and another conveying with wise precaution that monstrous snapping-turtle which those of our friends who wish to see will find among the specimens marked *Chelydra Serventina* in the great collection at Cantabridge.

CHAPTER XI.

VEXED WITH A DEVIL.

IT was necessary at once to summon a physician to ad
vise as to the treatment of Myrtle, who had received a
shock, bodily and mental, not lightly to be got rid of, and
very probably to be followed by serious and varied disturbances. Her very tranquillity was suspicious, for there
must be something of exhaustion in it, and the reaction
must come sooner or later.

Old Dr. Lemuel Hurlbut, at the age of ninety-two, very
deaf, very nearly blind, very feeble, liable to odd lapses of
memory, was yet a wise counsellor in doubtful and difficult
cases, and on rare occasions was still called upon to exercise
his ancient skill. Here was a case in which a few words
from him might soothe the patient and give confidence to
all who were interested in her. Miss Silence Withers
went herself to see him.

"Miss Withers, father, wants to talk with you about
her niece, Miss Hazard," said Dr. Fordyce Hurlbut.

Miss Withers, Miss Withers? — O, Silence Withers,
— lives up at The Poplars. How's the Deacon, Miss
Withers?" [Ob. 1810.]

"My grandfather is not living, Dr. Hurlbut," she
screamed into his ear.

"Dead, is he? Well, it is n't long since he was with
us; and they come and go, — they come and go. I remember his father, Major Gideon Withers. He had a

great red feather on training-days, — that was what made me remember him. Who did you say was sick and wanted to see me, Fordyce?"

"Myrtle Hazard, father, — she has had a narrow escape from drowning, and it has left her in a rather nervous state. They would like to have you go up to The Poplars and take a look at her. You remember Myrtle Hazard? She is the great-granddaughter of your old friend the Deacon."

He had to wait a minute before his thoughts would come to order; with a little time, the proper answer would be evolved by the slow automatic movement of the rusted mental machinery.

After the silent moment: "Myrtle Hazard, Myrtle Hazard, — yes, yes, to be sure! The old Withers stock, — good constitutions, — a little apt to be nervous, one or two of 'em. I've given 'em a good deal of valerian and assafœtida, — not quite so much since the new blood came in. There is n't the change in folks people think, — same thing over and over again. I've seen six fingers on a child that had a six-fingered great-uncle, and I've seen that child's grandchild born with six fingers. Does this girl like to have her own way pretty well, like the rest of the family?"

"A little too well, I suspect, father. You will remember all about her when you come to see her and talk with her. She would like to talk with you, and her aunt wants to see you too; they think there's nobody like the 'old Doctor.'"

He was not too old to be pleased with this preference, and said he was willing to go when they were ready. With no small labor of preparation he was at last got to the house, and crept with his son's aid up to the little room over the water, where his patient was still lying.

There was a little too much color in Myrtle's cheeks, and a glistening lustre in her eyes that told of unnatural excitement. It gave a strange brilliancy to her beauty, and might have deceived an unpractised observer. The old man looked at her long and curiously, his imperfect sight excusing the closeness of his scrutiny.

He laid his trembling hand upon her forehead, and then felt her pulse with his shrivelled fingers. He asked her various questions about herself, which she answered with a tone not quite so calm as natural, but willingly and intelligently. They thought she seemed to the old Doctor to be doing very well, for he spoke cheerfully to her, and treated her in such a way that neither she nor any of those around her could be alarmed. The younger physician was disposed to think she was only suffering from temporary excitement, and that it would soon pass off.

They left the room to talk it over.

"It does not amount to much, I suppose, father," said Dr. Fordyce Hurlbut. "You made the pulse about ninety, — a little hard, — did n't you, as I did? Rest, and low diet for a day or two, and all will be right, won't it?"

Was it the feeling of sympathy, or was it the pride of superior sagacity, that changed the look of the old man's wrinkled features? "Not so fast, — not so fast, Fordyce," he said. "I 've seen that look on another face of the same blood, — it 's a great many years ago, and she was dead before you were born, my boy, — but I 've seen that look, and it meant trouble then, and I 'm afraid it means trouble now. I see some danger of a brain fever. And if she does n't have that, then look out for some hysteric fits that

will make mischief. Take that handkerchief off of her
head, and cut her hair close, and keep her temples cool,
and put some drawing plasters to the soles of her feet, and
give her some of my *pilulæ compositæ*, and follow them
with some doses of *sal polychrest*. I 've been through it
all before in that same house. Live folks are only dead
folks warmed over. I can see 'em all in that girl's face,
— Handsome Judith, to begin with. And that queer
woman, the Deacon's mother, — there 's where she gets
that hystericky look. Yes, and the black-eyed woman
with the Indian blood in her, — look out for that, — look
out for that. And — and — my son, do you remember
Major Gideon Withers?" [Ob. 1780.]

"Why no, father, I can't say that I remember the
Major ; but I know the picture very well. Does she
remind you of him?"

He paused again, until the thoughts came slowly straggling up to the point where the question left him. He
shook his head solemnly, and turned his dim eyes on his
son's face.

"Four generations — four generations, man and wife, —
yes, five generations, for old Selah Withers took me in his
arms when I was a child, and called me 'little gal,' for I
was in girl's clothes, — five generations before this Hazard
child I 've looked on with these old eyes. And it seems
to me that I can see something of almost every one of 'em
in this child's face, — it 's the forehead of this one, and it 's
the eyes of that one, and it 's that other's mouth, and the
look that I remember in another, and when she speaks,
why, I 've heard that same voice before — yes, yes — as
long ago as when I was first married ; for I remember
Rachel used to think I praised Handsome Judith's voice

more than it deserved, — and her face too, for that matter You remember Rachel, my first wife, — don't you, For dyce?"

"No, father, I don't remember her, but I know her portrait." (As he was the son of the old Doctor's second wife, he could hardly be expected to remember her predecessor.)

The old Doctor's sagacity was not in fault about the somewhat threatening aspect of Myrtle's condition. His directions were followed implicitly; for with the exception of the fact of sluggishness rather than loss of memory, and of that confusion of dates which in slighter degrees is often felt as early as middle-life, and increases in most persons from year to year, his mind was still penetrating, and his advice almost as trustworthy, as in his best days.

It was very fortunate that the old Doctor ordered Myrtle's hair to be cut, and Miss Silence took the scissors and trimmed it at once. So, whenever she got well and was seen about, there would be no mystery about the loss of her locks, — the Doctor had been afraid of brain fever, and ordered them to cut her hair.

Many things are uncertain in this world, and among them the effect of a large proportion of the remedies prescribed by physicians. Whether it was by the use of the means ordered by the old Doctor, or by the efforts of nature, or by both together, at any rate the first danger was averted, and the immediate risk from brain fever soon passed over. But the impression upon her mind and body had been too profound to be dissipated by a few days' rest. The hysteric stage which the wise old man had apprehended began to manifest itself by its usual signs, if any thing can be called usual in a condition the natural order of which is disorder and anomaly.

And now the reader, if such there be, who believes in the absolute independence and self-determination of the will, and the consequent total responsibility of every human being for every irregular nervous action and ill-governed muscular contraction, may as well lay down this narrative, or he may lose all faith in poor Myrtle Hazard, and all patience with the writer who tells her story.

The mental excitement so long sustained, followed by a violent shock to the system, coming just at the period of rapid development, gave rise to that morbid condition, accompanied with a series of mental and moral perversions, which in ignorant ages and communities is attributed to the influence of evil spirits, but for the better-instructed is the malady which they call hysteria. Few households have ripened a growth of womanhood without witnessing some of its manifestations, and its phenomena are largely traded in by scientific pretenders and religious fanatics. Into this cloud, with all its risks and all its humiliations, Myrtle Hazard is about to enter. Will she pass through it unharmed, or wander from her path, and fall over one of those fearful precipices which lie before her?

After the ancient physician had settled the general plan of treatment, its details and practical application were left to the care of his son. Dr. Fordyce Hurlbut was a widower, not yet forty years old, a man of a fine masculine aspect and a vigorous nature. He was a favorite with his female patients, — perhaps many of them would have said because he was good-looking and pleasant in his manners, but some thought in virtue of a special magnetic power to which certain temperaments were impressible, though there was no explaining it. But he himself never claimed any such personal gift, and never attempted any of the exploits

6 *   x

which some thought were in his power if he chose to **exercise** his faculty in that direction.   This girl was, as it **were,** a child to him, for he had seen her grow up from infancy, and had often held her on his knee in her early years. The first thing he did was to get her a nurse, for he **saw** that neither of the two women about her exercised a quieting influence upon her nerves.   So he got her old friend, Nurse Byloe, to come and take care of her.

The old nurse looked calm enough at one or two of **his** first visits, but the next morning her face showed that something had been going wrong.   " Well, what has been the trouble, Nurse ? " the Doctor said, as soon as he could get her out of the room.

" She 's been attackted, Doctor, sence you been here, dreadful.   It 's them high stirricks, Doctor, 'n' I never see 'em higher, nor more of 'em.   Laughin' as ef she would bust.   Cryin' as ef she 'd lost all her friends, 'n' was a follerin' their corpse to their graves.   And spassums, — sech spassums !   And ketchin' at her throat, 'n' sayin' there was a great ball a risin' into it from her stommick. One time she had a kind o' lockjaw like.   And one time she stretched herself out 'n' laid jest as stiff as ef she was dead.   And she says now that her head feels as ef a nail had been driv' into it, — into the left temple, she says, and that 's what makes her look so distressed now."

The Doctor came once more to her bedside.   He saw that her forehead was contracted, and that she was evidently suffering from severe pain somewhere.

" Where is your uneasiness, Myrtle ? " he asked.

She moved her hand very slowly, and pressed it on her left temple.   He laid his hand upon the same spot, kept it there a moment, and then removed it.   She took it gently

with he. own, and placed it on her temple again. As he
sat watching her, he saw that her features were growing
easier, and in a short time her deep, even breathing showed
that she was asleep.

"It beats all," the old Nurse said. "Why, she's been a
complainin' ever sence daylight, and she hain't slep' not a
wink afore, sence twelve o'clock las' night! It 's jes' like
them magnetizers, — I never heerd you was one o' them
kind, Dr. Hulburt."

"I can't say how it is, Nurse, — I nave heard people
say my hand was magnetic, but I n ver thought of its
quieting her so quickly. No sleep since twelve o'clock
last night, you say?"

"Not a wink, 'n' actin' as ef she was posse.sed a good
deal o' the time. You read your Bible, Doctor, don't you?
You're pious? Do you remember about that woman in
Scriptur' out of whom the Lord cast seven devils? Wel,
I should ha' thought there was seventy devils in that gal
last night, from the way she carr'd on. And now she lays
there jest as peaceful as a new-born babe, — that is, accordin'
to the sayin' about 'em; for as to peaceful new-born babes,
I never see one that come t' anything, that did n't screech
as ef the haouse was afire 'n' it wanted to call all the fire-
ingines within ten mild."

The Doctor smiled, but he became thoughtful in a moment. Did he possess a hitherto unexercised personal
power, which put the key of this young girl's nervous
system into his hands? The remarkable tranquillizing
effect of the contact of his hand with her forehead looked
like an immediate physical action. It might have been a
mere coincidence, however. He would not form an opinion until his next visit.

At that next visit it did seem as if some of Nurse Byloe's seventy devils had possession of the girl. All the strange spasmodic movements, the chokings, the odd sounds, the wild talk, the laughing and crying, were in full blast. All the remedies which had been ordered seemed to have been of no avail. The Doctor could hardly refuse trying his *quasi* magnetic influence, and placed the tips of his fingers on her forehead. The result was the same that had followed the similar proceeding the day before, — the storm was soon calmed, and after a little time she fell into a quiet sleep, as in the first instance.

Here was an awkward affair for the physician, to be sure! He held this power in his hands, which no remedy and no other person seemed to possess. How long would he be chained to her, and she to him, and what would be the consequence of the mysterious relation which must necessarily spring up between a man like him, in the plenitude of vital force, of strongly attractive personality, and a young girl organized for victory over the calmest blood and the steadiest resistance?

Every day after this made matters worse. There was something almost partaking of the miraculous in the influence he was acquiring over her. His " Peace, be still! " was obeyed by the stormy elements of this young soul, as if it had been a supernatural command. How could he resist the dictate of humanity which called him to make his visits more frequent, that her intervals of rest might be more numerous? How could he refuse to sit at her bedside for a while in the evening, that she might be quieted, instead of beginning the night sleepless and agitated?

The Doctor was a man of refined feeling as well as of principle, and he had besides a sacred memory in the deepest heart of his affections. It was the common belief in the village that he would never marry again, but that his first and only love was buried in the grave of the wife of his youth. It did not easily occur to him to suspect himself of any weakness with regard to this patient of his, little more than a child in years. It did not at once suggest itself to him that she, in her strange, excited condition, might fasten her wandering thoughts upon him, too far removed by his age, as it seemed, to strike the fancy of a young girl under almost any conceivable conditions.

Thus it was that many of those beautiful summer evenings found him sitting by his patient, the river rippling and singing beneath them, the moon shining over them, sweet odors from the thickets on the banks of the stream stealing in on the soft air that came through the open window, and every time they were thus together, the subtile influence which bound them to each other bringing them more and more into inexplicable harmonies and almost spiritual identity.

But all this did not hinder the development of new and strange conditions in Myrtle Hazard. Her will was losing its power. " I cannot help it " — the hysteric motto — was her constant reply. It is not pleasant to confess the truth, but she was rapidly undergoing a singular change of her moral nature. She had been a truthful child. If she had kept her secret about what she found in the garret, she thought she was exercising her rights, and she had never been obliged to tell any lies about it.

But now she seemed to have lost the healthy instincts for veracity and honesty. She feigned all sorts of odd symptoms, and showed a wonderful degree of cunning in giving an appearance of truth to them. It became next to

impossible to tell what was real and what was simulated
At one time she could not be touched ever so lightly without shrinking and crying out. At another time she would
squint, and again she would be half paralyzed for a time.
She would pretend to fast for days, living on food she had
concealed and took secretly in the night.

The nurse was getting worn out. Kitty Fagan would
have had the priest come to the house and sprinkle it with
holy water. The two women were beginning to get nervous themselves. The Rev. Mr. Stoker said in confidence
to Miss Silence, that there was reason to fear she might
have been given over for a time to the buffetings of Satan,
and that perhaps his (Mr. Stoker's) personal attentions
might be useful in that case. And so it appeared that the
" young doctor " was the only being left with whom she
had any complete relations and absolute sympathy. She
had become so passive in his hands that it seemed as if
her only healthy life was, as it were, transmitted through
him, and that she depended on the transfer of his nervous
power, as the plant upon the light for its essential living
processes.

The two young men who had met in so unexpected a
manner on board the ship Swordfish had been reasonably
discreet in relating their adventures. Myrtle Hazard may
or may not have had the plan they attributed to her; however that was, they had looked rather foolish when they
met, and had not thought it worth while to be very com-
municative about the matter when they returned. It had
at least given them a chance to become a little better acquainted with each other, and it was an opportunity which
the elder and more artful of the two meant to turn to ad
vantage.

Of all Myrtle's few friends only one was in the habit of eeing her often during this period, namely, Olive Eveleth a girl so quiet and sensible that she, if anybody, could be trusted with her. But Myrtle's whole character seemed to have changed, and Olive soon found that she was in some mystic way absorbed into another nature. Except when the physician's will was exerted upon her, she was drifting without any self-directing power, and then any one of those manifold impulses which would in some former ages have been counted as separate manifestations on the part of distinct demoniacal beings might take possession of her. Olive did little, therefore, but visit Myrtle from time to time to learn if any change had occurred in her condition. All this she reported to Cyprian, and all this was got out of him by Mr. William Murray Bradshaw.

That gentleman was far from being pleased with the look of things as they were represented. What if the Doctor, who was after all in the prime of life and younger-looking than some who were born half a dozen years after him, should get a hold on this young woman, — girl now, if you will, but in a very few years certain to come within possible, nay, not very improbable, matrimonial range of him? That would be pleasant, would n't it. It had happened sometimes, as he knew, that these magnetizing tricks had led to infatuation on the part of the subjects of the wonderful influence. So he concluded to be ill and consult the younger Dr. Hurlbut, and incidentally find out how the land lay.

The next question was, what to be ill with. Some not ungentlemanly malady, not hereditary, not incurable, not requiring any obvious change in habits of life. Dyspepsia would answer the purpose well enough: so Mr. Murray

Bradshaw picked up a medical book and read ten minutes
or more for that complaint. At the end of this time he
was an accomplished dyspeptic ; for lawyers half learn a
thing quicker than the members of any other profession.

He presented himself with a somewhat forlorn countenance to Dr. Fordyce Hurlbut, as suffering from some of the
less formidable symptoms of that affection. He got into a
very interesting conversation with him, especially about
some nervous feelings which had accompanied his attack of
indigestion. Thence to nervous complaints in general.
Thence to the case of the young lady at The Poplars whom
he was attending. The Doctor talked with a certain reserve, as became his professional relations with his patient ;
but it was plain enough that, if this kind of intercourse
went on much longer, it would be liable to end in some
emotional explosion or other, and there was no saying how
it would at last turn out.

Murray Bradshaw was afraid to meddle directly. He
knew something more about the history of Myrtle's adventure than any of his neighbors, and, among other things,
that it had given Mr. Byles Gridley a peculiar interest in
her, of which he could take advantage. He therefore artfully hinted his fears to the old man, and left his hint to
work itself out.

However suspicious Master Gridley was of him and his
motives, he thought it worth while to call up at The Poplars and inquire for himself of the nurse what was this new
relation growing up between the physician and his young
patient.

She imparted her opinion to him in a private conversation with great freedom. " Sech doin's ! sech doin's ! The
gal 's jest as much bewitched as ever any gal was sence

them that was possessed in Scriptur'. And every day it 's
wus and wus. Ef that Doctor don't stop comin', she won't
breathe without his helpin' her to before long. And, Mr
Gridley, — I don't like to say so, — but I can't help thinkin' he 's gettin' a little bewitched too. I don't believe he
means to take no kind of advantage of her ; but, Mr. Gridley, you 've seen them millers fly round and round a
candle, and you know how it ginerally comes out. Men is
men and gals is gals. I would n't trust no man, not ef he
was much under a hundred year old, — and as for a
gal — ! "

"*Mulieri ne mortuæ quidem credendum est,*" said Mr.
Gridley. "You would n't trust a woman even if she was
dead, hey, Nurse ? "

"Not till she was buried, 'n' the grass growin' a foot
high over her," said Nurse Byloe, "unless I 'd know'd her
sence she was a baby. I 've know'd this one sence she was
two or three year old ; but this gal ain't Myrtle Hazard no
longer, — she 's bewitched into somethin' different. I 'll
tell ye what, Mr. Gridley ; you get old Dr. Hulburt to come
and see her once a day for a week, and get the young doctor to stay away. I 'll resk it. She 'll have some dreadful
tantrums at fust, but she 'll come to it in two or three
days."

Master Byles Gridley groaned in spirit. He had come
to this village to end his days in peace, and here he was
ust going to make a martyr of himself for the sake of a
young person to whom he was under no obligation, except
hat he had saved her from the consequences of her own
foolish act, at the expense of a great overturn of all his
domestic habits. There was no help for it. The nurse
was right, and he must perform the disagreeable duty of

letting the Doctor know that he was getting into a track which might very probably lead to mischief, and that he must back out as fast as he could.

At 2 P. M. Gifted Hopkins presented the following note at the Doctor's door: —

"Mr. Byles Gridley would be much obliged to Dr. Fordyce Hurlbut if he would call at his study this evening."

"Odd, is n't it, father, the old man's asking me to come and see him? Those old stub-twist constitutions never want patching."

"Old man! old man! Who's that you call old, — not Byles Gridley, hey? Old! old! Sixty year, more or less! How old was Floyer when he died, Fordyce? Ninety-odd, was n't it? Had the asthma though, or he'd have lived to be as old as Dr. Holyoke, — a hundred year and over. That's old. But men live to be a good deal more than that sometimes. What does Byles Gridley want of you, did you say?"

"I'm sure I can't tell, father; I'll go and find out." So he went over to Mrs. Hopkins's in the evening, and was shown up into the study.

Master Gridley treated the Doctor to a cup of such tea as bachelors sometimes keep hid away in mysterious caddies. He presently began asking certain questions about the grand climacteric, which eventful period of life he was fast approaching. Then he discoursed of medicine, ancient and modern, tasking the Doctor's knowledge not a little and evincing a good deal of acquaintance with old doctrines and authors. He had a few curious old medical books in his library, which he said he should like to show Dr Hurlbut.

" There, now ! What do you say to this copy of Joan-
nes de Ketam, Venice, 1522 ?   Look at these woodcuts, —
the first anatomical pictures ever printed, Doctor, unless
these others of Jacobus Berengarius are older !   See this
scene of the plague-patient, the doctor smelling at his
pouncet-box, the old nurse standing square at the bedside,
the young nurse with the bowl, holding back and turning
her head away, and the old burial-hag behind her, shoving
her forward, — a very curious book, Doctor, and has the
first phrenological picture in it ever made.   Take a look,
too, at my Vesalius, — not the Leyden edition, Doctor, but
the one with the grand old original figures, — so good that
they laid them to Titian.   And look here, Doctor, I could
n't help getting this great folio Albinus, 1747, — and the
nineteenth century can't touch it, Doctor, — can't touch it
for completeness and magnificence, — so all the learned
professors tell me !   Brave old fellows, Doctor, and put
their lives into their books as you gentlemen don't pretend
to do now-a-days.   And *good* old fellows, Doctor, — high-
minded, scrupulous, conscientious, punctilious, — remembered their duties to man and to woman, and felt all the
responsibilities of their confidential relation to families
Did you ever read the oldest of medical documents, — the
Oath of Hippocrates ? "

The Doctor thought he had read it, but did not remem
ber much about it.

" It 's worth reading, Doctor, — it 's worth remembering ;
and, old as it is, it is just as good to-day as it was when it
vas laid down as a rule of conduct four hundred years
before the Sermon on the Mount was delivered.   Let me
read it to you, Dr. Hurlbut."

There was something in Master Gridley's look that made

the Doctor feel a little nervous; he did not know just what
was coming.

Master Gridley took out his great Hippocrates, the
edition of Foesius, and opened to the place. He turned
so as to face the Doctor, and read the famous Oath aloud,
Englishing it as he went along. When he came to these
words which follow, he pronounced them very slowly and
with special emphasis.

"*My life shall be pure and holy.*"

"*Into whatever house I enter, I will go for the good of the
patient: I will abstain from inflicting any voluntary injury,
and from leading away any, whether man or woman, bond
or free.*"

The Doctor changed color as he listened, and the moisture broke out on his forehead.

Master Gridley saw it, and followed up his advantage.
" Dr. Fordyce Hurlbut, are you not in danger of violating
the sanctities of your honorable calling, and leading astray
a young person committed to your sacred keeping?"

While saying these words, Master Gridley looked full
upon him, with a face so charged with grave meaning, so
impressed with the gravity of his warning accents, that
the Doctor felt as if he were before some dread tribunal,
and remained silent. He was a member of the Rev. Mr.
Stoker's church, and the words he had just listened to were
those of a sinful old heathen who had never heard a sermon in his life; but they stung him, for all that, as the
parable of the prophet stung the royal transgressor.

He spoke at length, for the plain honest words had
touched the right spring of consciousness at the right moment; not too early, for he now saw whither he was tending, — not too late, for he was not yet in the inner spiral

of the passion which whirls men and women to their doom
in ever-narrowing coils, that will not unwind at the command of God or man.

He spoke as one who is humbled by self-accusation, yet
in a manly way, as became his honorable and truthful
character.

"Master Gridley," he said, "I stand convicted before
you. I know too well what you are thinking of. It .
true, I cannot continue my attendance on Myrtle — on
Miss Hazard, for you mean her — without peril to both of
us. She is not herself. God forbid that I should cease to
be myself! I have been thinking of a summer tour, and I
will at once set out upon it, and leave this patient in my
father's hands. I think he will find strength to visit her
under the circumstances."

The Doctor went off the next morning without saying a
word to Myrtle Hazard, and his father made the customary
visit in his place.

That night the spirit tare her, as may well be supposed,
and so the second night. But there was no help for it:
her doctor was gone, and the old physician, with great
effort, came instead, sat by her, spoke kindly to her, left
wise directions to her attendants, and above all assured
them that, if they would have a little patience, they would
see all this storm blow over.

On the third night after his visit, the spirit rent her sore,
and came out of her, or, in the phrase of to-day, she had a
fierce paroxysm, after which the violence of the conflict
ceased, and she might be called convalescent so far as that
was concerned.

But all this series of nervous disturbances left her in a
very impressible and excitable condition. This was just the

state to invite the spiritual manipulations of one of those theological practitioners who consider that the treatment of all morbid states of mind short of raving madness belongs to them and not to the doctors. This same condition was equally favorable for the operations of any professional experimenter who would use the flame of religious excitement to light the torch of an earthly passion. So many fingers that begin on the black keys stray to the white ones before the tune is played out!

If Myrtle Hazard was in charge of any angelic guardian, the time was at hand when she would need all celestial influences; for the Rev. Joseph Bellamy Stoker was about to take a deep interest in her spiritual welfare.

CHAPTER XII.

SKIRMISHING.

" SO the Rev. Joseph Bellamy Stoker has called upon
you, Susan Posey, has he? And wants you to come
and talk religion with him in his study, Susan Posey, does
he? Religion is a good thing, my dear, the best thing in
the world, and never better than when we are young, and
no young people need it more than young girls. There
are temptations to all, and to them as often as to any, Susan
Posey. And temptations come to them in places where
they don't look for them, and from persons they never
thought of as tempters. So I am very glad to have your
thoughts called to the subject of religion. ' Remember thy
Creator in the days of thy youth.'

" But Susan Posey, my dear, I think you had better not
break in upon the pious meditations of the Rev. Joseph
Bellamy Stoker in his private study. A monk's cell and
a minister's library are hardly the places for young ladies.
They distract the attention of these good men from their
devotions and their sermons. If you think you must go,
you had better take Mrs. Hopkins with you. She likes
religious conversation, and it will do her good too, and save
a great deal of time for the minister, conversing with two
at once. She is of discreet age, and will tell you when it
is time to come away, — you might stay too long, you know.
I 've known young persons stay a good deal too long at these
interviews, — a great deal too long, Susan Posey ! "

Such was the fatherly counsel of Master Byles Gridley

Susan was not very quick of apprehension, but she could not help seeing the justice of Master Gridley's remark, that for a young person to go and break in on the hours that a minister requires for his studies, without being accompanied by a mature friend who would remind her when it was time to go, would be taking an unfair advantage of his kindness in asking her to call upon him. She promised, therefore, that she would never go without having Mrs. Hopkins as her companion, and with this assurance her old friend rested satisfied.

It is altogether likely that he had some deeper reason for his advice than those with which he satisfied the simple nature of Susan Posey. Or that it will be easier to judge after a glance at the conditions and character of the minister and his household.

The Rev. Mr. Stoker had, in addition to the personal advantages already alluded to, some other qualities which might prove attractive to many women. He had, in particular, that art of sliding into easy intimacy with them which implies some knowledge of the female nature, and, above all, confidence in one's powers. There was little doubt, the gossips maintained, that many of the younger women of his parish would have been willing, in certain contingencies, to lift for him that other end of his yoke under which poor Mrs. Stoker was fainting, unequal to the burden.

That lady must have been some years older than her husband, — how many we need not inquire too curiously, — but in vitality she had long passed the prime in which he was still flourishing. She had borne him five children and cried her eyes hollow over the graves of three of them Household cares had dragged upon her; the routine of vil

lage life wearied her; the parishioners expected too much
of her as the minister's wife; she had wanted more fresh
air and more cheerful companionship; and her thoughts
had fed too much on death and sin, — good bitter tonics to
increase the appetite for virtue, but *not* good as food and
drink for the spirit.

But there was another grief which lay hidden far beneath
these obvious depressing influences. She felt that she was
no longer to her husband what she had been to him, and
felt it with something of self-reproach, — which was a
wrong to herself, for she had been a true and tender wife
Deeper than all the rest was still another feeling, which
had hardly risen into the region of inwardly articulated
thought, but lay unshaped beneath all the syllabled trains
of sleeping or waking consciousness.

The minister was often consulted by his parishioners upon
spiritual matters, and was in the habit of receiving in his
study visitors who came with such intent. Sometimes it
was old weak-eyed Deacon Rumrill, in great iron-bowed
spectacles, with hanging nether lip and tremulous voice,
who had got his brain into a muddle about the beast with
two horns, or the woman that fled into the wilderness, or
other points not settled to his mind in Scott's Commentary.
The minister was always very busy at such times, and
made short work of his deacon's doubts. Or it might be that
an ancient woman, a mother or a grandmother in Israel,
came with her questions and her perplexities to her pastor; and it was pretty certain that just at that moment he
was very deep in his next sermon, or had a pressing visit
to make.

But it would also happen occasionally that one of the
tenderer ewe-lambs of the flock needed comfort from the

presence of the shepherd.   Poor Mrs. Stoker noticed, or
thought she noticed, that the good man had more leisure
for the youthful and blooming sister than for the more discreet and venerable matron or spinster.   The sitting was
apt to be longer; and the worthy pastor would often linger awhile about the door, to speed the parting guest,
perhaps, but a little too much after the fashion of young
people who are not displeased with each other, and who
often find it as hard to cross a threshold single as a witch
finds it to get over a running stream.   More than once,
the pallid, faded wife had made an errand to the study,
and, after a keen look at the bright young cheeks, flushed
with the excitement of intimate spiritual communion, had
gone back to her chamber with her hand pressed against
her heart, and the bitterness of death in her soul.

The end of all these bodily and mental trials was, that
the minister's wife had fallen into a state of habitual inva-
lidism, such as only women, who feel all the nerves which
in men are as insensible as telegraph-wires, can experience.

The doctor did not know what to make of her case, —
whether she would live or die, — whether she would lan-
guish for years, or, all at once, roused by some strong impression, or in obedience to some unexplained movement
of the vital forces, take up her bed and walk.   For her
bed had become her home, where she lived as if it belonged
to her organism.   There she lay, a not unpleasing invalid
to contemplate, always looking resigned, patient, serene,
except when the one deeper grief was stirred, always
arrayed with simple neatness, and surrounded with little
tokens that showed the constant presence with her of
tasteful and thoughtful affection.   She did not know, nobody could know, how steadily, how silently all this arti-

ficial life was draining the veins and blanching the cheek of her daughter Bathsheba, one of the every-day, air-breathing angels without nimbus or aureole who belong to every story which lets us into a few households, as much as the stars and the flowers belong to everybody's verses.

Bathsheba's devotion to her mother brought its own reward, but it was not in the shape of outward commendation. Some of the more censorious members of her father's congregation were severe in their remarks upon her absorption in the supreme object of her care. It seems that this had prevented her from attending to other duties which they considered more imperative. They did n't see why she should n't keep a Sabbath school as well as the rest, and as to her not comin' to meetin' three times on Sabbath day like other folks, they could n't account for it, except because she calculated that she could get along without the means of grace, bein' a minister's daughter. Some went so far as to doubt if she had ever experienced religion, for all she was a professor. There was a goo many indulged a false hope. To this, others objected her life of utter self-denial and entire surrender to her duties towards her mother as some evidence of Christian character. But old Deacon Rumrill put down that heresy by showing conclusively from Scott's Commentary on Romans xi. 1 – 6, that this was altogether against her chance of being called, and that the better her disposition to perform good works, the more unlikely she was to be the subject of saving grace. Some of these severe critics were good people enough themselves, but they loved active work and stirring companionship, and would have found their real cross if they had been called to sit at an nvalid's bedside.

As for the Rev. Mr. Stoker, his duties did not allow
him to give so much time to his suffering wife as his
feelings would undoubtedly have prompted. He therefore relinquished the care of her (with great reluctance
we may naturally suppose) to Bathsheba, who had inherited not only her mother's youthful smile, but that
self-forgetfulness which, born with some of God's creatures, is, if not "grace," at least a manifestation of native
depravity which might well be mistaken for it.

The intimacy of mother and daughter was complete,
except on a single point. There was one subject on
which no word ever passed between them. The excuse of duties to others was by a tacit understanding a
mantle to cover all short-comings in the way of attention
from the husband and father, and no word ever passed
between them implying a suspicion of the loyalty of his
affections. Bathsheba came at last so to fill with her
tenderness the space left empty in the neglected heart,
that her mother only spoke her habitual feeling when she
said, "I should think you were in love with me, my darling, if you were not my daughter."

This was a dangerous state of things for the minister.
Strange suggestions and unsafe speculations began to mingle with his dreams and reveries. The thought once admitted that another's life is becoming superfluous and a burden, feeds like a ravenous vulture on the soul. Woe to the
man or woman whose days are passed in watching the
hour-glass through which the sands run too slowly for
longings that are like a skulking procession of bloodless
murders! Without affirming such horrors of the Rev.
Mr. Stoker, it would not be libellous to say that his fancy
was tampering with future possibilities, as it constantly

happens with those who are getting themselves into training for some act of folly, or some crime, it may be, which
will in its own time evolve itself as an idea in the consciousness, and by and by ripen into fact.

It must not be taken for granted that he was actually
on the road to some fearful deed, or that he was an utterly
lost soul. He was ready to yield to temptation if it came
in his way ; he would even court it, but he did not shape
out any plan very definitely in his mind, as a more desperate sinner would have done. He liked the pleasur-
able excitement of emotional relations with his pretty
lambs, and enjoyed it under the name of religious communion. There is a border land where one can stand on
the territory of legitimate instincts and affections, and
yet be so near the pleasant garden of the Adversary,
that his dangerous fruits and flowers are within easy
reach. Once tasted, the next step is like to be the scal-
ing of the wall. The Rev. Mr. Stoker was very fond
of this border land. His imagination was wandering over
it too often when his pen was travelling almost of itself
along the weary parallels of the page before him. All
at once a blinding flash would come over him, the lines
of his sermon would run together, the fresh manuscript
would shrivel like a dead leaf, and the rows of hard-
hearted theology on the shelves before him, and the
broken-backed Concordance, and the Holy Book itself,
would fade away as he gave himself up to the enchant-
ment of his delirious dream.

The reader will probably consider it a discreet arrangement that pretty Susan Posey should seek her
pastor in grave company. Mrs. Hopkins willingly consented to the arrangement which had been proposed, and

agreed to go with the young lady on her visit to the Rev
Mr. Stoker's study. They were both arrayed in their
field-day splendors on this occasion. Susan was lovely in
her light curls and blue ribbons, and the becoming dress
which could not help betraying the modestly emphasized
crescendos and gently graded *diminuendos* of her figure.
She was as round as if she had been turned in a lathe,
and as delicately finished as if she had been modelled
for a Flora. She had naturally an airy toss of the head
and a springy movement of the joints, such as some girls
study in the glass (and make dreadful work of it), so
that she danced all over without knowing it, like a little
lively bobolink on a bulrush. In short, she looked fit to
spoil a homily for Saint Anthony himself.

Mrs. Hopkins was not less perfect in her somewhat
different style. She might be called impressive and imposing in her grand costume, which she wore for this
visit. It was a black silk dress, with a crape shawl, a
firmly defensive bonnet, and an alpaca umbrella with
a stern-looking and decided knob presiding as its handle.
The dried-leaf rustle of her silk dress was suggestive
of the ripe autumn of life, bringing with it those golden
fruits of wisdom and experience which the grave teachers
of mankind so justly prefer to the idle blossoms of adoles-
cence.

It is needless to say that the visit was conducted with
the most perfect propriety in all respects. Mrs. Hopkins
was disposed to take upon herself a large share of the
conversation. The minister, on the other hand, would
have devoted himself more particularly to Miss Susan,
but, with a very natural make-believe obtuseness, the good
woman drew his fire so constantly that few of his remarks

and hardly any of his insinuating looks, reached the tender object at which they were aimed. It is probable that his features or tones betrayed some impatience at having thus been foiled of his purpose, for Mrs. Hopkins thought he looked all the time as if he wanted to get rid of her. The three parted, therefore, not in the best humor all round. Mrs. Hopkins declared she'd see the minister in Jericho before she'd fix herself up as if she was goin' to a weddin' to go and see *him* again. Why, he did n't make any more of her than if she'd been a tabby-cat. She believed some of these ministers thought women's souls dried up like peas in a pod by the time they was forty year old; anyhow, they did n't seem to care any great about 'em, except while they was green and tender. It was all Miss Se-usan, Miss Se-usan, Miss Se-usan, my dear! but as for her, she might jest as well have gone with her apron on, for any notice he took of her. She did n't care, she was n't goin' to be left out when there was talkin' goin' on, anyhow.

Susan Posey, on her part, said she did n't like him a bit. He looked so sweet at her, and held his head on one side, — law! just as if he had been a young beau! And, — don't tell, — but he whispered that he wished the next time I came I would n't bring that Hopkins woman!

It would not be fair to repeat what the minister said to himself; but we may own as much as this, that, if worthy Mrs. Hopkins had heard it, she would have treated him to a string of adjectives which would have greatly enlarged his conceptions of the fema'e vocabulary.

CHAPTER XIII.

BATTLE.

IN tracing the history of a human soul through its com
monplace nervous perturbations, still more through its
spiritual humiliations, there is danger that we shall feel a
certain contempt for the subject of such weakness. It is
easy to laugh at the erring impulses of a young girl; but
you who remember when —— ——, only fifteen years
old, untouched by passion, unsullied in name, was found
in the shallow brook where she had sternly and surely
sought her death, — (too true! too true! — *ejus animæ
Jesu miserere!* — but a generation has passed since then,)
— will not smile so scornfully.

Myrtle Hazard no longer required the physician's visits,
but her mind was very far from being poised in the just
balance of its faculties. She was of a good natural constitution and a fine temperament; but she had been over-
wrought by all that she had passed through, and, though
happening to have been born in another land, *she was of
American descent.* Now, it has long been noticed that
there is something in the influences, climatic or other, here
prevailing, which predisposes to morbid religious excitement. The graver reader will not object to seeing the
exact statement of a competent witness belonging to a
by-gone century, confirmed as it is by all that we see
about us.

"There is no Experienced Minister of the Gospel who
hath not in the Cases of *Tempted Souls* often had this Ex

perience, that the ill Cases of their distempered *Bodies* are the frequent Occasion and Original of their Temptations." " The Vitiated Humours in many Persons, yield the *Steams* whereinto *Satan* does insinuate himself, till he has gained a sort of *Possession* in them, or at least an Opportunity to shoot into the Mind as many *Fiery Darts* as may cause a sad Life unto them; yea, 't is well if *Self-Murder* be not the sad end into which these hurred (?) People are thus precipitated. *New England*, a country where *Splenetic* Maladies are prevailing and pernicious, perhaps above any other, hath afforded Numberless Instances, of even *pious People*, who have contracted these *Melancholy Indispositions* which have unhinged them from all Service or Comfort; yea, not a few Persons have been hurried thereby to lay *Violent Hands* upon themselves at the last. These are among the *unsearchable Judgments of God!* "

Such are the words of the Rev. Cotton Mather.

The minister had hardly recovered from his vexatious defeat in the skirmish where the Widow Hopkins was his principal opponent, when he received a note from Miss Silence Withers, which promised another and more important field of conflict. It contained a request that he would visit Myrtle Hazard, who seemed to be in a very excitable and impressible condition, and who might perhaps be easily brought under those influences which she had resisted from her early years, through inborn perversity of character.

When the Rev. Mr. Stoker received this note, he turned very pale, — which was a bad sign. Then he drew a long breath or two, and presently a flush tingled up to his cheek, where it remained a fixed burning glow. This may have

7 *

been from the deep interest he felt in Myrtle's spiritual welfare; but he had often been sent for by aged sinners in
more immediate peril, apparently, without any such disturbance of the circulation.

To know whether a minister, young or still in flower, is
in safe or dangerous paths, there are two psychometers, a
comparison between which will give as infallible a return
as the dry and wet bulbs of the ingenious " Hygrodeik."
The first is the black broadcloth forming the knees of his
pantaloons; the second, the patch of carpet before his
mirror. If the first is unworn and the second is frayed
and threadbare, pray for him. If the first is worn and
shiny, while the second keeps its pattern and texture, get
him to pray for you.

The Rev. Mr. Stoker should have gone down on his
knees then and there, and sought fervently for the grace
which he was like to need in the dangerous path just
opening before him. He did not do this; but he stood up
before his looking-glass and parted his hair as carefully as
if he had been separating the saints of his congregation
from the sinners, to send the list to the statistical columns
of a religious newspaper. He selected a professional
ueckcloth, as spotlessly pure as if it had been washed in
innocency, and adjusted it in a tie which was like the
white rose of Sharon. Myrtle Hazard was, he thought,
on the whole, the handsomest girl he had ever seen; Susan Posey was to her as a buttercup from the meadow is
to a tiger-lily. He knew the nature of the nervous
disturbances through which she had been passing, and
that she must be in a singularly impressible condition.
He felt sure that he could establish intimate spiritual relations with her by drawing out her repressed sympathies

by feeding the fires of her religious imagination, by exercising all those lesser arts of fascination which are so
familiar to the Don Giovannis, and not always unknown
to the San Giovannis.

As for the hard doctrines which he used to produce sen-
sations with in the pulpit, it would have been a great pity
to worry so lovely a girl, in such a nervous state, with
them. He remembered a savory text about being made
all things to all men, which would bear application particularly well to the case of this young woman. He knew
how to weaken his divinity, on occasion, as well as an old
housewife to weaken her tea, lest it should keep people
awake.

The Rev. Mr. Stoker was a man of emotions. He
loved to feel his heart beat; he loved all the forms of non-
alcoholic drunkenness, which are so much better than the
vinous, because they taste themselves so keenly, whereas
the other (according to the statement of experts who are
familiar with its curious phenomena) has a certain sense
of unreality connected with it. He delighted in the reflex stimulus of the excitement he produced in others by
working on their feelings. A powerful preacher is open
to the same sense of enjoyment — an awful, tremulous,
goose-flesh sort of state, but still enjoyment — that a
great tragedian feels when he curdles the blood of his
audience.

Mr. Stoker was noted for the vividness of his descrip-
tions of the future which was in store for the great bulk
of his fellow-townsmen and fellow-worldsmen. He had
three sermons on this subject, known to all the country
round as the *sweating* sermon, the *fainting* sermon, and
the *convulsion-fit* sermon, from the various effects said to

have been produced by them when delivered before large
audiences. It might be supposed that his reputation as a
terrorist would have interfered with his attempts to ingra-
tiate himself with his young favorites. But the tragedian
who is fearful as Richard or as Iago finds that no hin-
drance to his success in the part of Romeo. Indeed,
women rather take to terrible people; prize-fighters, pi-
rates, highwaymen, rebel generals, Grand Turks, and
Bluebeards generally have a fascination for the sex; your
virgin has a natural instinct to saddle your lion. The fact,
therefore, that the young girl had sat under his tremendous pulpitings, through the sweating sermon, the fainting
sermon, and the convulsion-fit sermon, did not secure her
against the influence of his milder approaches.

Myrtle was naturally surprised at receiving a visit from
him; but she was in just that unbalanced state in which
almost any impression is welcome. He showed so much
interest, first in her health, then in her thoughts and feelings, always following her lead in the conversation, that
before he left her she felt as if she had made a great discovery; namely, that this man, so formidable behind the guns
of his wooden bastion, was a most tender-hearted and sym-
pathizing person when he came out of it unarmed. How
delightful he was as he sat talking in the twilight in low
and tender tones, with respectful pauses of listening, in
which he looked as if he too had just made a discovery, —
of an angel, to wit, to whom he could not help unbosoming
his tenderest emotions, as to a being from another sphere!

It was a new experience to Myrtle. She was all ready
for the spiritual manipulations of an expert. The excita-
bility which had been showing itself in spasms and strange
paroxysms had been transferred to those nervous centres

whatever they may be, cerebral or ganglionic, which are concerned in the emotional movements of the religious nature. It was taking her at an unfair disadvantage, no doubt. In the old communion, some priest might have wrought upon her while in this condition, and we might have had at this very moment among us another Saint Theresa or Jacqueline Pascal. She found but a dangerous substitute in the spiritual companionship of a saint like the Rev. Joseph Bellamy Stoker.

People think the confessional is unknown in our Protestant churches. It is a great mistake. The principal change is, that there is no screen between the penitent and the father confessor. The minister knew his rights, and very soon asserted them. He gave Aunt Silence to understand that he could talk more at ease if he and his young disciple were left alone together. Cynthia Badlam did not like this arrangement. She was afraid to speak about it; but she glared at them aslant, with the look of a biting horse when his eyes follow one sideways until they are all white but one little vicious spark of pupil.

It was not very long before the Rev. Mr. Stoker had established pretty intimate relations with the household at The Poplars. He had reason to think, he assured Miss Silence, that Myrtle was in a state of mind which promised a complete transformation of her character. He used the phrases of his sect, of course, in talking with the elderly lady; but the language which he employed with the young girl was free from those mechanical expressions which would have been like to offend or disgust her.

As to his rougher formulæ, he knew better than to apply them to a creature of her fine texture. If he had been disposed to do so, her simple questions and answers

to his inquiries would have made it difficult. But it was
in her bright and beautiful eyes, in her handsome features,
and her winning voice, that he found his chief obstacle.
How could he look upon her face in its loveliness, and
talk to her as if she must be under the wrath and curse
of God for the mere fact of her existence? It seemed
more natural, and it certainly was more entertaining, to
question her in such a way as to find out what kind of
theology had grown up in her mind as the result of her
training in the complex scheme of his doctrinal school.
And as he knew that the merest child, so soon as it begins
to think at all, works out for itself something like a theory
of human nature, he pretty soon began sounding Myrtle's
thoughts on this matter.

What was her own idea, he would be pleased to know,
about her natural condition as one born of a sinful race,
and her inherited liabilities on that account?

Myrtle smiled like a little heathen, as she was, according to the standard of her earlier teachings. That kind
of talk used to worry her when she was a child, sometimes.
Yes, she remembered its coming back to her in a dream
she had, when — when — (She did not finish her sentence.) Did *he* think she hated every kind of goodness
and loved every kind of evil? Did *he* think she was
hateful to the Being who made her?

The minister looked straight into the bright, brave, tender eyes, and answered, "Nothing in heaven or on earth
could help loving you, Myrtle!"

Pretty well for a beginning!

Myrtle saw nothing but pious fervor in this florid sentiment. But as she was honest and clear-sighted, she
could not accept a statement which seemed so plainly in

contradiction with his common teachings, without bringing his flattering assertion to the test of another question.

Did he suppose, she asked, that any persons could be Christians, who could not tell the day or the year of their change from children of darkness to children of light.

The shrewd clergyman, whose creed could be lax enough on occasion, had provided himself with authorities of all kinds to meet these awkward questions in casuistical divinity. He had hunted up recipes for spiritual neuralgia, spasms, indigestion, psora, hypochondriasis, just as doctors do for their bodily counterparts.

To be sure they could. Why, what did the great Richard Baxter say in his book on Infant Baptism? That at a meeting of many eminent Christians, some of them very famous ministers, when it was desired that every one should give an account of the time and manner of his conversion, there was but one of them all could do it. And as for himself, Mr. Baxter said, he could not remember the day or the year when he began to be sincere, as he called it. Why, did n't President Wheelock say to a young man who consulted him, that some persons might be true Christians without suspecting it?

All this was so very different from the uncompromising way in which religious doctrines used to be presented to the young girl from the pulpit, that it naturally opened her heart and warmed her affections. Remember, if she needs excuse, that the defeated instincts of a strong nature were rushing in upon her, clamorous for their rights, and that she was not yet mature enough to understand and manage them. The paths of love and religion are at the fork of a road which every maiden travels. If some young hand does not open the turnpike gate of the first, she is pretty sure to try the other, which has no toll-bar. It is also very commonly noticed that these two paths, after diverging awhile, run into each other. True love leads many wandering souls into the better way. Nor is it rare to see those who started in company for the gates of pearl seated together on the banks that border the avenue to that other portal, gathering the roses for which it is so famous.

It was with the most curious interest that the minister listened to the various heresies into which her reflections had led her. Somehow or other they did not sound so dangerous coming from her lips as when they were uttered by the coarser people of the less rigorous denominations, or preached in the sermons of heretical clergymen. He found it impossible to think of her in connection with those denunciations of sinners for which his discourses had been noted. Some of the sharp old church-members began to complain that his exhortations were losing their pungency. The truth was, he was preaching for Myrtle Hazard. He was getting bewitched and driven beside himself by the intoxication of his relations with her.

All this time she was utterly unconscious of any charm that she was exercising, or of being herself subject to any personal fascination. She loved to read the books of ecstatic contemplation which he furnished her. She loved to sing the languishing hymns which he selected for her. She oved to listen to his devotional rhapsodies, hardly knowng sometimes whether she were in the body, or out of the body, while he lifted her upon the wings of his passion-kindled rhetoric. The time came when she had learned to listen for his step, when her eyes glistened at meeting him, when the words he uttered were treasured as from something more than a common mortal, and the book he had touched was like a saintly relic. It never suggested itself to her for an instant that this was anything more than such a friendship as Mercy might have cultivated with Great-Heart. She gave her confidence simply because she was very young and innocent. The green tendrils of the growing vine must wind round something.

The seasons had been changing their scenery while the events we have told were occurring, and the loveliest days of autumn were now shining. To those who know the "Indian summer" of our Northern States, it is needless to describe the influence it exerts on the senses and the soul. The stillness of the landscape in that beautiful time is as if the planet were *sleeping*, like a top, before it begins to rock with the storms of autumn. All natures seem to find themselves more truly in its light; love grows more tender, religion more spiritual, memory sees farther back into the past, grief revisits its mossy marbles, the poet harvests the ripe thoughts which he will tie in sheaves of verses by his winter fireside.

The minister had got into the way of taking frequent walks with Myrtle, whose health had seemed to require the open air, and who was fast regaining her natural look. Under the canopy of the scarlet, orange, and crimson leaved maples, of the purple and violet clad oaks, of the birches in their robes of sunshine, and the beeches in their clinging drapery of sober brown, they walked together while he discoursed of the joys of heaven, the sweet communion of kindred souls, the ineffable bliss of a world where love would be immortal and beauty should never know decay. And while she listened, the strange light of the leaves irradiated the youthful figure of Myrtle, as when

K

the stained window let in its colors on Madeline, the rose bloom and the amethyst and the glory.

"Yes! we shall be angels together," exclaimed the Rev. Mr. Stoker. "Our souls were made for immortal union. I know it; I feel it in every throb of my heart. Even in this world you are as an angel to me, lifting me into the heaven where I shall meet you again, or it will not be heaven. O, if on earth our communion could have been such as it must be hereafter! O Myrtle, Myrtle!"

He stretched out his hands as if to clasp hers between them in the rapture of his devotion. Was it the light reflected from the glossy leaves of the poison sumach which overhung the path that made his cheek look so pale? Was he going to kneel to her?

Myrtle turned her dark eyes on him with a simple wonder that saw an excess of saintly ardor in these demonstrations, and drew back from it.

"I think of heaven always as the place where I shall meet my mother," she said calmly.

These words recalled the man to himself for a moment and he was silent. Presently he seated himself on a stone. His lips were tremulous as he said, in a low tone, "Sit down by me, Myrtle."

"No," she answered, with something which chilled him in her voice, "we will not stay here any longer; it is time to go home."

"*Full time!*" muttered Cynthia Badlam, whose watchful eyes had been upon them, peering through a screen of yellow leaves, that turned her face pale as if with deadly passion.

CHAPTER XIV.

FLANK MOVEMENT.

MISS CYNTHIA BADLAM was in the habit of occasionally visiting the Widow Hopkins. Some said — but then people will talk, especially in the country where they have not much else to do, except in haying-time. She had always known the widow, long before Mr. Gridley came there to board, or any other special event happened in her family. No matter what people said.

Miss Badlam called to see Mrs. Hopkins, then, and the two had a long talk together, of which only a portion is on record. Here are such fragments as have been preserved.

"What would I do about it? Why, I'd put a stop to such carry'n's on, mighty quick, if I had to tie the girl to the bedpost, and have a bulldog that would take the seat out of any pair of black pantaloons that come within forty rod of her, — *that's* what *I'd* do about it! He undertook to be mighty sweet with our Susan one while, but ever sence he's been talkin' religion with Myrtle Hazard he's let us alone. Do as I did when he asked our Susan to come to his study, — stick close to your girl and you'll put a stop to all this business. He won't make love to two at once, unless they're both pretty young, I'll warrant. Follow her round, Miss Cynthy, and keep your eyes on her."

"I have watched her like a cat, Mrs. Hopkins, but I can't follow her everywhere, — she won't stand what

Susan Posey 'll stand. There 's no use *our* talking to her — we 've done with that at our house. You never know what that Indian blood of hers will make her do. She 's too high-strung for us to bit and bridle. I don't want to see her name in the paper again, alongside of that —— " (She did not finish the sentence.) " I 'd rather have her fished dead out of the river, or find her where she found her uncle Malachi ! "

" You don't think, Miss Cynthy, that the man means to inveigle the girl with the notion of marryin' her by and by, after poor Mrs. Stoker 's dead and gone ? "

" The Lord in heaven forbid ! " exclaimed Miss Cynthia, throwing up her hands. " A child of fifteen years old, if she is a woman to look at ! "

" It 's too bad, — it 's too bad to think of, Miss Cynthy ; and there 's that poor woman dyin' by inches, and Miss Bathsheby settin' with her day and night, — she has n't got a bit of her father in her, it 's all her mother, — and that man, instead of bein' with her to comfort her as any man ought to be with his wife, — *in sickness and in health*, that 's what he promised. I 'm sure when my poor husband was sick . . . . To think of that man goin' about to *talk religion* to all the prettiest girls he can find in the parish, and his wife at home like to leave him so soon, — it 's a shame, — so it is, come now ! Miss Cynthy, there 's one of the best men and one of the learnedest men that ever lived that 's a real friend of Myrtle Hazard, and a better friend to her than she knows of, — for ever sence he brought her home, he feels jest like a father to her, — and that man is Mr. Gridley, that lives in this house. It 's him I 'll speak to about the minister's carry'n's on. He knows about his talking sweet to our Susan, and

he 'll put things to rights! He 's a master hand when
he does once take hold of anything, I tell you that! Jest
get him to shet up them books of his, and take hold of
anybody's troubles, and you 'll see how he 'll straighten
'em out."

There was a pattering of little feet on the stairs, and the
two small twins, "Sossy" and "Minthy," in the home
dialect, came hand in hand into the room, Miss Susan
leaving them at the threshold, not wishing to interrupt
the two ladies, and being much interested also in listening
to Mr. Gifted Hopkins, who was reading some of his
last poems to her, with great delight to both of them.

The good woman rose to take them from Susan, and
guide their uncertain steps. "My babies, I call 'em,
Miss Cynthy. Ain't they nice children? Come to go to
bed, little dears? Only a few minutes, Miss Cynthy."

She took them into the bedroom on the same floor,
where they slept, and, leaving the door open, began un-
dressing them. Cynthia turned her rocking-chair round so
as to face the open door. She looked on while the little
creatures were being undressed; she heard the few words
they lisped as their infant prayer; she saw them laid in
their beds, and heard their pretty good-night.

A lone woman to whom all the sweet cares of maternity
have been denied cannot look upon a sight like this without feeling the void in her own heart where a mother's
affection should have nestled. Cynthia sat perfectly still,
without rocking, and watched kind Mrs. Hopkins at her
quasi parental task. A tear stole down her rigid face as
she saw the rounded limbs of the children bared in their
white beauty, and their little heads laid on the pillow.
They were sleeping quietly when Mrs. Hopkins left the

room for a moment on some errand of her own. Cynthia rose softly from her chair, stole swiftly to the bedside, and printed a long, burning kiss on each of their foreheads.

When Mrs. Hopkins came back, she found the maiden lady sitting in her place just as she left her, but rocking in her chair and sobbing as one in sudden pangs of grief.

" It *is* a great trouble, Miss Cynthy," she said, — " a great trouble to have such a child as Myrtle to think of and to care for. If she was like our Susan Posey, now ! — but we must do the best we can ; and if Mr. Gridley once sets himself to it, you may depend upon it he 'll make it all come right. I would n't take on about it if I was you. You let me speak to our Mr. Gridley. We all have our troubles. It is n't everybody that can ride to heaven in a C-spring shay, as my poor husband used to say ; and life 's a road that 's got a good many thank-you-ma'ams to go bumpin' over, says he."

Miss Badlam acquiesced in the philosophical reflections of the late Mr. Ammi Hopkins, and left it to his widow to carry out her own suggestion in reference to consulting Master Gridley. The good woman took the first opportunity she had to introduce the matter, a little diffusely, as is often the way of widows who keep boarders.

" There 's something going on I don't like, Mr. Gridley. They tell me that Minister Stoker is following round after Myrtle Hazard, talking religion at her jest about the same way he 'd have liked to with our Susan, I calculate. If he wants to talk religion to me or Silence Withers, — well, no, I don't feel sure about Silence, — she ain't as young as she used to be, but then ag'in she ain't so fur gone as some, and she 's got money, — but if he wants to talk religion with me, he may come and welcome. But as for Myrtle

Hazard, she's been sick, and it's left her a little flighty by what they say, and to have a minister round her all the time ravin' about the next world as if he had a latch-key to the front door of it, is no way to make her come to herself again. I've seen more than one young girl sent off to the asylum by that sort of work, when, if I'd only had 'em, I'd have made 'em sweep the stairs, and mix the puddin's, and tend the babies, and milk the cow, and keep 'em too busy all day to be thinkin' about themselves, and have 'em dress up nice evenin's and see some young folks and have a good time, and go to meetin' Sundays, and then have done with the minister, unless it was old Father Pemberton. He knows forty times as much about heaven as that Stoker man does, or ever's like to, — why don't they run after him, I should like to know? Ministers are men, come now; and I don't want to say anything against women, Mr. Gridley, but women are women, that's the fact of it, and half of 'em are hystericky when they're young; and I've heard old Dr. Hurlbut say many a time that he had to lay in an extra stock of valerian and assafœtida whenever there was a young minister round, — for there's plenty of religious ravin', says he, that's nothin' but hysterics."

[Mr. Froude thinks that was the trouble with Bloody Queen Mary, but the old physician did not get the idea from him.]

"Well, and what do you propose to do about the Rev. Joseph Bellamy Stoker and his young proselyte, Miss Myrtle Hazard?" said Mr Gridley, when Mrs. Hopkins at last gave him a chance to speak.

"Mr. Gridley" — Mrs. Hopkins looked full upon him as she spoke, — "people used to say that you was a good

man and a great man and one of the learnedest men alive,
but that you did n't know much nor care for much except
books.   I know you used to live pretty much to yourself
when you first came to board in this house.   But you 've
been very good to my son ; . . . . and if Gifted lives till
you . . . . till you are in . . . . your grave, ... he
will write a poem — I know he will — that will tell your
goodness to babes unborn."

[Here Master Gridley groaned, and repeated to himself
silently,

> " Scindentur vestes, gemmæ frangentur et aurum,
> Carmina quum tribuent fama perennis erit."

All this inwardly, and without interrupting the worthy
woman's talk.]

"And if ever Gifted makes a book, — don t say anything
about it, Mr. Gridley, for goodness' sake, for he would n't
have anybody know it, only I can't help thinking that some
time or other he will print a book, — and if he does, I
know whose name he 'll put at the head of it, — ' Dedicated to B. G., with the gratitude and respect — '   There,
now, I had n't any business to say a word about it, and it 's
only jest in case he does, you know.   I 'm sure you de-
serve it all.   You 've helped him with the best of advice.
And you 've been kind to me when I was in trouble.   And
you 've been like a grandfather " [Master Gridley winced,
— why could n't the woman have said *father?* — that
grand struck his ear like a spade going into the gravel]
" to those babes, poor little souls ! left on my door-step like
a couple of breakfast rolls, — only you know it 's the baker
left *them*.   I believe in you, Mr. Gridley, as I believe in
my Maker and in Father Pemberton, — but, poor man
he 's old, and you won't be old these twenty years yet."

[Master Gridley shook his head as if to say that was n't so, but felt comforted and refreshed.]

"You 've got to help Myrtle Hazard again. You brought her home when she come so nigh drowning. You got the old doctor to go and see her when she come so nigh being bewitched with the magnetism and nonsense, whatever they call it, and the young doctor was so nigh bein' crazy, too. I know, for Nurse Byloe told me all about it. And now Myrtle 's gettin' run away with by that pesky Minister Stoker. Cynthy Badlam was here yesterday crying and sobbing as if her heart would break about it. For my part, I did n't think Cynthy cared so much for the girl as all that, but I saw her takin' on dreadfully with my own eyes. That man 's like a hen-hawk among the chickens, — first he picks up one, and then he picks up another. I should like to know if nobody but young folks has souls to be saved, and specially young women!"

"Tell me all you know about Myrtle Hazard and Joseph Bellamy Stoker," said Master Gridley.

Thereupon that good lady related all that Miss Badlam had imparted to her, of which the reader knows the worst, being the interview of which the keen spinster had been a witness, having followed them for the express purpose of knowing, in her own phrase, what the minister was up to.

It is not to be supposed that Myrtle had forgotten the discreet kindness of Master Gridley in bringing her back and making the best of her adventure. He, on his part, had acquired a kind of right to consider himself her adviser, and had begun to take a pleasure in the thought that he, he worn-out and useless old pedant, as he had been in the way of considering himself, might perhaps do something

8

even more important than his previous achievement to save this young girl from the dangers that surrounded her. He loved his classics and his old books; he took an interest, too, in the newspapers and periodicals that brought the fermenting thought and the electric life of the great world into his lonely study; but these things just about him were getting strong hold on him, and most of all the fortunes of this beautiful young woman. How strange! For a whole generation he had lived in no nearer relation to his fellow-creatures than that of a half-fossilized teacher; and all at once he found himself face to face with the very most intense form of life, the counsellor of threatened innocence, the champion of imperilled loveliness. What business was it of his? growled the lower nature, of which he had said in "Thoughts on the Universe," — "*Every man leads or is led by something that goes on four legs.*"

Then he remembered the grand line of the African freedman, that makes all human interests everybody's business, and had a sudden sense of dilatation and evolution, as it were, in all his dimensions, as if he were a head taller, and a foot bigger round the chest, and took in an extra gallon of air at every breath. Then — you who have written a book that holds your heart-leaves between its pages will understand the movement — he took down "Thoughts on the Universe" for a refreshing draught from his own well-spring. He opened as chance ordered it, and his eyes fell on the following passage: —

"*The true American formula was well phrased by the late Samuel Patch, the Western Empedocles, 'Some things can be done as well as others.' A homely utterance, but it has virtue to overthrow all dynasties and hierarchies. These were all built up on the Old-World dogma that some thing can NOT be done as well as others.*"

"There, now!" he said, talking to himself in his usual way, "is n't that good? It always seems to me that I find something to the point when I open that book. 'Some things can be done as well as others,' can they? Suppose I should try what I can do by visiting Miss Myrtle Hazard? I think I may say I am old and incombustible enough to be trusted. She does not seem to be a safe neighbor to very inflammable bodies!"

Myrtle was sitting in the room long known as the Study, or the Library, when Master Byles Gridley called at The Poplars to see her. Miss Cynthia, who received him, led him to this apartment and left him alone with Myrtle. She welcomed him very cordially, but colored as she did so, — his visit was a surprise. She was at work on a piece of embroidery. Her first instinctive movement was to thrust it out of sight with the thought of concealment; but she checked this, and before the blush of detection had reached her cheek, the blush of ingenuous shame for her weakness had caught and passed it, and was in full possession. She sat with her worsted pattern held bravely in sight, and her cheek as bright as its liveliest crimson.

"Miss Cynthia has let me in upon you," he said, "or I should not have ventured to disturb you in this way. A work of art, is it, Miss Myrtle Hazard?"

"Only a pair of slippers, Mr. Gridley, — for my pastor."

"Oh! oh! That is well. A good old man. I have a great regard for the Rev. Eliphalet Pemberton. I wish all ministers were as good and simple and pure-hearted as the Rev. Eliphalet Pemberton. And I wish all the young people thought as much about their elders as you do, Miss Myrtle Hazard. We that are old love little acts of kind-ness. You gave me more pleasure than you knew of, my dear, when you worked that handsome cushion for me. The old minister will be greatly pleased, — poor old man ! "

" But, Mr. Gridley, I must not let you think these are for Father Pemberton. They are for — Mr. — Stoker."

" The Rev. Joseph Bellamy Stoker ! He is not an old man, the Rev. Joseph Bellamy Stoker. He may perhaps be a widower before a great while. — Does he know that you are working those slippers for him ? "

" Dear me ! no, Mr. Gridley. I meant them for a surprise to him. He has been so kind to me, and understands me so much better than I thought anybody did. He is so different from what I thought ; he makes religion so perfectly simple, it seems as if everybody would agree with him, if they could only hear him talk."

" Greatly interested in the souls of his people, is n't he ? "

" Too much, almost, I am afraid. He says he has been too hard in his sermons sometimes, but it was for fear he should not impress his hearers enough."

" Don't you think he worries himself about the souls of young women rather more than for those of old ones, Myrtle ? "

There was something in the tone of this question that helped its slightly sarcastic expression. Myrtle's jealousy for her minister's sincerity was roused.

" How can you ask that, Mr. Gridley ? I am sure I wish you or anybody could have heard him talk as I have There is no age in souls, he says ; and I am sure that it would do anybody good to hear him, old or young."

" No age in souls, — no age in souls. Souls of forty as young as souls of fifteen ; that 's it." Master Gridley did not say this loud. But he did speak as follows : " I am glad to hear what you say of the Rev. Joseph Bellamy

Stoker's love of being useful to people of all ages. You have had comfort in his companionship, and there are others who might be very glad to profit by it. I know a very excellent person who has had trials, and is greatly interested in religious conversation. Do you think he would be willing to let this friend of mine share in the privileges of spiritual intercourse which you enjoy ? "

There was but one answer possible. Of course 1 e would.

" I hope it is so, my dear young lady. But listen to me one moment. I love you, my dear child, do you know, as if I were your own — grandfather." (There was moral heroism in that word.) " I love you as if you were of my own blood; and so long as you trust me, and suffer me, I mean to keep watch against all dangers that threaten you in mind, body, or estate. You may wonder at me, you may sometimes doubt me; but until you say you distrust me, when any trouble comes near you, you will find me there. Now, my dear child, you ought to know that the Rev. Joseph Bellamy Stoker has the reputation of being too fond of prosecuting religious inquiries with young and handsome women."

Myrtle's eyes fell, — a new suspicion seemed to have suggested itself.

" He wanted to get up a spiritual intimacy with our Susan Posey, — a very pretty girl, as you know."

Myrtle tossed her head almost imperceptibly, and bit her lip.

" I suppose there are a dozen young people that have been talked about with him. He preaches cruel sermons in his pulpit, cruel as death, and cold-blooded enough to freeze any mother's blood if nature did not tell her he lied, and then smooths it all over with the first good-looking young woman he can get to listen to him."

Myrtle had dropped the slipper she was working on.

"Tell me, my dear, would you be willing to give up meeting this man alone, and gratify my friend, and avoid all occasion of reproach?"

"Of course I would," said Myrtle, her eyes flashing, for her doubts, her shame, her pride, were all excited. " Who is your friend, Mr. Gridley?"

"An excellent woman, — Mrs. Hopkins. You know her, Gifted Hopkins's mother, with whom I am residing. Shall the minister be given to understand that you will see him hereafter in her company?"

Myrtle came pretty near a turn of her old nervous perturbations. "As you say," she answered. "Is there nobody that I can trust, or is everybody hunting me like a bird?" She hid her face in her hands.

"You can trust me, my dear," said Byles Gridley. "Take your needle, my child, and work at your pattern, — it will come out a rose by and by. Life is like that, Myrtle, one stitch at a time, taken patiently, and the pattern will come out all right like the embroidery. You can trust me. Good by, my dear."

"Let her finish the slippers," the old man said to himself as he trudged home, " and make 'em big enough for Father Pemberton. He shall have his feet in 'em yet, or my name is n't Byles Gridley!"

CHAPTER XV.

ARRIVAL OF REINFORCEMENTS.

MYRTLE HAZARD waited until the steps of Master Byles Gridley had ceased to be heard, as he walked in his emphatic way through the long entry of the old mansion. Then she went to her little chamber and sat down in a sort of revery. She could not doubt his sincerity, and there was something in her own consciousness which responded to the suspicions he had expressed with regard to the questionable impulses of the Rev. Joseph Bellamy Stoker.

It is not in the words that others say to us, but in those other words which these make us say to ourselves, that we find our gravest lessons and our sharpest rebukes. The hint another gives us finds whole trains of thought which have been getting themselves ready to be shaped in inwardly articulated words, and only awaited the touch of a burning syllable, as the mottoes of a pyrotechnist only wait for a spark to become letters of fire.

The artist who takes your photograph must carry you with him into his "developing" room, and he will give you a more exact illustration of the truth just mentioned. There is nothing to be seen on the glass just taken from the camera. But there is a potential, though invisible, picture hid in the creamy film which covers it. Watch him as he pours a wash over it, and you will see that miracle wrought which is at once a surprise and a charm, — the sudden appearance of your own features where a moment before was a blank without a vestige of intelligence or beauty.

In some such way the grave warnings of Master Byles Gridley had called up a fully shaped, but hitherto unword-ed, train of thought in the consciousness of Myrtle Hazard. It was not merely their significance, it was mainly because they were spoken at the fitting time. If they had been uttered a few weeks earlier, when Myrtle was taking the first stitch on the embroidered slippers, they would have been as useless as the artist's developing solution on a plate which had never been exposed in the camera. But she had been of late in training for her lesson in ways that neither she nor anybody else dreamed of. The reader who has shrugged his (or her) shoulders over the last illustra-tion will perhaps hear this one which follows more cheer-fully. The physician in the Arabian Nights made his patient play at ball with a bat, the hollow handle of which contained drugs of marvellous efficacy. Whether it was the drugs that made the sick man get well, or the exercise, is not of so much consequence as the fact that he did at any rate get well.

These walks which Myrtle had taken with her reverend counsellor had given her a new taste for the open air, which was what she needed just now more than confessions of faith or spiritual paroxysms. And so it happened that, while he had been stimulating all those imaginative and emotional elements of her nature which responded to the keys he loved to play upon, the restoring influences of the sweet autumnal air, the mellow sunshine, the soothing aspects of the woods and fields and sky, had been quietly doing their work. The color was fast returning to her cheek, and the discords of her feelings and her thoughts gradually resolv-ing themselves into the harmonious and cheerful rhythms of bodily and mental health. It needed but the timely word from the fitting lips to change the whole programme of her daily mode of being. The word had been spoken. She saw its truth; but how hard it is to tear away a cherished illusion, to cast out an unworthy intimate! How hard for any! — but for a girl so young, and who had as yet found so little to love and trust, how cruelly hard!

She sat, still and stony, like an Egyptian statue. Her eyes were fixed on a vacant chair opposite the one on which she was sitting. It was a very singular and fantastic old chair, said to have been brought over by the first emigrant of her race. The legs and arms were curiously turned in spirals, the suggestions of which were half pleasing and half repulsive. Instead of the claw-feet common in furniture of a later date, each of its legs rested on a misshapen reptile, which it seemed to flatten by its weight, as if it were squeezing the breath out of the ugly creature. Over this chair hung the portrait of her beautiful ancestress, her neck and arms, the specialty of her beauty, bare, except for a bracelet on the left wrist, and her shapely figure set off by the ample folds of a rich crimson brocade. Over Myrtle's bed hung that other portrait, which was to her almost as the pictures of the *Mater Dolorosa* to trustful souls of the Roman faith. She had longed for these pictures while she was in her strange hysteric condition, and they had been hung up in her chamber.

The night was far gone, as she knew by the declining of the constellations which she had seen shining brightly almost overhead in the early evening, when she awoke, and found herself still sitting in the very attitude in which she was sitting hours before. Her lamp had burned out, and the starlight but dimly illuminated her chamber. She started to find herself sitting there, chilled and stiffened by

long remaining in one posture; and as her consciousness
returned, a great fear seized her, and she sprang for a
match. It broke with the quick movement she made to
kindle it, and she snatched another as if a fiend were after
her. It flashed and went out. O the terror, the terror!
The darkness seemed alive with fearful presences. The
lurid glare of her own eyeballs flashed backwards into her
brain. She tried one more match; it kindled as it should,
and she lighted another lamp. Her first impulse was to
assure herself that nothing was changed in the familiar
objects around her. She held the lamp up to the picture
of Judith Pride. The beauty looked at her, it seemed as if
with a kind of lofty recognition in her eyes; but there she
was, as always. She turned the light upon the pale face
of the martyr-portrait. It looked troubled and faded, as it
seemed to Myrtle, but still it was the same face she remembered from her childhood. Then she threw the light on
the old chair, and, shuddering, caught up a shawl and flung
it over the spiral-wound arms and legs, and the flattened
reptiles on which it stood.

In those dead hours of the night which had passed over
her sitting there, still and stony, as it should seem, she had
had strange visitors. *Two women* had been with her, as
real as any that breathed the breath of life,—so it appeared to her, — yet both had long been what is called, in
our poor language, *dead.* One came in all the glory of
her ripened beauty, bare-necked, bare-armed, full dressed
by nature in that splendid animal equipment which in its
day had captivated the eyes of all the lusty lovers of complete muliebrity. The other, — how delicate, how trans
lucent, how aerial she seemed! yet real and true to the
lineaments of her whom the young girl looked upon as her
hereditary protector.

The beautiful woman turned, and, with a face full of loathing and scorn, pointed to one of the reptiles beneath the feet of the chair. And while Myrtle's eyes followed hers, the flattened and half-crushed creature seemed to swell and spread like his relative in the old fable, like the black dog in Faust, until he became of tenfold size, and at last of colossal proportions. And, fearful to relate, the batrachian features humanized themselves as the monster grew, and, shaping themselves more and more into a remembered similitude, Myrtle saw in them a hideous likeness of — No! no! it was too horrible! Was that the face which had been so close to hers but yesterday? were those the lips, the breath from which had stirred her growing curls as he leaned over her while they read together some passionate stanza from a hymn that was as much like a love-song as it dared to be in godly company? A shudder of disgust — the natural repugnance of loveliness for deformity — ran all through her, and she shrieked, as she thought, and threw herself at the feet of that other figure. She felt herself lifted from the floor, and then a cold thin hand seemed to take hers. The warm life went out of her, and she was to herself as a dimly conscious shadow that glided with passive acquiescence wherever it was led. Presently she found herself in a half-lighted apartment, where there were books on the shelves around, and a desk with loose manuscripts lying on it, and a little mirror with a worn bit of carpet before it. And while she looked, a great serpent writhed in through the half-open door, and made the circuit of the room, laying one huge ring all round it, and then, going round again, laid another ring over the first, and so on until he was wound all round the room like the spiral of a mighty cable, leaving a hol-

low in the centre; and then the serpent seemed to arch
his neck in the air, and bring his head close down to Myrtle's face; and the features were not those of a serpent,
but of a man, and it hissed out the words she had read
that very day in a little note which said, " Come to my
study to-morrow, and we will read hymns together."

Again she was back in her little chamber, she did not
know how, and the two women were looking into her eyes
with strange meaning in their own. Something in them
seemed to plead with her to yield to their influence, and
her choice wavered which of them to follow, for each
would have led her her own way, — whither she knew
not. It was the strife of her "Vision," only in another
form, — the contest of two lives her blood inherited for
the mastery of her soul. The might of beauty conquered.
Myrtle resigned herself to the guidance of the lovely
phantom, which seemed so much fuller of the unextin-
guished fire of life, and so like herself as she would grow
to be when noon should have ripened her into maturity.

Doors opened softly before them; they climbed stairs,
and threaded corridors, and penetrated crypts, strange yet
familiar to her eyes, which seemed to her as if they could
see, as it were, in darkness. Then came a confused sense
of eager search for something that she knew was hidden,
whether in the cleft of a rock, or under the boards of a
floor, or in some hiding-place among the skeleton rafters,
or in a forgotten drawer, or in a heap of rubbish, she could
not tell; but somewhere there was something which she
was to find, and which, once found, was to be her talisman. She was in the midst of this eager search when
she awoke.

The impression was left so strongly on her mind that

with all her fears, she could not resist the desire to make
an effort to find what meaning there was in this frightfully
real dream. Her courage came back as her senses assured her that all around her was natural, as when she left
it. She determined to follow the lead of the strange hint
her nightmare had given her.

In one of the upper chambers of the old mansion there
stood a tall, upright desk of the ancient pattern, with
folding doors above and large drawers below. "That
desk is yours, Myrtle," her uncle Malachi had once said to
her; "and there is a trick or two about it that it will pay
you to study." Many a time Myrtle had puzzled herself
about the mystery of the old desk. All the little drawers, of which there were a considerable number, she had
pulled out, and every crevice, as she thought, she had
carefully examined. She determined to make one more
trial. It was the dead of the night, and this was a fearful
old place to be wandering about; but she was possessed
with an urgent feeling which would not let her wait until
daylight.

She stole like a ghost from her chamber. She glided
along the narrow entries as she had seemed to move in her
dream. She opened the folding doors of the great upright
lesk. She had always before examined it by daylight,
and though she had so often pulled all the little drawers out,
she had never thoroughly explored the recesses which received them. But in her new-born passion of search, she
held her light so as to illuminate all these deeper spaces.
At once she thought she saw the marks of pressure with
a finger. She pressed her own finger on this place, and,
as it yielded with a slight click, a small mahogany pilaster
sprang forward, revealing its well-kept secret that it was

the mask of a tall, deep, very narrow drawer. There was something heavy in it, and, as Myrtle turned it over, a golden bracelet fell into her hand. She recognized it at once as that which had been long ago the ornament of the fair woman whose portrait hung in her chamber. She clasped it upon her wrist, and from that moment she felt as if she were the captive of the lovely phantom who had been with her in her dream.

"The old man walked last night, God save us!" said Kitty Fagan to Biddy Finnegan, the day after Myrtle's nightmare and her curious discovery.

CHAPTER XVI.

VICTORY.

IT seems probable enough that Myrtle's whole spiritual adventure was an unconscious dramatization of a few simple facts which her imagination tangled together into a kind of vital coherence. The philosopher who goes to the bottom of things will remark that all the elements of her fantastic melodrama had been furnished her while waking Master Byles Gridley's penetrating and stinging caution was the text, and the grotesque carvings and the portraits furnished the " properties " with which her own mind had wrought up this scenic show.

The philosopher who goes to the bottom of things might not find it so easy to account for the change which came over Myrtle Hazard from the hour when she clasped the bracelet of Judith Pride upon her wrist. She felt a sudden loathing of the man whom she had idealized as a saint. A young girl's caprice? Possibly. A return of the natural instincts of girlhood with returning health? Perhaps so. An impression produced by her dream? An effect of an influx from another sphere of being? The working of Master Byles Gridley's emphatic warning? The magic of her new talisman?

We may safely leave these questions for the present. As we have to tell, not what Mrytle Hazard ought to have done, and why she should have done it, but what she did do our task is a simpler one than it would be to lay bare all the springs of her action. Until this period, she had hardly thought of herself as a born beauty. The flatteries she had received from time to time were like the chips and splinters under the green wood, when the chill women pretended to make a fire in the best parlor at The Poplars, which had a way of burning themselves out, hardly warming, much less kindling, the fore-stick and the back-log.

Myrtle had a tinge of what some call superstition, and she began to look upon her strange acquisition as a kind of amulet. Its suggestions betrayed themselves in one of her first movements. Nothing could be soberer than the cut of the dresses which the propriety of the severe household had established as the rule of her costume. But the girl was no sooner out of bed than a passion came over her to see herself in that less jealous arrangement of drapery which the Beauty of the last century had insisted on as presenting her most fittingly to the artist. She rolled up the sleeves of her dress, she turned down its prim collar and neck, and glanced from her glass to the portrait, from the portrait back to the glass. Myrtle was not blind nor dull, though young, and in many things untaught. She did not say in so many words, " I too am a beauty," but she could not help seeing that she had many of the attractions of feature and form which had made the original of the picture before her famous. The same stately carriage of the head, the same full-rounded neck, the same more than hinted outlines of figure, the same finely-shaped arms and hands, and something very like the same features startled her by their identity in the permanent image of the canvas and the fleeting one of the mirror.

The world was hers then, — for she had not read roman- ces and love-letters without finding that beauty governs It in all times and places. Who was this middle-aged minister that had been hanging round her and talking to her about heaven, when there was not a single joy of earth that she had as yet tasted ? A man that had been saying all his fine things to Miss Susan Posey, too, had he, before he had bestowed his attentions on her ? And to a dozen other girls, too, nobody knows who !

The revulsion was a very sudden one. Such changes of feeling are apt to be sudden in young people whose nerves have been tampered with, and Myrtle was not of a temperament or an age to act with much deliberation where a pique came in to the aid of a resolve. Master Gridley guessed sagaciously what would be the effect of his revelation, when he told her of the particular attentions the minister had paid to pretty Susan Posey and various other young women.

The Rev. Mr. Stoker had parted his hair wonderfully that morning, and made himself as captivating as his professional costume allowed. He had drawn down the shades of his windows so as to let in that subdued light which is merciful to crow's-feet and similar embellishments, and wheeled up his sofa so that two could sit at the table and read from the some book.

At eleven o'clock he was pacing the room with a certain feverish impatience, casting a glance now and then at the mirror as he passed it. At last the bell rang, and he himself went to answer it, his heart throbbing with expectation of meeting his lovely visitor.

Myrtle Hazard appeared by an envoy extraordinary, the bearer of sealed despatches. Mistress Kitty Fagan was the young lady's substitute, and she delivered into the hand of the astonished clergyman the following missive : —

"To the Rev. Mr. Stoker.

"Reverend Sir,—I shall not come to your study this day. I do not feel that I have any more need of religious counsel at this time, and I am told by a friend that there are *others* who will be glad to hear you talk on this subject. I hear that Mrs. Hopkins is interested in religious subjects, and would have been glad to see you in my company. As I cannot go with her, perhaps *Miss Susan Posey* will take my place. I thank you for all the good things you have said to me, and that you have given me so much of your company. I hope we shall sing hymns together in heaven some time, if we are good enough, but I want to wait for that awhile, for I do not feel quite ready. I am not going to see you any more alone, reverend sir. I think this is best, and I have good advice. I want to see more of young people of my own age, and I have a friend, Mr. Gridley, who I think is older than you are, that takes an interest in me ; and as you have many *others* that you must be interested in, he can take the place of a *father* better than you can do. I return to you the hymn-book, — I read one of those you marked, and do not care to read any more.

"Respectfully yours,

"Myrtle Hazard."

The Rev. Mr. Stoker uttered a cry of rage as he finished this awkwardly written, but tolerably intelligible letter. What could he do about it? It would hardly do to stab Myrtle Hazard, and shoot Byles Gridley, and strangle Mrs. Hopkins, every one of which homicides he felt at the moment that he could have committed. And here he was in a frantic paroxysm, and the next day was Sunday, and his morning's discourse was unwritten. His savage medi æval theology came to his relief, and he clutched out of a heap of yellow manuscripts his well-worn " convulsion-fit " sermon. He preached it the next day as if it did his heart good, but Myrtle Hazard did not hear it, for she had gone to St. Bartholomew s with Olive Eveleth.

CHAPTER XVII.

SAINT AND SINNER.

IT happened a little after this time that the minister's invalid wife improved somewhat unexpectedly in health, and, as Bathsheba was beginning to suffer from imprisonment in her sick-chamber, the physician advised very strongly that she should vary the monotony of her life by going out of the house daily for fresh air and cheerful companionship.   She was therefore frequently at the house of Olive Eveleth; and as Myrtle wanted to see young people, and had her own way now as never before, the three girls often met at the parsonage.   Thus they became more and more intimate, and grew more and more into each other's affections.

These girls presented three types of spiritual character which are to be found in all our towns and villages.   Olive had been carefully trained, and at the proper age *confirmed.* Bathsheba had been prayed for, and in due time startled and *converted.*   Myrtle was a simple daughter of Eve, with many impulses like those of the other two girls, and some that required more watching.   She was not so safe, perhaps, as either of the other girls, for this world or the next; but she was on some accounts more interesting, as being a more genuine representative of that inexperienced and too easily deluded, yet always cherished, mother of our race, whom we must after all accept as embodying the creative idea of woman, and who might have been alive and happy now (though at a great age) but for a single fatal error.

The Rev. Ambrose Eveleth, Rector of Saint Bartholomew's, Olive's father, was one of a class numerous in the Anglican Church, a cultivated man, with pure tastes, with simple habits, a good reader, a neat writer, a safe thinker, with a snug and well-fenced mental pasturage, which his sermons kept cropped moderately close without any exhausting demand upon the soil. Olive had grown insensibly into her religious maturity, as into her bodily and intellectual developments, which one might suppose was the natural order of things in a well-regulated Christian household, where the children are brought up in the nurture and admonition of the Lord.

Bathsheba had been worried over and perplexed and depressed with vague apprehensions about her condition, conveyed in mysterious phrases and graveyard expressions of countenance, until about the age of fourteen years, when she had one of those emotional paroxysms very commonly considered in some Protestant sects as essential to the formation of religious character. It began with a shivering sense of enormous guilt, inherited and practised from her earliest infancy. Just as every breath she ever drew had been malignantly poisoning the air with carbonic acid, so her every thought and feeling had been tainting the universe with sin. This spiritual chill or *rigor* had in due order been followed by the fever-flush of hope, and that in its turn had ushered in the last stage, — the free opening of all the spiritual pores in the peaceful relaxation of self-surrender.

Good Christians are made by many very different processes. Bathsheba had taken ner religion after the fashion of her sect; bit it was genuine, in spite of the cavils of the formalists, who could not understand that the spirit which kept her at her mother's bedside was the same as that which poured the tears of Mary of Magdala on the feet of her Lord, and led her forth at early dawn with the other Mary to visit his sepulchre.

Myrtle was a child of nature, and of course, according to the out-worn formulæ which still shame the distorted religion of humanity, hateful to the Father in Heaven who made her. She had grown up in antagonism with all that surrounded her. She had been talked to about her corrupt nature and her sinful heart, until the words had become an offence and an insult. Bathsheba knew her father's fondness for young company too well to suppose that his intercourse with Myrtle had gone beyond the sentimental and poetical stage, and was not displeased when she found that there was some breach between them. Myrtle herself did not profess to have passed through the technical stages of the customary spiritual paroxysm. Still, the gentle daughter of the terrible preacher loved her and judged her kindly. She was modest enough to think that perhaps the natural state of some girls might be at least as good as her own after the spiritual change of which she had been the subject. A manifest heresy, but not new, nor unamiable, nor inexplicable.

The excellent Bishop Joseph Hall, a painful preacher and solid divine of Puritan tendencies, declares that he prefers good-nature before grace in the election of a wife; because, saith he, " it will be a hard Task, where the Nature is peevish and froward, for Grace to make an entire Conquest whilst Life lasteth." An opinion apparently entertained by many modern ecclesiastics, and one which may be considered very encouraging to those young ladies of the politer circles who have a fancy for marrying bishops and other fashionable clergymen. Not of course that "grace" is so rare a gift among the young ladies of the upper social sphere; but they are in the habit of using the word with a somewhat different meaning from that which the good Bishop attached to it.

CHAPTER XVIII.

THE VILLAGE POET.

IT was impossible for Myrtle to be frequently at Olive's without often meeting Olive's brother, and her reappearance with the bloom on her cheek was a signal which her other admirers were not likely to overlook as a hint to recommence their flattering demonstrations; and so it was that she found herself all at once the centre of attraction to three young men with whom we have made some acquaintance, namely, Cyprian Eveleth, Gifted Hopkins, and Murray Bradshaw.

When the three girls were together at the house of Olive, it gave Cyprian a chance to see something of Myrtle in the most natural way. Indeed, they all became used to meeting him in a brotherly sort of relation; only, as he was not the brother of two of them, it gave him the inside track, as the sporting men say, with reference to any rivals for the good-will of either of these. Of course neither Bathsheba nor Myrtle thought of him in any other light than as Olive's brother, and would have been surprised with the manifestation on his part of any other feeling, if it existed. So he became very nearly as intimate with them as Olive was, and hardly thought of his intimacy as anything more than friendship, until one day Myrtle sang some hymns so sweetly that Cyprian dreamed about her that night; and what young person does not know that the woman or the man once idealized and glorified in the exalted state of the imagination belonging to sleep becomes dangerous to the sensibilities in the waking hours that follow? Yet something drew Cyprian to the gentler and more subdued nature of Bathsheba, so that he often thought, like a gayer personage than himself, whose divided affections are famous in song, that he could have been blessed to share her faithful heart, if Myrtle had not bewitched him with her unconscious and innocent sorceries. As for poor, modest Bathsheba, she thought nothing of herself, but was almost as much fascinated by Myrtle as if she had been one of the sex she was born to make in love with her.

The first rival Cyprian was to encounter in his admiration of Myrtle Hazard was Mr. Gifted Hopkins. This young gentleman had the enormous advantage of that all-subduing accomplishment, the poetical endowment. No woman, it is pretty generally understood, can resist the youth or man who addresses her in verse. The thought that she is the object of a poet's love is one which fills a woman's ambition more completely than all that wealth or office or social eminence can offer. Do the young millionnaires and the members of the General Court get letters from unknown ladies, every day, asking for their autographs and photographs? Well, then!

Mr. Gifted Hopkins, being a poet, felt that it was so, to the very depth of his soul. Could he not confer that immortality so dear to the human heart? Not quite yet, perhaps, — though the "Banner and Oracle" gave him already "an elevated niche in the Temple of Fame," to quote its own words, — but in that glorious summer of his genius, of which these spring blossoms were the promise. It was a most formidable battery, then, which Cyprian's first rival opened upon the fortress of Myrtle's affections.

His second rival, Mr. William Murray Bradshaw, had made a half-playful bet with his fair relative, Mrs. Clymer Ketchum, that he would bag a girl within twelve months of date who should unite three desirable qualities, specified in the bet, in a higher degree than any one of the five who were on the matrimonial programme which she had laid out for him, — and Myrtle was the girl with whom he meant to win the bet. When a young fellow like him, cool and clever, makes up his mind to bring down his bird, it is no joke, but a very serious and a tolerably certain piece of business. Not being made a fool of by any boyish nonsense, — passion and all that, — he has a great advantage. Many a woman rejects a man because he is in love with her, and accepts another because he is not. The first is thinking too much of himself and his emotions, — the other makes a study of her and her friends, and learns what ropes to pull. But then it must be remembered that Murray Bradshaw had a poet for his rival, to say nothing of the brother of a bosom friend.

The qualities of a young poet are so exceptional, and such interesting objects of study, that a narrative like this can well afford to linger awhile in the delineation of this most envied of all the forms of genius. And by contrasting the powers and limitations of two such young persons as Gifted Hopkins and Cyprian Eveleth, we may better appreciate the nature of that divine inspiration which gives to poetry the superiority it claims over every other form of human expression.

Gifted Hopkins had shown an ear for rhythm, and for the simpler forms of music, from his earliest childhood He began beating with his heels the accents of the psalm tunes sung at meeting at a very tender age, — a habit indeed, of which he had afterwards to correct himself, as, though it shows a sensibility to rhythmical impulses like that which is beautifully illustrated when a circle join hands and emphasize by vigorous downward movements the leading syllables in the tune of Auld Lang Syne, yet it is apt to be *too* expressive when a large number of boots join in the performance. He showed a remarkable talent for playing on one of the less complex musical instruments, too limited in compass to satisfy exacting ears, but affording excellent discipline to those who wish to write in the simpler metrical forms, — the same which summons the hero from his repose and stirs his blood in battle.

By the time he was twelve years old he was struck with the pleasing resemblance of certain vocal sounds which, without being the same, yet had a curious relation which made them agree marvellously well in couples ; as *eyes* with *skies ;* as *heart* with *art*, also with *part* and *smart ;* and so of numerous others, twenty or thirty pairs, perhaps, which number he considerably increased as he grew older, until he may have had fifty or more such pairs at his command.

The union of so extensive a catalogue of words which matched each other, and of an ear so nice that it could tell if there were nine or eleven syllables in an heroic line, instead of the legitimate ten, constituted a rare combination of talents in the opinion of those upon whose judgment he relied. He was naturally led to try his powers in the expression of some just thought or natural sentiment in the shape of verse, that wonderful medium of imparting thought and feeling to his fellow-creatures which a bountiul Providence had made his rare and inestimable endow ment.

It was at about this period of his life, that is to say when he was of the age of thirteen, or we may perhaps say fourteen years, for we do not wish to overstate his precocity, that he experienced a sensation so entirely novel, that, to the best of his belief, it was such as no other young person had ever known, at least in anything like the same degree. This extraordinary emotion was brought on by the sight of Myrtle Hazard, with whom he had never before had any near relations, as they had been at different schools, and Myrtle was too reserved to be very generally known among the young people of his age.

Then it was that he broke forth in his virgin effort, " Lines to M——e," which were published in the village paper, and were claimed by all possible girls but the right one; namely, by two Mary Annes, one Minnie, one Mehitable, and one Marthie, as she saw fit to spell the name borrowed from her who was troubled about many things.

The success of these lines, which were in that form of verse known to the hymn-books as " common metre," was such as to convince the youth that, whatever occupation he might be compelled to follow for a time to obtain a liveli-hood or to assist his worthy parent, his true destiny was the glorious career of a poet. It was a most pleasing circumstance, that his mother, while she fully recognized the propriety of his being diligent in the prosaic line of business to which circumstances had called him, was yet as much convinced as he himself that he was destined to achieve literary fame. She had read Watts and Select Hymns all through, she said, and she did n't see but what Gifted could make the verses come out jest as slick, and the sound of the rhymes jest as pooty, as Izik Watts or 'he Selectmen, whoever they was, — she was sure they could n't be the selectmen of this town, wherever they belonged. It is pleasant to say that the young man, though favored by nature with this rarest of talents, did not forget the humbler duties that Heaven, which dresses few singing birds in the golden plumes of fortune, had laid upon him. After having received a moderate amount of instruction at one of the less ambitious educational institutions of the town, supplemented, it is true, by the judicious and gratuitous hints of Master Gridley, the young poet, in obedience to a feeling which did him the highest credit, relinquished, at least for the time, the Groves of Academus, and offered his youth at the shrine of Plutus, that is, left off studying and took to business. He became what they call a "clerk" in what they call a "store" up in the huckleberry districts, and kept such accounts as were required by the business of the establishment. His principal occupation was, however, to attend to the details of commerce as it was transacted over the counter. This industry enabled him, to his great praise be it spoken, to assist his excellent parent, to clothe himself in a becoming manner, so that he made a really handsome figure on Sundays and was always of presentable aspect, likewise to purchase a book now and then, and to subscribe for that leading periodical which furnishes the best models to the youth of the country in the various modes of composition.

Though Master Gridley was very kind to the young man, he was rather disposed to check the exuberance of his poetical aspirations. The truth was, that the old classical scholar did not care a great deal for modern English poetry. Give him an Ode of Horace, or a scrap from the Greek Anthology, and he would recite it with great inflation of spirits ; but he did not think very much of " your

Keatses, and your Tennysons, and the whole Hasheesh
crazy lot," as he called the dreamily sensuous idealists who
belong to the same century that brought in ether and chlo-
roform.   He rather shook his head at Gifted Hopkins for
indulging so largely in metrical composition.

" Better stick to your ciphering, my young friend," he
said to him, one day.   " Figures of speech are all very
well, in their way ; but if you undertake to deal much in
them, you 'll figure down your prospects into a mighty
small sum.   There 's some danger that it will take all the
sense out of you, if you keep writing verses at this rate.
You young scribblers think any kind of nonsense will do
for the public, if it only has a string of rhymes tacked to it.
Cut off the bobs of your kite, Gifted Hopkins, and see if it
does n't pitch, and stagger, and come down head-foremost.
Don't write any stuff with rhyming tails to it that won't
make a decent show for itself after you 've chopped all the
rhyming tails off.   That 's my advice, Gifted Hopkins.   Is
there any book you would like to have out of my library ?
Have you ever read Spenser's Faery Queen ? "

He had tried, the young man answered, on the recom-
mendation of Cyprian Eveleth, but had found it rather
hard reading.

Master Gridley lifted his eyebrows very slightly, remembering that some had called Spenser the poet's poet.
" What a pity," he said to himself, " that this Gifted Hopkins has n't got the brains of that William Murray Bradshaw !   What 's the reason, I wonder, that all the little
earthen pots blow their covers off and froth over in rhymes
at such a great rate, while the big iron pots keep their lids
on, and do all their simmering inside ? "

That is the way these old pedants will talk, after all

their youth and all their poetry, if they ever had any, are
gone.   The smiles of woman, in the mean time, encourage
the young poet to smite the lyre.   Fame beckoned him upward from her templed steep.   The rhymes which rose
before him unbidden were as the rounds of Jacob's ladder,
on which he would climb to a heaven of glory.

Master Gridley threw cold water on the young man's
too sanguine anticipations of success.   " All up with the
boy, if he 's going to take to rhyming when he ought to be
doing up papers of brown sugar and weighing out pounds
of tea.   Poor-house, — that 's what it 'll end in.   Poets, to
be sure !   Sausage-makers !   Empty skins of old phrases,
— stuff 'em with odds and ends of old thoughts that never
were good for anything, — cut 'em up in lengths and sell
'em to fools !   And if they ain't big fools enough to buy
'em, give 'em away ; and if you can't do that, pay folks to
take 'em.   Bah ! what a fine style of genius common-sense
is !   There 's a passage in the book that would fit half
these addle-headed rhymesters.   What is that saying of
mine about ' squinting brains ' ? "

He took down " Thoughts on the Universe," and
read : —

" Of Squinting Brains.

" *Where there is one man who squints with his eyes, there
are a dozen who squint with their brains.   It is an infirmity in one of the eyes, making the two unequal in power,
that makes men squint.   Just so it is an inequality in the
two halves of the brain that makes some men idiots and
others rascals.   I know a fellow whose right half is a genius
but his other hemisphere belongs to a fool ; and I had a
friend perfectly honest on one side, but who was sent to*

jail because the other had an inveterate tendency in the direction of picking pockets and appropriating æs alienum."

All this, talking and reading to himself in his usual fashion.

The poetical faculty which was so freely developed in Gifted Hopkins had never manifested itself in Cyprian Eveleth, whose look and voice might, to a stranger, have seemed more likely to imply an imaginative nature. Cyprian was dark, slender, sensitive, contemplative, a lover of lonely walks, — one who listened for the whispers of Nature and watched her shadows, and was alive to the symbolisms she writes over everything. But Cyprian had never shown the talent or the inclination for writing in verse.

He was on the pleasantest terms with the young poet, and being somewhat older, and having had the advantage of academic and college culture, often gave him useful hints as to the cultivation of his powers, such as genius frequently requires at the hands of humbler intelligences. Cyprian was incapable of jealousy ; and although the name of Gifted Hopkins was getting to be known beyond the immediate neighborhood, and his autograph had been requested by more than one young lady living in another county, he never thought of envying the young poet's spreading popularity.

That the poet himself was flattered by these marks of public favor may be inferred from the growing confidence with which he expressed himself in his conversations with Cyprian, more especially in one which was held at the " store " where he officiated as " clerk."

" I become more and more assured, Cyprian," he said

æaning over the counter, "that I was born to be a poet. I feel it in my marrow. I must succeed. I must win the laurel of fame. I must taste the sweets of — "

"Molasses," said a bareheaded girl of ten who entered at that moment, bearing in her hand a cracked pitcher, — "ma wants three gills of molasses."

Gifted Hopkins dropped his subject and took up a tin measure. He served the little maid with a benignity quite charming to witness, made an entry on a slate of .08, and resumed the conversation.

"Yes, I am sure of it, Cyprian. The very last piece I wrote was copied in two papers. It was 'Contemplations in Autumn,' and — don't think I am too vain — one young lady has told me that it reminded her of Pollok. You never wrote in verse, did you, Cyprian?"

"I never wrote at all, Gifted, except school and college exercises, and a letter now and then. Do you find it an easy and pleasant exercise to make rhymes?"

"Pleasant! Poetry is to me a delight and a passion. I never know what I am going to write when I sit down. And presently the rhymes begin pounding in my brain, — it seems as if there were a hundred couples of them, paired like so many dancers, — and then these rhymes seem to take possession of me, like a surprise party, and bring in all sorts of beautiful thoughts, and I write and write, and the verses run measuring themselves out like — "

"Ribbins, — any narrer blue ribbins, Mr. Hopkins? Five eighths of a yard, if you please, Mr. Hopkins. How's your folks?" Then, in a lower tone, "Those last verses of yours in the Bannernoracle were sweet pooty."

Gifted Hopkins meted out the five eighths of blue ribbon

9 *

by the aid of certain brass nails on the counter. He gave good measure, not prodigal, for he was loyal to his employer but putting a very moderate strain on the ribbon, and letting the thumb-nail slide with a contempt of infinitesimals which betokened a large soul in its genial mood.

The young lady departed, after casting upon him one of those bewitching glances which the young poet — let us rather say the poet, without making odious distinctions — is in the confirmed habit of receiving from dear woman.

Mr. Gifted Hopkins resumed: "I do not know where this talent, as my friends call it, of mine, comes from. My father used to carry a chain for a surveyor sometimes, and there is a ten-foot pole in the house he used to measure land with. I don't see why *that* should make me a poet. My mother was always fond of Dr. Watts's hymns; but so are other young men's mothers, and yet *they* don't show poetical genius. But wherever I got it, it comes as easy to me to write in verse as to write in prose, almost. Don't you ever feel a longing to send your thoughts forth in verse, Cyprian?"

"I wish I had a greater facility of expression very often," Cyprian answered; "but when I have my best thoughts I do not find that I have words that seem fitting to clothe them. I have imagined a great many poems, Gifted, but I never wrote a rhyming verse, or verse of any kind. Did you ever hear Olive play 'Songs without Words'? If you have ever heard her, you will know what I mean by unrhymed and unversed poetry."

"I am sure I don't know what you mean, Cyprian, by poetry without rhyme or verse, any more than I should if you talked about pictures that were painted on nothing, or statues that were made out of nothing. How can you tell that anything is poetry, I should like to know, if there is neither a regular line with just so many syllables, nor a rhyme? Of course you can't. *I* never have any thoughts too beautiful to put in verse: nothing can be too beautiful for it."

Cyprian left the conversation at this point. It was getting more suggestive than interpenetrating, and he thought he might talk the matter over better with Olive. Just then a little boy came in, and bargained with Gifted for a Jews-harp, which, having obtained, he placed against his teeth, and began playing upon it with a pleasure almost equal to that of the young poet reciting his own verses.

"A little too much like my friend Gifted Hopkins's poetry," Cyprian said, as he left the "store." "All in one note, pretty much. Not a great many tunes, — ' Hi Betty Martin,' ' Yankee Doodle,' and one or two more like them. But many people seem to like them, and I don't doubt it is as exciting to Gifted to write them as it is to a great genius to express itself in a poem."

Cyprian was, perhaps, too exacting. He loved too well the sweet intricacies of Spenser, the majestic and subtly interwoven harmonies of Milton. These made him impatient of the simpler strains of Gifted Hopkins.

Though he himself never wrote verses, he had some qualities which his friend the poet may have undervalued in comparison with the talent of modelling the symmetries of verse and adjusting the correspondences of rhyme. He had kept in a singular degree all the sensibilities of childhood, its simplicity, its reverence. It seemed as if nothing of all that he met in his daily life was common or unclean to him, for there was no mordant in his nature for what was coarse or vile, and all else he could not help idealizing into its own conception of itself, so to speak. He loved the leaf after its kind as well as the flower, and the root as well as the leaf, and did not exhaust his capacity of affection or admiration on the blossom or bud upon which his friend the poet lavished the wealth of his verse. Thus Nature took him into her confidence. She loves the men of science well, and tells them all her family secrets, — who is the father of this or that member of the group, who is brother, sister, cousin, and so on, through all the circle of relationship. But there are others to whom she tells her *dreams ;* not what species or genus her lily belongs to, but what vague thought it has when it dresses in white, or what memory of its birthplace that is which we call its fragrance. Cyprian was one of these. Yet he was not a complete nature. He required another and a wholly different one to be the complement of his own. Olive came as near it as a sister could, but — we must borrow an old image — moonlight is no more than a cold and vacant glimmer on the sun-dial, which only answers to the great flaming orb of day. If Cyprian could but find some true, sweet-tempered, well-balanced woman, richer in feeling than in those special imaginative gifts which made the outward world at times unreal to him in the intense reality of his own inner life, how he could enrich and adorn her existence, — how she could direct and chasten and elevate the character of all his thoughts and actions !

" Bathsheba," said Olive, " it seems to me that Cyprian is getting more and more fascinated with Myrtle Hazard. He has never got over the fancy he took to her when he first saw her in her red jacket, and called her the fire-hang. bird. Would n't they suit each other by and by, after Myrtle has come to herself and grown into a beautiful and noble woman, as I feel sure she will in due time ? "

"Myrtle is very lovely," Bathsheba answered, "but is n't she a little too — flighty — for one like your brother? Cyprian is n't more like other young men than Myrtle is like other young girls. I have thought sometimes — I wondered whether out-of-the-way people and common ones do not get along best together. Does n't Cyprian want some more every-day kind of girl to keep him straight? Myrtle is beautiful, — beautiful, — fascinates everybody. Has Mr. Bradshaw been following after her lately? He is taken with her too. Did n't you ever think she would have to give in to Murray Bradshaw at last? He looks to me like a man that would hold on desperately as a lover."

If Myrtle Hazard, instead of being a half-finished school-girl, hardly sixteen years old, had been a young woman of eighteen or nineteen, it would have been plain sailing enough for Murray Bradshaw. But he knew what a distance their ages seemed just now to put between them, — a distance which would grow practically less and less with every year, and he did not wish to risk anything so long as there was no danger of interference. He rather encouraged Gifted Hopkins to write poetry to Myrtle. " Go in, Gifted," he said, " there 's no telling what may come of it," — and Gifted did go in at a great rate.

Murray Bradshaw did not write poetry himself, but he read poetry with a good deal of effect, and he would sometimes take a hint from one of Gifted Hopkins's last productions to recite a passionate lyric of Byron or Moore, into which he would artfully throw so much meaning that Myrtle was almost as much puzzled, in her simplicity, to know what it meant, as she had been by the religious fervors of the Rev. Mr. Stoker.

He spoke well of Cyprian Eveleth. A good young man, — limited, but exemplary. Would succeed well as rector of a small parish. That required little talent, but a good deal of the humbler sort of virtue. As for himself, he confessed to ambition, — yes, a great deal of ambition. A failing, he supposed, but not the worst of failings. He felt the instinct to handle the larger interests of society. The village would perhaps lose sight of him for a time; but he meant to emerge sooner or later in the higher spheres of government or diplomacy. Myrtle must keep his secret. Nobody else knew it. He could not help making a confidant of her, — a thing he had never done before with any other person as to his plans in life. Perhaps she might watch his career with more interest from her acquaintance with him. He loved to think that there was one woman at least who would be pleased to hear of his success if he succeeded, as with life and health he would, — who would share his disappointment if fate should not favor him. — So he wound and wreathed himself into her thoughts.

It was not very long before Myrtle began to accept the idea that she was the one person in the world whose peculiar duty it was to sympathize with the aspiring young man whose humble beginnings she had the honor of witnessing. And it is not very far from being the solitary confidant, and the single source of inspiration, to the growth of a livelier interest, where a young man and a young woman are in question.

Myrtle was at this time her own mistress as never before. The three young men had access to her as she walked to and from meeting and in her frequent rambles besides the opportunities Cyprian had of meeting her in his sister's company, and the convenient visits which, in connection with the great lawsuit, Murray Bradshaw could make, without question, at The Poplars.

It was not long before Cyprian perceived that he could never pass a certain boundary of intimacy with Myrtle. Very pleasant and sisterly always she was with him; but she never looked as if she might mean more than she said, and cherished a little spark of sensibility which might be fanned into the flame of love. Cyprian felt this so certainly that he was on the point of telling his grief to Bathsheba, who looked to him as if she would sympathize as heartily with him as his own sister, and whose sympathy would have a certain flavor in it, — something which one cannot find in the heart of the dearest sister that ever lived. But Bathsheba was herself sensitive, and changed color when Cyprian ventured a hint or two in the direction of his thought, so that he never got so far as to unburden his heart to her about Myrtle, whom she admired so sincerely that she could not have helped feeling a great interest in his passion towards her.

As for Gifted Hopkins, the roses that were beginning to bloom fresher and fresher every day in Myrtle's cheeks unfolded themselves more and more freely, to speak metaphorically, in his song. Every week she would receive a delicately tinted note with lines to " Myrtle awaking," or to " Myrtle retiring," (one string of verses a little too Musidora-ish, and which soon found itself in the condition of a cinder, perhaps reduced to that state by spontaneous combustion,) or to " The Flower of the Tropics," or to the " Nymph of the River-side," or other poetical alias, such as bards affect in their sieges of the female heart.

Gifted Hopkins was of a sanguine temperament. As

he read and re-read his verses it certainly seemed to him that they must reach the heart of the angelic being to whom they were addressed. That she was slow in confessing the impression they made upon her, was a favorable sign ; so many girls called his poems " sweet pooty," that those charming words, though soothing, no longer stirred him deeply. Myrtle's silence showed that the impression his verses had made was deep. Time would develop her sentiments ; they were both young ; his position was humble as yet ; but when he had become famous through the land — O blissful thought ! — the bard of Oxbow Village would bear a name that any woman would be proud to assume, and the M. H. which her delicate hands had wrought on the kerchiefs she wore would yet perhaps be read, not Myrtle Hazard, but Myrtle Hopkins !

CHAPTER XIX.

SUSAN'S YOUNG MAN.

THERE seems no reasonable doubt that Myrtle Hazard might have made a safe thing of it with Gifted Hopkins, (if so inclined,) provided that she had only been se cured against interference. But the constant habit of reading his verses to Susan Posey was not without its risk to so excitable a nature as that of the young poet. Poets were always capable of divided affections, and Cowley's " Chronicle " is a confession that would fit the whole tribe of them. It is true that Gifted had no right to regard Susan's heart as open to the wiles of any new-comer. He knew that she considered herself, and was considered by another, as pledged and plighted. Yet she was such a devoted listener, her sympathies were so easily roused, her blue eyes glistened so tenderly at the least poetical hint, such as " Never, O never," " My aching heart," " Go, let me weep," — any of those touching phrases out of the long catalogue which readily suggests itself, — that her influence was getting to be such that Myrtle (if really anxious to secure him) might look upon it with apprehension, and the owner of Susan's heart (if of a jealous disposition) might have thought it worth while to make a visit to Oxbow Village to see after his property.

It may seem not impossible that some friend had suggested as much as this to the young lady's lover. The caution would have been unnecessary, or at least premature. Susan was loyal as ever to her absent friend

ʀ

Gifted Hopkins had never yet presumed upon the familiar relations existing between them to attempt to shake her allegiance. It is quite as likely, after all, that the young gentleman about to make his appearance in Oxbow Village visited the place of his own accord, without a hint from anybody. But the fact concerns us more than the reason of it, just now.

"Who do you think is coming, Mr. Gridley? Who *do* you think is coming?" said Susan Posey, her face covered with a carnation such as the first season may see in a city belle, but not the second.

"Well, Susan Posey, I suppose I must guess, though I am rather slow at that business. Perhaps the Governor. No, I don't think it can be the Governor, for you would n't look so happy if it was only his Excellency. It must be the President, Susan Posey, — President James Buchanan. Have n't I guessed right, now, tell me, my dear?"

"O Mr. Gridley, you are too bad, — what do I care for governors and presidents? I know somebody that's worth fifty million thousand presidents, — and *he*'s coming, — my Clement is coming," said Susan, who had by this time learned to consider the awful Byles Gridley as her next friend and faithful counsellor.

Susan could not stay long in the house after she got her note informing her that her friend was soon to be with her. Everybody told everything to Olive Eveleth, and Susan must run over to the Parsonage to tell her that there was a young gentleman coming to Oxbow Village; upon which Olive asked who it was, exactly as if she did not know; whereupon Susan dropped her eyes and said, "Clement, — I mean Mr. Lindsay."

That was a fair piece of news now, and Olive had her

bonnet on five minutes after Susan was gone, and was on her way to Bathsheba's, — it was too bad that the poor girl who lived so out of the world should n't know anything of what was going on in it. Bathsheba had been in all the morning, and the Doctor had said she must take the air every day ; so Bathsheba had on *her* bonnet a little after Olive had gone, and walked straight up to The Poplars to tell Myrtle Hazard that a certain young gentleman, Clement Lindsay, was coming to Oxbow Village.

It was perhaps fortunate that there was no special significance to Myrtle in the name of Clement Lindsay. Since the adventure which had brought these two young persons together, and, after coming so near a disaster, had ended in a mere humiliation and disappointment, and but for Master Gridley's discreet kindness might have led to foolish scandal, Myrtle had never referred to it in any way. Nobody really knew what her plans had been except Olive. and Cyprian, who had observed a very kind silence about the whole matter. The common version of the story was harmless, and near enough to the truth, — down the river, — boat upset, — pulled out, — taken care of by some women in a house farther down, — sick, brain fever, — pretty near it, anyhow, — old Dr. Hurlbut called in, — had her hair cut, — hystericky, etc., etc.

Myrtle was contented with this statement, and asked no questions, and it was a perfectly understood thing that nobody alluded to the subject in her presence. It followed from all this that the name of Clement Lindsay had no peculiar meaning for her. Nor was she like to recognize him as the youth in whose company she had gone through her mortal peril, for all her recollections were confused and dreamlike from the moment when she awoke and found her-

self in the foaming rapids just above the fall, until that
when her senses returned, and she saw Master Byles Gridley standing over her with that look of tenderness in his
square features which had lingered in her recollection, and
made her feel towards him as if she were his daughter.

Now this had its advantage; for as Clement was Susan's
young man, and had been so for two or three years, it
would have been a great pity to have any such curious
relations established between him and Myrtle Hazard as a
consciousness on both sides of what had happened would
naturally suggest.

"Who is this Clement Lindsay, Bathsheba?" Myrtle
asked.

"Why, Myrtle, don't you remember about Susan Posey's
is-to-be, — the young man that has been — well, I don't
know, but I suppose engaged to her ever since they were
children almost?"

"Yes, yes, I remember now. O dear! I have forgotten
so many things, I should think I had been dead and was
coming back to life again. Do you know anything about
him, Bathsheba? Did n't somebody say he was very handsome? I wonder if he is really in love with Susan Posey.
Such a simple thing! I want to see him. I have seen so
few young men."

As Myrtle said these words, she lifted the sleeve a
little on her left arm, by a half-instinctive and half-volun-
tary movement. The glimmering gold of Judith Pride's
bracelet flashed out the yellow gleam which has been the
reddening of so many hands and the blackening of so many
souls since that innocent sin-breeder was first picked up
'n the land of Havilah. There came a sudden light into
her eye, such as Bathsheba had never seen there before

It looked to her as if Myrtle were saying unconsciously to herself that she had the power of beauty, and would like to try its influence on the handsome young man whom she was soon to meet, even at the risk of unseating poor little Susan in his affections. This pained the gentle and humble-minded girl, who, without having tasted the world's pleasures, had meekly consecrated herself to the lowly duties which lay nearest to her. For Bathsheba's phrasing of life was in the monosyllables of a rigid faith. Her conceptions of the human soul were all simplicity and purity, but elementary. She could not conceive the vast license the creative energy allows itself in mingling the instincts which, after long conflict, may come into harmonious adjustment. The flash which Myrtle's eye had caught from the gleam of the golden bracelet filled Bathsheba with a sudden fear that she was like to be led away by the vanities of that world lying in wickedness of which the minister's daughter had heard so much and seen so little.

Not that Bathsheba made any fine moral speeches to herself. She only felt a slight shock, such as a word or a look from one we love too often gives us, — such as a child's trivial gesture or movement makes a parent feel, — that impalpable something which in the slightest possible inflection of a syllable or gradation of a tone will some-times leave a sting behind it, even in a trusting heart. This was all. But it was true that what she saw meant a great deal. It meant the dawning in Myrtle Hazard of one of her as yet unlived *secondary lives*. Bathsheba's virgin perceptions had caught a faint early ray of its glimmering twilight.

She answered, after a very slight pause, which this explanation has made seem so long, that she had never seen the young gentleman, and that she did not know about Susan's sentiments. Only, as they had kept so long to each other, she supposed there must be love between them.

Myrtle fell into a revery, with certain *tableaux* glowing along its perspectives which poor little Susan Posey would have shivered to look upon, if they could have been transferred from the purple clouds of Myrtle's imagination to the pale silvery mists of Susan's pretty fancies. She sat in her day-dream long after Bathsheba had left her, her eyes fixed, not on the faded portrait of her beatified ancestress, but on that other canvas where the dead Beauty seemed to live in all the splendors of her full-blown womanhood.

The young man whose name had set her thoughts roving *was* handsome, as the glance at him already given might have foreshadowed. But his features had a graver impress than his age seemed to account for, and the sober tone of his letter to Susan implied that something had given him a maturity beyond his years. The story was not an uncommon one. At sixteen he had dreamed — and told his dream. At eighteen he had awoke, and found, as he believed, that a young heart had grown to his so that its life was dependent on his own. Whether it would have perished if its filaments had been gently disentangled from the object to which they had attached themselves, experienced judges of such matters may perhaps question. To justify Clement in his estimate of the danger of such an experiment, we must remember that to young people in their teens a first passion is a portentous and unprecedented phenomenon. The young man may have been mistaken in thinking that Susan would die if he left her, and may have done more than his duty in sacrificing himself; but if so, it was the mistake of a generous youth who estimated the depth of another's feelings by his own. He measured the depth of his own rather by what he felt they might be, than by that of any abysses they had yet sounded.

Clement was called a " genius " by those who knew him, and was consequently in danger of being spoiled early. The risk is great enough anywhere, but greatest in a new country, where there is an almost universal want of fixed standards of excellence.

He was by nature an artist; a shaper with the pencil or the chisel, a planner, a contriver capable of turning his hand to almost any work of eye and hand. It would not have been strange if he thought he could do everything, having gifts which were capable of various application, — and being an American citizen. But though he was a good draughtsman, and had made some reliefs and modelled some figures, he called himself only an architect. He had given himself up to his art, not merely from a love of it and talent for it, but with a kind of heroic devotion, because he thought his country wanted a race of builders to clothe the new forms of religious, social, and national life afresh from the forest, the quarry, and the mine. Some thought he would succeed, others that he would be a brilliant failure.

" Grand notions, — grand notions," the master with whom he studied said. " Large ground plan of life, — splendid elevation. A little wild in some of his fancies, perhaps, but he's only a boy, and he's the kind of boy that sometimes grows to be a pretty big man. Wait and see, —

wait and see. He works days, and we can let him dream
nights. There's a good deal of him, anyhow." His fellow-
students were puzzled. Those who thought of their calling
as a trade, and looked forward to the time when they
should be embodying the ideals of municipal authorities
in brick and stone, or making contracts with wealthy
citizens, doubted whether Clement would have a sharp
eye enough for business. "Too many whims, you know.
All sorts of queer ideas in his head, — as if a boy like him
were going to make things all over again ! "

No doubt there was something of youthful extravagance
in his plans and expectations. But it was the untamed
enthusiasm which is the source of all great thoughts and
deeds, — a beautiful delirium which age commonly tames
down, and for which the cold shower-bath the world furnishes *gratis* proves a pretty certain cure.

Creation is always preceded by chaos. The youthful
architect's mind was confused by the multitude of suggestions which were crowding in upon it, and which he had
not yet had time or developed mature strength sufficient to
reduce to order. The young American of any freshness
of intellect is stimulated to dangerous excess by the conditions of life into which he is born. There is a double
proportion of oxygen in the New-World air. The chemists
have not found it out yet, but human brains and breathing-
organs have long since made the discovery.

Clement knew that his hasty entanglement had limited
his possibilities of happiness in one direction, and he felt
that there was a certain grandeur in the recompense of
working out his defeated instincts through the ambitious
medium of his noble art. Had not Pharaohs chosen it
to proclaim their longings for immortality, Caesars their

passion for pomp and luxury, and priests to symbolize
their conceptions of the heavenly mansions? His dreams
were on a grand scale; such, after all, are the best
possessions of youth. Had he but been free, or mated
with a nature akin to his own, he would have felt himself as truly the heir of creation as any young man that
lived. But his lot was cast, and his youth had all the
serious aspect to himself of thoughtful manhood. In the
region of his art alone he hoped always to find freedom and
a companionship which his home life could never give him.

Clement meant to have visited his beloved before he left
Alderbank, but was called unexpectedly back to the city
Happily Susan was not exacting; she looked up to him
with too great a feeling of distance between them to dare
to question his actions. Perhaps she found a partial con-
olation in the company of Mr. Gifted Hopkins, who tried
his new poems on her, which was the next best thing to
addressing them to her. " Would that you were with us
at this delightful season," she wrote in the autumn; " but no,
your Susan must not repine. Yet, in the beautiful words of
our native poet,

> ' O would, O would that thou wast here,
> For absence makes thee doubly dear;
> Ah! what is life while thou 'rt away?
> 'T is night without the orb of day!' "

The poet referred to, it need hardly be said, was our
young and promising friend G. H., as he sometimes modestly signed himself. The letter, it is unnecessary to state.
was voluminous, — for a woman can tell her love, or other
matter of interest, over and over again in as many forms
as another poet, not G. H., found for his grief in ringing
the musical changes of " In Memoriam."

10

The answers to Susan's letters were kind, but not **very**
long. They convinced her that it was a simple impossi-
bility that Clement could come to Oxbow Village, on
account of the great pressure of the work he had to keep
him in the city, and the plans he *must* finish at any rate.
But at last the work was partially got rid of, and Clement
was coming; yes, it was so nice, and, O dear! should n't
she be real happy to see him?

To Susan he appeared as a kind of divinity, — almost
too grand for human nature's daily food. Yet, if the sim
ple-hearted girl could have told herself the whole truth in
plain words, she would have confessed to certain doubts
which from time to time, and oftener of late, cast a shadow
on her seemingly bright future. With all the pleasure that
the thought of meeting Clement gave her, she felt a little
tremor, a certain degree of awe, in contemplating his visit.
If she could have clothed her self-humiliation in the gold
and purple of the " Portuguese Sonnets," it would have
been another matter ; but the trouble with the most common sources of disquiet is that they have no wardrobe of
flaming phraseology to air themselves in; the inward
burning goes on without the relief and gratifying display
of the crater.

" A *friend* of mine is coming to the village," she said to
Mr. Gifted Hopkins. " I want you to see him. He is a
genius, — as some other young men are." (This was obviously personal, and the youthful poet blushed with ingenuous delight.) " I have known him for ever so many years
He and I are *very good friends.*" The poet knew that
this meant an exclusive relation between them ; and though
the fact was no surprise to him, his countenance fell a
little. The truth was, that his admiration was divided

between Myrtle, who seemed to him divine and adorable, but distant, and Susan, who listened to his frequent poems, whom he was in the habit of seeing in artless domestic costumes, and whose attractions had been gaining upon him of late in the enforced absence of his divinity.

He retired pensive from this interview, and, flinging himself at his desk, attempted wreaking his thoughts upon expression, to borrow the language of one of his brother bards, in a passionate lyric which he began thus : —

"ANOTHER'S!

"Another's ! O the pang, the smart !
Fate owes to Love a deathless grudge, —
The barbéd fang has rent a heart
Which — which —

"judge — judge, — no, not judge. Budge, drudge, fudge — What a disgusting language English is ! Nothing fit to couple with such a word as grudge ! And the gush of an impassioned moment arrested in full flow, stopped short, corked up, for want of a paltry rhyme ! Judge, — budge, — drudge, — nudge, — oh ! — smudge, — misery ! — fudge. In vain, — futile, — no use, — all up for to-night !"

While the poet, headed off in this way by the poverty of his native tongue, sought inspiration by retiring into the world of dreams, — went to bed, in short, — his more fortunate rival was just entering the village, where he was to make his brief residence at the house of Deacon Rumrill, who, having been a loser by the devouring element, was glad to receive a stray boarder when any such were looking about for quarters.

For some reason or other he was restless that evening, and took out a volume he had brought with him to beguile the earlier hours of the night. It was too late when he

arrived to disturb the quiet of Mrs. Hopkins's household
and whatever may have been Clement's impatience, he
held it in check, and sat tranquilly until midnight over the
pages of the book with which he had prudently provided
himself.

"Hope you slept well last night," said the old Deacon,
when Mr. Clement came down to breakfast the next morn‑
ing.

"Very well, thank you, — that is, after I got to bed.
But I sat up pretty late reading my favorite Scott. I am
apt to forget how the hours pass when I have one of his
books in my hand."

The worthy Deacon looked at Mr. Clement with a
sudden accession of interest.

"You could n't find better reading, young man. Scott
is *my* favorite author. A great man. I have got his like‑
ness in a gilt frame hanging up in the other room. I have
read him all through three times."

The young man's countenance brightened. He had not
expected to find so much taste for elegant literature in an
old village deacon.

"What are your favorites among his writings, Deacon?
I suppose you have your particular likings, as the rest of us
have."

The Deacon was flattered by the question. "Well," he
answered, "I can hardly tell you. I like pretty much
everything Scott ever wrote. Sometimes I think it is one
thing, and sometimes another. Great on Paul's Epistles
— don't you think so?"

The honest fact was, that Clement remembered very
little about "Paul's Letters to his Kinsfolk," — a book of
Sir Walter's less famous than many of his others; but he

signified his polite assent to the Deacon's statement, rather wondering at his choice of a favorite, and smiling at his queer way of talking about the Letters as Epistles.

"I am afraid Scott is not so much read now-a-days as he once was, and as he ought to be," said Mr. Clement. "Such character, such nature and so much grace — "

"That 's it, — that 's it, young man," the Deacon broke in, — "Natur' and Grace, — Natur' and Grace. Nobody ever knew better what those two words meant than Scott did, and I 'm very glad to see you 've chosen such good wholesome reading. You can't set up too late, young man, to read Scott. If I had twenty children, they should all begin reading Scott as soon as they were old enough to spell 'sin,' — and that 's the first word my little ones learned, next to 'pa' and 'ma.' Nothing like beginning the lessons of life in good season."

"What a grim old satirist!" Clement said to himself. "I wonder if the old man reads other novelists. — Do tell me, Deacon, if you have read Thackeray's last story?"

"Thackery's story? Published by the American Tract Society?"

"Not exactly," Clement answered, smiling, and quite delighted to find such an unexpected vein of grave pleasantry about the demure-looking church-dignitary; for the Deacon asked his question without moving a muscle, and took no cognizance whatever of the young man's tone and smile. First-class humorists are, as is well known, remarkable for the immovable solemnity of their features. Clement promised himself not a little amusement from the curiously sedate drollery of the venerable Deacon, who, it was plain from his conversation, had cultivated a literary taste which would make him a more agreeable companion

than the common ecclesiastics of his grade in country vil.
lages.

After breakfast, Mr. Clement walked forth in the direction of Mrs. Hopkins's house, thinking as he went of the
pleasant surprise his visit would bring to his longing and
doubtless pensive Susan; for though she knew he was
coming, she did not know that he was at that moment in
Oxbow Village.

As he drew near the house, the first thing he saw was
Susan Posey, almost running against her just as he turned
a corner. She looked wonderfully lively and rosy, for the
weather was getting keen and the frosts had begun to bite.
A young gentleman was walking at her side, and reading
to her from a paper he held in his hand. Both looked
deeply interested, — so much so that Clement felt half
ashamed of himself for intruding upon them so abruptly.

But lovers are lovers, and Clement could not help join-
ing them. The first thing, of course, was the utterance
of two simultaneous exclamations, " Why, Clement!"
" Why, Susan!" What might have come next in the programme, but for the presence of a third party, is matter
of conjecture; but what did come next was a mighty awkward look on the part of Susan Posey, and the following
short speech : —

" Mr. Lindsay, let me introduce Mr. Hopkins, my friend,
the poet I've written to you about. He was just reading
two of his poems to me. Some other time, Gifted — Mr
Hopkins."

" O no, Mr. Hopkins, — pray go on," said Clement.
' I'm very fond of poetry."

The poet did not require much urging, and began at
once reciting over again the stanzas which were afterwards

so much admired in the " Banner and Oracle," — the first
verse being, as the readers of that paper will remember, —

> " She moves in splendor, like the ray
>   That flashes from unclouded skies,
> And all the charms of night and day
>   Are mingled in her hair and eyes.'

Clement, who must have been in an agony of impatience
to be alone with his beloved, commanded his feelings ad-
mirably. He signified his approbation of the poem by
saying that the lines were smooth and the rhymes absolutely without blemish. The stanzas reminded him forcibly
of one of the greatest poets of the century.

Gifted flushed hot with pleasure. He had tasted the
blood of his own rhymes ; and when a poet gets as far as
that, it is like wringing the bag of exhilarating gas from
the lips of a fellow sucking at it, to drag his piece away
from him.

" Perhaps you will like these lines still better," he said ;
" the style is more modern : —

> ' O daughter of the spicéd South,
>   Her bubbly grapes have spilled the wine
>   That staineth with its hue divine
> The red flower of thy perfect mouth.' "

And so on, through a series of stanzas like these, with the
pulp of two rhymes between the upper and lower crust of
two others.

Clement was cornered. It was necessary to say something for the poet's sake, — perhaps for Susan's ; for she
was in a certain sense responsible for the poems of a youth
of genius, of whom she had spoken so often and so en-
thusiastically.

"Very good, Mr. Hopkins, and a form of verse little used, I should think, until of late years. You modelled this piece on the style of a famous living English poet, did you not?"

"Indeed I did not, Mr. Lindsay, — I never imitate. Originality is, if I may be allowed to say so much for myself, my peculiar *forte*. Why, the critics allow as much as that. See here, Mr. Lindsay."

Mr. Gifted Hopkins pulled out his pocket-book, and, taking therefrom a cutting from a newspaper, — which dropped helplessly open of itself, as if tired of the process, being very tender in the joints or creases, by reason of having been often folded and unfolded, — read aloud as follows : —

"The bard of Oxbow Village — our valued correspondent who writes over the signature of G. H. — is, in our opinion, more remarkable for his *originality* than for any other of his numerous gifts."

Clement was apparently silenced by this, and the poet a little elated with a sense of triumph. Susan could not help sharing his feeling of satisfaction, and without meaning it in the least, nay, without knowing it, for she was as simple and pure as new milk, edged a little bit — the merest infinitesimal atom — nearer to Gifted Hopkins, who was on one side of her, while Clement walked on the other. Women love the conquering party, — it is the way of their sex. And poets, as we have seen, are wellnigh irresistible when they exert their dangerous power of fascination upon the female heart. But Clement was above jealousy ; and, if he perceived anything of this movement, took no notice of it.

He saw a good deal of his pretty Susan that day. She was tender in her expressions and manners as usual, but there was a little something in her looks and language

from time to time that Clement did not know exactly what
to make of. She colored once or twice when the young
poet's name was mentioned. She was not so full of her
little plans for the future as she had sometimes been,
" everything was so uncertain," she said. Clement asked
himself whether she felt quite as sure that her attachment
would last as she once did. But there were no reproaches,
not even any explanations, which are about as bad between
lovers. There was nothing but an undefined feeling on
his side that she did not cling quite so closely to him, perhaps, as he had once thought, and that, if he had happened to have been drowned that day when he went down
with the beautiful young woman, it was just conceivable
that Susan, who would have cried dreadfully, no doubt,
would in time have listened to consolation from some other
young man, — possibly from the young poet whose verses
he had been admiring. Easy-crying widows take new
husbands soonest ; there is nothing like wet weather for
transplanting, as Master Gridley used to say. Susan had
a fluent natural gift for tears, as Clement well knew, after
the exercise of which she used to brighten up like the rose
which had been washed, just washed in a shower, mentioned by Cowper.

As for the poet, he learned more of his own sentiments
during this visit of Clement's than he had ever before
known. He wandered about with a dreadfully disconsolate
look upon his countenance. He showed a falling-off in
his appetite at tea-time, which surprised and disturbed his
mother, for she had filled the house with fragrant suggestions of good things coming, in honor of Mr. Lindsay
who was to be her guest at tea. And chiefly the genteel
form of doughnut called in the native dialect *cymbal* (*Qu.*

10 *   o

Symbol? B. G.) which graced the board with its plastic
forms, suggestive of the most pleasing objects, — the spiral
ringlets pendent from the brow of beauty, — the magic
circlet, which is the pledge of plighted affection, — the
indissoluble knot, which typifies the union of hearts, which
organs were also largely represented; this exceptional
delicacy would at any other time have claimed his special
notice. But his mother remarked that he paid little attention to these, and his, " No, I thank you," when it came to
the preserved " damsels," as some call them, carried a
pang with it to the maternal bosom. The most touching
evidence of his unhappiness — whether intentional or the
result of accident was not evident — was a *broken heart*,
which he left upon his plate, the meaning of which was as
plain as anything in the language of flowers. His thoughts
were gloomy during that day, running a good deal on the
more picturesque and impressive methods of bidding a
voluntary farewell to a world which had allured him with
visions of beauty only to snatch them from his impassioned
gaze. His mother saw something of this, and got from
him a few disjointed words, which led her to lock up the
clothes-line and hide her late husband's razors, — an affectionate, yet perhaps unnecessary precaution, for self-elimi-
nation contemplated from this point of view by those who
have the natural outlet of verse to relieve them is rarely
followed by a casualty. It may rather be considered
as implying a more than average chance for longevity; as
those who meditate an imposing finish naturally save themselves for it, and are therefore careful of their health until
the time comes, and this is apt to be indefinitely postponed
so long as there is a poem to write or a proof to be corrected.

CHAPTER XX.

THE SECOND MEETING.

"MISS EVELETH requests the pleasure of Mr Lindsay's company to meet a few friends on the evening of the Feast of St. Ambrose, December 7th, Wednesday.

"THE PARSONAGE, December 6th."

It was the luckiest thing in the world. They always made a little festival of that evening at the Rev. Ambrose Eveleth's, in honor of his canonized namesake, and because they liked to have a good time. It came this year just at the right moment, for here was a distinguished stranger visiting in the place. Oxbow Village seemed to be running over with its one extra young man, — as may be seen sometimes in larger villages, and even in cities of moderate dimensions.

Mr. William Murray Bradshaw had called on Clement the day after his arrival. He had already met the Deacon in the street, and asked some questions about his transient boarder.

A very interesting young man, the Deacon said, much given to the reading of pious books. Up late at night after he came, reading Scott's Commentary. Appeared to be as fond of serious works as other young folks were of their novels and romances and other immoral publications. He, the Deacon, thought of having a few religious friends to meet the young gentleman, if he felt so disposed; and should like to have him, Mr. Bradshaw, come in and

take a part in the exercises. — Mr. Bradshaw was unfortu-
nately engaged. He thought the young gentleman could
hardly find time for such a meeting during his brief visit.

Mr. Bradshaw expected naturally to see a youth of im
perfect constitution, and cachectic or dyspeptic tendencies,
who was in training to furnish one of those biographies
beginning with the statement that, from his infancy, the
subject of it showed no inclination for boyish amusements,
and so on, until he dies out, for the simple reason that there
was not enough of him to live. Very interesting, no
doubt, Master Byles Gridley would have said, but had no
more to do with good, hearty, sound life than the history
of those very little people to be seen in museums preserved in jars of alcohol, like brandy peaches.

When Mr. Clement Lindsay presented himself, Mr.
Bradshaw was a good deal surprised to see a young fellow
of such a mould. He pleased himself with the idea that
he knew a man of mark at sight, and he set down Clement
in that category at his first glance. The young man met
his penetrating and questioning look with a frank, ingenuous, open aspect, before which he felt himself disarmed,
as it were, and thrown upon other means of analysis. He
would try him a little in talk.

"I hope you like these people you are with. What sort
of a man do you find my old friend the Deacon?"

Clement laughed. "A very queer old character. Loves
his joke as well, and is as sly in making it, as if he had
studied Joe Miller instead of the Catechism."

Mr. Bradshaw looked at the young man to know what
he meant. Mr Lindsay talked in a very easy way for a
serious young person. He was puzzled. He did not see
to the bottom of this description of the Deacon. Witt

a lawyer's instinct, he kept his doubts to himself and tried his witness with a new question.

" Did you talk about books at all with the old man ? "

" To be sure I did. Would you believe it, — that aged saint is a great novel-reader. So he tells me. What is more, he brings up his children to that sort of reading, from the time when they first begin to spell. If anybody else had told me such a story about an old country deacon, I would n't have believed it; but he said so himself, to me, at breakfast this morning."

Mr Bradshaw felt as if either he or Mr. Lindsay must certainly be in the first stage of mild insanity, and he did not think that he himself could be out of his wits. He must try one more question. He had become so mystified that he forgot himself, and began putting his interrogation n legal form.

" Will you state, if you please — I beg your pardon — may I ask who is your own favorite author ? "

" I think just now I like to read Scott better than almost anybody."

" Do you mean the Rev. Thomas Scott, author of the Commentary ? "

Clement stared at Mr. Bradshaw, and wondered whether he was trying to make a fool of him. The young lawyer hardly looked as if he could be a fool himself.

" I mean Sir Walter Scott," he said, dryly.

" Oh ! " said Mr. Bradshaw. He saw that there had been a slight misunderstanding between the young man and his worthy host, but it was none of his business, and there were other subjects of interest to talk about.

" You know one of our charming young ladies very well, I believe, Mr Lindsay. 1 think you are an old acquaintance of Miss Posey, whom we all consider sc pretty."

Poor Clement! The question pierced to the very marrow of his soul, but it was put with the utmost suavity and courtesy, and honeyed with a compliment to the young lady, too, so that there was no avoiding a direct and pleasant answer to it.

"Yes," he said, "I have known the young lady you speak of for a long time, and very well, — in fact, as you must have heard, we are something more than friends. My visit here is principally on her account "

"You must give the rest of us a chance to see something of you during your visit, Mr. Lindsay. I hope you are invited to Miss Eveleth's to-morrow evening?"

"Yes, I got a note this morning. Tell me, Mr. Bradshaw, who is there that I shall meet if I go? I have no doubt there are girls here in the village I should like to see, and perhaps some young fellows that I should like to talk with. You know all that's prettiest and pleasantest, of course."

"O, we're a little place, Mr. Lindsay. A few nice people, the rest *comme ça*, you know. High-bush blackberries and low-bush blackberries, — you understand, — just so everywhere, — high-bush here and there, low-bush plenty. You must see the two parsons' daughters, — Saint Ambrose's and Saint Joseph's, — and another girl I want particularly to introduce you to. You shall form your own opinion of her. *I* call her handsome and stylish, but you have got spoiled, you know. Our young poet, too, one we raised in this place, Mr. Lindsay, and a superior article of poet, as we think, — that is, some of us, for the rest of us are jealous of him, because the girls are all dying for him and want his autograph. — And Cyp, — yes, you must talk to Cyp, — he has ideas. But don'" forget to get hold of old Byles — Master Gridley I mean — before you go. Big head. Brains enough for a cabinet minister, and fit out a college faculty with what was left over. Be sure you see old Byles. Set him talking about his book, — 'Thoughts on the Universe.' Did n't sell much, but has got knowing things in it. I 'll show you a copy, and then you can tell him you know it, and he will take to you. Come in and get your dinner with me to-morrow. We will dine late, as the city folks do, and after that we will go over to the Rector's. I should like to show you some of our village people.

Mr. Bradshaw liked the thought of showing the young man to some of his friends there. As Clement was already " done for," or " bowled out," as the young lawyer would have expressed the fact of his being pledged in the matrimonial direction, there was nothing to be apprehended on the score of rivalry. And although Clement was particularly good-looking, and would have been called a distinguishable youth anywhere, Mr. Bradshaw considered himself far more than his match, in all probability, in social accomplishments. He expected, therefore, a certain amount of reflex credit for bringing such a fine young fellow in his company, and a second instalment of reputation from outshining him in conversation. This was rather nice calculating, but Murray Bradshaw always calculated. With most men life is like backgammon, half skill, and half luck, but with him it was like chess. He never pushed a pawn without reckoning the cost, and when his mind was least busy it was sure to be half a dozen moves ahead of the game as it was standing.

Mr. Bradshaw gave Clement a pretty dinner enough for such a place as Oxbow Village. He offered him some good wine, and would have made him talk so as to show his lining, to use one of his own expressions, but Clement had apparently been through that trifling experience, and could not be coaxed into saying more than he meant to say. Murray Bradshaw was very curious to find out how it was that he had become the victim of such a rudimentary miss as Susan Posey. Could she be an heiress in disguise? Why no, of course not; had not he made all proper inquiries about that when Susan came to town? A small inheritance from an aunt or uncle, or some such relative, enough to make her a desirable party in the eyes of certain villagers perhaps, but nothing to allure a man like this, whose face and figure as marketable possessions were worth say a hundred thousand in the girl's own right, as Mr. Bradshaw put it roughly, with another hundred thousand if his talent is what some say, and if his connection is a desirable one, a fancy price, — anything he would fetch. Of course not. Must have got caught when he was a child. Why the *diavolo* did n't he break it off, then?

There was no fault to find with the modest entertainment at the Parsonage. A splendid banquet in a great house is an admirable thing, provided always its getting up did not cost the entertainer an inward conflict, nor its recollection a twinge of economical regret, nor its bills a cramp of anxiety. A simple evening party in the smallest village is just as admirable in its degree, when the parlor is cheerfully lighted, and the board prettily spread, and the guests are made to feel comfortable without being reminded that anybody is making a painful effort.

We know several of the young people who were there, and need not trouble ourselves for the others. Myrtle Hazard had promised to come. She had her own way of

late as never before ; in fact, the women were afraid of her
Miss Silence felt that she could not be responsible for her
any longer. She had hopes for a time that Myrtle would
go through the customary spiritual paroxysm under the
influence of the Rev. Mr. Stoker's assiduous exhortations ;
but since she had broken off with him, Miss Silence had
looked upon her as little better than a backslider. And
now that the girl was beginning to show the tendencies
which seemed to come straight down to her from the belle
of the last century, (whose rich physical developments
seemed to the under-vitalized spinster as in themselves a
kind of offence against propriety,) the forlorn woman folded
her thin hands and looked on hopelessly, hardly venturing
a remonstrance for fear of some new explosion. As for
Cynthia, she was comparatively easy since she had, through
Mr. Byles Gridley, upset the minister's questionable arrangement of religious intimacy. She had, in fact, in a
quiet way, given Mr. Bradshaw to understand that he would
probably meet Myrtle at the Parsonage if he dropped in at
their small gathering.

Clement walked over to Mrs. Hopkins's after his dinner
with the young lawyer, and asked if Susan was ready to
go with him. At the sound of his voice, Gifted Hopkins
smote his forehead, and called himself, in subdued tones, a
miserable being. His imagination wavered uncertain for
a while between pictures of various modes of ridding him
self of existence, and fearful deeds involving the life of
others. He had no fell purpose of actually doing either,
but there was a gloomy pleasure in contemplating them as
possibilities, and in mentally sketching the " Lines written
n Despair " which would be found in what was but an
nour oefore the pocket of the youthful bard, G. H., victim

of a hopeless passion. All this emotion was in the nature of a surprise to the young man. He had fully believed himself desperately in love with Myrtle Hazard; and it was not until Clement came into the family circle with the right of eminent domain over the realm of Susan's affections, that this unfortunate discovered that Susan's pretty ways and morning dress and love of poetry and liking for his company had been too much for him, and that he was henceforth to be wretched during the remainder of his natural life, except so far as he could unburden himself in song.

Mr. William Murray Bradshaw had asked the privilege of waiting upon Myrtle to the little party at the Eveleths. Myrtle was not insensible to the attractions of the young lawyer, though she had never thought of herself except as a child in her relations with any of these older persons. But she was not the same girl that she had been but a few months before. She had achieved her independence by her audacious and most dangerous enterprise. She had gone through strange nervous trials and spiritual experiences which had matured her more rapidly than years of common life would have done. She had got back her health, bringing with it a riper wealth of womanhood. She had found her destiny in the consciousness that she inherited the beauty belonging to her blood, and which, after sleeping for a generation or two as if to rest from the glare of the pageant that follows beauty through its long career of triumph, had come to the light again in her life, and was to repeat the legends of the olden time in her own history.

Myrtle's wardrobe had very little of ornament, such as the *modistes* of the town would have thought essential to render a young girl like her presentable. There were a few heirlooms of old date, however, which she had kept a⁰ ouriosities until now, and which she looked over until she found some lace and other convertible material, with which she enlivened her costume a little for the evening. As she clasped the antique bracelet around her wrist, she felt as if it were an amulet that gave her the power of charming which had been so long obsolete in her lineage. At the bottom of her heart she cherished a secret longing to try her fascinations on the young lawyer. Who could blame her? It was not an inwardly expressed intention, — it was the simple instinctive movement to subjugate the strongest of the other sex who had come in her way, which, as already said, is as natural to a woman as it is to a man to be captivated by the loveliest of those to whom he dares to aspire.

Before William Murray Bradshaw and Myrtle Hazard had reached the Parsonage, the girl's cheeks were flushed and her dark eyes were flashing with a new excitement. The young man had not made love to her directly, but he had interested her in herself by a delicate and tender flattery of manner, and so set her fancies working that she was .aken with him as never before, and wishing that the Parsonage had been a mile farther from The Poplars. It was impossible for a young girl like Myrtle to conceal the pleasure she received from listening to her seductive admirer, who was trying all his trained skill upon his artless companion. Murray Bradshaw felt sure that the game was in his hands if he played it with only common prudence. There was no need of hurrying this child, — it might startle her to make downright love abruptly; and now that he had an ally in her own household, and was to have access to her with a freedom he had never before enjoyed, there was a refined pleasure in playing his fish, —

this gamest of golden-scaled creatures, — which had risen to his fly, and which he wished to hook, but not to land, until he was sure it would be worth his while.

They entered the little parlor at the Parsonage looking so beaming, that Olive and Bathsheba exchanged glances which implied so much that it would take a full page to tell it with all the potentialities involved.

" How magnificent Myrtle is this evening, Bathsheba ! " said Cyprian Eveleth, pensively.

" What a handsome pair they are, Cyprian ! " said Bathsheba cheerfully.

Cyprian sighed.   " She always fascinates me whenever I look upon her. Is n't she the very picture of what a poet's love should be, — a poem herself, — a glorious lyric, — all light and music ! See what a smile the creature has ! And her voice ! When did you ever hear such tones ? And when was it ever so full of life before."

Bathsheba sighed.   " I do not know any poets but Gifted Hopkins.   Does not Myrtle look more in her place by the side of Murray Bradshaw than she would with Gifted hitched on her arm ? "

Just then the poet made his appearance. He looked depressed, as if it had cost him an effort to come. He was, however, charged with a message which he must deliver to the hostess of the evening.

" They 're coming presently," he said.   " That young man and Susan. Wants you to introduce him, Mr. Bradshaw."

The bell rang presently, and Murray Bradshaw slipped out into the entry to meet the two lovers.

" How are you, my fortunate friend ? " he said, as he met them at the door. " Of course you 're well and hap py as mortal man can be in this vale of tears. Charming, ravishing, quite delicious, that way of dressing your hair, Miss Posey! Nice girls here this evening, Mr. Lindsay Looked lovely when I came out of the parlor. Can't say how they will show after this young lady puts in an appearance." In reply to which florid speeches Susan blushed, not knowing what else to do, and Clement smiled as naturally as if he had been sitting for his photograph.

He felt, in a vague way, that he and Susan were being patronized, which is not a pleasant feeling to persons with a certain pride of character. There was no expression of contempt about Mr. Bradshaw's manner or language at which he could take offence. Only he had the air of a man who praises his neighbor without stint, with a calm consciousness that he himself is out of reach of comparison in the possessions or qualities which he is admiring in the other. Clement was right in his obscure perception of Mr. Bradshaw's feeling while he was making his phrases. That gentleman was, in another moment, to have the tin gling delight of showing the grand creature he had just begun to tame. He was going to extinguish the pallid light of Susan's prettiness in the brightness of Myrtle's beauty. He would bring this young man, neutralized and rendered entirely harmless by his irrevocable pledge to a slight girl, face to face with a masterpiece of young womanhood, and say to him, not in words, but as plainly as speech could have told him, " Behold my captive ! "

It was a proud moment for Murray Bradshaw. He had seen, or thought that he had seen, the assured evidence of a speedy triumph over all the obstacles of Myrtle's youth and his own present seeming slight excess of matu-ty. Unless he were very greatly mistaken, he could now walk the course; the plate was his, no matter what might be the entries. And this youth, this handsome, spirited-looking, noble-aired young fellow, whose artist-eye could not miss a line of Myrtle's proud and almost defiant beauty, was to be the witness of his power, and to look in admiration upon his prize! He introduced him to the others, reserving her for the last. She was at that moment talking with the worthy Rector, and turned when Mr. Bradshaw spoke to her.

"Miss Hazard, will you allow me to present to you my friend, Mr. Clement Lindsay?"

They looked full upon each other, and spoke the common words of salutation. It was a strange meeting; but we who profess to tell the truth must tell strange things, or we shall be liars.

In poor little Susan's letter there was some allusion to a bust of Innocence which the young artist had begun, but of which he had said nothing in his answer to her. He had roughed out a block of marble for that impersonation; sculpture was a delight to him, though secondary to his main pursuit. After his memorable adventure, the image of the girl he had rescued so haunted him that the pale ideal which was to work itself out in the bust faded away in its perpetual presence, and — alas, poor Susan! — in obedience to the impulse that he could not control, he left Innocence sleeping in the marble, and began modelling a figure of proud and noble and imperious beauty, to which he gave the name of Liberty.

The original which had inspired his conception was before him. These were the lips to which his own had clung when he brought her back from the land of shadows The hyacinthine curl of her lengthening locks had added something to her beauty; but it was the same face which had haunted him. This was the form he had borne seemingly lifeless in his arms, and the bosom which heaved so visibly before him was that which his eyes —— they were the calm eyes of a sculptor, but of a sculptor hardly twenty years old.

Yes, — her bosom was heaving. She had an unexplained feeling of suffocation, and drew great breaths, — she could not have said why, — but she could not help it; and presently she became giddy, and had a great noise in her ears, and rolled her eyes about, and was on the point of going into an hysteric spasm. They called Dr. Hurlbut, who was making himself agreeable to Olive just then, to come and see what was the matter with Myrtle.

"A little nervous turn, — that is all," he said. "Open the window. Loose the ribbon round her neck. Rub her hands. Sprinkle some water on her forehead. A few drops of cologne. Room too warm for her, — that's all, I think."

Myrtle came to herself after a time without anything like a regular paroxysm. But she was excitable, and whatever the cause of the disturbance may have been, it seemed prudent that she should go home early; and the excellent Rector insisted on caring for her, much to the discontent of Mr. William Murray Bradshaw.

"Demonish odd," said this gentleman, was n't it, Mr Lindsay, that Miss Hazard should go off in that way? Did you ever see her before?

"I — I — have seen that young lady before," Clement answered.

"Where did you meet her?" Mr. Bradshaw asked, with eager interest.

"I met her in the Valley of the Shadow of Death," Clement answered, very solemnly. — "I leave this place to-morrow morning. Have you any commands for the city?"

("Knows how to shut a fellow up pretty well for a young one, does n't he?" Mr. Bradshaw thought to himself.)

"Thank you, no," he answered, recovering himself. "Rather a melancholy place to make acquaintance in, I should think, that Valley you spoke of. I should like to know about it."

Mr. Clement had the power of looking steadily into another person's eyes in a way that was by no means encouraging to curiosity or favorable to the process of cross-examination. Mr. Bradshaw was not disposed to press his question in the face of the calm, repressive look the young man gave him.

"If he was n't bagged, I should n't like the shape of things any too well," he said to himself.

The conversation between Mr. Clement Lindsay and Miss Susan Posey, as they walked home together, was not very brilliant. "I am going to-morrow morning," he said, "and I must bid you good by to-night." Perhaps it is as well to leave two lovers to themselves, under these circumstances.

Before he went he spoke to his worthy host, whose moderate demands he had to satisfy, and with whom he wished to exchange a few words.

"And by the way, Deacon, I have no use for this book, and as it is in a good type, perhaps you would like it. Your favorite, Scott, and one of his greatest works. I have another edition of it at home, and don't care for this volume."

" Thank you, thank you, Mr. Lindsay, much obleeged.
I shall read that copy for your sake, — the best of books
next to the Bible itself."

After Mr. Lindsay had gone, the Deacon looked at the
back of the book. " Scott's Works, Vol. IX." He opened
it at hazard, and happened to fall on a well-known page
from which he began reading aloud, slowly,

> " When Izrul, of the Lord beloved,
> Out of the land of bondage came."

The whole hymn pleased the grave Deacon. He had
never seen this work of the author of the Commentary. No
matter ; anything that such a good man wrote must be
good reading, and he would save it up for Sunday. The
consequence of this was, that, when the Rev. Mr. Stoker
stopped in on his way to meeting on the " Sabbath," he
turned white with horror at the spectacle of the senior
Deacon of his church sitting, open-mouthed and wide-eyed,
absorbed in the pages of " Ivanhoe," which he found enor-
mously interesting ; but, so far as he had yet read, not
occupied with religious matters so much as he had expected.

Myrtle had no explanation to give of her nervous attack.
Mr. Bradshaw called the day after the party, but did not
see her. He met her walking, and thought she seemed a
little more distant than common. That would never do.
He called again at The Poplars a few days afterwards,
and was met in the entry by Miss Cynthia, with whom he
had a long conversation on matters involving Myrtle's
interests and their own.

11

CHAPTER XXI.

MADNESS?

MR. CLEMENT LINDSAY returned to the city and his usual labors in a state of strange mental agitation. He had received an impression for which he was unprepared. He had seen for the second time a young girl whom, for the peace of his own mind, and for the happiness of others, he should never again have looked upon until Time had taught their young hearts the lesson which all hearts must learn, sooner or later.

What shall the unfortunate person do who has met with one of those disappointments, or been betrayed into one of those positions, which do violence to all the tenderest feelings, blighting the happiness of youth, and the prospects of after years?

If the person is a young man, he has various resources. He can take to the philosophic meerschaum, and nicotize himself at brief intervals into a kind of buzzing and blurry insensibility, until he begins to "color" at last like the bowl of his own pipe, and even his mind gets the tobacco flavor. Or he can have recourse to the more suggestive stimulants, which will dress his future up for him in shining possibilities that glitter like Masonic regalia, until the morning light and the waking headache reveal his illusion. Some kind of spiritual anæsthetic he must have, if he holds his grief fast tied to his heart-strings. But as grief must be fed with thought, or starve to death, it is the best plan to keep the mind so busy in other ways that it has no time

to attend to the wants of that ravening passion. To sit
down and passively endure it, is apt to end in putting all
the mental machinery into disorder.

Clement Lindsay had thought that his battle of life was
already fought, and that he had conquered. He believed
that he had subdued himself completely, and that he was
ready, without betraying a shadow of disappointment, to
take the insufficient nature which destiny had assigned
him in his companion, and share with it all of his own
larger being it was capable, not of comprehending, but of
apprehending.

He had deceived himself. The battle was not fought
and won. There had been a struggle, and what seemed to
be a victory, but the enemy — intrenched in the very citadel of life — had rallied, and would make another desperate attempt to retrieve his defeat.

The haste with which the young man had quitted the
village was only a proof that he felt his danger. He
believed that, if he came into the presence of Myrtle Hazard for the third time, he should be no longer master of his
feelings. Some explanation must take place between
them, and how was it possible that it should be without
emotion? and in what do all emotions shared by a young
man with such a young girl as this tend to find their last
expression?

Clement determined to stun his sensibilities by work.
He would give himself no leisure to indulge in idle dreams
of what might have been. His plans were never so carefully finished, and his studies were never so continuous as
now. But the passion still wrought within him, and, if he
drove it from his waking thoughts haunted his sleep until
he could endure it no longer, and must give it some mani-

festation. He had covered up the bust of Liberty so closely, that not an outline betrayed itself through the heavy folds of drapery in which it was wrapped. His thoughts recurred to his unfinished marble, as offering the one mode in which he could find a silent outlet to the feelings and thoughts which it was torture to keep imprisoned in his soul. The cold stone would tell them, but without passion ; and having got the image which possessed him out of himself into a lifeless form, it seemed as if he might be delivered from a presence which, lovely as it was, stood between him and all that made him seem honorable and worthy to himself.

He uncovered the bust which he had but half shaped, and struck the first flake from the glittering marble. The toil, once begun, fascinated him strangely, and after the day's work was done, and at every interval he could snatch from his duties, he wrought at his secret task.

" Clement is graver than ever," the young men said at the office. " What 's the matter, do you suppose ? Turned off by the girl they say he means to marry by and by ? How pale he looks too ! Must have something worrying him : he used to look as fresh as a clove pink."

The master with whom he studied saw that he was losing color, and looking very much worn, and determined to find out, if he could, whether he was not overworking himself. He soon discovered that his light was seen burning late into the night, that he was neglecting his natural rest, and always busy with some unknown task, not called for in his routine of duty or legitimate study.

Something is wearing on you, Clement," he said. " You are killing yourself with undertaking too much. Will you let me know what keeps you so busy when you ought to be asleep, or taking your ease and comfort in some way or other ? "

Nobody but himself had ever seen his marble or its model. He had now almost finished it, laboring at it with such sleepless devotion, and he was willing to let his master have a sight of his first effort of the kind, — for he was not a sculptor, it must be remembered, though he had modelled in clay, not without some success, from time to time.

" Come with me," he said.

The master climbed the stairs with him up to his modest chamber. A closely shrouded bust stood on its pedestal in the light of the solitary window.

" That is my ideal personage," Clement said. " Wait one moment, and you shall see how far I have caught the character of our uncrowned queen."

The master expected, very naturally, to see the conventional young woman with classical wreath or feather head-dress, whom we have placed upon our smallest coin, so that our children may all grow up loving Liberty.

As Clement withdrew the drapery that covered his work, the master stared at it in amazement. He looked at it long and earnestly, and at length turned his eyes, a little moistened by some feeling which thus betrayed itself, upon his scholar.

" This is no ideal, Clement. It is the portrait of a very young but very beautiful woman. No common feeling could have guided your hand in shaping such a portrait from memory. This must be that friend of yours of whom I have often heard as an amiable young person. Pardon me, for you know that nobody cares more for you than I do, — I hope that you are happy in all your relations with this young friend of yours. How could one be otherwise?"

It was hard to bear, very hard. He forced a smile. "You are partly right," he said. "There is a resemblance, I trust, to a living person, for I had one in my mind."

"Did n't you tell me once, Clement, that you were attempting a bust of Innocence? I do not see any block in your room but this. Is that done?"

"Done *with!*" Clement answered; and, as he said it, the thought stung through him that this was the very stone which was to have worn the pleasant blandness of pretty Susan's guileless countenance. How the new features had effaced the recollection of the others!

In a few days more Clement had finished his bust. His hours were again vacant to his thick-coming fancies. While he had been busy with his marble, his hands had required his attention, and he must think closely of every detail upon which he was at work. But at length his task was done, and he could contemplate what he had made of it. It was a triumph for one so little exercised in sculpture. The master had told him so, and his own eye could not deceive him. He might never succeed in any repetition of his effort, but this once he most certainly had succeeded. He could not disguise from himself the source of this extraordinary good fortune in so doubtful and difficult an attempt. Nor could he resist the desire of contemplating the portrait bust, which — it was foolish to talk about ideals — was not Liberty, but Myrtle Hazard.

It was too nearly like the story of the ancient sculptor. his own work was an over-match for its artist. Clemen had made a mistake in supposing that by giving his dream a material form he should drive it from the possession of his mind. The image in which he had fixed his recollection of its original served only to keep her living presence before him. He thought of her as she clasped her arms around him, and they were swallowed up in the rushing waters, coming so near to passing into the unknown world together. He thought of her as he stretched her lifeless form upon the bank, and looked for one brief moment on her unsunned loveliness, — " a sight to dream of, not to tell." He thought of her as his last fleeting glimpse had shown her, beautiful, not with the blossomy prettiness that passes away with the spring sunshine, but with a rich vitality of which noble outlines and winning expression were only the natural accidents. And that singular impression which the sight of him had produced upon her, — how strange! How could she but have listened to him, — to him, who was, as it were, a second creator to her, for he had brought her back from the gates of the unseen realm, — if he had recalled to her the dread moments they had passed in each other's arms, with death, not love, in all their thoughts. And if then he had told her how her image had remained with him, how it had colored all his visions, and mingled with all his conceptions, would not those dark eyes have melted as they were turned upon him? Nay, how could he keep the thought away, that she would not have been insensible to his passion, if he could have suffered its flame to kindle in his heart? Did it not seem as if Death had spared them for Love, and that Love should lead them together through life's long journey to the gates of Death?

Never! never! never! Their fates were fixed. For him, poor insect as he was, a solitary flight by day, and a return at evening to his wingless mate! For her — he thought he saw her doom.

Could he give her up to the cold embraces of that passionless egotist, who, as he perceived plainly enough, was casting his shining net all around her? Clement read Murray Bradshaw correctly. He could not perhaps have spread his character out in set words, as we must do for him, for it takes a long apprenticeship to learn to describe analytically what we know as soon as we see it; but he felt in his inner consciousness all that we must tell for him. Fascinating, agreeable, artful, knowing, capable of winning a woman infinitely above himself, incapable of understanding her, — O, if he could but touch him with the angel's spear, and bid him take his true shape before her whom he was gradually enveloping in the silken meshes of his subtle web! He would make a place for her in the world, — O yes, doubtless. He would be proud of her in company, would dress her handsomely, and show her off in the best lights. But from the very hour that he felt his power over her firmly established, he would begin to remodel her after his own worldly pattern. He would dismantle her of her womanly ideals, and give her in their place his table of market-values. He would teach her to submit her sensibilities to her selfish interest, and her tastes to the fashion of the moment, no matter which world or half-world it came from. " As the husband is, the wife is," — he would subdue her to what he worked in.

All this Clement saw, as in apocalyptic vision, stored up for the wife of Murray Bradshaw, if he read him rightly, as he felt sure he did, from the few times he had seen him. He would be rich by and by, very probably. He

looked like one of those young men who are sharp
and hard enough to come to fortune. Then she would
have to take her place in the great social exhibition where
the gilded cages are daily opened that the animals may
be seen, feeding on the sight of stereotyped toilets and
the sound of impoverished tattle. O misery of semi-pro ·
vincial fashionable life, where wealth is at its wit's end to
avoid being tired of an existence which has all the labor
of keeping up appearances, without the piquant profligacy
which saves it at least from being utterly vapid! How
many fashionable women at the end of a long season
would be ready to welcome heaven itself as a relief from
the desperate monotony of dressing, dawdling, and driving!

This could not go on so forever. Clement had placed
a red curtain so as to throw a rose-bloom on his marble,
and give it an aspect which his fancy turned to the semblance of life. He would sit and look at the features his
own hand had so faithfully wrought, until it seemed as if
the lips moved, sometimes as if they were smiling, sometimes as if they were ready to speak to him. His companions began to whisper strange things of him in the
studio, — that his eye was getting an unnatural light, —
that he talked as if to imaginary listeners, — in short, that
there was a look as if something were going wrong with
his brain, which it might be feared would spoil his fine
intelligence. It was the undecided battle, and the enemy,
as in his noblest moments he had considered the growing
passion, was getting the better of him.

He was sitting one afternoon before the fatal bust which
had smiled and whispered away his peace, when the post-
man brought him a letter. It was from the simple girl

11 *

to whom he had given his promise. We know how she used to prattle in her harmless way about her innocent feelings, and the trifling matters that were going on in her little village world. But now she wrote in sadness. Something, she did not too clearly explain what, had grieved her, and she gave free expression to her feelings. "I have no one that loves me but you," she said; "and if you leave me I must droop and die. Are you true to me, dearest Clement, — true as when we promised each other that we would love while life lasted? Or have you forgotten one who will never cease to remember that she was once your own Susan?"

Clement dropped the letter from his hand, and sat a long hour looking at the exquisitely wrought features of her who had come between him and honor and his plighted word.

At length he arose, and, lifting the bust tenderly from its pedestal, laid it upon the cloth with which it had been covered. He wrapped it closely, fold upon fold, as the mother whom man condemns and God pities wraps the child she loves before she lifts her hand against its life. Then he took a heavy hammer and shattered his lovely idol into shapeless fragments. The strife was over.

CHAPTER XXII.

⁎ CHANGE OF PROGRAMME.

MR. WILLIAM MURRAY BRADSHAW was in pretty intimate relations with Miss Cynthia Badlam. It was well understood between them that it might be of very great advantage to both of them if he should in due time become the accepted lover of Myrtle Hazard. So long as he could be reasonably secure against interference, he did not wish to hurry her in making her decision. Two things he did wish to be sure of, if possible, before asking her the great question; — first, that she would answer it in the affirmative; and secondly, that certain contingencies, the turning of which was not as yet absolutely capable of being predicted, should happen as he expected. Cynthia had the power of furthering his wishes in many direct and indirect ways, and he felt sure of her co-operation. She had some reason to fear his enmity if she displeased him, and he had taken good care to make her understand that her interests would be greatly promoted by the success of the plan which he had formed, and which was confided to her alone.

He kept the most careful eye on every possible source of disturbance to this quietly maturing plan. He had no objection to have Gifted Hopkins about Myrtle as much as she would endure to have him. The youthful bard entertained her very innocently with his bursts of poetry, but she was in no danger from a young person so intimately associated with the yard-stick, the blunt scissors, and the brown-paper parcel. There was Cyprian too, about whom he did not feel any very particular solicitude. Myrtle had evidently found out that she was handsome and stylish and all that, and it was not very likely she would take up with such a bashful, humble, country youth as this. He could expect nothing beyond a possible rectorate in the remote distance, with one of those little pony chapels to preach in, which, if it were set up on a stout pole, would pass for a good-sized martin-house. Cyprian might do to practise on, but there was no danger of her looking at him in a serious way. As for that youth, Clement Lindsay, if he had not taken himself off as he did, Murray Bradshaw confessed to himself that he should have felt uneasy. He was too good-looking, and too clever a young fellow to have knocking about among fragile susceptibilities. But on reflection he saw there could be no danger.

"All up with him, — poor diavolo! Can't understand it — such a little sixpenny miss — pretty enough boiled parsnip blonde, if one likes that sort of thing — pleases some of the old boys, apparently. Look out, Mr. L. — remember Susanna and the Elders. Good!

"Safe enough if something new does n't turn up. Youngish. Sixteen 's a little early. Seventeen will do. Marry a girl while she 's in the gristle, and you can shape her bones for her. Splendid creature — without her trimmings. Wants training. Must learn to dance, and sing something besides psalm-tunes."

Mr. Bradshaw began humming the hymn, "When I can read my title clear," adding some variations of his own, "That 's the solo for my *prima donna!*"

In the mean time Myrtle seemed to be showing some new developments. One would have said that the in-

stincts of the coquette, or at least of the city belle, were
coming uppermost in her nature.   Her little nervous
attack passed away, and she gained strength and beauty
every day.   She was becoming conscious of her gifts of
fascination, and seemed to please herself with the homage
of her rustic admirers.   Why was it that no one of them
had the look and bearing of that young man she had seen
but a moment the other evening?   To think that he should
have taken up with such a weakling as Susan Posey!
She sighed, and not so much thought as felt how kind it
would have been in Heaven to have made her such a man.
But the image of the delicate blonde stood between her
and all serious thought of Clement Lindsay.   She saw the
wedding in the distance, and very foolishly thought to herself that she could not and would not go to it.

But Clement Lindsay was gone, and she must content
herself with such worshippers as the village afforded.
Murray Bradshaw was surprised and confounded at the
easy way in which she received his compliments, and
played with his advances, after the fashion of the trained
ball-room belles, who know how to be almost caressing in
manner, and yet are really as far off from the deluded victim of their suavities as the topmost statue of the Milan
cathedral from the peasant that kneels on its floor.   He
admired her all the more for this, and yet he saw that she
would be a harder prize to win than he had once thought
If he made up his mind that he would have her, he must
go armed with all implements, from the red hackle to the
harpoon.

The change which surprised Murray Bradshaw could
not fail to be noticed by all those about her.   Miss Silence
had long ago come to pantomime, — rolling up of eyes,

clasping of hands, making of sad mouths, and the rest, —
but left her to her own way, as already the property
of that great firm of World & Co. which drives such
sharp bargains for young souls with the better angels.
Cynthia studied her for her own purposes, but had never
gained her confidence. The Irish servant saw that some
change had come over her, and thought of the great ladies
she had sometimes looked upon in the old country. They
all had a kind of superstitious feeling about Myrtle's bracelet, of which she had told them the story, but which Kitty
half believed was put in the drawer by the fairies, who
brought her ribbons and partridge feathers, and other
slight adornments with which she contrived to set off her
simple costume, so as to produce those effects which an
eye for color and cunning fingers can bring out of almost
nothing.

Gifted Hopkins was now in a sad, vacillating condition,
between the two great attractions to which he was exposed.
Myrtle looked so immensely handsome one Sunday when
he saw her going to church, — not to meeting, for she
would not go, except when she knew Father Pemberton
was going to be the preacher, — that the young poet was
on the point of going down on his knees to her, and telling
her that his heart was hers and hers alone. But he suddenly remembered that he had on his best trowsers; and
the idea of carrying the marks of his devotion in the shape
of two dusty impressions on his most valued article of apparel turned the scale against the demonstration. It happened the next morning, that Susan Posey wore the most
becoming ribbon she had displayed for a long time, and
Gifted was so taken with her pretty looks that he might
very probably have made the same speech to her that h

had been on the point of making to Myrtle the day before, but that he remembered her plighted affections, and thought what he should have to say for himself when Clement Lindsay, in a frenzy of rage and jealousy, stood before him, probably armed with as many deadly instruments as a lawyer mentions by name in an indictment for murder.

Cyprian Eveleth looked very differently on the new manifestations Myrtle was making of her tastes and inclinations. He had always felt dazzled, as well as attracted, by her; but now there was something in her expression and manner which made him feel still more strongly that they were intended for different spheres of life. He could not but own that she was born for a brilliant destiny, — that no ball-room would throw a light from its chandeliers too strong for her, — that no circle would be too brilliant for her to illuminate by her presence. Love does not thrive without hope, and Cyprian was beginning to see that it was idle in him to think of folding these wide wings of Myrtle's so that they would be shut up in any cage he could ever offer her. He began to doubt whether, after all, he might not find a meeker and humbler nature better adapted to his own. And so it happened that one evening after the three girls, Olive, Myrtle, and Bathsheba, had been together at the Parsonage, and Cyprian, availing himself of a brother's privilege, had joined them, he found he had been talking most of the evening with the gentle girl whose voice had grown so soft and sweet, during her long ministry in the sick-chamber, that it seemed to him more like music than speech. It would not be fair to say that Myrtle was piqued to see that Cyprian was devoting himself to Bathsheba. Her ambition was already reaching beyond her little village circle, and she had an inward sense that Cyprian found a form of sympathy in the minister's simple-minded daughter which he could not ask from a young woman of her own aspirations.

Such was the state of affairs when Master Byles Gridley was one morning surprised by an early call from Myrtle. He had a volume of Walton's Polyglot open before him, and was reading Job in the original, when she entered.

"Why, bless me, is that my young friend Miss Myrtle Hazard?" he exclaimed. "I might call you *Keren-Happuch*, which is Hebrew for Child of Beauty, and not be very far out of the way, — Job's youngest daughter, my dear. And what brings my young friend out in such good season this morning? Nothing going wrong up at our ancient mansion, The Poplars, I trust?"

"I want to talk with you, dear Master Gridley," she answered. She looked as if she did not know just how to begin.

"Anything that interests you, Myrtle, interests me. I think you have some project in that young head of yours, my child. Let us have it, in all its dimensions, length, breadth, and thickness. I think I can guess, Myrtle, that we have a little plan of some kind or other. We don't visit Papa Job quite so early as this without some special cause, — do we, Miss Keren-Happuch?"

"I want to go to the city — to school," Myrtle said, with the directness which belonged to her nature.

"That is precisely what I want you to do myself, Miss Myrtle Hazard. I don't like to lose you from the village but I think we must spare you for a while."

"You 're the best and dearest man that ever lived. What could have made you think of such a thing for me, Mr. Gridley?"

" Because you are ignorant, my child, — partly. I want
to see you fitted to take a look at the world without feeling
like a little country miss. Has your Aunt Silence promised
to bear your expenses while you are in the city? It will
cost a good deal of money."

" I have not said a word to her about it. I am sure I
don't know what she would say. But I have some money,
Mr. Gridley."

She showed him a purse with gold, telling him how she
came by it. " There is some silver besides. Will it be
enough?"

" No, no, my child, we must not meddle with that. Your
aunt will let me put it in the bank for you, I think, where
it will be safe. But that shall not make any difference.
I have got a little money lying idle, which you may just as
well have the use of as not. You can pay it back perhaps
some time or other; if you did not, it would not make much
difference. I am pretty much alone in the world, and except a book now and then — *Aut liberos aut libros*, as our
valiant heretic has it, — you ought to know a little Latin,
Myrtle, but never mind — I have not much occasion for
money. You shall go to the best school that any of our
cities can offer, Myrtle, and you shall stay there until we
agree that you are fitted to come back to us an ornament
to Oxbow Village, and to larger places than this if you are
called there. We have had some talk about it, your Aunt
Silence and I, and it is all settled. Your aunt does not
feel very rich just now, or perhaps she would do more for
you. She has many pious and poor friends, and it keeps
her funds low. Never mind, my child, we will have it all
arranged for you, and you shall begin the year 1860 in
Madam Delacoste's institution for young ladies. Too many

Q

rich girls and fashionable ones there, I fear, but you must see some of all kinds, and there are very good instructors in the school, — I know one, — he was a college boy with me, — and you will find pleasant and good companions there, so he tells me; only don't be in a hurry to choose your friends, for the least desirable young persons are very apt to cluster about a new-comer."

Myrtle was bewildered with the suddenness of the prospect thus held out to her. It is a wonder that she did not bestow an embrace upon the worthy old master. Perhaps she had too much tact. It is a pretty way enough of telling one that he belongs to a past generation, but it does tell him that not over-pleasing fact. Like the title of Emeritus Professor, it is a tribute to be accepted, hardly to be longed for.

When the curtain rises again, it will show Miss Hazard in a new character, and surrounded by a new world.

CHAPTER XXIII.

MYRTLE HAZARD AT THE CITY SCHOOL.

MR. BRADSHAW was obliged to leave town for a week or two on business connected with the great land-claim. On his return, feeling in pretty good spirits, as the prospects looked favorable, he went to make a call at The Poplars. He asked first for Miss Hazard.

"Bliss your soul, Mr. Bridshaw," answered Mistress Kitty Fagan, " she 's been gahn nigh a wake. It 's to the city, to the big school, they 've sint her."

This announcement seemed to make a deep impression on Murray Bradshaw, for his feelings found utterance in one of the most energetic forms of language to which ears polite or impolite are accustomed. He next asked for Miss Silence, who soon presented herself. Mr. Bradshaw asked, in a rather excited way, "Is it possible, Miss Withers, that your niece has quitted you to go to a city school ? "

Miss Silence answered, with her chief-mourner expression, and her death-chamber tone : " Yes, she has left us for a season. I trust it may not be her destruction. I had hoped in former years that she would become a missionary, but I have given up all expectation of that now Two whole years, from the age of four to that of six, I had prevailed upon her to give up sugar, — the money so saved to go to a graduate of our institution — who was afterwards —— he labored among the cannibal-islanders. I thought she seemed to take pleasure in this small act of self-denial, but I have since suspected that Kitty gave her secret lumps. It was by Mr. Gridley's advice that she went, and by his pecuniary assistance. What could I do? She was bent on going, and I was afraid she would have fits, or do something dreadful, if I did not let her have her way. I am afraid she will come back to us spoiled. She has seemed so fond of dress lately, and once she spoke of learning — yes, Mr. Bradshaw, of learning to — dance! I wept when I heard of it. Yes, I wept."

That was such a tremendous thing to think of, and especially to speak of in Mr. Bradshaw's presence, — for the most pathetic image in the world to many women is that of themselves in tears, — that it brought a return of the same overflow, which served as a substitute for conversation until Miss Badlam entered the apartment.

Miss Cynthia followed the same general course of remark. They could not help Myrtle's going if they tried. She had always maintained that, if they had only once broke her will when she was little, they would have kept the upper hand of her; but her will never *was* broke. They came pretty near it once, but the child would n't give in.

Miss Cynthia went to the door with Mr. Bradshaw, and the conversation immediately became short and informal.

"Demonish pretty business! All up for a year or more, — hey?"

"Don't blame me, — I could n't stop her."

"Give me her address, — I'll write to her. Any young men teach in the school?"

"Can't tell you. She'll write to Olive and Bathsheba and I'll find out all about it."

Murray Bradshaw went home and wrote a long letter to Mrs. Clymer Ketchum, of 24 Carat Place, containing many interesting remarks and inquiries, some of the latter relating to Madam Delacoste's institution for the education of young ladies.

While this was going on at Oxbow Village, Myrtle was establishing herself at the rather fashionable school to which Mr. Gridley had recommended her. Mrs. or Madam Delacoste's boarding-school had a name which on the whole it deserved pretty well. She had some very good instructors for girls who wished to get up useful knowledge in case they might marry professors or ministers. They had a chance to learn music, dancing, drawing, and the way of behaving in company. There was a chance, too, to pick up available acquaintances, for many rich people sent their daughters to the school, and it was something to have been bred in their company.

There was the usual division of the scholars into a first and second set, according to the social position, mainly depending upon the fortune, of the families to which they belonged. The wholesale dealer's daughter very naturally considered herself as belonging to a different order from the retail dealer's daughter. The keeper of a great hotel and the editor of a widely circulated newspaper were considered as ranking with the wholesale dealers, and their daughters belonged also to the untitled nobility which has the dollar for its armorial bearing. The second set had most of the good scholars, and some of the prettiest girls; but nobody knew anything about their families, who lived off the great streets and avenues, or vegetated in country towns.

Myrtle Hazard's advent made something like a sensatiou. They did not know exactly what to make of her. Hazard? Hazard? No great firm of that name. No leading hote kept by any Hazard, was there? No newspaper of note edited by anybody called Hazard, was there? Came from where? Oxbow Village. O, rural district. Yes. — Still they could not help owning that she was handsome, — a concession which of course had to be made with reservations.

"Don't you think she's vurry good-lookin'?" said a Boston girl to a New York girl. "I think she's real pooty."

"I dew, indeed. I did n't think she was haäf so handsome the fĕeest time I saw her," answered the New York girl.

"What a pity she had n't been bawn in Bawston!"

"Yes, and moved very young to Ne Yock!"

"And married a sarsaparilla man, and lived in Fiff Avenoo, and moved in the fust society."

"Better dew that than be strong-mainded, and dew your own cook'n, and live in your own kitch'n."

"Don't forgit to send your card when you are Mrs. Old Dr. Jacob!"

"Indeed I shaän't. What's the name of the alley, and which bell?" The New York girl took out a memorandum-book as if to put it down.

"Had n't you better let me write it for you, dear?" said the Boston girl. "It is as well to have it legible, you know."

"Take it," said the New York girl. "There's tew York shill'ns in it when I hand it to you."

"Your whŏle quarter's allowance, I bullieve, — ain' it?" said the Boston girl.

" Elegant manners, correct deportment, and propriety of language will be strictly attended to in this institution The most correct standards of pronunciation will be inculcated by precept and example. It will be the special aim of the teachers to educate their pupils out of all provincialisms, so that they may be recognized as well-bred English scholars wherever the language is spoken in its purity." — *Extract from the Prospectus of Madam Delacoste's Boarding-School.*

Myrtle Hazard was a puzzle to all the girls. Striking, they all agreed, but then the criticisms began. Many of the girls chattered a little broken French, and one of them, Miss Euphrosyne De Lacy, had been half educated in Paris, so that she had all the phrases which are to social operators what his cutting instruments are to the surgeon Her face she allowed was handsome ; but her style, according to this oracle, was a little *bourgeoise*, and her air not exactly *comme il faut.* More specifically, she was guilty of *contours fortement prononcés,* — *corsage de paysanne,* — *quelque chose de sauvage,* etc., etc. This girl prided herself on her figure.

Miss Bella Pool, (*La Belle Poule* as the demi-Parisian girl had christened her,) the beauty of the school, did not think so much of Myrtle's face, but considered her figure as better than the De Lacy girl's.

The two sets, first and second, fought over her as the Greeks and Trojans over a dead hero, or the Yale College societies over a live freshman. She was nobody by her connections, it is true, so far as they could find out, but then, on the other hand, she had the walk of a queen, and she looked as if a few stylish dresses and a season or two vould make her a belle of the first water. She had that

air of indifference to their little looks and whispered comments which is surest to disarm all the critics of a small
tattling community. On the other hand, she came to this
school to learn, and not to play; and the modest and more
plainly dressed girls, whose fathers did not sell by the car-
go, or keep victualling establishments for some hundreds of
people, considered her as rather in sympathy with them than
with the daughters of the rough-and-tumble millionnaires
who were grappling and rolling over each other in the gold-
en dust of the great city markets.

She did not mean to belong exclusively to either of their
sets. She came with that sense of manifold deficiencies,
and eager ambition to supply them, which carries any
learner upward, as if on wings, over the heads of the
mechanical plodders and the indifferent routinists. She
learned, therefore, in a way to surprise the experienced
instructors. Her somewhat rude sketching soon began
to show something of the artist's touch. Her voice, which
had only been taught to warble the simplest melodies, after
a little training began to show its force and sweetness and
flexibility in the airs that enchant drawing-room audiences.
She caught with great readiness the manner of the easiest
girls, unconsciously, for she inherited old social instincts
which became nature with the briefest exercise. Not
much license of dress was allowed in the educational establishment of Madam Delacoste, but every girl had an
opportunity to show her taste within the conventional limits prescribed. And Myrtle soon began to challenge remark
by a certain air she contrived to give her dresses, and th
skill with which she blended their colors.

"Tell you what, girls," said Miss Berengaria Topping
'emale representative of the great dynasty that ruled ove'

the world-famous Planet Hotel, "she's got style, lots of it. I call her perfectly splendid, when she's got up in her swell clothes. That oriole's wing she wears in her bonnet makes her look gorgeous, — she'll be a stunning Pocahontas for the next *tableau.*"

Miss Rose Bugbee, whose family opulence grew out of the only merchantable article a Hebrew is never known to seek profit from, thought she could be made presentable in the first circles if taken in hand in good season. So it came about that, before many weeks had passed over her as a scholar in the great educational establishment, she might be considered as on the whole the most popular girl in the whole bevy of them. The studious ones admired her for her facility of learning, and her extraordinary appetite for every form of instruction, and the showy girls, who were only enduring school as the purgatory that opened into the celestial world of society, recognized in her a very handsome young person, who would be like to make a sensation sooner or later.

There were, however, it must be confessed, a few who considered themselves the thickest of the cream of the school-girls, who submitted her to a more trying ordeal than any she had yet passed.

" How many horses does your papa keep ? " asked Miss Florence Smythe. " We keep nine and a pony for Edgar."

Myrtle had to explain that she had no papa, and that they did not keep any horses. Thereupon Miss Florence Smythe lost her desire to form an acquaintance, and wrote home to her mother (who was an ex-bonnet-maker) that the school was getting common, she was afraid, — they were letting in persons one knew nothing about.

12

Miss Clara Browne had a similar curiosity about the amount of plate used in the household from which Myrtle came. *Her* father had just bought a complete silver service. Myrtle had to own that they used a good deal of china at her own home, — old china, which had been a hundred years in the family, some of it.

"A hundred years old!" exclaimed Miss Clara Browne. "What queer-looking stuff it must be! Why, everything in our house is just as new and bright! Papaä had all our pictures painted on purpose for us. Have you got any handsome pictures in your house?"

"We have a good many portraits of members of the family," she said "some of them older than the china."

"How very very odd! What do the dear old things look like?"

"One was a great beauty in her time."

"How jolly!"

"Another was a young woman who was put to death for her religion, — burned to ashes at the stake in Queen Mary's time."

"How very very wicked! It was n't nice a bit, was it? Ain't you telling me stories? Was that a hundred years ago? — But you 've got some new pictures and things, have n't you? Who furnished your parlors?"

"My great-grandfather, or his father, I believe."

"Stuff and nonsense. I don't believe it. What color are your carriage-horses?"

"Our woman, Kitty Fagan, told somebody once we did n't keep any horse but a cow."

"Not keep any horses! Do for pity's sake let me look at your feet."

Myrtle put out as neat a little foot as a shoemaker ever

fitted with a pair of number two. What she would have been tempted to do with it, if she had been a boy, we will not stop to guess. After all, the questions amused her quite as much as the answers instructed Miss Clara Browne. Of that young lady's ancestral claims to distinction there is no need of discoursing. Her " papaä " commonly said *sir* in talking with a gentleman, and her " mammaä " would once in a while forget, and go down the area steps instead of entering at the proper door ; but they lived behind a brown stone front, which veneers everybody's antecedents with a facing of respectability.

Miss Clara Browne wrote home to *her* mother in the same terms as Miss Florence Smythe, — that the school was getting dreadful common, and they were letting in very queer folks.

Still another trial awaited Myrtle, and one which not one girl in a thousand would have been so unprepared to meet. She knew absolutely nothing of certain things with which the vast majority of young persons were quite familiar.

There were literary young ladies, who had read everything of Dickens and Thackeray, and something at least of Sir Walter, and occasionally, perhaps, a French novel, which they had better have let alone. One of the talking young ladies of this set began upon Myrtle one day.

" O, is n't Pickwick nice ? " she asked.

" I don't know," Myrtle replied ; " I never tasted any."

The girl stared at her as if she were a crazy creature " Tasted any ! Why, I mean the Pickwick Papers, Dickens's story. Don't you think they 're nice ' "

Poor Myrtle had to confess that she had never read them, and did n't know anything about them.

"What! did you never read any novels?" said the young lady.

"O, to be sure I have," said Myrtle, blushing as she thought of the great trunk and its contents. "I have read Caleb Williams, and Evelina, and Tristram Shandy" (naughty girl!), "and the Castle of Otranto, and the Mysteries of Udolpho, and the Vicar of Wakefield, and Don Quixote —"

The young lady burst out laughing. "Stop! stop! for mercy's sake," she cried. "You must be somebody that 's been dead and buried and come back to life again. Why you 're Rip Van Winkle in a petticoat! You ought to powder your hair and wear patches."

"We 've got the oddest girl here," this young lady wrote home. "She has n't read any book that is n't a thousand years old. One of the girls says she wears a trilobite for a breastpin; some horrid old stone, I believe that is, that was a bug ever so long ago. Her name, she says, is Myrtle Hazard, but I call her Rip Van Myrtle."

Notwithstanding the quiet life which these young girls were compelled to lead, they did once in a while have their gatherings, at which a few young gentlemen were admitted. One of these took place about a month after Myrtle had joined the school. The girls were all in their best, and by and by they were to have a *tableau*. Myrtle came out in all her force. She dressed herself as nearly as she dared like the handsome woman of the past generation whom she resembled. The very spirit of the dead beauty seemed to animate every feature and every movement of the young girl whose position in the school was assured from that moment. She had a good solid foundation to build upon in the jealousy of two or three of the leading girls of the style of pretensions illustrated by some of their talk which has been given. There is no possible success without some opposition as a fulcrum : force is always aggressive, and crowds something or other, if it does not hit or trample on it.

The cruelest cut of all was the remark attributed to Mr. Livingston Jenkins, who was what the opposition girls just referred to called the great " swell " among the privileged young gentlemen who were present at the gathering.

" Rip Van Myrtle, you call that handsome girl, do you, Miss Clara? By Jove, she 's the stylishest of the whole lot, to say nothing of being a first-class beauty. Of course you know I except one, Miss Clara. If a girl can go to sleep and wake up after twenty years looking like that, I know a good many who had better begin their nap without waiting. If I were Florence Smythe, I 'd try it, and begin now, — eh, Clara ? "

Miss Browne felt the praise of Myrtle to be slightly alleviated by the depreciation of Miss Smythe, who had long been a rival of her own. A little later in the evening Miss Smythe enjoyed almost precisely the same sensation, produced in a very economical way by Mr. Livingston Jenkins's repeating pretty nearly the same sentiments to her, only with a change in the arrangement of the proper names. The two young ladies were left feeling comparatively comfortable with regard to each other, each intending to repeat Mr. Livingston Jenkins's remark about her friend to such of her other friends as enjoyed clever sayings, but not at all comfortable with reference to Myrtle Hazard, who was evidently considered by the leading swell" of their circle as the most noticeable personage of the assembly. The individual exception in each case did very well as a matter of politeness, but they knew well enough what he meant.

It seemed to Myrtle Hazard, that evening, that she felt the bracelet on her wrist glow with a strange, unaccustomed warmth. It was as if it had just been unclasped from the arm of a young woman full of red blood and tingling all over with swift nerve-currents. Life had never looked to her as it did that evening. It was the swan's first breasting the water, — bred on the desert sand, with vague dreams of lake and river, and strange longings as the mirage came and dissolved, and at length afloat upon the sparkling wave. She felt as if she had for the first time found her destiny. It was to please, and so to command, — to rule with gentle sway in virtue of the royal gift of beauty, — to enchant with the commonest exercise of speech, through the rare quality of a voice which could not help being always gracious and winning, of a manner which came to he as an inheritance of which she had just found the title. She read in the eyes of all that she was more than any other the centre of admiration. Blame her who may, the world was a very splendid vision as it opened before her eyes in its long vista of pleasures and of triumphs. How different the light of these bright saloons from the glimmer of the dim chamber at The Poplars! Silence Withers was at that very moment looking at the portraits of Anne Holyoake and of Judith Pride. "The old picture seems to me to be fading faster than ever," she was thinking. But when she held her lamp before the other, it seemed to her that the picture never was so fresh before, and that the proud smile upon its lips was more full of conscious triumph than she remembered it. A reflex, doubtless, of her own thoughts for she believed that the martyr was weeping even in heaven over her lost descendant, and that the beauty, changed to the nature of the malignant spiritual company with which she had long consorted in the under-world, was pleasing herself with the thought that Myrtle was in due time to bring her news from the Satanic province overhead, where she herself had so long indulged in the profligacy of *embonpoint* and loveliness.

The evening at the school-party was to terminate with some *tableaux*. The girl who had suggested that Myrtle would look "stunning" or "gorgeous" or "jolly," or whatever the expression was, as Pocahontas, was not far out of the way, and it was so evident to the managing heads that she would make a fine appearance in that character, that the "Rescue of Captain John Smith" was specially got up to show her off.

Myrtle had sufficient reason to believe that there was a hint of Indian blood in her veins. It was one of those family legends which some of the members are a little proud of, and others are willing to leave uninvestigated. But with Myrtle it was a fixed belief that she felt perfectly distinct currents of her ancestral blood at intervals, and she had sometimes thought there were instincts and vague recollections which must have come from the old warriors and hunters and their dusky brides. The Indians who visited the neighborhood recognized something of their own race in her dark eyes, as the reader may remember they told the persons who were searching after her. It had almost frightened her sometimes to find how like a wild creature she felt when alone in the woods. Her senses had much of that delicacy for which the red people are noted, and she often thought she could follow the trail of an enemy, if she wished to track one through the forest, as unerringly as if she were a Pequot or a Mohegan.

It was a strange feeling that came over Myrtle, as they dressed her for the part she was to take. Had she never worn that painted robe before? Was it the first time that these strings of wampum had ever rattled upon her neck and arms? And could it be that the plume of eagle's feathers with which they crowned her dark, fast-lengthening locks had never shadowed her forehead until now? She felt herself carried back into the dim ages when the wilderness was yet untrodden save by the feet of its native lords. Think of her wild fancy as we may, she felt as if that dusky woman of her midnight vision on the river were breathing for one hour through her lips. If this belief had lasted, it is plain enough where it would have carried her. But it came into her imagination and vivifying consciousness with the putting on of her unwonted costume, and might well leave her when she put it off. It is not for us, who tell only what happened, to solve these mysteries of the seeming admission of unhoused souls into the fleshly tenements belonging to air-breathing personalities. A very little more, and from that evening forward the question would have been treated in full in all the works on medical jurisprudence published throughout the limits of Christendom. The story must be told or we should not be honest with the reader.

TABLEAU 1. Captain John Smith (Miss Euphrosyne de Lacy) was to be represented prostrate and bound, ready for execution; Powhatan (Miss Florence Smythe) sitting upon a log; savages with clubs (Misses Clara Browne, A. Van Boodle, E. Van Boodle, Heister, Booster

etc., etc.) standing around; Pocahontas holding the knife
in her hand, ready to cut the cords with which Captain
John Smith is bound. — Curtain.

TABLEAU 2. Captain John Smith released and kneel-
ing before Pocahontas, whose hand is extended in the act
of raising him and presenting him to her father. Savages
in various attitudes of surprise. Clubs fallen from their
hands. Strontian flame to be kindled. — Curtain.

This was a portion of the programme for the evening,
as arranged behind the scenes. The first part went off
with wonderful *éclat*, and at its close there were loud cries
for Pocahontas. She appeared for a moment. Bouquets
were flung to her; and a wreath, which one of the young
ladies had expected for herself in another part, was tossed
upon the stage, and laid at her feet. The curtain fell.

"Put the wreath on her for the next *tableau*," some
of them whispered, just as the curtain was going to rise,
and one of the girls hastened to place it upon her head.

The disappointed young lady could not endure it, and,
in a spasm of jealous passion, sprang at Myrtle, snatched
it from her head, and trampled it under her feet at the
very instant the curtain was rising. With a cry which
some said had the blood-chilling tone of an Indian's
battle-shriek, Myrtle caught the knife up, and raised her
arm against the girl who had thus rudely assailed her.
The girl sank to the ground, covering her eyes in her terror.
Myrtle, with her arm still lifted, and the blade glistening
in her hand, stood over her, rigid as if she had been suddenly changed to stone. Many of those looking on thought
all this was a part of the show, and were thrilled with the
wonderful acting. Before those immediately around her
had had time to recover from the palsy of their fright

Myrtle had flung the knife away from her, and was kneel-
ing, her head bowed and her hands crossed upon her
breast. The audience went into a rapture of applause as
the curtain came suddenly down; but Myrtle had forgotten all but the dread peril she had just passed, and
was thanking God that his angel — her own protecting
spirit, as it seemed to her — had stayed the arm which

passion such as her nature had never known, such as she
believed was alien to her truest self, had lifted with dead-
liest purpose. She alone knew how extreme the danger had
been. "She meant to scare her, — that's all," they said.
But Myrtle tore the eagle's feathers from her hair, and
stripped off her colored beads, and threw off her painted
robe. The metempsychosis was far too real for her to let
her wear the semblance of the savage from whom, as she
believed, had come the lawless impulse at the thought
of which her soul recoiled in horror.

"Pocahontas has got a horrid headache," the managing
young ladies gave it out, "and can't come to time for the
last *tableau*." So this all passed over, not only without
loss of credit to Myrtle, but with no small addition to her
local fame, — for it must have been acting; "and was n't it
stunning to see her with that knife, looking as if she was
going to stab Bella, or to scalp her, or something?"

As Master Gridley had predicted, and as is the case
commonly with new-comers at colleges and schools, Myrtle
had come first in contact with those who were least agreeable to meet. The low-bred youth who amuse themselves
with scurvy tricks on freshmen, and the vulgar girls who
try to show off their gentility to those whom they think less
important than themselves, are exceptions in every institu
tion; but they make themselves odiously prominent befor

the quiet and modest young people have had time to gain the new scholar's confidence.   Myrtle found friends in due time, some of them daughters of rich people, some poor girls, who came with the same sincerity of purpose as her-self.   But not one was her match in the facility of acquir-ing knowledge.   Not one promised to make such a mark in society, if she found an opening into its loftier circles She was by no means ignorant of her natural gifts, and she cultivated them with the ambition which would not let her rest.

During her stay at the great school, she made but one visit to Oxbow Village.   She did not try to startle the good people with her accomplishments, but they were surprised at the change which had taken place in her. Her dress was hardly more showy, for she was but a school-girl, but it fitted her more gracefully.   She had gained a softness of expression, and an ease in conver-sation, which produced their effect on all with whom she came in contact.   Her aunt's voice lost something of its plaintiveness in talking with her.   Miss Cynthia listened with involuntary interest to her stories of school and school-mates.   Master Byles Gridley accepted her as the great success of his life, and determined to make her his chief heiress, if there was any occasion for so doing.   Cyprian told Bathsheba that Myrtle must come to be a great lady. Gifted Hopkins confessed to Susan Posey that he was afraid of her, since she had been to the great city school. She knew too much and looked too much like a queen, for a village boy to talk with.

Mr. William Murray Bradshaw tried all his fascinations upon her, but she parried compliments so well, and put off all his nearer advances so dexterously, that he could not

advance beyond the region of florid courtesy, and never got
a chance, if so disposed, to risk a question which he would
not ask rashly, believing that, if Myrtle once said *No, there*
would be little chance of her ever saying *Yes*.

CHAPTER XXIV.

MUSTERING OF FORCES.

NOT long after the tableau performance had made Myrtle Hazard's name famous in the school and among the friends of the scholars, she received the very flattering attention of a call from Mrs. Clymer Ketchum, of 24 Carat Place. This was in consequence of a suggestion from Mr. Livingston Jenkins, a particular friend of the family.

"They 've got a demonish splendid school-girl over there," he said to that lady, — "made the stunningest-looking Pocahontas at the show there the other day. Demonish plucky-looking filly as ever you saw. Had a row with another girl, — gave the war-whoop, and went at her with a knife. Festive, — hey? Say she only meant to scare her, — *looked* as if she meant to stick her, anyhow. Splendid style. Why can't you go over to the shop and make em trot her out?"

The lady promised Mr. Livingston Jenkins that she certainly would, just as soon as she could find a moment's leisure, — which, as she had nothing in the world to do, was not likely to be very soon. Myrtle in the mean time was busy with her studies, little dreaming what an extraordinary honor was awaiting her.

That rare accident in the lives of people who have nothing to do, a leisure morning, did at last occur. An elegant carriage, with a coachman in a wonderful cape, seated on a box lofty as a throne, and wearing a hat-band as brilliant as a coronet, stopped at the portal of Madam Delacoste's establishment. A card was sent in bearing the open sesame of Mrs. Clymer Ketchum, the great lady of 24 Carat Place. Miss Myrtle Hazard was summoned as a matter of course, and the fashionable woman and the young girl sat half an hour together in lively conversation.

Myrtle was fascinated by her visitor, who had that flattering manner which, to those not experienced in the world's ways, seems to imply unfathomable depths of disinterested devotion. Then it was so delightful to look upon a perfectly appointed woman, — one who was as artistically composed as a poem or an opera, — in whose costume a kind of various rhythm undulated in one fluent harmony, from the spray that nodded on her bonnet to the rosette that blossomed on her sandal. As for the lady, she was captivated with Myrtle. There is nothing that your fashionable woman, who has ground and polished her own spark of life into as many and as glittering social facets as it will bear, has a greater passion for than a large rough diamond, which knows nothing of the sea of light it imprisons, and which it will be her pride to have cut into a brilliant under her own eye, and to show the world for its admiration and her own reflected glory. Mrs. Clymer Ketchum had taken the entire inventory of Myrtle's natural endowments before the interview was over. She had no marriageable children, and she was thinking what a killing bait Myrtle would be at one of her stylish parties.

She soon got another letter from Mr. William Murray Bradshaw, which explained the interest he had taken in Madam Delacoste's school, — all which she knew pretty nearly beforehand, for she had found out a good part of

Myrtle's history in the half-hour they had spent in com
pany.

"I had a particular reason for my inquiries about the
school," he wrote. "There is a young girl there I take
an interest in. She is handsome and interesting, and —
though it is a shame to mention such a thing — has possibilities in the way of fortune not to be undervalued.
Why can't you make her acquaintance and be civil to
her? A country girl, but fine old stock, and will make
a figure some time or other, I tell you. Myrtle Hazard,
— that's her name. A mere school-girl. Don't be malicious and badger me about her, but be polite to her.
Some of these country girls have got ' blue blood' in them,
let me tell you, and show it plain enough."

("In huckleberry season!") said Mrs. Clymer Ketchum, in a parenthesis, — and went on reading.

"Don't think I'm one of your love-in-a-cottage sort, to
have my head turned by a village beauty. I've got
a career before me, Mrs. K., and I know it. But this is
one of my pets, and I want you to keep an eye on her.
Perhaps when she leaves school you wouldn't mind asking her to come and stay with you a little while. Possibly
I may come and see how she is getting on if you do, —
won't that tempt you, Mrs. C. K.?"

Mrs. Clymer Ketchum wrote back to her relative how
he had already made the young lady's acquaintance.

"Livingston Jenkins (you remember him) picked her
out of the whole lot of girls as the ' prettiest filly in the
stable.' That's his horrid way of talking. But your
young milkmaid is really charming, and will come into
form like a Derby three-year-old. There, now, I've
caught that odious creature's horse-talk, myself. You're
dead in love with this girl, Murray, you know you are

" After all, I don't know but you're right. You would
make a good country lawyer enough, I don't doubt. I
used to think you had your ambitions, but never mind.
If you choose to risk yourself on 'possibilities,' it is not
my affair, and she's a beauty, — there's no mistake about
that.

" There are some desirable *partis* at the school with
your dulcinea. There's Rose Bugbee. That last name
is a good one to be married from. Rose is a nice girl, —
there are only two of them. The estate will cut up like
one of the animals it was made out of, — you know, —
the sandwich-quadruped. Then there's Berengaria. Old
Topping owns the Planet Hotel among other things, —
so big, they say, there's always a bell ringing from somebody's room day and night the year round. Only child
— unit and six ciphers — carries diamonds loose in her
pocket — that's the story — good-looking — lively — a little slangy — called Livingston Jenkins ' Living Jingo' to
his face one day. I want you to see my lot before you do
anything serious. You owe something to the family, Mr.
William Murray Bradshaw! But you must suit yourself,
after all : if you are contented with a humble position in
life, it is nobody's business that I know of. Only I know
what life is, Murray B. Getting married is jumping overboard, any way you look at it, and if you must save some
woman from drowning an old maid, try to find one *with a
ork jacket*, or she'll carry you down with her."

Murray Bradshaw was calculating enough, but he shook
his head over this letter. It was too demonish cold-blooded
for him, he said to himself. (Men cannot pardon women
for saying aloud what they do not hesitate to think in si
lence themselves.) Never mind, — he must have Mrs

Clymer Ketchum's house and influence for his own pur
poses.   Myrtle Hazard must become her guest, and then
if circumstances were favorable, he was certain of obtaining her aid in his project.

The opportunity to invite Myrtle to the great mansion
presented itself unexpectedly.   Early in the spring of 1861
there were some cases of sickness in Madam Delacoste's establishment, which led to closing the school for a while.
Mrs. Clymer Ketchum took advantage of the dispersion of
the scholars to ask Myrtle to come and spend some weeks
with her.   There were reasons why this was more agreeable to the young girl than returning to Oxbow Village, and
she very gladly accepted the invitation.

It was very remarkable that a man living as Master
Byles Gridley had lived for so long a time should all at
once display such liberality as he showed to a young
woman who had no claim upon him, except that he had
rescued her from the consequences of her own imprudence
and warned her against impending dangers.   Perhaps he
cared more for her than if the obligation had been the
other way, — students of human nature say it is commonly
so.   At any rate, either he had ampler resources than it
was commonly supposed, or he was imprudently giving
way to his generous impulses, or he thought he was making
advances which would in due time be returned to him.
Whatever the reason was, he furnished her with means,
not only for her necessary expenses, but sufficient to afford
her many of the elegances which she would be like to
want in the fashionable society with which she was for a
short time to mingle.

Mrs. Clymer Ketchum was so well pleased with the
young lady she was entertaining, that she thought it worth

while to give a party while Myrtle was staying with her
She had her jealousies and rivalries, as women of the world
will, sometimes, and these may have had their share in
leading her to take the trouble a large party involved.
She was tired of the airs of Mrs. Pinnikle, who was of the
great Apex family, and her terribly accomplished daughter
Rhadamantha, and wanted to crush the young lady, and
jaundice her mother, with a girl twice as brilliant and ten
times handsomer. She was very willing, also, to take the
nonsense out of the Capsheaf girls, who thought themselves
the most stylish personages of their city world, and would
bite their lips well to see themselves distanced by a country miss.

In the mean time circumstances were promising to bring
into Myrtle's neighborhood several of her old friends and
admirers. Mrs. Clymer Ketchum had written to Murray
Bradshaw that she had asked his pretty milkmaid to come
and stay awhile with her, but he had been away on business, and only arrived in the city a day or two before
the party. But other young fellows had found out the
attractions of the girl who was "hanging out at the Clymer
Ketchum concern," and callers were plenty, reducing *tête-
à-têtes* in a corresponding ratio. He did get one opportunity, however, and used it well. They had so many things
to talk about in common, that she could not help finding
him good company. She might well be pleased, for he
was an adept in the curious art of being agreeable, as other
people are in chess or billiards, and had made a special
study of her tastes, as a physician studies a patient's constitution. What he wanted was to get her thoroughly interested in himself, and to maintain her in a receptive
condition until such time as he should be ready for a fina

move. Any day might furnish the decisive motive; in the mean time he wished only to hold her as against all others.

It was well for her, perhaps, that others had flattered her into a certain consciousness of her own value. She felt her veins full of the same rich blood as that which had flushed the cheeks of handsome Judith in the long summer of her triumph. Whether it was vanity, or pride, or only the instinctive sense of inherited force and attraction, it was the best of defences. The golden bracelet on her wrist seemed to have brought as much protection with it as if it had been a shield over her heart.

But far away in Oxbow Village other events were in preparation. The "fugitive pieces" of Mr. Gifted Hopkins had now reached a number so considerable. that, if collected and printed in large type, with plenty of what the unpleasant printers call "fat," — meaning thereby blank spaces, — upon a good, substantial, not to say thick paper, they might perhaps make a volume which would have substance enough to bear the title, printed lengthwise along the back, "Hopkins's Poems." Such a volume that author had in contemplation. It was to be the literary event of the year 1861.

He could not mature such a project, one which he had been for some time contemplating, without consulting Mr. Byles Gridley, who, though he had not unfrequently repressed the young poet's too ardent ambition, had yet always been kind and helpful.

Mr. Gridley was seated in his large arm-chair, indulging himself in the perusal of a page or two of his own work before repeatedly referred to. His eye was glistening, for 't had just rested on the following passage : —

" *There is infinite pathos in unsuccessful authorship
The book that perishes unread is the deaf mute of litera
ture.   The great asylum of Oblivion is full of such, making
inaudible signs to each other in leaky garrets and unattain-
able dusty upper shelves.*"

He shut the book, for the page grew a little dim as he
finished this elegiac sentence, and sighed to think how
much more keenly he felt its truth than when it was written, — than on that memorable morning when he saw the
advertisement in all the papers, " This day published,
' Thoughts on the Universe.   By Byles Gridley, A. M.' "

At that moment he heard a knock at his door.   He
closed his eyelids forcibly for ten seconds, opened them,
and said cheerfully, " Come in ! "

Gifted Hopkins entered.   He had a collection of manuscripts in his hands which it seemed to him would fill
a vast number of pages.   He did not know that manuscript is to type what fresh dandelions are to the dish of
greens that comes to table, of which last Nurse Byloe, who
considered them very wholesome spring grazing for her
patients, used to say that they " biled down dreadful."

" I have brought the autographs of my poems, Master
Gridley, to consult you about making arrangements for
publication.   They have been so well received by the public and the leading critics of this part of the State, that I
think of having them printed in a volume.   I am going to
the city for that purpose.   My mother has given her consent.   I wish to ask you several business questions.   Shall
I part with the copyright for a downright sum of money
which I understand some prefer doing, or publish on
shares, or take a percentage on the sales ?   These, I be
lieve, are the different ways taken by authors."

Mr. Gridley was altogether too considerate to reply with the words which would most naturally have come to his lips. He waited as if he were gravely pondering the important questions just put to him, all the while looking at Gifted with a tenderness which no one who had not buried one of his soul's children could have felt for a young author trying to get clothing for his newborn intellectual offspring.

" I think," he said presently, " you had better talk with an intelligent and liberal publisher, and be guided by his advice. I can put you in correspondence with such a person, and you had better trust him than me a great deal. Why don't you send your manuscript by mail?"

" *What*, Mr. Gridley? Trust my poems, some of which are unpublished, to the post-office? No, sir, I could never make up my mind to such a risk. I mean to go to the city myself, and read them to some of the leading publishers. I don't want to pledge myself to any one of them. I should like to set them bidding against each other for the copyright, if I sell it at all."

Mr. Gridley gazed upon the innocent youth with a sweet wonder in his eyes that made him look like an angel, a little damaged in the features by time, but full of celestial feelings.

" It will cost you something to make this trip, Gifted Have you the means to pay for your journey and your stay at a city hotel?"

Gifted blushed. " My mother has laid by a small sum for me," he said. " She knows some of my poems by heart, and she wants to see them all in print."

Master Gridley closed his eyes very firmly again, as if thinking, and opened them as soon as the foolish film had left them. He had read many a page of "Thoughts on the Universe" to his own old mother, long, long years ago, and she had often listened with tears of modest pride that Heaven had favored her with a son so full of genius.

"I'll tell you what, Gifted," he said. "I have been thinking for a good while that I would make a visit to the city, and if you have made up your mind to try what you can do with the publishers, I will take you with me as a companion. It will be a saving to you and your good mother, for I shall bear the expenses of the expedition."

Gifted Hopkins came very near going down on his knees. He was so overcome with gratitude that it seemed as if his very coat-tails wagged with his emotion.

"Take it quietly," said Master Gridley. "Don't make a fool of yourself. Tell your mother to have some clean shirts and things ready for you, and we will be off day after to-morrow morning."

Gifted hastened to impart the joyful news to his mother, and to break the fact to Susan Posey that he was about to leave them for a while, and rush into the deliriums and dangers of the great city.

Susan smiled. Gifted hardly knew whether to be pleased with her sympathy, or vexed that she did not take his leaving more to heart. The smile held out bravely for about a quarter of a minute. Then there came on a little twitching at the corners of the mouth. Then the blue eyes began to shine with a kind of veiled glimmer. Then the blood came up into her cheeks with a great rush, as if the heart had sent up a herald with a red flag from the citadel to know what was going on at the outworks. The message that went back was of discomfiture and capitulation. Poor Susan was overcome, and gave herself up to weeping and sobbing.

The sight was too much for the young poet. In a wild burst of passion he seized her hand, and pressed it to his lips, exclaiming, " Would that you could be mine forever ! " and Susan forgot all that she ought to have remembered, and, looking half reproachfully but half tenderly through her tears, said, in tones of 'nfinite sweetness, " O Gifted ! '

CHAPTER XXV.

THE POET AND THE PUBLISHER.

IT was settled that Master Byles Gridley and Mr. Gifted Hopkins should leave early in the morning of the day appointed, to take the nearest train to the city. Mrs. Hopkins labored hard to get them ready, so that they might make a genteel appearance among the great people whom they would meet in society. She brushed up Mr. Gridley's best black suit, and bound the cuffs of his dress-coat, which were getting a little worried. She held his honest-looking hat to the fire, and smoothed it while it was warm, until one would have thought it had just been ironed by the hatter himself. She had his boots and shoes brought into a more brilliant condition than they had ever known: if Gifted helped, it was to his credit as much as if he had shown his gratitude by polishing off a copy of verses in praise of his benefactor.

When she had got Mr. Gridley's encumbrances in readiness for the journey, she devoted herself to fitting out her son Gifted. First, she had down from the garret a capacious trunk, of solid wood, but covered with leather, and adorned with brass-headed nails, by the cunning disposition of which, also, the paternal initials stood out on the rounded lid, in the most conspicuous manner. It was his father's trunk, and the first thing that went into it, as the widow lifted the cover, and the smothering shut-up smell struck an old chord of associations, was a single tear-drop. How well she remembered the time when she first unpacked it for her young husband, and the white shirt bosoms showed their snowy plaits! O dear, dear!

But women decant their affection, sweet and sound, out of the old bottles into the new ones, — off from the lees of the past generation, clear and bright, into the clean vessels just made ready to receive it. Gifted Hopkins was his mother's idol, and no wonder. She had not only the common attachment of a parent for him, as her offspring, but she felt that her race was to be rendered illustrious by his genius, and thought proudly of the time when some future biographer would mention her own humble name, to be held in lasting remembrance as that of the mother of Hopkins.

So she took great pains to equip this brilliant but inexperienced young man with everything he could by any possibility need during his absence. The great trunk filled itself until it bulged with its contents like a boa-constrictor who has swallowed his blanket. Best clothes and common clothes, thick clothes and thin clothes, flannels and linens, socks and collars, with handkerchiefs enough to keep the pickpockets busy for a week, with a paper of gingerbread and some lozenges for gastralgia, and "hot drops," and ruled paper to write letters on, and a little Bible, and a phial with *hiera picra*, and another with paregoric, and another with "camphire" for sprains and bruises, — Gifted went forth equipped for every climate from the tropic to the pole, and armed against every malady from Ague to Zoster. He carried also the paternal watch, a solid silver bull's-eye, and a large pocket-book, tied round with a long tape, and, by way of precaution, pinned into his breast-pocket. He talked about having a pistol, in case he were attacked by any of the ruffians who are so numerous in the city, but Mr. Gridley told him, No! he would certainly shoot himself, and he should n't think of letting him take a pistol.

They went forth, Mentor and Telemachus, at the appointed time, to dare the perils of the railroad and the snares of the city. Mrs. Hopkins was firm up to near the last moment, when a little quiver in her voice set her eyes off, and her face broke up all at once, so that she had to hide it behind her handkerchief. Susan Posey showed the truthfulness of her character in her words to Gifted at parting. "Farewell," she said, "and think of me sometimes while absent. My heart is another's, but my friendship, Gifted — my friendship — "

Both were deeply affected. He took her hand and would have raised it to his lips; but she did not forget herself, and gently withdrew it, exclaiming, "O Gifted!" this time with a tone of tender reproach which made him feel like a profligate. He tore himself away, and when at a safe distance flung her a kiss, which she rewarded with a tearful smile.

Master Byles Gridley must have had some good dividends from some of his property of late. There is no other way of accounting for the handsome style in which he did things on their arrival in the city. He went to a tailor's and ordered a new suit to be sent home as soon as possible, for he knew his wardrobe was a little rusty. He looked Gifted over from head to foot, and suggested such improvements as would recommend him to the fastidious eyes of the selecter sort of people, and put him in his own tailor's hands, at the same time saying that all bills were to be sent to him, B. Gridley, Esq., parlor No. 6, at the Planet House. Thus it came to pass that in three day

from their arrival they were both in an eminently presentable condition. In the mean time the prudent Mr. Gridley had been keeping the young man busy, and amusing
himself by showing him such of the sights of the city and
its suburbs as he thought would combine instruction with
entertainment.

When they were both properly equipped and ready for
the best company, Mr. Gridley said to the young poet, who
had found it very hard to contain his impatience, that they
would now call together on the publisher to whom he
wished to introduce him, and they set out accordingly.

"My name is Gridley," he said with modest gravity, as
he entered the publisher's private room. "I have a note
of introduction here from one of your authors, as I think
he called himself, — a very popular writer for whom you
publish."

The publisher rose and came forward in the most cordial and respectful manner. "Mr. Gridley? — Professor Byles Gridley, — author of 'Thoughts on the Universe'?"

The brave-hearted old man colored as if he had been
a young girl. His dead book rose before him like an ap-
parition. He groped in modest confusion for an answer.
"A child I buried long ago, my dear sir," he said. "Its
title-page was its tombstone. I have brought this young
friend with me, — this is Mr. Gifted Hopkins of Oxbow
Village, — who wishes to converse with you about —"

"I have come, sir —" the young poet began, interrupting him.

"Let me look at your manuscript, if you please, Mr.
Popkins," said the publisher, interrupting in his turn.

"Hopkins, if you please, sir," Gifted suggested mildly,

proceeding to extract the manuscript, which had got wedged into his pocket, and seemed to be holding on with all its might. He was wondering all the time over the extraordinary clairvoyance of the publisher, who had looked through so many thick folds, broadcloth, lining, brown paper, and seen his poems lying hidden in his breast-pocket. The idea that a young person coming on such an errand should have to explain his intentions would have seemed very odd to the publisher. He knew the look which belongs to this class of enthusiasts just as a horse-dealer knows the look of a green purchaser with the equine fever raging in his veins. If a young author had come to him with a scrap of manuscript hidden in his boots, like Major André's papers, the publisher would have taken one glance at him and said, "Out with it!"

While he was battling for the refractory scroll with his pocket, which turned half wrong side out, and acted as things always do when people are nervous and in a hurry, the publisher directed his conversation again to Master Byles Gridley.

"A remarkable book, that of yours, Mr. Gridley,— would have a great run if it were well handled. Came out twenty years too soon,—that was the trouble. One of our leading scholars was speaking of it to me the other day. 'We must have a new edition,' he said; 'people are just ripe for that book.' Did you ever think of that? Change the form of it a little, and give it a new title, and it will be a popular book. Five thousand or more, very likely."

Mr. Gridley felt as if he had been rapidly struck on the forehead with a dozen distinct blows from a hammer no quite big enough to stun him. He sat still without saying word. He had forgotten for the moment all about poor Gifted Hopkins, who had got out his manuscript at last, and was calming the disturbed corners of it. Coming to himself a little, he took a large and beautiful silk handkerchief, one of his new purchases, from his pocket, and applied it to his face, for the weather seemed to have grown very warm all at once. Then he remembered the errand on which he had come, and thought of this youth, who had got to receive his first hard lesson in life, and whom he had brought to this kind man that it should be gently administered.

"You surprise me," he said, — "you surprise me. Dead and buried. Dead and buried. I had sometimes thought that — at some future period, after I was gone, it might — but I hardly know what to say about your suggestions. But here is my young friend, Mr. Hopkins, who would like to talk with you, and I will leave him in your hands. I am at the Planet House, if you should care to call upon me. Good morning. Mr. Hopkins will explain everything to you more at his ease, without me, I am confident."

Master Gridley could not quite make up his mind to stay through the interview between the young poet and the publisher. The flush of hope was bright in Gifted's eye and cheek, and the good man knew that young hearts are apt to be over-sanguine, and that one who enters a shower-bath often feels very differently from the same person when he has pulled the string.

"I have brought you my Poems in the original autographs, sir," said Mr. Gifted Hopkins.

He laid the manuscript on the table, caressing the eaves still with one hand, as loath to let it go.

"What disposition had you thought of making of them?" the publisher asked, in a pleasant tone. He was as kind a man as lived, though he worked the chief engine in a chamber of torture.

"I wish to read you a few specimens of the poems," he said, "with reference to their proposed publication in a volume."

"By all means," said the kind publisher, who determined to be very patient with the *protégé* of the hitherto little-known, but remarkable writer, Professor Gridley. At the same time he extended his foot in an accidental sort of way, and pressed it on the right-hand knob of three which were arranged in a line beneath the table. A little bell in a distant apartment — the little bell marked C — gave one slight note, loud enough to start a small boy up, who looked at the clock, and knew that he was to go and call the publisher in just twenty-five minutes. "A, five minutes; B, ten minutes; C, twenty-five minutes"; — that was the youngster's working formula. Mr. Hopkins was treated to the full allowance of time, as being introduced by Professor Gridley.

The young man laid open the manuscript so that the title-page, written out very handsomely in his own hand should win the eye of the publisher.

BLOSSOMS OF THE SOUL.

A WREATH OF VERSE; *Original.*

BY GIFTED HOPKINS.

"A youth to Fortune and to Fame unknown."

Gray.

"Shall I read you some of the rhymed pieces first, or some of the blank-verse poems, sir?" Gifted asked.

" Read what you think is best, — a specimen of **your**
first-class style of composition."

" I will read you the very last poem I have **written**," he
said, and he began : —

"THE TRIUMPH OF SONG.

" I met that gold-haired maiden, all too dear;
   And I to her : Lo! thou art very fair,
   Fairer than all the ladies in the world
   That fan the sweetened air with scented **fans,**
   And I am scorchéd with exceeding love,
   Yea, crispéd till my bones are dry as straw.
   Look not away with that high-archéd brow,
   But turn its whiteness that I may behold,
   And lift thy great eyes till they blaze on **mine,**
   And lay thy finger on thy perfect mouth,
   And let thy lucent ears of carven pearl
   Drink in the murmured music of my soul,
   As the lush grass drinks in the globéd dew ;
   For I have many scrolls of sweetest rhyme
   I will unroll and make thee glad to hear.
   " Then she : O shaper of the marvellous **phrase**
   That openeth woman's heart as doth a key,
   I dare not hear thee — lest the bolt should **slide**
   That locks another's heart within my own.
   Go, leave me, — and she let her eyelids fall
   And the great tears rolled from her large blue **eyes.**
   " Then I: If thou not hear me, I shall die,
   Yea, in my desperate mood may lift my hand
   And do myself a hurt no leech can mend ;
   For poets ever were of dark resolve,
   And swift stern deed —
                That maiden heard **no more,**
   But spake: Alas! my heart is very weak,
   And but for — Stay !   And if some dreadful **morn,**
   After great search and shouting thorough the **wold,**
   We found thee missing, — strangled, — drowned i' the mere, —
   Then should I go distraught and be clean mad !

O poet, read! read all thy wondrous scroll.
Yea, read the verse that maketh glad to hear!
Then I began and read two sweet, brief hours,
And she forgot all love save only mine!"

"Is all this from real life?" asked the publisher.

"It — no, sir — not exactly from real life — that is
the leading female person is not wholly fictitious — and
the incident is one which might have happened. Shall I
read you the poems referred to in the one you have just
heard, sir?"

"Allow me, one moment. Two hours' reading, I think,
you said. I fear I shall hardly be able to spare quite time
to hear them all. Let me ask what you intend doing with
these productions, Mr. — — — rr — Popkins."

"Hopkins, if you please, sir, not Popkins," said Gifted,
plaintively. He expressed his willingness to dispose of
the copyright, to publish on shares, or perhaps to receive a
certain percentage on the profits.

"Suppose we take a glass of wine together, Mr. — —
Hopkins, before we talk business," the publisher said, opening a little cupboard and taking therefrom a decanter and
two glasses. He saw the young man was looking nervous.
He waited a few minutes, until the wine had comforted
his epigastrium, and diffused its gentle glow through his
unspoiled and consequently susceptible organization.

"Come with me," he said.

Gifted followed him into a dingy apartment in the attic,
where one sat at a great table heaped and piled with
manuscripts. By him was a huge basket, half full of
manuscripts also. As they entered he dropped another
manuscript into the basket and looked up.

"Tell me," said Gifted, "what are these papers, and

who is he that looks upon them and drops them into the basket?"

"These are the manuscript poems that we receive, and the one sitting at the table is commonly spoken of among us as The Butcher. The poems he drops into the basket are those rejected as of no account."

"But does he not read the poems before he rejects them?"

"He tastes them. Do you eat a cheese before you buy it?"

"And what becomes of all those that he drops into the basket?"

If they are not claimed by their author in proper season, they go to the devil."

"What!" said Gifted, with his eyes stretched very round.

"To the paper factory, where they have a horrid machine they call the devil, that tears everything to bits, — as the critics treat our authors, sometimes, — *sometimes*, Mr. Hopkins."

Gifted devoted a moment to silent reflection.

After this instructive sight they returned together to the publisher's private room. The wine had now warmed the youthful poet's præcordia, so that he began to feel a renewed confidence in his genius and his fortunes.

"I should like to know what that critic of yours would say to *my* manuscript," he said boldly.

"You can try it if you want to," the publisher replied, with an ominous dryness of manner which the sanguine youth did not perceive, or, perceiving, did not heed.

"How can we manage to get an impartial judgment?"

"O, I'll arrange that. He always goes to his luncheon about this time. Raw meat and vitriol punch, — that's what the authors say. Wait till we hear him go, and

13 *

then I will lay your manuscript so that he will come
to it among the first after he gets back. You shall see
with your own eyes what treatment it gets. I hope it may
please him, but you shall see."

They went back to the publisher's private room and
talked awhile. Then the little office-boy came up with
some vague message about a gentleman — business —
wants to see you, sir, etc., according to the established
programme; all in a vacant, mechanical sort of way, as
if he were a talking-machine just running down.

The publisher told the boy that he was engaged, and
the gentleman must wait. Very soon they heard The
Butcher's heavy footstep as he went out to get his raw
meat and vitriol punch.

"Now, then," said the publisher, and led forth the con-
fiding literary lamb once more, to enter the fatal door of
the critical shambles.

"Hand me your manuscript, if you please, Mr. Hop·
kins. I will lay it so that it shall be the third of these
that are coming to hand. Our friend here is a pretty good
judge of verse, and knows a merchantable article about as
quick as any man in his line of business. If he forms
a favorable opinion of your poems, we will talk over your
propositions."

Gifted was conscious of a very slight tremor as he saw
his precious manuscript deposited on the table, under two
others, and over a pile of similar productions. Still he
could not help feeling that the critic would be struck by
his title. The quotation from Gray must touch his feelings. The very first piece in the collection could not fat.
to arrest him. He looked a little excited, but he was in
good spirits.

" We will be looking about here when our friend comes back," the publisher said. " He is a very methodical person, and will sit down and go right to work just as if we were not here. We can watch him, and if he should express any particular interest in your poems, I will, if you say so, carry you up to him and reveal the fact that you are the author of the works that please him."

They waited patiently until The Butcher returned, apparently refreshed by his ferocious refection, and sat down at his table. He looked comforted, and not in ill humor. The publisher and the poet talked in low tones, as if on business of their own, and watched him as he returned to his labor.

The Butcher took the first manuscript that came to hand, read a stanza here and there, turned over the leaves, turned back and tried again, — shook his head — held it for an instant over the basket, as if doubtful, — and let it softly drop. He took up the second manuscript, opened it in several places, seemed rather pleased with what he read, and laid it aside for further examination.

He took up the third. " Blossoms of the Soul," etc. He glared at it in a dreadfully ogreish way. Both the lookers-on held their breath. Gifted Hopkins felt as if half a glass more of that warm sherry would not hurt him. There was a sinking at the pit of his stomach, as if he was in a swing, as high as he could go, close up to the swallows' nests and spiders' webs. The Butcher opened the manuscript at random, read ten seconds, and gave a short low grunt. He opened again, read ten seconds, and gave another grunt, this time a little longer and louder. He opened once more, read five seconds, and, with something that sounded like the snort of a dangerous animal, cast it impatiently into the basket, and took up the manuscript that came next in order.

Gifted Hopkins stood as if paralyzed for a moment.

"Safe, perfectly safe," the publisher said to him in a whisper. "I'll get it for you presently. Come in and take another glass of wine," he said, leading him back to his own office.

"No, I thank you," he said faintly, "I can bear it. But this is dreadful, sir. Is this the way that genius is welcomed to the world of letters?"

The publisher explained to him, in the kindest manner, that there was an enormous over-production of verse, and that it took a great part of one man's time simply to overhaul the cart-loads of it that were trying to get themselves into print with the *imprimatur* of his famous house. "You are young, Mr. Hopkins. I advise you not to try to force your article of poetry on the market. The B—, our friend, there, that is, knows a thing that will sell as soon as he sees it. You are in independent circumstances, perhaps? If so, you can print — at your own expense — whatever you choose. May I take the liberty to ask your — profession?"

Gifted explained that he was "clerk" in a "store," where they sold dry goods and West India goods, and goods promiscuous.

"O, well, then," the publisher said, "you will understand me. Do you know a good article of brown sugar when you see it?"

Gifted Hopkins rather thought he did. He knew at sight whether it was a fair, salable article or not.

"Just so. Now our friend, there, knows verses that are salable and unsalable as well as you do brown sugar. —

Keep quiet now, and I will go and get your manuscript for you.

"There, Mr. Hopkins, take your poems, — they will give you a reputation in your village, I don't doubt, which is pleasant, but it will cost you a good deal of money to print them in a volume. You are very young : you can afford to wait. Your genius is not ripe yet, I am confident, Mr. Hopkins. These verses are very well for a beginning, but a man of promise like you, Mr. Hopkins, must n't throw away his chance by premature publication ! I should like to make you a present of a few of the books we publish. By and by, perhaps, we can work you into our series of poets ; but the best pears ripen slowly, and so with genius. — Where shall I send the volumes ?"

Gifted answered, to parlor number No. 6, Planet Hotel, where he soon presented himself to Master Gridley, who could guess pretty well what was coming. But he let him tell his story.

"Shall I try the other publishers?" said the disconsolate youth.

"I would n't, my young friend, I would n't. You have seen the best one of them all. He is right about it, quite right : you are young, and had better wait. Look here, Gifted, here is something to please you. We are going to visit the gay world together. See what has been left here this forenoon."

He showed him two elegant notes of invitation requesting the pleasure of Professor Byles Gridley's and of Mr. Gifted Hopkins's company on Thursday evening, as the guests of Mrs. Clymer Ketchum, of 24 Carat Place

CHAPTER XXVI.

MRS. CLYMER KETCHUM'S PARTY.

MYRTLE HAZARD had flowered out as beyond question the handsomest girl of the season. There were hints from different quarters that she might possibly be an heiress. Vague stories were about of some contingency which might possibly throw a fortune into her lap. The young men about town talked of her at the clubs in their free-and-easy way, but all agreed that she was the girl of the new crop, — "best filly this grass," as Livingston Jenkins put it. The general understanding seemed to be that the young lawyer who had followed her to the city was going to capture her. She seemed to favor him certainly as much as anybody. But Myrtle saw many young men now, and it was not so easy as it would once have been to make out who was an especial favorite.

There had been times when Murray Bradshaw would have offered his heart and hand to Myrtle at once, if he had felt sure that she would accept him. But he preferred playing the safe game now, and only wanted to feel sure of her. He had done his best to be agreeable, and could hardly doubt that he had made an impression. He dressed well when in the city, — even elegantly, — he had many of the lesser social accomplishments, was a good dancer and compared favorably in all such matters with the more dashing young fellows in society. He was a better talker han most of them, and he knew more about the girl he was dealing with than they could know. "You have only got to say the word, Murray," Mrs. Clymer Ketchum said to her relative, "and you can have her. But don't be rash. I believe you can get Berengaria if you try; and there's something better there than possibilities." Murray Bradshaw laughed, and told Mrs. Clymer Ketchum not to worry about him; he knew what he was doing.

It so happened that Myrtle met Master Byles Gridley walking with Mr. Gifted Hopkins the day before the party. She longed to have a talk with her old friend, and was glad to have a chance of pleasing her poetical admirer. She therefore begged her hostess to invite them both to her party to please her, which she promised to do at once. Thus the two elegant notes were accounted for.

Mrs. Clymer Ketchum, though her acquaintances were chiefly in the world of fortune and of fashion, had yet a certain weakness for what she called clever people. She therefore always variegated her parties with a streak of young artists and writers, and a literary lady or two; and, if she could lay hands on a first-class celebrity, was as happy as an Amazon who had captured a Centaur.

"There's a demonish clever young fellow by the name of Lindsay," Mr. Livingston Jenkins said to her a little before the day of the party. "Better ask him. They say he's the rising talent in his line, architecture mainly, but has done some remarkable things in the way of sculpture. There's some story about a bust he made that was quite wonderful. I'll find his address for you." So Mr. Clement Lindsay got his invitation, and thus Mrs. Clymer Ketchum's party promised to bring together a number of persons with whom we are acquainted. and who were acquainted with each other.

Mrs. Clymer Ketchum knew how to give a party. Let

her only have *carte blanche* for flowers, music, and cham-
pagne, she used to tell her lord, and she would see to the
rest, — lighting the rooms, tables, and toilet.   He need n't
be afraid : all he had to do was to keep out of the way.

Subdivision of labor is one of the triumphs of modern
civilization.   Labor was beautifully subdivided in this
lady's household.   It was old Ketchum's business to make
money, and he understood it.   It was Mrs. K.'s business
to spend money, and she knew how to do it.   The rooms
blazed with light like a conflagration ; the flowers burned
like lamps of many-colored flame ; the music throbbed into
the hearts of the promenaders and tingled through all the
muscles of the dancers.

Mrs. Clymer Ketchum was in her glory.   Her *point d'
Alençon* must have spoiled ever so many French girls'
eyes.   Her bosom heaved beneath a kind of breastplate
glittering with a heavy dew of diamonds.   She glistened
and sparkled with every movement, so that the admirer
forgot to question too closely whether the eyes matched the
brilliants, or the cheeks glowed like the roses.   Not far
from the great lady stood Myrtle Hazard.   She was
dressed as the fashion of the day demanded, but she had
added certain audacious touches of her own, reminiscences
of the time when the dead beauty had flourished, and
which first provoked the question and then the admiration
of the young people who had a natural eye for effect.   Over
the long white glove on her left arm was clasped a rich
bracelet, of so quaint an antique pattern that nobody had
seen anything like it, and as some one whispered that it
was "the last thing out," it was greatly admired by the
fashion-plate multitude, as well as by the few who had
a taste of their own.   If the soul of Judith Pride, long

divorced from its once beautifully moulded dust, ever lived in dim consciousness through any of those who inherited her blood, it was then and there that she breathed through the lips of Myrtle Hazard. The young girl almost trembled with the ecstasy of this new mode of being, soliciting every sense with light, with perfume, with melody, — all that could make her feel the wonderful complex music of a fresh life when all its chords first vibrate together in harmony. Miss Rhadamantha Pinnikle, whose mother was an Apex (of whose race it was said that they always made an obeisance when the family name was mentioned, and had all their portraits painted with halos round their heads), found herself extinguished in this new radiance. Miss Victoria Capsheaf stuck to the wall as if she had been a fresco on it. The fifty-year-old dynasties were dismayed and dismounted. Myrtle fossilized them as suddenly as if she had been a Gorgon, instead of a beauty.

The guests in whom we may have some interest were in the mean time making ready for the party, which was expected to be a brilliant one; for 24 Carat Place was well known for the handsome style of its entertainments.

Clement Lindsay was a little surprised by his invitation. He had, however, been made a lion of several times of late, and was very willing to amuse himself once in a while with a peep into the great world. It was but an empty show to him at best, for his lot was cast, and he expected to lead a quiet domestic life after his student days were over.

Master Byles Gridley had known what society was in his earlier time, and understood very well that all a gentleman of his age had to do was to dress himself in his usual plain way, only taking a little more care in his ar

rangements than was needed in the latitude of Oxbow Vil
lage. But Gifted must be looked after, that he should not
provoke the unamiable comments of the city youth by any
defect or extravagance of costume. The young gentleman
had bought a light sky-blue neckerchief, and a very large
breast-pin containing a gem which he was assured by the
vendor was a genuine stone. He considered that both
these would be eminently effective articles of dress, and
Mr. Gridley had some trouble to convince him that a
white tie and plain shirt-buttons would be more fitted to
the occasion.

On the morning of the day of the great party Mr. William Murray Bradshaw received a brief telegram, which
seemed to cause him great emotion, as he changed color,
uttered a forcible exclamation, and began walking up and
down his room in a very nervous kind of way. It was a
foreshadowing of a certain event now pretty sure to happen.
Whatever bearing this telegram may have had upon his
plans, he made up his mind that he would contrive an opportunity somehow that very evening to propose himself
as a suitor to Myrtle Hazard. He could not say that he
felt as absolutely certain of getting the right answer as he
had felt at some previous periods. Myrtle knew her price,
he said to himself, a great deal better than when she was a
simple country girl. The flatteries with which she had
been surrounded, and the effect of all the new appliances
of beauty, which had set her off so that she could not help
seeing her own attractions, rendered her harder to please
and to satisfy. A little experience in society teaches a
young girl the arts and the phrases which all the Lotharios
have in common. Murray Bradshaw was ready to land
his fish now, but he was not quite sure that she was yet

hooked, and he had a feeling that by this time she knew
every fly in his book. However, as he had made up his
mind not to wait another day, he addressed himself to the
trial before him with a determination to succeed, if any
means at his command would insure success. He arrayed
himself with faultless elegance : nothing must be neglected
on such an occasion. He went forth firm and grave as a
general going into a battle where all is to be lost or won
He entered the blazing saloon with the unfailing smile
upon his lips, to which he set them as he set his watch to
a particular hour and minute.

The rooms were pretty well filled when he arrived and
made his bow before the blazing, rustling, glistening, waving, blushing appearance under which palpitated, with the
pleasing excitement of the magic scene over which its
owner presided, the heart of Mrs. Clymer Ketchum. He
turned to Myrtle Hazard, and if he had ever doubted
which way his inclinations led him, he could doubt no
longer. How much dress and how much light can a woman bear? That is the way to measure her beauty. A
plain girl in a simple dress, if she has only a pleasant
voice, may seem almost a beauty in the rosy twilight
The nearer she comes to being handsome, the more ornament she will bear, and the more she may defy the sunshine or the chandelier. Murray Bradshaw was fairly dazzled with the brilliant effect of Myrtle in full dress. He
did not know before what handsome arms she had, — Ju-
lith Pride's famous arms, — which the high-colored young
men in top-boots used to swear were the handsomest pair
in New England, — right over again. He did not know
before with what defiant effect she would light up, standing
as she did directly under a huge lustre, in full flower of

flame, like a burning azalea.   He was not a man who intended to let his sentiments carry him away from the
serious interests of his future, yet, as he looked upon Myrtle Hazard, his heart gave one throb which made him feel
in every pulse that this was a woman who in her own
right, simply as a woman, could challenge the homage of
the proudest young man of her time.   He hardly knew
till this moment how much of passion mingled with other
and calmer motives of admiration.   He could say *I love
you* as truly as such a man could ever speak these words,
meaning that he admired her, that he was attracted to her,
that he should be proud of her as his wife, that he should
value himself always as the proprietor of so rare a person,
that no appendage to his existence would take so high a
place in his thoughts.   This implied also, what is of great
consequence to a young woman's happiness in the married
state, that she would be treated with uniform politeness,
with satisfactory evidences of affection, and with a degree
of confidence quite equal to what a reasonable woman
should expect from a very superior man, her husband.

If Myrtle could have looked through the window in the
breast against which only authors are privileged to flatten
their features, it is for the reader to judge how far the programme would have satisfied her.   Less than this, a great
deal less, does appear to satisfy many young women ; and
it may be that the interior just drawn, fairly judged, belongs to a model lover and husband.   Whether it does or
not, Myrtle did not see this picture.   There was a beautifully embroidered shirt-bosom in front of that window
through which we have just looked, that intercepted all
sight of what was going on within.   She only saw a man,
young, handsome, courtly, with a winning tongue, with a

ambitious spirit, whose every look and tone implied his admiration of herself, and who was associated with her past
life in such a way that they alone appeared like old friends
in the midst of that cold alien throng.   It seemed as if he
could not have chosen a more auspicious hour than this;
for she never looked so captivating, and her presence must
inspire his lips with the eloquence of love.   And she —
was not this delirious atmosphere of light and music just
the influence to which he would wish to subject her before
trying the last experiment of all which can stir the soul of
a woman?   He knew the mechanism of that impressiona-
ble state which served Coleridge so excellently well. -

> " All impulses of soul and sense
> Had thrilled my guileless Genevieve ;
> The music, and the doleful tale,
> The rich and balmy eve," —

though he hardly expected such startling results as happened in that case, — which might be taken as an awful
warning not to sing moving ballads to young ladies of susceptible feelings, unless one is prepared for very serious
consequences.   Without expecting that Myrtle would rush
into his arms, he did think that she could not help listening
to him in the intervals of the delicious music, in some
recess where the roses and jasmines and heliotropes made
the air heavy with sweetness, and the crimson curtains
drooped in heavy folds that half hid their forms from the
curious eyes all round them.   Her heart would swell like
Genevieve's as he told her in simple phrase that she was
his life, his love, his all, — for in some two or three words
like these he meant to put his appeal, and not in fine poet
'cal phrases : that would do for Gifted Hopkins and rhym
ing tomtits of that feather.

Full of his purpose, involving the plans of his whole life, implying, as he saw clearly, a brilliant future or a disastrous disappointment, with a great unexploded mine of consequences under his feet, and the spark ready to fall into it, he walked about the gilded saloon with a smile upon his lips so perfectly natural and pleasant, that one would have said he was as vacant of any aim, except a sort of superficial good-natured disposition to be amused, as the blankest-eyed simpleton who had tied himself up in a white cravat and come to bore and be bored.

Yet under this pleasant smile his mind was so busy with its thoughts that he had forgotten all about the guests from Oxbow Village who, as Myrtle had told him, were to come this evening. His eye was all at once caught by a familiar figure, and he recognized Master Byles Gridley, accompanied by Mr. Gifted Hopkins, at the door of the saloon. He stepped forward at once to meet and to present them.

Mr. Gridley in evening costume made an eminently dignified and respectable appearance. There was an unusual look of benignity upon his firmly moulded features, and an air of ease which rather surprised Mr. Bradshaw, who did not know all the social experiences which had formed a part of the old Master's history. The greeting between them was courteous, but somewhat formal, as Mr. Bradshaw was acting as one of the masters of ceremony. He nodded to Gifted in an easy way, and led them both into the immediate Presence.

"This is my friend Professor Gridley, Mrs. Ketchum, whom I have the honor of introducing to you, — a very distinguished scholar, as I have no doubt you are well aware. And this is my friend Mr. Gifted Hopkins, a young poet of distinction, whose fame will reach you by and by, if it has not come to your ears already."

The two gentlemen went through the usual forms, the poet a little crushed by the Presence, but doing his best. While the lady was making polite speeches to them, Myrtle Hazard came forward. She was greatly delighted to meet her old friend, and even looked upon the young poet with a degree of pleasure she would hardly have expected to receive from his company. They both brought with them so many reminiscences of familiar scenes and events, that it was like going back for the moment to Oxbow Village. But Myrtle did not belong to herself that evening, and had no opportunity to enter into conversation just then with either of them. There was to be dancing by and by, and the younger people were getting impatient that it should begin. At last the music sounded the well-known summons, and the floors began to ring to the tread of the dancers. As usual on such occasions there were a large number of non-combatants, who stood as spectators around those who were engaged in the campaign of the evening. Mr. Byles Gridley looked on gravely, thinking of the minuets and the gavots of his younger days. Mr. Gifted Hopkins, who had never acquired the desirable accomplishment of dancing, gazed with dazzled and admiring eyes at the wonderful evolutions of the graceful performers. The music stirred him a good deal ; he had also been introduced to one or two young persons as Mr. Hopkins, the poet, and he began to feel a kind of excitement, such as was often the prelude of a lyric burst from his pen. Others might have wealth and beauty, he thought to himself, but what were these to the gift of genius ? In fifty years the wealth of these people would have passed into other hands. In fifty years all these beauties would be dead, or wrinkled and double-wrinkled great-grandmothers. And when they were all gone and forgotten, the name of Hopkins would be still fresh in the world's memory. Inspiring thought. A smile of triumph rose to his lips; he felt that the village boy who could look forward to fame as his inheritance was richer than all the millionnaires, and that the words he should set in verse would have an enduring lustre to which the whiteness of pearls was cloudy, and the sparkle of diamonds dull.

He raised his eyes, which had been cast down in reflection, to look upon these less favored children of Fortune, to whom she had given nothing but perishable inheritances. Two or three pairs of eyes, he observed, were fastened upon him. His mouth perhaps betrayed a little self-consciousness, but he tried to show his features in an aspect of dignified self-possession. There seemed to be remarks and questionings going on, which he supposed to be something like the following : —

Which is it? Which is it? — Why, that one, there, — that young fellow, — don't you see? — What young fellow are you two looking at? Who is he? What is he? — Why, that is *Hopkins*, the poet. — Hopkins, the poet! Let me see him! Let *me* see him! — Hopkins? What! Gifted Hopkins? etc., etc.

Gifted Hopkins did not hear these words except in fancy, but he did unquestionably find a considerable number of eyes concentrated upon him, which he very naturally interpreted as an evidence that he had already begun to enjoy a foretaste of the fame of which he should hereafter have his full allowance. Some seemed to be glancing furtively, some appeared as if they wished to speak, and all the time the number of those looking at him seemed to be increasing. A vision came through his fancy of himself as standing on a platform, and having persons who wished to look upon him and shake hands with him presented, as he had heard was the way with great people when going about the country. But this was only a suggestion, and by no means a serious thought, for that would have implied infatuation.

Gifted Hopkins was quite right in believing that he attracted many eyes. At last those of Myrtle Hazard were called to him, and she perceived that an accident was making him unenviably conspicuous. The bow of his rather large white neck-tie had slid round and got beneath his left ear. A not very good-natured or well-bred young fellow had pointed out the subject of this slight misfortune to one or two others of not much better taste or breeding, and thus the unusual attention the youthful poet was receiving explained itself. Myrtle no sooner saw the little accident of which her rural friend was the victim, than she left her place in the dance with a simple courage which did her credit. "I want to speak to you a minute," she said. "Come into this alcove."

And the courageous young lady not only told Gifted what had happened to him, but found a pin somehow, as women always do on a pinch, and had him in presentable condition again almost before the bewildered young man knew what was the matter. On reflection it occurred to him, as it has to other provincial young persons going to great cities, that he might perhaps have been hasty in thinking himself an object of general curiosity as yet. There had hardly been time for his name to have become very widely known. Still, the feeling had been pleasant for the moment, and had given him an idea of what the rapture would be, when, wherever he went, the monster digit (to hint a classical phrase) of the collective admiring

14

public would be lifted to point him out, and the whisper would pass from one to another, "That's him! That's Hopkins!"

Mr. Murray Bradshaw had been watching the opportunity for carrying out his intentions, with his pleasant smile covering up all that was passing in his mind, and Master Byles Gridley, looking equally unconcerned, had been watching him. The young man's time came at last. Some were at the supper-table, some were promenading, some were talking, when he managed to get Myrtle a little apart from the rest, and led her towards one of the recesses in the apartment, where two chairs were invitingly placed. Her cheeks were flushed, her eyes were sparkling, — the influences to which he had trusted had not been thrown away upon her. He had no idea of letting his purpose be seen until he was fully ready. It required all his self-mastery to avoid betraying himself by look or tone, but he was so natural that Myrtle was thrown wholly off her guard. He meant to make her pleased with herself at the outset, and that not by point-blank flattery, of which she had had more than enough of late, but rather by suggestion and inference, so that she should find herself feeling happy without knowing how. It would be easy to glide from that to the impression she had produced upon him, and get the two feelings more or less mingled in her mind. And so the simple confession he meant to make would at length evolve itself logically, and hold by a natural connection to the first agreeable train of thought which he had called up. Not the way, certainly, that most young men would arrange their great trial scene; but Murray Bradshaw was a lawyer in love as much as in business, and considered himself as pleading a cause before a jury of

Myrtle Hazard's conflicting motives. What would any lawyer do in a jury case, but begin by giving the twelve honest men and true to understand, in the first place, that their intelligence and virtue were conceded by all, and that he himself had perfect confidence in them, and leave them to shape their verdict in accordance with these propositions and his own side of the case?

Myrtle had, perhaps, never so seriously inclined her ear to the honeyed accents of the young pleader. He flattered her with so much tact, that she thought she heard an unconscious echo through his lips of an admiration which he only shared with all around him. But in him he made it seem discriminating, deliberate, not blind, but very real. This it evidently was which had led him to trust her with his ambitions and his plans, — they might be delusions, but he could never keep them from her, and she was the one woman in the world to whom he thought he could safely give his confidence.

The dread moment was close at hand. Myrtle was listening with an instinctive premonition of what was coming, — ten thousand mothers and grandmothers and great-grandmothers, and so on, had passed through it all in preceding generations until time reached backwards to the sturdy savage who asked no questions of any kind, but knocked down the primeval great grandmother of all, and carried her off to his hole in the rock, or into the tree where he had made his nest. Why should not the coming question announce itself by stirring in the pulses and thrilling in the nerves of the descendant of all these grandmothers?

She was leaning imperceptibly towards him, drawn by the mere blind elemental force, as the plummet was at tracted to the side of Schehallion. Her lips were parted, and she breathed a little faster than so healthy a girl ought to breathe in a state of repose. The steady nerves of William Murray Bradshaw felt unwonted thrills and tremors tingling through them, as he came nearer and nearer the few simple words with which he was to make Myrtle Hazard the mistress of his destiny. His tones were becoming lower and more serious ; there were slight breaks once or twice in the conversation ; Myrtle had cast down her eyes.

"There is but one word more to add," he murmured softly, as he bent towards her —

A grave voice interrupted him. "Excuse me, Mr. Bradshaw," said Master Byles Gridley, "I wish to present a young gentleman to my friend here. I promised to show him the most charming young person I have the honor to be acquainted with, and I must redeem my pledge. Miss Hazard, I have the pleasure of introducing to your acquaintance my distinguished young friend, Mr. Clement Lindsay."

Once more, for the third time, these two young persons stood face to face. Myrtle was no longer liable to those nervous seizures which any sudden impression was liable to produce when she was in her half-hysteric state of mind and body. She turned to the new-comer, who found himself unexpectedly submitted to a test which he would never have risked of his own will. He must go through it, cruel as it was, with the easy self-command which belongs to a gentleman in the most trying social exigencies. He addressed her, therefore, in the usual terms of courtesy, and then turned and greeted Mr. Bradshaw, whom he had never met since their coming together at Oxbow Village

Myrtle was conscious, the instant she looked upon Clement Lindsay, of the existence of some peculiar relation between them ; but what, she could not tell. Whatever it was, it broke the charm which had been weaving between her and Murray Bradshaw. He was not foolish enough to make a scene. What fault could he find with Clement Lindsay, who had only done as any gentleman would do with a lady to whom he had just been introduced, — addressed a few polite words to her? After saying those words, Clement had turned very courteously to him, and they had spoken with each other. But Murray Bradshaw could not help seeing that Myrtle had transferred her attention, at least for the moment, from him to the new-comer. He folded his arms and waited, — but he waited in vain. The hidden attraction which drew Clement to the young girl with whom he had passed into the Valley of the Shadow of Death overmastered all other feelings, and he gave himself up to the fascination of her presence.

The inward rage of Murray Bradshaw at being interrupted just at the moment when he was, as he thought, about to cry checkmate and finish the first great game he had ever played, may well be imagined. But it could not be helped. Myrtle had exercised the customary privilege of young ladies at parties, and had turned from talking with one to talking with another, — that was all. Fortunately for him the young man who had been introduced at such a most critical moment was not one from whom he need apprehend any serious interference. He felt grateful beyond measure to pretty Susan Posey, who, as he had good reason for believing, retained her hold upon her early lover, and was looking forward with bashful interest to the time when she should become Mrs. Lindsay. It was better to put up quietly with his disappointment; and, if he could get no favorable opportunity that evening to resume his conversation at the interesting point where he left it off, he would call the next day and bring matters to a conclusion.

He called accordingly the next morning, but was disappointed in not seeing Myrtle. She had hardly slept that night, and was suffering from a bad headache, which last reason was her excuse for not seeing company.

He called again, the following day, and learned that Miss Hazard had just left the city, and gone on a visit to Oxbow Village.

CHAPTER XXVII.

MINE AND COUNTERMINE.

WHAT the nature of the telegram was which had produced such an effect on the feelings and plans of Mr. William Murray Bradshaw nobody especially interested knew but himself. We may conjecture that it announced some fact, which had leaked out a little prematurely, relating to the issue of the great land-case in which the firm was interested. However that might be, Mr. Bradshaw no sooner heard that Myrtle had suddenly left the city for Oxbow Village, — for what reason he puzzled himself to guess, — than he determined to follow her at once, and take up the conversation he had begun at the party where it left off. And as the young poet had received his quietus for the present at the publisher's, and as Master Gridley had nothing specially to detain him, they too returned at about the same time, and so our old acquaintances were once more together within the familiar precincts where we have been accustomed to see them.

Master Gridley did not like playing the part of a spy, but it must be remembered that he was an old college officer, and had something of the detective's sagacity, and a certain cunning derived from the habit of keeping an eye on mischievous students. If any underhand contrivance was at work, involving the welfare of any one in whom he was interested, he was a dangerous person for the plotters, for he had plenty of time to attend to them, and would be apt to take a kind of pleasure in matching his wits against another crafty person's, — such a one, for instance, as Mr. Macchiavelli Bradshaw

Perhaps he caught some words of that gentleman's con- versation at the party; at any rate, he could not fail to observe his manner. When he found that the young man had followed Myrtle back to the village, he suspected something more than a coincidence. When he learned that he was assiduously visiting The Poplars, and that he was in close communication with Miss Cynthia Badlam, he felt sure that he was pressing the siege of Myrtle's heart. But that there was some difficulty in the way was equally clear to him, for he ascertained, through channels which the attentive reader will soon have means of conjec- turing, that Myrtle had seen him but once in the week following his return, and that in the presence of her dragons. She had various excuses when he called, — headaches, perhaps, among the rest, as these are staple articles on such occasions. But Master Gridley knew his man too well to think that slight obstacles would prevent his going forward to effect his purpose.

" I think he will get her, if he holds on," the old man said to himself, "and he won't let go in a hurry. If there were any real love about it — but surely he is inca- pable of such a human weakness as the tender passion. What does all this sudden concentration upon the girl mean? He knows something about her that we don't know, — that must be it. What did he hide that paper for, a year ago and more? Could that have anything to do with his pursuit of Myrtle Hazard to-day?"

Master Gridley paused as he asked this question of himself, for a luminous idea had struck him. Consulting daily with Cynthia Badlam, was he? Could there be a conspiracy between these two persons to conceal some important fact, or to keep something back until it would be for their common interest to have it made known?

Now Mistress Kitty Fagan was devoted, heart and soul, to Myrtle Hazard, and ever since she had received the young girl from Mr. Gridley's hands, when he brought her back safe and sound after her memorable adventure, had considered him as Myrtle's best friend and natural protector. These simple creatures, whose thoughts are not taken up, like those of educated people, with the care of a great museum of dead phrases, are very quick to see the live facts which are going on about them. Mr. Gridley had met her, more or less accidentally, several times of late, and inquired very particularly about Myrtle, and how she got along at the house since her return, and whether she was getting over her headaches, and how they treated her in the family.

" Bliss your heart, Mr. Gridley," Kitty said to him on one of these occasions, " it's ahltogither changed intirely. Sure Miss Myrtle does jist iverythin' she likes, an' Miss Withers niver middles with her at ahl, excip' jist to roll up her eyes an' look as if she was the hid-moorner at a funeril whiniver Miss Myrtle says she wants to do this or that, or to go here or there. It's Miss Badlam that's ahlwiz after her, an' a-watchin' her, — she thinks she's cunnin'er than a cat, but there's other folks that's got eyes an' ears as good as hers. It's that Mr. Bridshaw that's a puttin' his head together with Miss Badlam for somethin' or other, an' I don't believe there's no good in it, — for what does the fox an' the cat be a whisperin about, as if they was thaves an' incind'ries, if there ain't no mischief hatchin'?"

14 *　　　　　　　　　　u

" Why, Kitty," he said, " what mischief do you think is going on, and who is to be harmed?"

" O Mr. Gridley," she answered, " if there ain't some body to be chated somehow, then I don't know an honest man and woman from two rogues.   An' have n't I heard Miss Myrtle's name whispered as if there was somethin goin' on agin' her, an' they was afraid the tahk would go out through the doors, an' up through the chimbley?   I don't want to tell no tales, Mr. Gridley, nor to hurt no honest body, for I 'm a poor woman, Mr. Gridley, but I comes of dacent folks, an' I vallies my repitation an' charácter as much as if I was dressed in silks and satins instead of this mane old gown, savin' your presence, which is the best I 've got, an' niver a dollar to buy another.   But if iver I hears a word, Mr. Gridley, that manes any kind of a mischief to Miss Myrtle, — the Lard bliss her soul an' keep ahl the divils away from her! — I 'll be runnin' straight down here to tell ye ahl about it, — be right sure o' that, Mr. Gridley."

" Nothing must happen to Myrtle," he said, " that we can help.   If you see anything more that looks wrong, you had better come down here at once and let me know, as you say you will.   *At once*, you understand.   And, Kitty, I am a little particular about the dress of people who come to see me, so that if you would just take the trouble to get you a tidy pattern of gingham or calico, or whatever you like of that sort for a gown, you would please me ; and perhaps this little trifle will be a convenience to you when you come to pay for it."

Kitty thanked him with all the national accompaniments, and trotted off to the store, where Mr. Gifted Hopkins displayed the native amiability of his temper by tumbling down everything in the shape of ginghams and calicos they had on the shelves, without a murmur at the taste of his customer, who found it hard to get a pattern sufficiently emphatic for her taste. She succeeded at last, and laid down a five-dollar bill as if she were as used to the pleasing figure on its face as to the sight of her own five digits.

Master Byles Gridley had struck a spade deeper than he knew into his first countermine, for Kitty had none of those delicate scruples about the means of obtaining information which might have embarrassed a diplomatist of higher degree.

CHAPTER XXVIII.

MR. BRADSHAW CALLS ON MISS BADLAM.

"IS Miss Hazard in, Kitty?"

"Indade she's in, Mr. Bridshaw, but she won't see nobody."

"What's the meaning of that, Kitty? Here is the third time within three days you've told me I could n't see her. She saw Mr. Gridley yesterday, I know; why won't she see me to-day?"

"Y' must ask Miss Myrtle what the rason is, — it's none o' my business, Mr. Bridshaw. That's the order she give me."

"Is Miss Badlam in?"

"Indade she's in, Mr. Bridshaw, an' I'll go cahl her."

"Bedad," said Kitty Fagan to herself, "the cat an' the fox is goin' to have another o' thim big tahks togither, an' sure the old hole for the stove-pipe has niver been stopped up yet."

Mr. Bradshaw and Miss Cynthia went into the parlor together, and Mistress Kitty retired to her kitchen. There was a deep closet belonging to this apartment, separated by a partition from the parlor. There was a round hole high up in this partition through which a stove-pipe had once passed. Mistress Kitty placed a stool just under this opening, upon which, as on a pedestal, she posed herself with great precaution in the attitude of the goddess of other people's secrets, that is to say, with her head a little on one side, so as to bring her liveliest ear close to the opening. The conversation which took place in the hearing of the invisible third party began in a singularly free-and-easy manner on Mr. Bradshaw's part.

" What the d is the reason I can't see Myrtle, Cynthia?"

" That's more than I can tell you, Mr. Bradshaw. I can watch her goings on, but I can't account for her tantrums."

" You say she has had some of her old nervous whims, — has the doctor been to see her?"

" No indeed. She has kept to herself a good deal, but I don't think there's anything in particular the matter with her. She looks well enough, only she seems a little queer, — as girls do that have taken a fancy into their heads that they're in love, you know, — absent-minded, — does n't seem to be interested in things as you would expect after being away so long."

Mr. Bradshaw looked as if this did not please him particularly. If he was the object of her thoughts she would not avoid him, surely.

" Have you kept your eye on her steadily?"

" I don't believe there is an hour we can't account for, — Kitty and I between us."

" Are you sure you can depend on Kitty?"

[" Depind on Kitty, is it? O, an' to be sure ye can depind on Kitty to kape watch at the stove-pipe hole, an' to tell all y'r plottin's an' contrivin's to them that'll get the cheese out o' y'r mousetrap for ye before ye catch any poor cratur in it." This was the inaudible comment of the unseen third party.]

" Of course I can depend on her as far as I trust her. All she knows is that she must look out for the girl to see that she does not run away or do herself a mischief. The

Biddies don't know much, but they know enough to keep a watch on the — "

" Chickens." Mr. Bradshaw playfully finished the sentence for Miss Cynthia.

[" An' on the foxes, an' the cats, an' the wazels, an' the hen-hahks, an' ahl the other bastes," added the invisible witness, in unheard soliloquy.]

" I ain't sure whether she 's quite as stupid as she looks,' said the suspicious young lawyer. " There 's a little cunning twinkle in her eye sometimes that makes me think she might be up to a trick on occasion. Does she ever listen about to hear what people are saying ? "

" Don't trouble yourself about Kitty Fagan, for pity's sake, Mr. Bradshaw. The Biddies are all alike, and they 're all as stupid as owls, except when you tell 'em just what to do, and how to do it. A pack of priest-ridden fools ! "

The hot Celtic blood in Kitty Fagan's heart gave a leap. The stout muscles gave an involuntary jerk. The substantial frame felt the thrill all through, and the rickety stool on which she was standing creaked sharply under its burden.

Murray Bradshaw started. He got up and opened softly all the doors leading from the room, one after another, and looked out.

" I thought I heard a noise as if somebody was moving Cynthia. It 's just as well to keep our own matters to ourselves."

" If you wait till this old house keeps still, Mr. Bradshaw, you might as well wait till the river has run by It 's as full of rats and mice as an old cheese is of mites There 's a hundred old rats in this house, and that 's wha you hear."

[" An' one old cat ; that 's what *I* hear." Third party.]

" I told you, Cynthia, I must be off on this business to-morrow. I want to know that everything is safe before I go. And, besides, I have got something to say to you that 's important, — very important, mind you."

He got up once more and opened every door softly and looked out. He fixed his eye suspiciously on a large sofa at the other side of the room, and went, looking half ashamed of his extreme precaution, and peeped under it, to see if there was any one hidden there to listen. Then he came back and drew his chair close up to the table at which Miss Badlam had seated herself. The conversation which followed was in a low tone, and a portion of it must be given in another place in the words of the third party. The beginning of it we are able to supply in this connection.

" Look here, Cynthia ; you know what I am going for It 's all right, I feel sure, for I have had private means of finding out. It 's a sure thing ; but I must go once more to see that the other fellows don't try any trick on us. You understand what is for my advantage is for yours, and, if I go wrong, you go overboard with me. Now I must leave the — you know — behind me. I can't leave it in the house or the office : they might burn up. I won't have it about me when I am travelling. Draw your chair a little more this way. Now listen."

[" Indade I will," said the third party to herself. The reader will find out in due time whether she listened to any purpose or no.]

In the mean time Myrtle, who for some reason was rather nervous and restless, had found a pair of half-finished slippers which she had left behind her. The color came into her cheeks when she remembered the state of mind she was in when she was working on them for the Rev. Mr. Stoker. She recollected Master Gridley's mistake about their destination, and determined to follow the hint he had given. It would please him better if she sent them to good Father Pemberton, she felt sure, than if he should get them himself. So she enlarged them somewhat, (for the old man did not pinch his feet, as the younger clergyman was in the habit of doing, and was, besides, of portly dimensions, as the old orthodox three-deckers were apt to be,) and worked E. P. very handsomely into the pattern, and sent them to him with her love and respect, to his great delight; for old ministers do not have quite so many tokens of affection from fair hands as younger ones.

What made Myrtle nervous and restless? Why had she quitted the city so abruptly, and fled to her old home, leaving all the gayeties behind her which had so attracted and dazzled her?

She had not betrayed herself at the third meeting with the young man who stood in such an extraordinary relation to her, — who had actually given her life from his own breath, — as when she met him for the second time. Whether his introduction to her at the party, just at the instant when Murray Bradshaw was about to make a declaration, saved her from being in another moment the promised bride of that young gentleman, or not, we will not be so rash as to say. It looked, certainly, as if he was in a fair way to carry his point; but perhaps she would have hesitated, or shrunk back, when the great question came to stare her in the face.

She was excited, at any rate, by the conversation, so

that, when Clement was presented to her, her thoughts could not at once be all called away from her other admirer, and she was saved from all danger of that sudden disturbance which had followed their second meeting. Whatever impression he made upon her developed itself gradually, — still, she felt strangely drawn towards him. It was not simply in his good looks, in his good manners, in his conversation, that she found this attraction, but there was a singular fascination which she felt might be dangerous to her peace, without explaining it to herself in words. She could hardly be in love with this young artist; she knew that his affections were plighted to another, — a fact which keeps most young women from indulging unruly fancies; yet her mind was possessed by his image to such an extent that it left little room for that of Mr. William Murray Bradshaw.

Myrtle Hazard had been just ready to enter on a career of worldly vanity and ambition. It is hard to blame her, for we know how she came by the tendency. She had every quality, too, which fitted her to shine in the gay world; and the general law is, that those who have the power have the instinct to use it. We do not suppose that the bracelet on her arm was an amulet, but it was a symbol. It reminded her of her descent; it kept alive the desire to live over the joys and excitements of a bygone generation. If she had accepted Murray Bradshaw, she would have pledged herself to a worldly life. If she had refused him, it would perhaps have given her a taste of power that might have turned her into a coquette. This new impression saved her for the time. She had come back to her nest in the village like a frightened bird; her heart was throbbing, her nerves were thrilling, her dreams were agitated; she wanted to be quiet, and could not listen to the flatteries or entreaties of her old lover.

It was a strong will and a subtle intellect that had arrayed their force and skill against the ill-defended citadel of Myrtle's heart. Murray Bradshaw was perfectly determined, and not to be kept back by any trivial hindrances, such as her present unwillingness to accept him or even her repugnance to him, if a freak of the moment had carried her so far. It was a settled thing: Myrtle Hazard must become Mrs. Bradshaw; and nobody could deny that, if he gave her his name, they had a chance, at least, for a brilliant future.

CHAPTER XXIX.

MISTRESS KITTY FAGAN CALLS ON MASTER BYLES GRIDLEY.

"I'D like to go down to the store this mornin', Miss Withers, plase. Sure I 've niver a shoe to my fut, only jist these two that I 've got on, an' one other pair, and thim is so full of holes that whin I 'm standin' in 'em I 'm outside of 'em intirely."

"You can go, Kitty," Miss Silence answered, funereally.

Thereupon Kitty Fagan proceeded to array herself in her most tidy apparel, including a pair of shoes not exactly answering to her description, and set out straight for the house of the Widow Hopkins. Arrived at that respectable mansion, she inquired for Mr. Gridley, and was informed that he was at home. Had a message for him, — could she see him in his study? She could if she would wait a little while. Mr. Gridley was busy just at this minute. Sit down, Kitty, and warm yourself at the cooking-stove.

Mistress Kitty accepted Mrs. Hopkins's hospitable offer, and presently began orienting herself, and getting ready to make herself agreeable. The kind-hearted Mrs. Hopkins had gathered about her several other pensioners besides the twins. These two little people, it may be here mentioned, were just taking a morning airing in charge of Susar Posey, who strolled along in company with Gifted Hopkins on his way to "the store."

Mistress Kitty soon began the conversational blandish

ments so natural to her good-humored race. "It's a little
blarney that 'll jist suit th' old lady," she said to herself,
as she made her first conciliatory advance.

"An' sure an' it's a beautiful kitten you ve got there,
Mrs. Hopkins. An' it's a splindid mouser she is, I 'll be
bound. Does n't she look as if she 'd clane the house out
o' them little bastes, — bad luck to 'em!"

Mrs. Hopkins looked benignantly upon the more than
middle-aged tabby, slumbering as if she had never known
an enemy, and turned smiling to Mistress Kitty. "Why
bless your heart, Kitty, our old puss would n't know a
mouse by sight, if you showed her one. If I was a mouse,
I 'd as lieves have a nest in one of that old cat's ears as
anywhere else. You could n't find a safer place for one."

"Indade, an' to be sure she 's too big an' too handsome
a pussy to be after wastin' her time on them little bastes.
It 's that little tarrier dog of yours, Mrs. Hopkins, that
will be after worryin' the mice an' the rats, an' the thaves
too, I 'll warrant. Is n't he a fust-rate-lookin' watch-dog,
an' a rig'ler rat-hound?"

Mrs. Hopkins looked at the little short-legged and short-
winded animal of miscellaneous extraction with an expression of contempt and affection, mingled about half and
half. "*Worry* 'em! If they wanted to *sleep*, I rather guess
he would worry 'em! If barkin' would do their job for
'em, nary a mouse nor rat would board free gratis in my
house as they do now. Noisy little good-for-nothing tike,
— ain't you, Fret?"

Mistress Kitty was put back a little by two such signal
failures. There was another chance, however, to make
ner point, which she presently availed herself of, — feeling
pretty sure this time that she should effect a lodgement

Mrs. Hopkins's parrot had been observing Kitty, first with one eye and then with the other, evidently preparing to make a remark, but awkward with a stranger. "That's a beautiful par't y 've got there," Kitty said, buoyant with the certainty that she was on safe ground this time; "and tahks like a book, I 'll be bound. Poll! Poll! Poor Poll!"

She put forth her hand to caress the intelligent and affable bird, which, instead of responding as expected, "squawked," as our phonetic language has it, and, opening a beak imitated from a tooth-drawing instrument of the good old days, made a shrewd nip at Kitty's forefinger. She drew it back with a jerk.

"An' is that the way your par't tahks, Mrs. Hopkins?"

"Talks, bless you, Kitty! why, that parrot has n't said a word this ten year. He used to say Poor Poll! when we first had him, but he found it was easier to squawk, and that's all he ever does now-a-days, — except bite once in a while."

"Well, an' to be sure," Kitty answered, radiant as she rose from her defeats, "if you 'll kape a cat that does n't know a mouse when she sees it, an' a dog that only barks for his livin', and a par't that only squawks an' bites an' niver spakes a word, ye must be the best-hearted woman that's alive, an' bliss ye, if ye was only a good Catholic, the Holy Father 'd make a saint of ye in less than no ime!"

So Mistress Kitty Fagan got in her bit of Celtic flattery, in spite of her three successive discomfitures.

"You may come up now, Kitty," said Mr. Gridley over the stairs. He had just finished and sealed a letter.

"Well, Kitty, how are things going on up at The Pop-

lars? And how does our young lady seem to be of
late?"

"Whisht! whisht! your honor."

Mr. Bradshaw's lessons had not been thrown away on
his attentive listener. She opened every door in the room,
"by your lave," as she said. She looked all over the walls
to see if there was any old stove-pipe hole or other avenue
to eye or ear. Then she went, in her excess of caution, to
the window. She saw nothing noteworthy except Mr.
Gifted Hopkins and the charge he convoyed, large and
small, in the distance. The whole living fleet was station-
ary for the moment, he leaning on the fence with his cheek
on his hand, in one of the attitudes of the late Lord Byron ;
she, very near him, listening, apparently, in the pose of
Mignon aspirant au ciel, as rendered by Carlo Dolce
Scheffer.

Kitty came back, apparently satisfied, and stood close to
Mr. Gridley, who told her to sit down, which she did, first
making a catch at her apron to dust the chair with, and
then remembering that she had left that part of her costume at home. — Automatic movements, curious.

Mistress Kitty began telling in an undertone of the
meeting between Mr. Bradshaw and Miss Badlam, and of
the arrangements she made for herself as the reporter of
the occasion. She then repeated to him, in her own way,
that part of the conversation which has been already laid
before the reader. There is no need of going over the
whole of this again in Kitty's version, but we may fit what
followed into the joints of what has been already told.

"He cahled her Cynthy, d' ye see, Mr. Gridley, an
tahked to her jist as asy as if they was two rogues, and she
knowed it as well as he did. An' so, says he, I 'm goin

away, says he, an' I 'm goin' to be gahn siveral days,
or perhaps longer, says he, an' you 'd better kape it,
says he."

"Keep *what*, Kitty? What was it he wanted her to
keep?" said Mr. Gridley, who no longer doubted that he
was on the trail of a plot, and meant to follow it. He was
getting impatient with the "says he's" with which Kitty
double-leaded her discourse.

"An' to be sure ain't I tellin' you, Mr. Gridley, jist as
fast as my breath will let me? An' so, says he, you 'd better kape it, says he, mixed up with your other paäpers,
says he," (Mr. Gridley started,) "an' thin we can find it in
the garret, says he, whinever we want it, says he. An' if
it ahl goes right out there, says he, it won't be lahng before
we shall want to find it, says he. And I can dipind on
you, says he, for we 're both in the same boat, says he, an'
you knows what I knows, says he, an' I knows what you
knows, says he. And thin he taks a stack o' paäpers out
of his pocket, an' he pulls out one of 'em, an' he says to
her, says he, that 's the paäper, says he, an' if you die, says
he, niver lose sight of that day or night, says he, for it 's life
an' dith to both of us, says he. An' thin he asks her if
she has n't got one o' them paäpers — what is 't they cahls
'em? — divilops, or some sich kind of a name — that they
wraps up their letters in ; an' she says no, she has n't got
none that 's big enough to hold it. So he says, give me a
shate o' paäper, says he. An' thin he takes the paäper
that she give him, an' he folds it up like one o' them — divilops, if that 's the name of 'em ; and thin he pulls a stick
o' salin'-wax out of his pocket, an' a stamp, an' he takes the
paäper an' puts it into th' other paäper, along with the
rest of the paäpers, an' thin he folds th' other paäper over

the paäpers, and thin he lights a candle, an' he milts the salin'-wax, and he sales up the paäper that was outside th other paäpers, an' he writes on the back of the paäper, an thin he hands it to Miss Badlam."

"Did you see the paper that he showed her before he fastened it up with the others, Kitty?"

"I did see it, indade, Mr. Gridley, and it's the truth I'm tellin' ye."

"Did you happen to notice anything about it, Kitty."

"I did, indade, Mr. Gridley. It was a longish kind of a paäper, and there was some blotches of ink on the back of it, — an' they looked like a face without any mouth, for, says I, there's two spots for the eyes, says I, and there's a spot for the nose, says I, and there's niver a spot for the mouth, says I."

This was the substance of what Master Byles Gridley got out of Kitty Fagan. It was enough, — yes, it was too much. There was some deep-laid plot between Murray Bradshaw and Cynthia Badlam, involving the interests of some of the persons connected with the late Malachi Withers; for that the paper described by Kitty was the same that he had seen the young man conceal in the *Corpus Juris Civilis*, it was impossible to doubt. If it had been a single spot on the back of it, or two, he might have doubted. But three large spots — "blotches" she had called them, disposed thus •.• — would not have happened to be on two different papers, in all human probability.

After grave consultation of all his mental faculties in committee of the whole, he arrived at the following conclusion, — that Miss Cynthia Badlam was the depositary of a secret involving interests which he felt it his business to defend, and of a document which was fraudulently with held and meant to be used for some unfair purpose. And most assuredly, Master Gridley said to himself, he held a master-key, which, just so certainly as he could make up his mind to use it, would open any secret in the keeping of Miss Cynthia Badlam.

He proceeded, therefore, without delay, to get ready for a visit to that lady, at The Poplars. He meant to go thoroughly armed, for he was a very provident old gentleman. His weapons were not exactly of the kind which a housebreaker would provide himself with, but of a somewhat peculiar nature.

Weapon number one was a slip of paper with a date and a few words written upon it. "I think this will fetch the document," he said to himself, "if it comes to the worst. Not if I can help it, — not if I can help it. But if I cannot get at the heart of this thing otherwise, why, I must come to this. Poor woman! — Poor woman!"

Weapon number two was a small phial containing spirits of hartshorn, *sal volatile*, very strong, that would stab through the nostrils, like a stiletto, deep into the gray kernels that lie in the core of the brain. Excellent in cases of sudden syncope or fainting, such as sometimes require the opening of windows, the dashing on of cold water, the cutting of stays, perhaps, with a scene of more or less tumultuous perturbation and afflux of clamorous womanhood.

So armed, Byles Gridley, A. M., champion of unprotected innocence, grasped his ivory-handled cane and sallied forth on his way to The Poplars.

CHAPTER XXX.

MASTER BYLES GRIDLEY CALLS ON MISS CYNTHIA BADLAM.

MISS CYNTHIA BADLAM was seated in a small parlor which she was accustomed to consider her own during her long residences at The Poplars. The entry stove warmed it but imperfectly, and she looked pinched and cold, for the evenings were still pretty sharp, and the old house let in the chill blasts, as old houses are in the habit of doing. She was sitting at her table, with a little trunk open before her. She had taken some papers from it, which she was looking over, when a knock at her door announced a visitor, and Master Byles Gridley entered the parlor.

As he came into the room, she gathered the papers together and replaced them in the trunk, which she locked, throwing an unfinished piece of needle-work over it, putting the key in her pocket, and gathering herself up for company. Something of all this Master Gridley saw through his round spectacles, but seemed not to see, and took his seat like a visitor making a call of politeness.

A visitor at such an hour, of the male sex, without special provocation, without social pretext, was an event in the life of the desolate spinster. Could it be — No it could not — and yet — and yet! Miss Cynthia threw back the rather common-looking but comfortable shawl which covered her shoulders, and showed her quite presentable figure, arrayed with a still lingering thought of that remote contingency which might yet offer itself at some unexpected moment; she adjusted the carefully plaited cap, which was not yet of the *lasciate ogni speranza* pattern, and as she obeyed these instincts of her sex, she smiled a welcome to the respectable, learned, and independent bachelor. Mr. Gridley had a frosty but kindly age before him, with a score or so of years to run, which it was after all not strange to fancy might be rendered more cheerful by the companionship of a well-conserved and amiably disposed woman, — if any such should happen to fall in his way.

That smile came very near disconcerting the plot of Master Byles Gridley. He had come on an inquisitor's errand, his heart secure, as he thought, against all blandishments, his will steeled to break down all resistance. He had come armed with an instrument of torture worse than the thumb-screw, worse than the pulleys which attempt the miracle of adding a cubit to the stature, worse than the brazier of live coals brought close to the naked soles of the feet, — an instrument which, instead of trifling with the nerves, would clutch all the nerve-*centres* and the heart itself in its gripe, and hold them until it got its answer, if the white lips had life enough left to shape one. And here was this unfortunate maiden lady smiling at him, setting her limited attractions in their best light, pleading with him in that natural language which makes any contumacious bachelor feel as guilty as Cain before any single woman. If Mr. Gridley had been alone, he would have taken a good sniff at his own bottle of *sal volatile;* for his kind heart sunk within him as he thought of the errand upon which he had come. It would not do to leave the subject of his vivisection under any illusion as to the nature of his designs.

" Good evening, Miss Badlam," he said, " I have come to visit you on a matter of business."

What was the internal panorama which had unrolled tself at the instant of his entrance, and which rolled up as suddenly at the sound of his serious voice and the look of his grave features ? It cannot be reproduced, though pages were given to it; for some of the pictures were near, and some were distant; some were clearly seen, and some were only hinted; some were not recognized in the intellect at all, and yet they were implied, as it were, be-hind the others. Many times we have all found ourselves glad or sorry, and yet we could not tell what thought it was that reflected the sunbeam or cast the shadow. Look into Cynthia's suddenly exalted consciousness and see the picture, actual and potential, unroll itself in all its details of the natural, the ridiculous, the selfish, the pitiful, the human. Glimpses, hints, echoes, suggestions, involving tender sentiments hitherto unknown, we may suppose, to that unclaimed sister's breast, — pleasant excitement of receiving congratulations from suddenly cordial friends; the fussy delights of buying furniture and shopping for new dresses, — (it seemed as if she could hear herself saying, " *Heavy* silks, — *best* goods, if you please,") — with delectable thumping down of flat-sided pieces of calico, cambric, " rep," and other stuffs, and rhythmic evolution of measured yards, followed by sharp snip of scissors, and that cry of rending tissues dearer to woman's ear than any earthly sound until she hears the voice of her own first-born, — (much of this potentially, remember,) — thoughts of a comfortable settlement, an imposing social condition, a cheerful household, and by and by an Indian summer of serene widowhood, — all these, and infinite other involved possibilities had mapped themselves in one long swift flash before Cynthia's inward eye, and all vanished as the old man spoke those few words. The look on his face, and the tone of his cold speech, had instantly swept them all away, like a tea-set sliding in a single crash from a slippery tray.

What could be the "business" on which he had come to her with that solemn face? she asked herself, as she returned his greeting and offered him a chair. She was conscious of a slight tremor as she put this question to her own intelligence.

"Are we like to be alone and undisturbed?" Mr. Gridley asked. It was a strange question, — men do act strangely sometimes. She hardly knew whether to turn red or white.

"Yes, there is nobody like to come in at present," she answered. She did not know what to make of it. What was coming next, — a declaration, or an accusation of murder?

"My business," Mr. Gridley said, very gravely, "relates to this. I wish to inspect papers which I have reason to believe exist, and which have reference to the affairs of the late Malachi Withers. Can you help me to get sight of any of these papers not to be found at the Registry of Deeds or the Probate Office?"

"Excuse me, Mr. Gridley, but may I ask you what particular concern you have with the affairs of my relative, Cousin Malachi Withers. that's been dead and buried these half-dozen years?"

"Perhaps it would take some time to answer that question fully, Miss Badlam. Some of these affairs do concern those I am interested in, if not myself directly."

"May I ask who the person or persons may be on whose account you wish to look at papers belonging to my late relative, Malachi Withers?"

"You can ask me almost anything, Miss Badlam, but I should really be very much obliged if you would answer my question first. Can you help me to get a sight of any papers relating to the estate of Malachi Withers, not to be found at the Registry of Deeds or the Probate Office, — any of which you may happen to have any private and particular knowledge?"

"I beg your pardon, Mr. Gridley; but I don't understand why you come to me with such questions. Lawyer Penhallow is the proper person, I should think, to go to. He and his partner that was — Mr. Wibird, you know — settled the estate, and he has got the papers, I suppose, if there are any, that ain't to be found in the offices you mention."

Mr. Gridley moved his chair a little, so as to bring Miss Badlam's face a little more squarely in view.

"Does Mr. William Murray Bradshaw know anything about any papers, such as I am referring to, that may have been sent to the office?"

The lady felt a little moisture stealing through all her pores, and at the same time a certain dryness of the vocal organs, so that her answer came in a slightly altered tone which neither of them could help noticing.

"You had better ask Mr. William Murray Bradshaw yourself about that," she answered. She felt the hook now, and her spines were rising, partly with apprehension, partly with irritation.

"Has that young gentleman ever delivered into your hands any papers relating to the affairs of the late Malachi Withers, for your safe keeping?"

" What do you mean by asking me these questions, Mr. Gridley ? I don't choose to be catechised about Murray Bradshaw's business. Go to him, if you please, if you want to find out about it."

" Excuse my persistence, Miss Badlam, but I must prevail upon you to answer my question. Has Mr. William Murray Bradshaw ever delivered into your hands any papers relating to the affairs of the late Malachi Withers, for your safe keeping ? "

" Do you suppose I am going to answer such questions as you are putting me because you repeat them over, Mr. Gridley ? Indeed I sha'n't. Ask him, if you please, whatever you wish to know about his doings."

She drew herself up and looked savagely at him. She had talked herself into her courage. There was a color in her cheeks and a sparkle in her eye ; she looked dangerous as a cobra.

"Miss Cynthia Badlam," Master Gridley said, very deliberately, " I am afraid we do not entirely understand each other. You must answer my question precisely, categorically, point-blank, and on the instant. Will you do this at once, or will you compel me to show you the absolute necessity of your doing it, at the expense of pain to both of us ? Six words from me will make you answer all my questions."

" You can't say six words, nor sixty, Mr. Gridley, that will make me answer one question I do not choose to. I defy you ! "

" I will not *say* one, Miss Cynthia Badlam. There are some things one does not like to speak in words. But I will show you a scrap of paper, containing just six words and a date, — not one word more nor one less. You shall

read them. Then I will burn the paper in the flame of
your lamp As soon after that as you feel ready, I will
ask the same question again."

Master Gridley took out from his pocket-book a scrap
of paper, and handed it to Cynthia Badlam. Her hand
shook as she received it, for she was frightened as well as
enraged, and she saw that Mr. Gridley was in earnest and
knew what he was doing.

She read the six words, he looking at her steadily all the
time, and watching her as if he had just given her a drop
of prussic acid.

No cry. No sound from her lips. She stared as if half
stunned for one moment, then turned her head and glared
at Mr. Gridley as if she would have murdered him if she
dared.   In another instant her face whitened, the scrap of
paper fluttered to the floor, and she would have followed it
but for the support of both Mr. Gridley's arms. He dis-
engaged one of them presently, and felt in his pocket for
the *sal volatile*. It served him excellently well, and stung
her back again to her senses very quickly. All her defiant
aspect had gone.

"Look!" he said, as he lighted the scrap of paper in
the flame. "You understand me, and you see that I must
be answered the next time I ask my question."

She opened her lips as if to speak. It was as when a
bell is rung in a vacuum, — no words came from them, —
only a faint gasping sound, an effort at speech. She was
caught tight in the heart-screw.

"Don't hurry yourself, Miss Cynthia," he said, with
a certain relenting tenderness of manner. "Here, take
another sniff of the smelling-salts. Be calm, be quiet, — I
am well disposed towards you, — I don't like to give you

trouble. There, now, I must have the answer to that question; but take your time, — take your time."

" Give me some water, — some water!" she said, in a strange hoarse whisper. There was a pitcher of water and a tumbler on an old marble sideboard near by. He filled the tumbler, and Cynthia emptied it as if she had just been taken from the rack, and could have swallowed a bucketful.

" What do you want to know?" she asked.

" I wish to know all that you can tell me about a certain paper, or certain papers, which I have reason to believe Mr. William Murray Bradshaw committed to your keeping."

" There is only one paper of any consequence. Do you want to make him kill me? or do you want to make me kill myself?"

" Neither, Miss Cynthia, neither. I wish to see that paper, but not for any bad purpose. Don't you think, on the whole, you have pretty good reason to trust me? I am a very quiet man, Miss Cynthia. Don't be afraid of me; only do what I ask, — it will be a great deal better for you in the end."

She thrust her trembling hand into her pocket, and took out the key of the little trunk. She drew the trunk towards her, put the key in the lock, and opened it. It seemed like pressing a knife into her own bosom and turning the blade. That little trunk held all the records of her life the forlorn spinster most cherished; — a few letters that came nearer to love-letters than any others she had ever received; an album, with flowers of the summers of 1840 and 1841 fading between its leaves; two papers containing locks of hair, half of a broken ring, and other insig-

15 *

nificant mementos which had their meaning, doubtless, .o her, — such a collection as is often priceless to one human heart, and passed by as worthless in the auctioneer's inven- tory. She took the papers out mechanically, and laid them on the table. Among them was an oblong packet, sealed with what appeared to be the office-seal of Messrs. Penhallow and Bradshaw.

"Will you allow me to take that envelope containing papers, Miss Badlam?" Mr. Gridley asked, with a suavity and courtesy in his tone and manner that showed how he felt for her sex and her helpless position.

She seemed to obey his will as if she had none of her own left. She passed the envelope to him, and stared at him vacantly while he examined it. He read on the back of the package: "*Withers Estate* — old papers — of no importance apparently. Examine hereafter."

"May I ask when, where, and of whom you obtained these papers, Miss Badlam?"

"Have pity on me, Mr. Gridley, — have pity on me. I am a lost woman if you do not. Spare me! for God's sake, spare me! There will no wrong come of all this, if you will but wait a little while. The paper will come to light when it is wanted, and all will be right. But do not make me answer any more questions, and let me keep this paper. O Mr. Gridley! I am in the power of a dreadful man —"

"You mean Mr. William Murray Bradshaw?"

"I mean him."

"Has there not been some understanding between you that he should become the approved suitor of Miss Myrtle Hazard?"

Cynthia wrung her hands and rocked herself backward

and forward in her misery, but answered not a word. What *could* she answer, if she had plotted with this " dreadful man " against a young and innocent girl, to deliver her over into his hands, at the risk of all her earthly hopes and happiness ?

Master Gridley waited long and patiently for any answer she might have the force to make. As she made none, he took upon himself to settle the whole matter without further torture of his helpless victim.

" This package must go into the hands of the parties who had the settlement of the estate of the late Malachi Withers. Mr. Penhallow is the survivor of the two gentlemen to whom that business was intrusted. How long is Mr. William Murray Bradshaw like to be away ? "

" Perhaps a few days, — perhaps weeks, — and then he will come back and kill me, — or — or — worse ! Don't take that paper, Mr. Gridley, — he is n't like you ! you would n't — but he would — he would send me to everlasting misery to gain his own end, or to save himself. And yet he is n't every way bad, and if he did marry Myrtle she 'd think there never was such a man, — for he can talk her heart out of her, and the wicked in him lies very deep and won't ever come out, perhaps, if the world goes right with him." The last part of this sentence showed how Cynthia talked with her own conscience ; all her mental and moral machinery lay open before the calm eyes of Master Byles Gridley.

His thoughts wandered a moment from the business before him ; he had just got a new study of human nature, which in spite of himself would be shaping itself into an axiom for an imagined new edition of " Thoughts on the Universe," — something like this, — *The greatest saint may be a sinner that never got down to "hard pan."* I was not the time to be framing axioms.

"Poh! poh!" he said to himself; "what are you about, making phrases, when you have got a piece of work like this in hand?" Then to Cynthia, with great gentleness and kindness of manner: "Have no fear about any consequences to yourself. Mr. Penhallow must see that paper — I mean those papers. You shall not be a loser nor a sufferer if you do your duty now in these premises."

Master Gridley, treating her, as far as circumstances permitted, like a gentleman, had shown no intention of taking the papers either stealthily or violently. It must be with her consent. He had laid the package down upon the table, waiting for her to give him leave to take it. But just as he spoke these last words, Cynthia, whose eye had been glancing furtively at it while he was thinking out his axiom, and taking her bearings to it pretty carefully, stretched her hand out, and, seizing the package, thrust it into the sanctuary of her bosom.

"Mr. Penhallow must see those papers, Miss Cynthia Badlam," Mr. Gridley repeated calmly. "If he says they or any of them can be returned to your keeping, well and good. But see them he must, for they have his office seal and belong in his custody, and, as you see by the writing on the back, they have not been examined. Now there may be something among them which is of immediate importance to the relatives of the late deceased Malachi Withers, and therefore they must be forthwith submitted to the inspection of the surviving partner of the firm of Wibird and Penhallow. This I propose to do, with your consent, this evening. It is now twenty-five minutes past eight by the true time, as my watch has it. At half pas·

eight exactly I shall have the honor of bidding you good evening, Miss Cynthia Badlam, whether you give me those papers or not. I shall go to the office of Jacob Penhallow, Esquire, and there make one of two communications to him ; to wit, these papers and the facts connected there, with, or another statement, the nature of which you may perhaps conjecture."

There is no need of our speculating as to what Mr. Byles Gridley, an honorable and humane man, would have done, or what would have been the nature of that communication which he offered as an alternative to the perplexed woman. He had not at any rate miscalculated the strength of his appeal, which Cynthia interpreted as he expected. She bore the heart-screw about two minutes. Then she took the package from her bosom, and gave it with averted face to Master Byles Gridley, who, on receiving it, made her a formal but not unkindly bow, and bade her good evening.

" One would think it had been lying out in the dew," he said, as he left the house and walked towards Mr Penhallow's residence.

CHAPTER XXXI.

MASTER BYLES GRIDLEY CONSULTS WITH JACOB PEN-
HALLOW, ESQUIRE.

LAWYER PENHALLOW was seated in his study
his day's work over, his feet in slippers, after the
comfortable but inelegant fashion which Sir Walter Scott
reprobates, amusing himself with a volume of old Reports
He was a knowing man enough, a keen country lawyer
but honest, and therefore less ready to suspect the honesty
of others. He had a great belief in his young partner's
ability, and, though he knew him to be astute, did not think
him capable of roguery.

It was at his request that Mr. Bradshaw had undertaken his journey, which, as he believed, — and as Mr
Bradshaw had still stronger evidence of a strictly confidential nature which led him to feel sure, — would end in the
final settlement of the great land claim in favor of their
client. The case had been dragging along from year to
year, like an English chancery suit; and while courts and
lawyers and witnesses had been sleeping, the property had
been steadily growing. A railroad had passed close to
one margin of the township, some mines had been opened
in the county, in which a village calling itself a city had
grown big enough to have a newspaper and Fourth of July
orations. It was plain that the successful issue of the long
process would make the heirs of the late Malachi Withers
possessors of an ample fortune, and it was also plain that
the firm of Penhallow and Bradshaw were like to receive

in such case, the largest fee that had gladdened the professional existence of its members.

Mr. Penhallow had his book open before him, but his
thoughts were wandering from the page. He was thinking of his absent partner, and the probable results of his
expedition. What would be the consequence if all this
property came into the possession of Silence Withers?
Could she have any liberal intentions with reference to
Myrtle Hazard, the young girl who had grown up with
her, or was the common impression true, that she was bent
on endowing an institution, and thus securing for herself a
favorable consideration in the higher courts, where her
beneficiaries would be, it might be supposed, influential ad-
vocates? He could not help thinking that Mr. Bradshaw
believed that Myrtle Hazard would eventually come to a
part at least of this inheritance. For the story was, that
he was paying his court to the young lady whenever he
got an opportunity, and that he was cultivating an intimacy
with Miss Cynthia Badlam. "Bradshaw would n't make
a move in that direction," Mr. Penhallow said to himself,
"until he felt pretty sure that it was going to be a paying
business. If he was only a young minister now, there 'd
be no difficulty about it. Let any man, young or old, in a
clerical white cravat, step up to Myrtle Hazard, and ask
her to be miserable in his company through this wretched
life, and Aunt Silence would very likely give them her
blessing, and add something to it that the man in the
white cravat would think worth even more than that was.
But I don't know what she 'll say to Bradshaw. Perhaps he 'd better have a hint to go to meeting a little more
regularly. However, I suppose he knows what he 's
about."

He was thinking all this over when a visitor was announced, and Mr. Byles Gridley entered the study.

"Good evening, Mr. Penhallow," Mr. Gridley said, wiping his forehead. "Quite warm, is n't it, this evening?"

"Warm!" said Mr. Penhallow, "I should think it would freeze pretty thick to-night. I should have asked you to come up to the fire and warm yourself. But take off your coat, Mr. Gridley, — very glad to see you. You don't come to the house half as often as you come to the office. Sit down, sit down."

Mr. Gridley took off his outside coat and sat down. "He does look warm, does n't he?" Mr. Penhallow thought. "Wonder what has heated up the old gentleman so. Find out quick enough, for he always goes straight to business."

"Mr. Penhallow," Mr. Gridley began at once, "I have come on a very grave matter, in which you are interested as well as myself, and I wish to lay the whole of it before you as explicitly as I can, so that we may settle this night before I go what is to be done. I am afraid the good standing of your partner, Mr. William Murray Bradshaw, is concerned in the matter. Would it be a surprise to you, if he had carried his acuteness in some particular case like the one I am to mention beyond the prescribed limits?"

The question was put so diplomatically that there was no chance for an indignant denial of the possibility of Mr. Bradshaw's being involved in any discreditable transaction.

"It is possible," he answered, "that Bradshaw's keen wits may have betrayed him into sharper practice than I should altogether approve in any business we carried on together. He is a very knowing young man, but I can't think he is foolish enough, to say nothing of his honesty to make any false step of the kind you seem to hint. I think he might on occasion go pretty near the line, but I don't believe he would cross it."

"Permit me a few questions, Mr. Penhallow. You se.-tled the estate of the late Malachi Withers, did you not?

"Mr. Wibird and myself settled it together."

"Have you received any papers from any of the family since the settlement of the estate? '

"Let me see. Yes; a roll of old plans of the Withers Place, and so forth, — not of much use, but labelled and kept. An old trunk with letters and account-books, some of them in Dutch, — mere curiosities. A year ago or more, I remember that Silence sent me over some papers she had found in an odd corner, — the old man hid things like a magpie. I looked over most of them, — trumpery not worth keeping, — old leases and so forth."

"Do you recollect giving some of them to Mr. Bradshaw to look over?"

"Now I come to think of it, I believe I did; but he reported to me, if I remember right, that they amounted to nothing."

"If any of those papers were of importance, should you think your junior partner ought to keep them from your knowledge?"

"I need not answer that question, Mr. Gridley. Will you be so good as to come at once to the facts on which you found your suspicions, and which lead you to put these questions to me?"

Thereupon Mr. Gridley proceeded to state succinctly the singular behavior of Murray Bradshaw in taking one paper from a number handed to him by Mr. Penhallow and concealing it in a volume. He related how he was jus'

w

on the point of taking out the volume which contained the paper, when Mr. Bradshaw entered and disconcerted him. He had, however, noticed three spots on the paper by which he should know it anywhere. He then repeated the substance of Kitty Fagan's story, accenting the fact that she too noticed three remarkable spots on the paper which Mr. Bradshaw had pointed out to Miss Badlam as the one so important to both of them. Here he rested the case for the moment.

Mr. Penhallow looked thoughtful. There was something questionable in the aspect of this business. It did obviously suggest the idea of an underhand arrangement with Miss Cynthia, possibly involving some very grave consequences. It would have been most desirable, he said, to have ascertained what these papers, or rather this particular paper, to which so much importance was attached, amounted to. Without that knowledge there was nothing, after all, which it might not be possible to explain. He might have laid aside the spotted paper to examine for some object of mere curiosity. It was certainly odd that the one the Fagan woman had seen should present three spots so like those on the other paper, but people did sometimes throw *treys* at backgammon, and that which not rarely happened with two dice of six faces *might* happen if they had sixty or six hundred faces. On the whole, he did not see that there was any ground, so far, for anything more than a vague suspicion. He thought it not unlikely that Mr. Bradshaw was a little smitten with the young lady up at The Poplars, and that he had made some diplomatic overtures to the duenna, after the approved method of suitors. She was young for Bradshaw, — very young, — but he knew his own affairs. If he chose to make love to a

child, it was natural enough that he should begin by court-
ing her nurse.

Master Byles Gridley lost himself for half a minute in
a most discreditable inward discussion as to whether Laura
Penhallow was probably one or two years older than Mr.
Bradshaw. That was his way, — he could not help it. He
could not think of anything without these mental paren-
theses. But he came back to business at the end of his
half-minute.

"I can lay the package before you at this moment, Mr.
Penhallow. I have induced that woman in whose charge
it was left to intrust it to my keeping, with the express intention of showing it to you. But it is protected by a seal,
as I have told you, which I should on no account presume
to meddle with."

Mr. Gridley took out the package of papers.

"How damp it is!" Mr. Penhallow said; "must have
been lying in some very moist neighborhood."

"Very," Mr. Gridley answered, with a peculiar expression which said, "Never mind about that."

"Did the party give you possession of these documents
without making any effort to retain them?" the lawyer
asked.

"Not precisely. It cost some effort to induce Miss Badlam to let them go out of her hands. I hope you think I
was justified in making the effort I did, not without a considerable strain upon my feelings, as well as her own, to get
hold of the papers?"

"That will depend something on what the papers prove
to be, Mr. Gridley. A man takes a certain responsibility
in doing just what you have done. If, for instance, it
should prove that this envelope contained matters relating

solely to private transactions between Mr. Bradshaw and Miss Badlam, concerning no one but themselves, — and if the words on the back of the envelope and the seal had been put there merely as a protection for a package containing private papers of a delicate but perfectly legitimate character — "

The lawyer paused, as careful experts do, after bending the bow of an hypothesis, before letting the arrow go. Mr. Gridley felt very warm indeed, uncomfortably so, and applied his handkerchief to his face. Could n't be anything in such a violent supposition as that, — and yet such a crafty fellow as that Bradshaw, — what trick was he not up to? Absurd! Cynthia was not acting, — Rachel would n't be equal to such a performance! — " why then, Mr. Gridley," the lawyer continued, " I don't see but what my partner would have you at an advantage, and, if disposed to make you uncomfortable, could do so pretty effectively. But this, you understand, is only a supposed case, and not a very likely one. I don't think it would have been prudent in you to meddle with that seal. But it is a very different matter with regard to myself. It makes no difference, so far as I am concerned, where this package came from, or how it was obtained. It is just as absolutely within my control as any piece of property I call my own. should not hesitate, if I saw fit, to break this seal at once, and proceed to the examination of any papers contained within the envelope. If I found any paper of the slightest importance relating to the estate, I should act as if it had never been out of my possession.

" Suppose, however, I chose to know what was in the package, and, having ascertained, act my judgment about returning it to the party from whom you obtained it. In such case I might see fit to restore, or cause it to be restored, to the party, without any marks of violence having been used being apparent.   If everything is not right, probably no questions would be asked by the party having charge of the package.   If there is no underhand work going on, and the papers are what they profess to be, nobody is compromised but yourself, so far as I can see, and you are compromised at any rate, Mr. Gridley, at least in the good graces of the party from whom you obtained the documents.   Tell that party that I took the package without opening it, and shall return it, very likely, without breaking the seal.   Will consider of the matter, say a couple of days.   Then you shall hear from me, and she shall hear from you.   So.   So.   Yes, that's it.   A nice business. A thing to sleep on.   You had better leave the whole matter of dealing with the package to me.   If I see fit to send it back with the seal unbroken, that is my affair.   But keep perfectly quiet, if you please, Mr. Gridley, about the whole matter.   Mr. Bradshaw is off, as you know, and the business on which he is gone is important, — very important.   He can be depended on for that ; he has acted all along as if he had a personal interest in the success of our firm beyond his legal relation to it."

Mr. Penhallow's light burned very late in the office that night, and the following one.   He looked troubled and absent-minded, and, when Miss Laura ventured to ask him how long Mr. Bradshaw was like to be gone, answered her in such a way that the girl who waited at table concluded that he did n t mean to have Miss Laury keep company with Mr. Bradshaw, or he 'd never have spoke so dreadful hash to her when she ahst about him.

CHAPTER XXXII.

SUSAN POSEY'S TRIAL.

A DAY or two after Myrtle Hazard returned to the village, Master Byles Gridley, accompanied by Gifted Hopkins, followed her, as has been already mentioned, to the same scene of the principal events of this narrative. The young man had been persuaded that it would be doing injustice to his talents to crowd their fruit prematurely upon the market. He carried his manuscript back with him, having relinquished the idea of publishing for the present. Master Byles Gridley, on the other hand, had in his pocket a very flattering proposal from the same pub lisher to whom he had introduced the young poet, for a new and revised edition of his work, "Thoughts on the Universe," which was to be remodelled in some respects, and to have a new title not quite so formidable to the average reader.

It would be hardly fair to Susan Posey to describe with what delight and innocent enthusiasm she welcomed back Gifted Hopkins. She had been so lonely since he was away! She had read such of his poems as she possessed — duplicates of his printed ones, or autographs which he had kindly written out for her — over and over again, not without the sweet tribute of feminine sensibility, which is the most precious of all testimonials to a poet's power over the heart. True, her love belonged to another, — but then she was so used to Gifted! She did so love to hear him read his poems, — and Clement had never written tha' "little bit of a poem to Susie," which she had asked him for so long ago! She received him therefore with open arms, — not literally, of course, which would have been a breach of duty and propriety, but in a figurative sense, which it is hoped no reader will interpret to her discredit.

The young poet was in need of consolation. It is true that he had seen many remarkable sights during his visit to the city; that he had got "smarted up," as his mother called it, a good deal; that he had been to Mrs. Clyme Ketchum's party, where he had looked upon life in all its splendors; and that he brought back many interesting experiences, which would serve to enliven his conversation for a long time. But he had failed in the great enterprise he had undertaken. He was forced to confess to his revered parent, and his esteemed friend Susan Posey, that his genius, which was freely acknowledged, was not thought to be quite ripe as yet. He told the young lady some particulars of his visit to the publisher, how he had listened with great interest to one of his poems, — " The Triumph of Song," — how he had treated him with marked and flattering attention; but that he advised him not to risk anything prematurely, giving him the hope that *by and by* he would be admitted into that series of illustrious authors which it was the publisher's privilege to present to the reading public. In short, he was advised not to print. That was the net total of the matter, and it was a pang to the susceptible heart of the poet. He had hoped to have ome home enriched by the sale of his copyright, and with he prospect of seeing his name before long on the back of a handsome volume.

Gifted's mother did all in her power to console him in his disappointment. There was plenty of jealous people always that wanted to keep young folks from rising in the world. Never mind, she did n't believe but what Gifted could make jest as good verses as any of them that they kept such a talk about. She had a fear that he might pine away in consequence of the mental excitement he had gone through, and solicited his appetite with her choicest appliances, — of which he partook in a measure which showed that there was no immediate cause of alarm.

But Susan Posey was more than a consoler, — she was an angel to him in this time of his disappointment. " Read me all the poems over again," she said, — " it is almost the only pleasure I have left, to hear you read your beautiful verses." Clement Lindsay had not written to Susan quite so often of late as at some former periods of the history of their love. Perhaps it was that which had made her look paler than usual for some little time. Something was evidently preying on her. Her only delight seemed to be in listening to Gifted as he read, sometimes with fine declamatory emphasis, sometimes in low, tremulous tones, the various poems enshrined in his manuscript. At other times she was sad, and more than once Mrs. Hopkins had seen a tear steal down her innocent cheek, when there seemed to be no special cause for grief. She ventured to speak of it to Master Byles Gridley.

" Our Susan 's in trouble, Mr. Gridley, for some reason or other that 's unbeknown to me, and I can't help wishing you could jest have a few words with her. You 're a kind of a grandfather, you know, to all the young folks, and they 'd tell you pretty much everything about themselves I calc'late she is n't at ease in her mind about somethin' or other, and I kind o' think, Mr. Gridley, you could coax it out of her."

"Was there ever anything like it?" said Master Byles Gridley to himself. "I shall have all the young folks in Oxbow Village to take care of at this rate! Susan Posey in trouble, too! Well, well, well, it's easier to get a birchbark canoe off the shallows than a big ship off the rocks. Susan Posey's trouble will be come at easily enough; but Myrtle Hazard floats in deeper water. We must make Susan Posey tell her own story, or let her tell it, for it will all come out of itself."

"I am going to dust the books in the open shelves this morning. I wonder if Miss Susan Posey would n't like to help for half an hour or so," Master Gridley remarked at the breakfast-table.

The amiable girl's very pleasant countenance lighted up at the thought of obliging the old man who had been so kind to her and so liberal to her friend, the poet. She would be delighted to help him; she would dust them all for him, if he wanted her to. No, Master Gridley said, he always wanted to have a hand in it; and, besides, such a little body as she was could not lift those great folios out of the lower shelves without overstraining herself; she might handle the musketry and the light artillery, but he must deal with the heavy guns himself. "As low down as the octavos, Susan Posey, you shall govern; below that, the Salic law."

Susan did not know much about the Salic law; but she knew he meant that he would dust the big books and she would attend to the little ones.

A very young and a very pretty girl is sometimes quite charming in a costume which thinks of nothing less than of being attractive. Susan appeared after breakfast in the

16

study, her head bound with a kerchief of bright pattern, a little jacket she had outgrown buttoned, in spite of opposition, close about her up to the throat, round which a white handkerchief was loosely tied, and a pair of old gauntlets protecting her hands, so that she suggested something between a gypsy, a jaunty *soubrette,* and the *fille du regiment.*

Master Gridley took out a great volume from the lower shelf, — a folio in massive oaken covers with clasps like prison hinges, bearing the stately colophon, white on a ground of vermilion, of Nicholas Jenson and his associates. He opened the volume, — paused over its blue and scarlet initial letter, — he turned page after page, admiring its brilliant characters, its broad, white marginal rivers, and the narrower white creek that separated the black-typed twin-columns, — he turned back to the beginning and read the commendatory paragraph, *"Nam ipsorum omnia fulgent tum correctione dignissima, tum cura imprimendo splendida ac miranda,"* and began reading, *"Incipit proemium super apparatum decretalium . . . . ."* when it suddenly occurred to him that this was not exactly doing what he had undertaken to do, and he began whisking an ancient bandanna about the ears of the venerable volume. All this time Miss Susan Posey was catching the little books 'by the small of their backs, pulling them out, opening them, and clapping them together, 'p-'p-'p! 'p-'p-'p! and carefully caressing all their edges with a regular professional dusting-cloth, so persuasively that they yielded up every particle that a year had drifted upon them, and came forth refreshed and rejuvenated. This process went on for a while, until Susan had worked down among the octavos, and Master Gridley had worked up among the quartos. He had got hold of Calmet's Dictionary, and was caught by the article Solomon, so that he forgot his occupation again. All at once it struck him that everything was very silent, — the 'p-'p-'p! of clapping the books had ceased, and the light rustle of Susan's dress was no longer heard. He looked up and saw her standing perfectly still, with a book in one hand and her duster in the other. She was lost in thought, and by the shadow on her face and the glistening of her blue eyes he knew it was her hidden sorrow that had just come back to her. Master Gridley shut up his book, leaving Solomon to his fate, like the worthy Benedictine he was reading, without discussing the question whether he was saved or not.

"Susan Posey, child, what is your trouble?"

Poor Susan was in the state of unstable equilibrium which the least touch upsets, and fell to crying. It took her some time to get down the waves of emotion so that speech would live upon them. At last it ventured out, — showing at intervals, like the boat rising on the billow, sinking into the hollow, and climbing again into notice.

"O Mr. Grid—ley — I can't — I can't — tell you or — any—body — what's the mat—mat—matter. — My heart will br—br—break."

"No, no, no, child," said Mr. Gridley, sympathetically stirred a little himself by the sight of Susan in tears and sobbing and catching her breath, "that must n't be, Susan Posey. Come off the steps, Susan Posey, and stop dusting the books, — I can finish them, — and tell me all about your troubles. I will try to help you out of them, and I have begun to think I know how to help young people pretty well. I have had some experience at it."

But Susan cried and sobbed all the more uncontrollably and convulsively. Master Gridley thought he had better

lead her at once to what he felt pretty sure was the source
of her grief, and that, when she had had her cry out, she
would probably make the hole in the ice he had broken big
enough in a very few minutes.

"I think something has gone wrong between you and
your friend, the young gentleman with whom you are in
intimate relations, my child, and I think you had better
talk freely with me, for I can perhaps give you a little
counsel that will be of service."

Susan cried herself quiet at last. "There's nobody in
the world like you, Mr. Gridley," she said, "and I've been
wanting to tell you something ever so long. My friend —
Mr. Clem — Clement Lindsay does n't care for me as he
used to, — I know he does n't. He has n't written to me
for — I don't know but it 's a month. And O Mr. Gridley !
he 's such a great man, and I am such a simple person, —
I can't help thinking — he would be happier with somebody else than poor little Susan Posey ! "

This last touch of self-pity overcame her, as it is so apt
to do those who indulge in that delightful misery, and she
broke up badly, as a horse-fancier would say, so that it
was some little time before she recovered her conversational road-gait.

"O Mr. Gridley," she began again, at length, "if I only
dared to tell him what I think, — that perhaps it would be
happier for us both — if we could forget each other !
Ought I not to tell him so? *Don't* you think he would
find another to make him happy? *Would n't* he forgive
me for telling him he was free? *Were* we not too young
to know each other's hearts when we promised each other
that we would love as long as we lived? *Sha'n't* I write
him a letter this very day and tell him all? *Do* you think

ıt would be wrong in me to do it? O Mr. Gridley, it makes me almost crazy to think about it. Clement must be free! I cannot, cannot hold him to a promise he does n't want to keep."

There were so many questions in this eloquent rhapsody of Susan's that they neutralized each other, as one might say, and Master Gridley had time for reflection. His thoughts went on something in this way: —

"Pretty clear case! Guess Mr. Clement can make up his mind to it. Put it well, did n't she? Not a word about our little Gifted! That's the trouble. Poets! how they do bewitch these school-girls! And having a chance every day, too, how could you expect her to stand it?" Then aloud: "Susan Posey, you are a good, honest little girl as ever was. I think you and Clement *were* too hasty in coming together for life before you knew what life meant. I think if you write Clement a letter, telling him that you cannot help fearing that you two are not perfectly adapted to each other, on account of certain differences for which neither of you is responsible, and that you propose that each should release the other from the pledge given so long ago, — in that case, I say, I believe he will think no worse of you for so doing, and may perhaps agree that it is best for both of you to seek your happiness elsewhere than in each other."

The book-dusting came to as abrupt a close as the reading of Lancelot. Susan went straight to her room, dried her tears so as to write in a fair hand, but had to stop every few lines and take a turn at the "dust-layers," as Mrs. Clymer Ketchum's friend used to call the fountains of sensibility. It would seem like betraying Susan's confidence to reveal the contents of this letter, but the reader may be assured that it was simple and sincere and very sweetly written, without the slightest allusion to any other young man, whether of the poetical or cheaper human varieties.

It was not long before Susan received a reply from Clement Lindsay. It was as kind and generous and noble as she could have asked. It was affectionate, as a very amiable brother's letter might be, and candidly appreciative of the reasons Susan had assigned for her proposal. He gave her back her freedom, — not that he should cease to feel an interest in her, always. He accepted his own release, not that he would ever think she could be indifferent to his future fortunes. And within a very brief period of time after sending his answer to Susan Posey, whether he wished to see her in person, or whether he had some other motive, he had packed his trunk, and made his excuses for an absence of uncertain length at the studio, and was on his way to Oxbow Village.

CHAPTER XXXIII.

JUST AS YOU EXPECTED.

THE spring of 1861 had now arrived, — that eventful spring which was to lift the curtain and show the first scene of the first act in the mighty drama which fixed the eyes of mankind during four bloody years. The little schemes of little people were going on in all our cities and villages without thought of the fearful convulsion which was soon coming to shatter the hopes and cloud the prospects of millions. Our little Oxbow Village, which held itself by no means the least of human centres, was the scene of its own commotions, as intense and exciting to those concerned as if the destiny of the nation had been involved in them.

Mr. Clement Lindsay appeared suddenly in that important locality, and repaired to his accustomed quarters at the house of Deacon Rumrill. That worthy person received him with a certain gravity of manner, caused by his recollection of the involuntary transgression into which Mr. Lindsay had led him by his present of Ivanhoe. He was, on the whole, glad to see him, for his finances were not yet wholly recovered from the injury inflicted on them by the devouring element. But he could not forget that his boarder had betrayed him into a breach of the fourth commandment, and that the strict eyes of his clergyman had detected him in the very commission of the offence. He had no sooner seen Mr. Clement comfortably installed, therefore, than he presented himself at the door of his chamber with the book, enveloped in strong paper and very securely tied round with a stout string.

"Here is your vollum, Mr. Lindsay," the Deacon said. "I understand it is not the work of that great and good mahn who I thought wrote it. I did not see anything immoral in it as fur as I read, but it belongs to what I consider a very dangerous class of publications. These novels and rómances are awfully destructive to our youth. I should recommend you, as a young man of principle, to burn the vollum. At least I hope you will not leave it about anywhere unless it is carefully tied up. I have written upon the paper round it to warn off all the young persons of my household from meddling with it."

True enough, Mr. Clement saw in strong black letters on the back of the paper wrapping his unfortunate Ivan-hoe, —

"DANGEROUS READING FOR CHRISTIAN YOUTH.

"TOUCH NOT THE UNCLEAN THING."

"I thought you said you had Scott's picture hung up in your parlor, Deacon Rumrill," he said, a little amused with the worthy man's fear and precautions.

"It is *the great* Scott's likeness that I have in my parlor," he said; "I will show it to you if you will come with me."

Mr. Clement followed the Deacon into that sacred apartment.

"That is the portrait of the great Scott," he said, pointing to an engraving of a heavy-looking person whose phrenological developments were a somewhat striking contrast to those of the distinguished Sir Walter.

"I will take good care that none of your young people

see this volume," Mr. Clement said ; " I trust you read it yourself, however, and found something to please you in it. I am sure you are safe from being harmed by any such book. Did n't you have to finish it, Deacon, after you had once begun ? "

" Well, I — I — perused a consid'able portion of the work," the Deacon answered, in a way that led Mr. Clement to think he had not stopped much short of *Finis.* " Anything new in the city ? "

" Nothing except what you 've all had, — Confederate States establishing an army and all that, — not very new either. What has been going on here lately, Deacon ? "

" Well, Mr. Lindsay, not a great deal. My new barn is pretty nigh done. I 've got as fine a litter of pigs as ever you see. I don't know whether you 're a judge of pigs or no. The Hazard gal 's come back, spilt, pooty much, I guess. Been to one o' them fashionable schools, — I 've heerd that she 's learnt to dance. I 've heerd say that that Hopkins boy 's round the Posey gal, — come to think, she 's the one you went with some when you was here, — I 'm gettin' kind o' forgetful. Old Doctor Hurlbut 's pretty low, — ninety-four year old, — born in '67, — folks ain't ginerally very spry after they 're ninety, but he held out wonderful."

" How 's Mr. Bradshaw ? "

" Well, the young squire, he 's off travellin' somewhere in the West, or to Washin'ton, or somewhere else, — I don't jestly know where. They say that he 's follerin' up the courts in the business about old Malachi's estate. I don' know much about it."

The news got round Oxbow Village very speedily that

Mr. Clement Lindsay, generally considered the accepted lover of Miss Susan Posey, had arrived in that place. Now it had come to be the common talk of the village that young Gifted Hopkins and Susan Posey were getting to be mighty thick with each other, and the prevailing idea was that Clement's visit had reference to that state of affairs. Some said that Susan had given her young man the mitten, meaning thereby that she had signified that his services as a suitor were dispensed with. Others thought there was only a wavering in her affection for her lover, and that he feared for her constancy, and had come to vindicate his rights.

Some of the young fellows, who were doubtless envious of Gifted's popularity with the fair sex, attempted in the most unjustifiable manner to play upon his susceptible nature. One of them informed him that he had seen that Lindsay fellah raound taown with the darndest big stick y' ever did see. Looked kind o' savage and wild like. Another one told him that perhaps he 'd better keep a little shady ; that are chap that had got the mittin was vraowlin' abaout with a pistil,— one o' them Darringers, — abaout as long as your thumb, an' 'll fire a bullet as big as a p'tatah-ball, — a fellah carries one in his breeches-pocket, an' shoots y' right threugh his own pahnts, withaout ever takin' on it aout of his pocket. The stable-keeper, who, it may be remembered, once exchanged a few playful words with Mr. Gridley, got a hint from some of these unfeeling young men, and offered the resources of his stable to the youth supposed to be in peril.

" I 've got a faäst colt, Mr. Hopkins, that 'll put twenty mild betwixt you an' this here village, as quick as any four huffs 'll dew it in this here caounty, if you *should* want

to get away suddin. I 've heern tell there was some lookin'
raound here that would n't be wholesome to meet, — jest
say the word, Mr. Hopkins, an' I 'll have ye on that are
colt's back in less than no time, an' start ye off full jump.
There 's a good many that 's kind o' worried for fear
something might happen to ye, Mr. Hopkins, — y' see fel-
lahs don't like to have other chaps cuttin' on 'em aout with
their gals."

Gifted Hopkins had become excessively nervous by this
time. It is true that everything in his intimacy with
Susan Posey, so far, might come under the general head of
friendship; but he was conscious that something more
was in both their thoughts. Susan had given him mysterious hints that her relations with Clement had undergone
a change, but had never had quite courage enough, perhaps had too much delicacy, to reveal the whole truth.

Gifted was walking home, deeply immersed in thoughts
excited by the hints which had been thus wantonly thrown
out to inflame his imagination, when all at once, on lifting
his eyes, he saw Clement Lindsay coming straight towards
him. Gifted was unarmed, except with a pair of blunt
scissors, which he carried habitually in his pocket. What
should he do? Should he fly? But he was never a good
runner, being apt to find himself scant o' breath, like Hamlet, after violent exercise. His demeanor on the occasion
did credit to his sense of his own virtuous conduct and his
self-possession. He put his hand out, while yet at a considerable distance, and marched up towards Clement, smiling with all the native amiability which belonged to him.

To his infinite relief, Clement put out *his* hand to grasp
the one offered him, and greeted the young poet in the
most frank and cordial manner.

"And how is Miss Susan Posey, Mr. Hopkins?" asked Clement, in the most cheerful tone. "It is a long while since I have seen her, and you must tell her that I hope I shall not leave the village without finding time to call upon her. She and I are good friends always, Mr. Hopkins, though perhaps I shall not be quite so often at your mother's as I was during my last visit to Oxbow Village."

Gifted felt somewhat as the subject of one of those old-fashioned forms of argument, formerly much employed to convince men of error in matters of religion, must have felt when the official who superintended the stretching-machine said, "Slack up!"

He told Mr. Clement all about Susan, and was on the point of saying that if he, Mr. Clement, did not claim any engrossing interest in her, he, Gifted, was ready to offer her the devotion of a poet's heart. Mr. Clement, however, had so many other questions to ask him about everybody in the village, more particularly concerning certain young persons in whom he seemed to be specially interested, that there was no chance to work in his own revelations of sentiment.

Clement Lindsay had come to Oxbow Village with a single purpose. He could now venture to trust himself in the presence of Myrtle Hazard. He was free, and he knew nothing to show that she had lost the liberty of disposing of her heart. But after an experience such as he had gone through, he was naturally distrustful of himself, and inclined to be cautious and reserved in yielding to a new passion. Should he tell her the true relations in which they stood to each other, — that she owed her life to him, and that he had very nearly sacrificed his own in saving hers? Why not? He had a claim on her grati tude for what he had done in her behalf, and out of this gratitude there might naturally spring a warmer feeling.

No, he could not try to win her affections by showing that he had paid for them beforehand. She seemed to be utterly unconscious of the fact that it was he who had been with her in the abyss of waters. If the thought came to her of itself, and she ever asked him, it would be time enough to tell her the story. If not, the moment might arrive when he could reveal to her the truth that he was her deliverer, without accusing himself of bribing her woman's heart to reward him for his services. He would wait for that moment.

It was the most natural thing in the world that Mr. Lindsay, a young gentleman from the city, should call to see Miss Hazard, a young lady whom he had met recently at a party. To that pleasing duty he addressed himself the evening after his arrival.

" The young gentleman's goin' a courtin, 'I calc'late," was the remark of the Deacon's wife when she saw what a comely figure Mr. Clement showed at the tea-table.

" A very hahnsome young mahn," the Deacon replied, " and looks as if he might know consid'able. An architect, you know, — a sort of a builder. Wonder if he has n't got any good plans for a hahnsome pigsty. I suppose he 'd charge somethin' for one, but it could n't be much, an' he could take it out in board."

" Better ask him," his wife said; " he looks mighty pleasant; there 's nothin' lost by askin', an' a good deal gct sometimes, grandma used to say."

The Deacon followed her advice. Mr. Clement was perfectly good-natured about it, asked the Deacon the number of snouts in his menagerie, got an idea of the accommodations required, and sketched the plan of a new and appropriate edifice for the *Porcellarium*, as Master Gridley afterwards pleasantly christened it, which was carried out by the carpenter, and stands to this day a monument of his obliging disposition, and a proof that there is nothing so humble that taste cannot be shown in it.

"What'll be your charge for the plan of the pigsty, Mr. Lindsay?" the Deacon inquired with an air of interest, — he might have become involved more deeply than he had intended. "How much should you call about right for the picter an' figgerin'?"

"O, you're quite welcome to my sketch of a plan, Deacon. I've seen much showier buildings tenanted by animals not very different from those your edifice is meant for."

Mr. Clement found the three ladies sitting together in the chill, dim parlor at The Poplars. They had one of the city papers spread out on the table, and Myrtle was reading aloud the last news from Charleston Harbor. She rose as Mr. Clement entered, and stepped forward to meet him. It was a strange impression this young man produced upon her, — not through the common channels of the intelligence, — not exactly that "magnetic" influence of which she had had experience at a former time. It did not overcome her as at the moment of their second meeting. But it was something she must struggle against, and she had force and pride and training enough now to maintain her usual tranquillity, in spite of a certain inward commotion which seemed to reach her breathing and her pulse by some strange, inexplicable mechanism.

Myrtle, it must be remembered, was no longer the sim-ple country girl who had run away at fifteen, but a young lady of seventeen, who had learned all that more than a year's diligence at a great school could teach her, who had been much with girls of taste and of culture, and was familiar with the style and manners of those who came from what considered itself the supreme order in the social hierarchy. Her natural love for picturesque adornment was qualified by a knowledge of the prevailing modes not usual in so small a place as Oxbow Village. All this had not failed to produce its impression on those about her. Persons who, like Miss Silence Withers, believe, not in education, inasmuch as there is no healthy nature to be educated, but in transformation, worry about their charges up to a certain period of their lives. Then, if the trans-formation does not come, they seem to think their cares and duties are at an end, and, considering their theories of human destiny, usually accept the situation with won-derful complacency. This was the stage which Miss Si-lence Withers had reached with reference to Myrtle. It made her infinitely more agreeable, or less disagreeable, as the reader may choose one or the other statement, than when she was always fretting about her "responsibility." She even began to take an interest in some of Myrtle's worldly experiences, and something like a smile would now and then disarrange the chief-mourner stillness of her features, as Myrtle would tell some lively story she had brought away from the gay society she had frequented.

Cynthia Badlam kept her keen eyes on her like a hawk. Murray Bradshaw was away, and here was this handsome and agreeable youth coming in to poach on the preserve of which she considered herself the gamekeeper. What did it mean? She had heard the story about Susan's being off with her old love and on with a new one. Ah ha! this is the game, is it?

Clement Lindsay passed not so much a pleasant evening, as one of strange, perplexed, and mingled delight and inward conflict. He had found his marble once more turned to flesh and blood, and breathing before him. This was the woman he was born for; her form was fit to model his proudest ideal from, — her eyes melted him when they rested for an instant on his face, — her voice reached the hidden sensibilities of his inmost nature; those which never betray their existence until the outward chord to which they vibrate in response sends its message to stir them. But was she not already pledged to that other, — that cold-blooded, contriving, venal, cynical, selfish, polished, fascinating man of the world, whose artful strategy would pass with nine women out of ten for the most romantic devotion?

If he had known the impression he made, he would have felt less anxiety with reference to this particular possibility. Miss Silence expressed herself gratified with his appearance, and thought he looked like a good young man, — he reminded her of a young friend of hers who — [It was the same who had gone to one of the cannibal islands as a missionary, — and stayed there.] Myrtle was very quiet. She had nothing to say about Clement, except that she had met him at a party in the city, and found him agreeable. Miss Cynthia wrote a letter to Murray Bradshaw that very evening, telling him that he had better come back to Oxbow Village as quickly as he could, unless he wished to find his place occupied by an intruder.

In the mean time, the country was watching the garrison in Charleston Harbor.   All at once the first gun of
the four years' cannonade hurled its ball against the walls
of Fort Sumter.   There was no hamlet in the land which
the reverberations of that cannon-roar did not reach.   There
was no valley so darkened by overshadowing hills that
it did not see the American flag hauled down on the 13th
of April.   There was no loyal heart in the North that did
not answer to the call of the country to its defenders
which went forth two days later.   The great tide of feeling reached the locality where the lesser events of our
narrative were occurring.   A meeting of the citizens
was instantly called.   The venerable Father Pemberton
opened it with a prayer that filled every soul with courage and high resolve.   The young farmers and mechanics
of that whole region joined the companies to which they
belonged, or organized in squads and marched at once, or
got ready to march, to the scene of conflict.

The contagion of warlike patriotism reached the most
peacefully inclined young persons.

"My country calls me," Gifted Hopkins said to Susan
Posey, "and I am preparing to obey her summons.   If
I can pass the medical examination, which it is possible I
may, though I fear my constitution *may* be thought too
weak, and if no obstacle impedes me, I think of marching
in the ranks of the Oxbow Invincibles.   If I go, Susan,
and I fall, will you not remember me . . . as one who . . .
cherished the tenderest . . sentiments . . . towards you
. . and who had looked forward to the time when . . .
when . . ."

His eyes told the rest.   He loved !

Susan forgot all the rules of reserve to which she had

been trained.   What were cold conventionalities at such a moment?   " Never! never !" she said, throwing her arms about his neck and mingling her tears with his, which were flowing freely.   " Your country does not need your sword, ... but it does need ... your pen.   Your poems will inspire ... our soldiers. ... The Oxbow Invincibles will march to victory, singing your songs. ... If you go .. and if you ... fall ... O Gifted ! ... I ... I ... yes, I ... shall die too ! "

His love was returned.   He was blest !

" Susan," he said, "my own Susan, I yield to your wishes, at every sacrifice.   Henceforth they will be my law.   Yes, I will stay and encourage my brave countrymen to go forward to the bloody field.   My voice shall urge them on to the battle-ground.   I will give my dearest breath to stimulate their ardor. ... O Susan !   My own, own Susan ! "

While these interesting events had been going on beneath the modest roof of the Widow Hopkins, affairs had been rapidly hastening to a similar conclusion under the statelier shadow of The Poplars.   Clement Lindsay was so well received at his first visit that he ventured to repeat it several times, with so short intervals that it implied something more than a common interest in one of the members of the household.   There was no room for doubt who this could be, and Myrtle Hazard could not help seeing that she was the object of his undisguised admiration.   The belief was now general in the village that Gifted Hopkins and Susan Posey were either engaged, or on the point of being so ; and it was equally understood that, whatever might be the explanation, she and her former lover had parted company in an amicable manner.

Love works very strange transformations in young women. Sometimes it leads them to try every mode of adding to their attractions, — their whole thought is how to be most lovely in the eyes they would fill so as to keep out all other images. Poor darlings! We smile at their little vanities, as if they were very trivial things compared with the last Congressman's speech or the great Election Sermon; but Nature knows well what she is about. The maiden's ribbon or ruffle means a great deal more for her than the judge's wig or the priest's surplice.

It was not in this way that the gentle emotion awaking in the breast of Myrtle Hazard betrayed itself. As the thought dawned in her consciousness that she was loved, a change came over her such as the spirit that protected her, according to the harmless fancy she had inherited, might have wept for joy to behold, if tears could flow from an gelic eyes. She forgot herself and her ambitions, — the thought of shining in the great world died out in the presence of new visions of a future in which she was not to be her own, — of feelings in the depth of which the shallow vanities which had drawn her young eyes to them for a while seemed less than nothing. Myrtle had not hitherto said to herself that Clement was her lover, yet her whole nature was expanding and deepening in the light of that friendship which any other eye could have known at a glance for the great passion.

Cynthia Badlam wrote a pressing letter to Murray Bradshaw. "There is no time to be lost; she is bewitched, and will be gone beyond hope if this business is not put a stop to."

Love moves in an accelerating ratio; and there comes a time when the progress of the passion escapes from all human formulæ, and brings two young hearts, which had been gradually drawing nearer and nearer together, into complete union, with a suddenness that puts an infinity between the moment when all is told and that which went just before.

They were sitting together by themselves in the dimly lighted parlor. They had told each other many experiences of their past lives, very freely, as two intimate friends of different sex might do. Clement had happened to allude to Susan, speaking very kindly and tenderly of her. He hoped this youth to whom she was attached would make her life happy. "You know how simple-hearted and good she is; her image will always be a pleasant one in my memory, — second to but one other."

Myrtle ought, according to the common rules of conversation, to have asked, *What other?* but she did not. She may have looked as if she wanted to ask, — she may have blushed or turned pale, — perhaps she could not trust her voice; but whatever the reason was, she sat still, with downcast eyes. Clement waited a reasonable time, but, finding it was of no use, began again.

"*Your* image is the one other, — the only one, let me say for all else fades in its presence, — your image fills all my thought. Will you trust your life and happiness with one who can offer you so little beside his love? You know my whole heart is yours."

Whether Myrtle said anything in reply or not, — whether she acted like Coleridge's Genevieve, — that is, "fled to him and wept," or suffered her feelings to betray them es in some less startling confession, we will leave untold. Her answer, spoken or silent, could not have been a cruel one, for in another moment Clement was pressing his lips to hers, after the manner of accepted lovers.

"Our lips have met to-day for the second time," he said, presently.

She looked at him in wonder. What did he mean? The second time! How assuredly he spoke! She looked him calmly in the face, and awaited his explanation.

"I have a singular story to tell you. On the morning of the 16th of June, now nearly two years ago, I was sitting in my room at Alderbank, some twenty miles down the river, when I heard a cry for help coming from the river. I ran down to the bank, and there I saw a boy in an old boat — "

When it came to the "boy" in the old boat, Myrtle's cheeks flamed so that she could not bear it, and she covered her face with both her hands. But Clement told his story calmly through to the end, sliding gently over its later incidents, for Myrtle's heart was throbbing violently, and her breath a little catching and sighing, as when she had first lived with the new life his breath had given her.

"Why did you ask me for myself, when you could have claimed me?" she said.

"I wanted a free gift, Myrtle," Clement answered, "and I have it."

They sat in silence, lost in the sense of that new life which had suddenly risen on their souls.

The door-bell rang sharply   Kitty Fagan answered its summons, and presently entered the parlor and announced that Mr. Bradshaw was in the library, and wished to see the ladies.

CHAPTER XXXIV.

MURRAY BRADSHAW PLAYS HIS LAST CARD.

"HOW can I see that man this evening, Mr. Lindsay?"

"May I not be *Clement*, dearest? I would not see him at all, Myrtle. I don't believe you will find much pleasure in listening to his fine speeches."

"I cannot endure it. — Kitty, tell him I am engaged, and cannot see him this evening. No, no! don't say engaged, say very much occupied."

Kitty departed, communing with herself in this wise: — "Ockipied, is it? An' that's what ye cahl it when ye 're kapin' company with one young gintleman an' don't want another young gintleman to come in an' help the two of ye? Ye won't get y'r pigs to market to-day, Mr. Bridshaw, no, nor to-morrow, nayther, Mr. Bridshaw. It's Mrs. Lindsay that Miss Myrtle is goin' to be, — an' a big cake there 'll be at the weddin', frosted all over, — won't ye be plased with a slice o' that, Mr. Bridshaw?"

With these reflections in her mind, Mistress Kitty delivered her message, not without a gleam of malicious intelligence in her look that stung Mr. Bradshaw sharply. He had noticed a hat in the entry, and a little stick by it which he remembered well as one he had seen carried by Clement Lindsay. But he was used to concealing his emotions, and he greeted the two older ladies who presently came into the library so pleasantly, that no one who had not studied his face long and carefully would have suspected the bitterness of heart that lay hidden far down beneath his deceptive smile. He told Miss Silence, with much apparent interest, the story of his journey. He gave her an account of the progress of the case in which the estate of which she inherited the principal portion was interested. He did not tell her that a final decision which would settle the right to the great claim might be expected at any moment, and he did not tell her that there was very little doubt that it would be in favor of the heirs of Malachi Withers. He was very sorry he could not see Miss Hazard that evening, — hoped he should be more fortunate to-morrow forenoon, when he intended to call again, — had a message for her from one of her former school friends, which he was anxious to give her. He exchanged certain looks and hints with Miss Cynthia, which led her to withdraw and bring down the papers he had intrusted to her. At the close of his visit, she followed him into the entry with a lamp, as was her common custom.

"What's the meaning of all this, Cynthia? Is that fellow making love to Myrtle?"

"I'm afraid so, Mr. Bradshaw. He's been here several times, and they seem to be getting intimate. I couldn't do anything to stop it."

"Give me the papers, — quick!"

Cynthia pulled the package from her pocket. Murray Bradshaw looked sharply at it. A little crumpled, — crowded into her pocket. Seal unbroken. All safe.

"I shall come again to-morrow forenoon. Another day and it will be all up. The decision of the court will be known. It won't be my fault if one visit is not enough. — You don't suppose Myrtle is in love with this fellow?"

"She acts as if she might be. You know he's broke

with Susan Posey, and there's nothing to hinder. If you ask my opinion, I think it's your last chance: she is n't a girl to half do things, and if she has taken to this man it will be hard to make her change her mind. But she's young, and she has had a liking for you, and if you manage it well there's no telling."

Two notes passed between Myrtle Hazard and Master Byles Gridley that evening. Mistress Kitty Fagan, who had kept her ears pretty wide open, carried them.

Murray Bradshaw went home in a very desperate state of feeling. He had laid his plans, as he thought, with perfect skill, and the certainty of their securing their end. These papers were to have been taken from the envelope, and found in the garret just at the right moment, either by Cynthia herself or one of the other members of the family, who was to be led on, as it were accidentally, to the discovery. The right moment must be close at hand. He was to offer his hand — and heart, of course — to Myrtle, and it was to be accepted. As soon as the decision of the land case was made known, or not long afterwards, there was to be a search in the garret for papers, and these were to be discovered in a certain dusty recess, where, of course, they would have been placed by Miss Cynthia.

And now the one condition which gave any value to these arrangements seemed like to fail. This obscure youth — this poor fool, who had been on the point of marrying a simpleton to whom he had made a boyish promise — was coming between him and the object of his long pursuit, — the woman who had every attraction to draw him to herself. It had been a matter of pride with Murray Bradshaw that he never lost his temper so as to interfere with the precise course of action which his cool judg ment approved; but now he was almost beside himself with passion. His labors, as he believed, had secured the favorable issue of the great case so long pending. He had followed Myrtle through her whole career, if not as her avowed lover, at least as one whose friendship promised to flower in love in due season. The moment had come when the scene and the characters in this village drama were to undergo a change as sudden and as brilliant as is seen in those fairy spectacles where the dark background changes to a golden palace and the sober dresses are replaced by robes of regal splendor. The change was fast approaching; but he, the enchanter, as he had thought himself, found his wand broken, and his power given to another.

He could not sleep during that night. He paced his room, a prey to jealousy and envy and rage, which his calm temperament had kept him from feeling in their intensity up to this miserable hour. He thought of all that a maddened nature can imagine to deaden its own intolerable anguish. Of revenge. If Myrtle rejected his suit, should he take her life on the spot, that she might never be another's, — that neither man nor woman should ever triumph over him, — the proud ambitious man, defeated, humbled, scorned? No! that was a meanness of egotism which only the most vulgar souls could be capable of. Should he challenge her lover? It was not the way of the people and time, and ended in absurd complications, if anybody was foolish enough to try it. Shoot him? The idea floated through his mind, for he thought of everything; but he was a lawyer, and not a fool, and had no idea of figuring in court as a criminal. Besides, he was not a murderer, — cunning was his natural weapon, not vio-

17   r

lence. He had a certain admiration of desperate crime in others, as showing nerve and force, but he did not feel it to be his own style of doing business.

During the night he made every arrangement for leaving the village the next day, in case he failed to make any impression on Myrtle Hazard and found that his chance was gone. He wrote a letter to his partner, telling him that he had left to join one of the regiments forming in the city He adjusted all his business matters so that his partner should find as little trouble as possible. A little before dawn he threw himself on the bed, but he could not sleep; and he rose at sunrise, and finished his preparations for his departure to the city.

The morning dragged along slowly. He would not go to the office, not wishing to meet his partner again. After breakfast he dressed himself with great care, for he meant to show himself in the best possible aspect. Just before he left the house to go to The Poplars, he took the sealed package from his trunk, broke open the envelope, took from it a single paper, — it had some spots on it which distinguished it from all the rest, — put it separately in his pocket, and then the envelope containing the other papers. The calm smile he wore on his features as he set forth cost him a greater effort than he had ever made before to put it on. He was moulding his face to the look with which he meant to present himself; and the muscles had been sternly fixed so long that it was a task to bring them to their habitual expression in company, — that of ingenuous good-nature.

He was shown into the parlor at The Poplars; and Kitty told Myrtle that he had called and inquired for her and was waiting down stairs.

"Tell him I will be down presently," she said. " And, Kitty, now mind just what I tell you. Leave your kitchen door open, so that you can hear anything fall in the parlor. If you hear a book fall, — it will be a heavy one, and will make some noise, — run straight up here to my little chamber, and hang this red scarf out of the window. The *left-hand side-sash*, mind, so that anybody can see it from the road. If Mr. Gridley calls, show him into the parlor, no matter who is there."

Kitty Fagan looked amazingly intelligent, and promised that she would do exactly as she was told. Myrtle followed her down stairs almost immediately, and went into the parlor, where Mr. Bradshaw was waiting.

Never in his calmest moments had he worn a more insinuating smile on his features than that with which he now greeted Myrtle. So gentle, so gracious, so full of trust, such a completely natural expression of a kind, genial character did it seem, that to any but an expert it would have appeared impossible that such an effect could be produced by the skilful balancing of half a dozen pairs of little muscles that manage the lips and the corners of the mouth. The tones of his voice were subdued into accord with the look of his features; his whole manner was fascinating, as far as any conscious effort could make it so. It was just one of those artificially pleasing effects that so often pass with such as have little experience of life for the genuine expression of character and feeling. But Myrtle had learned the look that shapes itself on the features of one who loves with a love that seeketh not its own, and she knew the difference between acting and reality. She met his insinuating approach with a courtesy so carefully ordered that it was of itself a sentence without appeal. Artful persons often interpret sincere ones by their own standard. Murray Bradshaw thought little of this somewhat formal address, — a few minutes would break this thin film to pieces. He was not only a suitor with a prize to gain, he was a colloquial artist about to employ all the resources of his specialty.

He introduced the conversation in the most natural and easy way, by giving her the message from a former school-mate to which he had referred, coloring it so delicately, as he delivered it, that it became an innocent-looking flat-tery. Myrtle found herself in a rose-colored atmosphere, not from Murray Bradshaw's admiration, as it seemed, but only reflected by his mind from another source. That was one of his arts, — always, if possible, to associate himself incidentally, as it appeared, and unavoidably, with an agreeable impression.

So Myrtle was betrayed into smiling and being pleased before he had said a word about himself or his affairs. Then he told her of the adventures and labors of his late expedition ; of certain evidence which at the very last moment he had unearthed, and which was very probably the turning-point in the case. He could not help feeling that she must eventually reap some benefit from the good fortune with which his efforts had been attended. The thought that it might yet be so had been a great source of encouragement to him, — it would always be a great happiness to him to remember that he had done anything to make her happy.

Myrtle was very glad that he had been so far successful, — she did not know that it made much difference to her but she was obliged to him for the desire of serving her hat he had expressed.

'My services are always yours, Miss Hazard. There is no sacrifice I would not willingly make for your benefit. I have never had but one feeling toward you. You cannot be ignorant of what that feeling is.

"I know, Mr. Bradshaw, it has been one of kindness. I have to thank you for many friendly attentions, for which I hope I have never been ungrateful."

"Kindness is not all that I feel towards you, Miss Hazard. If that were all, my lips would not tremble as they do now in telling you my feelings. I love you."

He sprang the great confession on Myrtle a little sooner than he had meant. It was so hard to go on making phrases! Myrtle changed color a little, for she was startled.

The seemingly involuntary movement she made brought her arm against a large dictionary, which lay very near the edge of the table on which it was resting. The book fell with a loud noise to the floor.

There it lay. The young man awaited her answer; he did not think of polite forms at such a moment.

"It cannot be, Mr. Bradshaw, — it must not be. I have known you long, and I am not ignorant of all your brilliant qualities, but you must not speak to me of love. Your regard, — your friendly interest, — tell me that I shall always have these, but do not distress me with offering more than these."

"I do not ask you to give me your love in return; I only ask you not to bid me despair. Let me believe that the time may come when you will listen to me, — no matter how distant. You are young, — you have a tender heart, — you would not doom one who only lives for you to wretchedness. So long that we have known each other It cannot be that any other has come between us — "

Myrtle blushed so deeply that there was no need of his finishing his question.

"Do you mean, Myrtle Hazard, that you have cast me aside for another? — for this stranger — this artist — who was with you yesterday when I came, bringing with me the story of all I had done for you, — yes, for you, — and was ignominiously refused the privilege of seeing you?" Rage and jealousy had got the better of him this time. He rose as he spoke, and looked upon her with such passion kindling in his eyes that he seemed ready for any desperate act.

"I have thanked you for any services you may have rendered me, Mr. Bradshaw," Myrtle answered, very calmly, "and I hope you will add one more to them by sparing me this rude questioning. I wished to treat you as a friend; I hope you will not render that impossible."

He had recovered himself for one more last effort. "I was impatient: overlook it, I beg you. I was thinking of all the happiness I have labored to secure for you, and of the ruin to us both it would be if you scornfully rejected the love I offer you, — if you refuse to leave me any hope for the future, — if you insist on throwing yourself away on this man, so lately pledged to another. I hold the key of all your earthly fortunes in my hand. My love for you inspired me in all that I have done, and, now that I come to lay the result of my labors at your feet, you turn from me, and offer my reward to a stranger. I do not ask you to say this day that you will be mine, — I would not force your inclinations, — but I do ask you that you will hold yourself free of all others, and listen to me as one who may yet be more than a friend. Say so much as this, Myrtle and you shall have such a future as you never dreamed of

Fortune, position, all that this world can give, shall be yours!"

"Never! never! If you could offer me the whole world, or take away from me all that the world can give, it would make no difference to me. I cannot tell what power you hold over me, whether of life and death, or of wealth and poverty; but after talking to me of love, I should not have thought you would have wronged me by suggesting any meaner motive. It is only because we have been on friendly terms so long that I have listened to you as I have done. You have said more than enough, and I beg you will allow me to put an end to this interview."

She rose to leave the room. But Murray Bradshaw had gone too far to control himself, — he listened only to the rage which blinded him.

"Not yet!" he said. "Stay one moment, and you shall know what your pride and self-will have cost you!"

Myrtle stood, arrested, whether by fear, or curiosity, or the passive subjection of her muscles to his imperious will, it would be hard to say.

Murray Bradshaw took out the spotted paper from his breast-pocket, and held it up before her. "Look here!" he exclaimed. "This would have made you rich, — it would have crowned you a queen in society, — it would have given you all, and more than all, that you ever dreamed of luxury, of splendor, of enjoyment; and I, who won it for you, would have taught you how to make life yield every bliss it had in store to your wishes. You re ject my offer unconditionally?"

Myrtle expressed her negative only by a slight contemptuous movement.

Murray Bradshaw walked deliberately to the fireplace, and laid the spotted paper upon the burning coals. It writhed and curled, blackened, flamed, and in a moment was a cinder dropping into ashes. He folded his arms, and stood looking at the wreck of Myrtle's future, the work of his cruel hand. Strangely enough, Myrtle herself was fascinated, as it were, by the apparent solemnity of this mysterious sacrifice. She had kept her eyes steadily on him all the time, and was still gazing at the altar on which her happiness had been in some way offered up, when the door was opened by Kitty Fagan, and Master Byles Gridley was ushered into the parlor.

"Too late, old man!" Murray Bradshaw exclaimed, in a hoarse and savage voice, as he passed out of the room, and strode through the entry and down the avenue. It was the last time the old gate of The Poplars was to open or close for him. The same day he left the village ; and the next time his name was mentioned it was as an officer in one of the regiments just raised and about marching to the seat of war.

CHAPTER XXXV.

THE SPOTTED PAPER.

WHAT Master Gridley may have said to Myrtle Hazard that served to calm her after this exciting scene cannot now be recalled. That Murray Bradshaw thought he was inflicting a deadly injury on her was plain enough. That Master Gridley did succeed in convincing her that no great harm had probably been done her is equally certain.

Like all bachelors who have lived a lonely life, Master Byles Gridley had his habits, which nothing short of some terrestrial convulsion — or perhaps, in his case, some instinct that drove him forth to help somebody in trouble — could possibly derange. After his breakfast, he always sat and read awhile, — the paper, if a new one came to hand or some pleasant old author, — if a little neglected by the world of readers, he felt more at ease with him, and loved him all the better.

But on the morning after his interview with Myrtle Hazard, he had received a letter which made him forget newspapers, old authors, almost everything, for the moment. It was from the publisher with whom he had had a conversation, it may be remembered, when he visited the city, and was to this effect: That Our Firm propose to print and stereotype the work originally published under the title of "Thoughts on the Universe"; said work to be remodelled according to the plan suggested by the Author, with the corrections, alterations, omissions, and addi-

17 *

tions proposed by him ; said work to be published under
the following title to wit · —— —— : said work to be
printed in 12mo, on paper of good quality, from new types,
etc., etc., and for every copy thereof printed the author to
receive, etc., etc.

Master Gridley sat as in a trance, reading this letter
over and over, to know if it could be really so. So it
really was. His book had disappeared from the market
long ago, as the elm seeds that carpet the ground and
never germinate disappear. At last it had got a certain
value as a curiosity for book-hunters. Some one of them,
keener-eyed than the rest, had seen that there was a meaning and virtue in this unsuccessful book, for which there
was a new audience educated since it had tried to breathe
before its time. Out of this had grown at last the publisher's proposal. It was too much : his heart swelled with
joy, and his eyes filled with tears.

How could he resist the temptation? He took down his
own particular copy of the book, which was yet to do him
honor as its parent, and began reading. As his eye fell on
one paragraph after another, he nodded approval of this
sentiment or opinion, he shook his head as if questioning
whether this other were not to be modified or left out, he
condemned a third as being no longer true for him as
when it was written, and he sanctioned a fourth with his
hearty approval. The reader may like a few specimens
from this early edition, now a rarity. He shall have them.
with Master Gridley's verbal comments. The book, as its
name implied, contained " Thoughts " rather than consecu-
tive trains of reasoning or continuous disquisitions. What
he read and remarked upon were a few of the more pointed
statements which stood out in the chapters he was turning

over. The worth of the book must not be judged by these almost random specimens.

" *The best thought, like the most perfect digestion, is done unconsciously.* — Develop that. — Ideas at compound interest in the mind. — Be aye sticking in *an idea,* — while you 're sleeping it 'll be growing. Seed of a thought to-day, — flower to-morrow— next week — ten years from now, etc. — Article by and by for the . . . .

" *Can the Infinite be supposed to shift the responsibility of the ultimate destiny of any created thing to the finite ? Our theologians pretend that it can. I doubt.* — Heretical Stet.

" *Protestantism means None of your business. But it is afraid of its own logic.* — Stet. No logical resting-place short of None of your business.

" *The supreme self-indulgence is to surrender the will to a spiritual director.* — Protestantism gave up a great luxury. — Did it though ?

" *Asiatic modes of thought and speech do not express the relations in which the American feels himself to stand to his Superiors in this or any other sphere of being. Republicanism must have its own religious phraseology, which is not that borrowed from Oriental despotisms.*

" *Idols and dogmas in place of character ; pills and theories in place of wholesome living. See the histories of theology and medicine* passim. — Hits 'em.

" ' *Of such is the kingdom of heaven.' Do you mean to say Jean Chauvin, that*

' *Heaven* LIES *about us in our infancy* ' *?*

" *Why do you complain of your organization ? Your soul was in a hurry, and made a rush for a body. There* *are patient spirits that have waited from eternity, **and** never found parents fit to be born of.* —- How do you know anything about all that? *Dele.*

" *What sweet, smooth voices the negroes have! A hundred generations fed on bananas. — Compare them with our apple-eating white folks! —* It won't do. Bananas came from the West Indies.

" *To tell a man's temperament by his handwriting. See if the dots of his i's run ahead or not, and if they do, how far. —* I have tried that — on myself.

" *Marrying into some families is the next thing to being canonized. —* Not so true now as twenty or thirty years ago. As many bladders, but more pins.

" *Fish and dandies only keep on ice. —* Who will take? Explain in note how all warmth approaching blood heat spoils fops and flounders.

" *Flying is a lost art among men and reptiles. Bats fly, and men ought to. Try a light turbine. Rise a mile straight, fall half a mile slanting, — rise half a mile straight, fall half a mile slanting, and so on. Or slant up and slant down. —* Poh! You ain't such a fool as to think that is new, — are you?

" Put in my telegraph project. Central station. Cables with insulated wires running to it from different quarters of the city. These form the centripetal system. From central station, wires to all the livery stables, messenger stands, provision shops, etc., etc. These form the centrifugal system. Any house may have a wire in the nearest cable at small cost.

" *Do you want to be remembered after the continents have gone under, and come up again, and dried, and bred new races? Have your name stamped on all your plates and cups and saucers. Nothing of you or yours will last like those. I never sit down at my table without looking at the china service, and saying, 'Here are my monuments. That butter-dish is my urn. This soup-plate is my memorial tablet.' — No need of a skeleton at my banquets! I feed from my tombstone and read my epitaph at the bottom of every teacup. — Good."*

He fell into a revery as he finished reading this last sentence. He thought of the dim and dread future, — all the changes that it would bring to him, to all the living, to the face of the globe, to the order of earthly things. He saw men of a new race, alien to all that had ever lived, excavating with strange, vast engines the old ocean-bed now become habitable land. And as the great scoops turned out the earth they had fetched up from the unexplored depths, a relic of a former simple civilization revealed the fact that here a tribe of human beings had lived and perished. — Only the coffee-cup he had in his hand half an hour ago. — Where would he be then? and Mrs. Hopkins, and Gifted, and Susan, and everybody? and President Buchanan? and the Boston State-House? and Broadway? — O Lord, Lord, Lord! And the sun perceptibly smaller, according to the astronomers, and the earth cooled down a number of degrees, and inconceivable arts practised by men of a type yet undreamed of, and all the fighting creeds merged in one great universal —

A knock at his door interrupted his revery. Miss Susan Posey informed him that a gentleman was waiting below who wished to see him.

"Show him up to my study, Susan Posey, if you please," said Master Gridley.

Mr. Penhallow presented himself at Mr. Gridley's door with a countenance expressive of a very high state of ex citement.

"You have heard the news, Mr. Gridley, I suppose?"

"What news, Mr. Penhallow?"

"First, that my partner has left very unexpectedly to enlist in a regiment just forming. Second, that the great land-case is decided in favor of the heirs of the late Malachi Withers."

"Your partner must have known about it yesterday?"

"He did, even before I knew it. He thought himself possessed of a very important document, as you know, of which he has made, or means to make, some use. You are aware of the artifice I employed to prevent any possible evil consequences from any action of his. I have the genuine document, of course. I wish you to go over with me to The Poplars, and I should be glad to have good old Father Pemberton go with us; for it is a serious matter, and will be a great surprise to more than one of the family.

They walked together to the old house, where the old clergyman had lived for more than half a century. He was used to being neglected by the people who ran after his younger colleague; and the attention paid him in asking him to be present on an important occasion, as he understood this to be, pleased him greatly. He smoothed his long white locks, and called a granddaughter to help make him look fitly for such an occasion, and, being at last got into his grandest Sunday aspect, took his faithful staff. and set out with the two gentlemen for The Poplars. On the way, Mr. Penhallow explained to him the occasion of their visit, and the general character of the facts he had to

announce. He wished the venerable minister to prepare
Miss Silence Withers for a revelation which would mate-
rially change her future prospects. He thought it might
be well, also, if he would say a few words to Myrtle Hazard, for whom a new life, with new and untried temptations, was about to open. His business was, as a lawyer
to make known to these parties the facts just come to his
own knowledge affecting their interests. He had asked
Mr. Gridley to go with him, as having intimate relations
with one of the parties referred to, and as having been the
principal agent in securing to that party the advantages
which were to accrue to her from the new turn of events.
" You are a second parent to her, Mr. Gridley," he said.
" Your vigilance, your shrewdness, and your — spectacles
have saved her. I hope she knows the full extent of her ob-
ligations to you, and that she will always look to you for
counsel in all her needs. She will want a wise friend, for
she is to begin the world anew."

What had happened, when she saw the three grave gentlemen at the door early in the forenoon, Mistress Kitty
Fagan could not guess. Something relating to Miss Myrtle, no doubt: she was n't goin' to be married right off to
Mr. Clement, — was she, — and no church, nor cake, nor
anything? The gentlemen were shown into the parlor.
" Ask Miss Withers to go into the library, Kitty," said
Master Gridley. " Dr. Pemberton wishes to speak with
her." The good old man was prepared for a scene with
Miss Silence. He announced to her, in a kind and delicate way, that she must make up her mind to the disappointment of certain expectations which she had long
entertained, and which, as her lawyer, Mr. Penhallow,
had come to inform her and others, were to be finally re
linquished from this hour.

To his great surprise, Miss Silence received this communication almost cheerfully. It seemed more like a relief
to her than anything else. Her one dread in this world
was her " responsibility "; and the thought that she might
have to account for ten talents hereafter, instead of one,
had often of late been a positive distress to her. There was
also in her mind a secret disgust at the thought of the hungry creatures who would swarm round her if she should
ever be in a position to bestow patronage. This had
grown upon her as the habits of lonely life gave her more
and more of that fastidious dislike to males in general, as
such, which is not rare in maidens who have seen the roses
of more summers than politeness cares to mention.

Father Pemberton then asked if he could see Miss Myrtle Hazard a few moments in the library before they went
into the parlor, where they were to meet Mr. Penhallow
and Mr. Gridley, for the purpose of receiving the lawyer's
communication.

What change was this which Myrtle had undergone
since love had touched her heart, and her visions of worldly enjoyment had faded before the thought of sharing and
ennobling the life of one who was worthy of her best affections, — of living for another, and of finding her own
noblest self in that divine office of woman? She had laid
aside the .bracelet which she had so long worn as a kind
of charm as well as an ornament. One would have said
her features had lost something of that look of imperious
beauty which had added to her resemblance to the dead
woman whose glowing portrait hung upon her wall. And
if it could be that, after so many generations, the blood of
her who had died for her faith could show in her descend
ant's veins, and the soul of that elect lady of her race

ook out from her far-removed offspring's dark eyes, such a transfusion of the martyr's life and spiritual being might well seem to manifest itself in Myrtle Hazard.

The large-hearted old man forgot his scholastic theory of human nature as he looked upon her face. He thought he saw in her the dawning of that grace which some are born with; which some, like Myrtle, only reach through many trials and dangers; which some seem to show for a while and then lose; which too many never reach while they wear the robes of earth, but which speaks of the kingdom of heaven already begun in the heart of a child of earth. He told her simply the story of the occurrences which had brought them together in the old house, with the message the lawyer was to deliver to its inmates. He wished to prepare her for what might have been too sudden a surprise.

But Myrtle was not wholly unprepared for some such revelation. There was little danger that any such announcement would throw her mind from its balance after the inward conflict though which she had been passing. For her lover had left her almost as soon as he had told her the story of his passion, and the relation in which he stood to her. He, too, had gone to answer his country's call to her children, not driven away by crime and shame and despair, but quitting all — his new-born happiness, the art in which he was an enthusiast, his prospects of success and honor — to obey the higher command of duty. War was to him, as to so many of the noble youth who went forth, only organized barbarism, hateful but for the sacred cause which alone redeemed it from the curse that blasted the first murderer. God only knew the sacrifice such young men as he made.

z

How brief Myrtle's dream had been! She almost doubted, at some moments, whether she would not awake from it, as from her other visions, and find it all unreal. There was no need of fearing any undue excitement of her mind after the alternations of feeling she had just experienced. Nothing seemed of much moment to her which could come from without, — her real world was within, and the light of its day and the breath of its life came from her love, made holy by the self-forgetfulness on both sides which was born with it.

Only one member of the household was in danger of finding the excitement more than she could bear. Miss Cynthia knew that all Murray Bradshaw's plans, in which he had taken care that she should have a personal interest, had utterly failed. What he had done with the means of revenge in his power, — if, indeed, they were still in his power, — she did not know. She only knew that there had been a terrible scene, and that he had gone, leaving it uncertain whether he would ever return. It was with fear and trembling that she heard the summons which went forth, that the whole family should meet in the parlor to listen to a statement from Mr. Penhallow. They all gathered as requested, and sat round the room, with the exception of Mistress Kitty Fagan, who knew her place too well to be sittin' down with the likes o' them, and stood with attentive ears in the doorway.

Mr. Penhallow then read from a printed paper the decision of the Supreme Court in the land-case so long pending, where the estate of the late Malachi Withers was the claimant, against certain parties pretending to hold under an ancient grant. The decision was in favor of the estate.

"This gives a great property to the heirs," Mr. Penhallow remarked, "and the question as to who these heirs are has to be opened. For the will under which Silence Withers, sister of the deceased, has inherited, is dated some years previous to the decease, and it was not very strange that a will of later date should be discovered. Such a will has been discovered. It is the instrument I have here."

Myrtle Hazard opened her eyes very widely, for the paper Mr. Penhallow held looked exactly like that which Murray Bradshaw had burned, and, what was curious, had some spots on it just like some she had noticed on that.

"This will," Mr. Penhallow said, "signed by witnesses dead or absent from this place, makes a disposition of the testator's property in some respects similar to that of the previous one, but with a single change, which proves to be of very great importance."

Mr. Penhallow proceeded to read the will. The important change in the disposition of the property was this. In case the land-claim was decided in favor of the estate, then, in addition to the small provision made for Myrtle Hazard, the property so coming to the estate should all go to her. There was no question about the genuineness and the legal sufficiency of this instrument. Its date was not very long after the preceding one, at a period when, as was well known, he had almost given up the hope of gaining his case, and when the property was of little value compared to that which it had at present.

A long silence followed this reading. Then, to the surprise of all, Miss Silence Withers rose, and went to Myrtle Hazard, and wished her joy with every appearance of sincerity. She was relieved of a great responsibility Myrtle was young and could bear it better. She hoped

that her young relative would live long to enjoy the blessings Providence had bestowed upon her, and to use them
for the good of the community, and especially the promotion
of the education of deserving youth.   If some fitting per
son could be found to advise Myrtle, whose affairs would
require much care, it would be a great relief to her.

They all went up to Myrtle and congratulated her on her
change of fortune.   Even Cynthia Badlam got out a phrase
or two which passed muster in the midst of the general
excitement.   As for Kitty Fagan, she could not say a
word, but caught Myrtle's hand and kissed it as if it belonged to her own saint, and then, suddenly applying her
apron to her eyes, retreated from a scene which was too
much for her, in a state of complete mental beatitude and
total bodily discomfiture.

Then Silence asked the old minister to make a prayer,
and he stretched his hands up to Heaven, and called down
all the blessings of Providence upon all the household, and
especially upon this young handmaiden, who was to be
tried with prosperity, and would need all aid from above
to keep her from its dangers.

Then Mr. Penhallow asked Myrtle if she had any
choice as to the friend who should have charge of her
affairs.

Myrtle turned to Master Byles Gridley, and said, "You
have been my friend and protector so far, — will you continue to be so hereafter?"

Master Gridley tried very hard to begin a few words
of thanks to her for her preference, but finding his voice a
little uncertain, contented himself with pressing her hand
and saying, "Most willingly, my dear daughter!"

CHAPTER XXXVI.

CONCLUSION.

THE same day the great news of Myrtle Hazard's accession to fortune came out, the secret was told that she had promised herself in marriage to Mr. Clement Lindsay. But her friends hardly knew how to congratulate her on this last event. Her lover was gone, to risk his life, not improbably to lose it, or to come home a wreck, crippled by wounds, or worn out with disease.

Some of them wondered to see her so cheerful in such a moment of trial. They could not know how the manly strength of Clement's determination had nerved her for womanly endurance. They had not learned that a great cause makes great souls, or reveals them to themselves, — a lesson taught by so many noble examples in the times that followed. Myrtle's only desire seemed to be to labor in some way to help the soldiers and their families. She appeared to have forgotten everything for this duty; she had no time for regrets, if she were disposed to indulge them, and she hardly asked a question as to the extent of the fortune which had fallen to her.

The next number of the "Banner and Oracle" contained two announcements which she read with some interest when her attention was called to them. They were as follows : —

" A fair and accomplished daughter of this village comes, by the late decision of the Supreme Court, into possession of a property estimated at a million of dollars or more. It consists of a large tract of land purchased many years ago by the late Malachi Withers, now become of immense value by the growth of a city in its neighborhood, the opening of mines. etc., etc. It is rumored that the lovely and highly educated heiress has formed a connection looking towards matrimony with a certain distinguished artist."

" Our distinguished young townsman, William Murray Bradshaw, Esq., has been among the first to respond to the call of the country for champions to defend her from traitors. We understand that he has obtained a captaincy in the —th Regiment, about to march to the threatened seat of war. May victory perch on his banners! "

The two lovers, parted by their own self-sacrificing choice in the very hour that promised to bring them so much happiness, labored for the common cause during all the terrible years of warfare, one in the camp and the field, the other in the not less needful work which the good women carried on at home, or wherever their services were needed. Clement — now Captain Lindsay — returned at the end of his first campaign charged with a special office. Some months later, after one of the great battles, he was sent home wounded. He wore the leaf on his shoulder which entitled him to be called Major Lindsay. He recovered from his wound only too rapidly, for Myrtle had visited him daily in the military hospital where he had resided for treatment; and it was bitter parting. The telegraph wires were thrilling almost hourly with messages of death, and the long pine boxes came by almost every train, — no need of asking what they held !

Once more he came, detailed on special duty, and this time with the eagle on his shoulder, — he was Colonel Lindsay. The lovers could not part again of their own free will. Some adventurous women had followed their husbands to the camp, and Myrtle looked as if she could play the part of the Maid of Saragossa on occasion. So Clement asked her if she would return with him as his wife ; and Myrtle answered, with as much willingness to submit as a maiden might fairly show under such circum-

stances, that she would do his bidding. Thereupon, with
the shortest possible legal notice, Father Pemberton was
sent for, and the ceremony was performed in the presence
of a few witnesses in the large parlor at The Poplars,
which was adorned with flowers, and hung round with all
the portraits of the dead members of the family, summoned
as witnesses to the celebration. One witness looked on
with unmoved features, yet Myrtle thought there was a
more heavenly smile on her faded lips than she had ever
seen before beaming from the canvas, — it was Ann Holyoake, the martyr to her faith, the guardian spirit of Myrtle's
visions, who seemed to breathe a holier benediction than
any words — even those of the good old Father Pemberton himself — could convey.

They went back together to the camp. From that period
until the end of the war, Myrtle passed her time between
the life of the tent and that of the hospital. In the offices
of mercy which she performed for the sick and the wounded
and the dying, the dross of her nature seemed to be burned
away. The conflict of mingled lives in her blood had
ceased. No lawless impulses usurped the place of that
serene resolve which had grown strong by every exercise
of its high prerogative. If she had been called now to die
for any worthy cause, her race would have been ennobled
by a second martyr, true to the blood of her who died under the cruel Queen.

Many sad sights she saw in the great hospital where
she passed some months at intervals, — one never to be
forgotten. An officer was brought into the ward where
she was in attendance. " Shot through the lungs, — pretty
nearly gone."

She went softly to his bedside. He was breathing with

great difficulty; his face was almost convulsed with the effort, but she recognized him in a moment; it was Murray Bradshaw, — Captain Bradshaw, — as she knew by the bars on his coat flung upon the bed where he had just been laid.

She addressed him by name, tenderly as if he had been a dear brother; she saw on his face that hers were to be the last kind words he would ever hear.

He turned his glazing eyes upon her. "Who are you?" he said in a feeble voice.

"An old friend," she answered; "you knew me as Myrtle Hazard."

He started. "You by my bedside! You caring for me! — for me, that burned the title to your fortune to ashes before your eyes! You can't forgive that, — I won't believe it! Don't you hate me, dying as I am?"

Myrtle was used to maintaining a perfect calmness of voice and countenance, and she held her feelings firmly down. "I have nothing to forgive you, Mr. Bradshaw. You may have meant to do me wrong, but Providence raised up a protector for me. The paper you burned was not the original, — it was a copy substituted for it — "

"And did the old man outwit me after all?" he cried out, rising suddenly in bed, and clasping his hands behind his head to give him a few more gasps of breath. "I knew he was cunning, but I thought I was his match. It must have been Byles Gridley, — nobody else. And so the old man beat me after all, and saved you from ruin Thank God that it came out so! Thank God! I can die now. Give me your hand, Myrtle."

She took his hand, and held it until it gently loosed its hold, and he ceased to breathe. Myrtle's creed was a sim

ple one, with more of trust and love in it than of systema‹
tized articles of belief. She cherished the fond hope that
these last words of one who had erred so miserably were a
token of some blessed change which the influences of the
better world might carry onward until he should have
outgrown the sins and the weaknesses of his earthly
career.

Soon after this she rejoined her husband in the camp.
From time to time they received stray copies of the " Banner and Oracle," which, to Myrtle especially, were full of
interest, even to the last advertisement. A few paragraphs
may be reproduced here which relate to persons who have
figured in this narrative.

" TEMPLE OF HYMEN.

"Married, on the 6th instant, Fordyce Hurlbut, M. D., to Olive, only daughter of the Rev. Ambrose Eveleth. The editor of this paper returns his ac-
knowledgments for a bountiful slice of the wedding-cake. May their shadows
never be less ! "

Not many weeks after this appeared the following : —

"Died in this place, on the 28th instant, the venerable Lemuel Hurlbut, M. D.,
at the great age of XCVI years.
"'With the ancient is wisdom, and in length of days understanding.'"

Myrtle recalled his kind care of her in her illness, and
paid the tribute of a sigh to his memory, — there was nothing in a death like his to call for any aching regret.

The usual routine of small occurrences was duly recorded in the village paper for some weeks longer, when
she was startled and shocked by receiving a number containing the following paragraph : —

" CALAMITOUS ACCIDENT !

" It is known to our readers that the steeple of the old meeting-house was
struck by lightning about a month ago. The frame of the building was a good
deal jarred by the shock, but no danger was apprehended from the injury it had
received. On Sunday last the congregation came together as usual. The Rev.
Mr. Stoker was alone in the pulpit, the Rev. Doctor Pemberton having been
detained by slight indisposition The sermon was from the text, ' The wolf also

shall dwell with the lamb, and the leopard shall lie down with the kid.' (**Isaiah xi.** 6.) The pastor described the millennium as the reign of love and peace, in eloquent and impressive language. He was in the midst of the prayer which follows the sermon, and had just put up a petition that the spirit of affection and faith and trust might grow up and prevail among the flock of which he was the shepherd, more especially those dear lambs whom he gathered with his arm and carried in his bosom, when the old sounding-board, which had hung safely for nearly a century, — loosened, no doubt by the bolt which had fallen on the church, — broke from its fastenings, and fell with a loud crash upon the pulpit, crushing the Rev. Mr. Stoker under its ruins. The scene that followed beggars description. Cries and shrieks resounded through the house. Two or three young women fainted entirely away. Mr. Penhallow, Deacon Rumrill, Gifted Hopkins, Esq., and others, came forward immediately, and after much effort succeeded in removing the wreck of the sounding-board, and extricating their unfortunate pastor. He was not fatally injured, it is hoped ; but, sad to relate, he received such a violent blow upon the spine of the back, that palsy of the lower extremities is like to ensue. He is at present lying entirely helpless. Every attention is paid to him by his affectionately devoted family.''

Myrtle had hardly got over the pain which the reading of this unfortunate occurrence gave her, when her eyes were gladdened by the following pleasing piece of intelligence, contained in a subsequent number of the village paper : —

"IMPOSING CEREMONY.

"The Reverend Doctor Pemberton performed the impressive rite of baptism upon the first-born child of our distinguished townsman, Gifted Hopkins, Esq., the Bard of Oxbow Village, and Mrs. Susan P. Hopkins, his amiable and respected lady. The babe conducted himself with singular propriety on this occasion. He received the Christian name of Byron Tennyson Browning. May he prove worthy of his name and his parentage!"

The end of the war came at last, and found Colonel Lindsay among its unharmed survivors. He returned with Myrtle to her native village, and they established themselves, at the request of Miss Silence Withers, in the old family mansion. Miss Cynthia, to whom Myrtle made a generous allowance, had gone to live in a town not many miles distant, where she had a kind of home on sufferance as well as at The Poplars. This was a convenience just then, because Nurse Byloe was invited to stay with them for a month or two ; and one nurse and two single women under the same roof keep each other in a stew all the time, as the old dame somewhat sharply remarked.

Master Byles Gridley had been appointed Myrtle's legal

protector, and, with the assistance of Mr. Penhallow, had
brought the property she inherited into a more manageable
and productive form ; so that, when Clement began his
fine studio behind the old mansion, he felt that at least he
could pursue his art, or arts, if he chose to give himself to
sculpture, without that dreadful hag, Necessity, standing by
him to pinch the features of all his ideals, and give them
something of her own likeness.

Silence Withers was more cheerful now that she had got
rid of her responsibility.   She embellished her spare person a little more than in former years.   These young people looked so happy !   Love was not so unendurable,
perhaps, after all.   No woman need despair, — especially
if she has a house over her, and a snug little property.   A
worthy man, a former missionary, of the best principles,
but of a slightly jocose and good-humored habit, thought
that he could piece his widowed years with the not insigni
ficant fraction of life left to Miss Silence, to their mutual
advantage.   He came to the village, therefore, where
Father Pemberton was very glad to have him supply the
pulpit in the place of his unfortunate disabled colleague.
The courtship soon began, and was brisk enough ; for the
good man knew there was no time to lose at his period of
life, — or hers either, for that matter.   It was a rather odd
specimen of love-making ; for he was constantly trying to
subdue his features to a gravity which they were not used
to, and she was as constantly endeavoring to be as lively
as possible, with the innocent desire of pleasing her light-
hearted suitor.

" *Vieille fille fait jeune mariée* "   Silence was ten years
younger as a bride than she had seemed as a lone woman.
One would have said she had got out of the coach next to

the hearse, and got into one some half a dozen behind it, — where there is often good and reasonably cheerful conversation going on about the virtues of the deceased, the probable amount of his property, or the little slips he may have committed, and where occasionally a subdued pleasantry at his expense sets the four waistcoats shaking that were lifting with sighs a half-hour ago in the house of mourning. But Miss Silence, that was, thought that two families, with all the possible complications which time might bring, would be better in separate establishments. She therefore proposed selling The Poplars to Myrtle and her husband, and removing to a house in the village, which would be large enough for them, at least for the present. So the young folks bought the old house, and paid a mighty good price for it; and enlarged it, and beautified and glorified it, and one fine morning went together down to the Widow Hopkins's, whose residence seemed in danger of being a little crowded, — for Gifted lived there with his Susan, — and what had happened might happen again, — and gave Master Byles Gridley a formal and most persuasively worded invitation to come up and make his home with them at The Poplars.

Now Master Gridley has been betrayed into palpable and undisguised weakness at least once in the presence of this assembly, who are looking upon him almost for the last time before they part from him, and see his face no more. Let us not inquire too curiously, then, how he received this kind proposition. It is enough, that, when he found that a new study had been built on purpose for him, and a sleeping-room attached to it so that he could live there without disturbing anybody if he chose, he consented to remove there for a while, and that he was there established amidst great rejoicing.

Cynthia Badlam had fallen of late into poor health. She found at last that she was going; and as she had a little property of her own, — as almost all poor relations have, only there is not enough of it, — she was much exercised in her mind as to the final arrangements to be made respecting its disposition. The Rev. Dr. Pemberton was one day surprised by a message, that she wished to have an interview with him. He rode over to the town in which she was residing, and there had a long conversation with her upon this matter. When this was settled, her mind seemed to be more at ease. She died with a comfortable assurance that she was going to a better world, and with a bitter conviction that it would be hard to find one that would offer her a worse lot than being a poor relation in this.

Her little property was left to Rev. Eliphalet Pemberton and Jacob Penhallow, Esq., to be by them employed for such charitable purposes as they should elect, educational or other. Father Pemberton preached an admirable funeral sermon, in which he praised her virtues, known to this people among whom she had long lived, and especially that crowning act by which she devoted all she had to purposes of charity and benevolence.

The old clergyman seemed to have renewed his youth since the misfortune of his colleague had incapacitated him from labor. He generally preached in the *forenoon* now, and to the great acceptance of the people, — for the truth was that the honest minister who had married Miss Silence was not young enough or good-looking enough to be an object of personal attentions like the Rev. Joseph Bellamy Stoker, — and the old minister appeared to great advantage contrasted with him in the pulpit. Poor Mr. Stoker was now helpless, faithfully and tenderly waited upon by his own wife, who had regained her health and strength, — in no small measure, perhaps, from the great need of sympathy and active aid which her unfortunate husband now experienced. It was an astonishment to herself when she found that she who had so long been served was able to serve another. Some who knew his errors thought his accident was a judgment; but others believed that it was only a mercy in disguise, — it snatched him roughly from his sin, but it opened his heart to gratitude towards her whom his neglect could not alienate, and through gratitude to repentance and better thoughts. Bathsheba had long ago promised herself to Cyprian Eveleth ; and, as he was about to become the rector of a parish in the next town, the marriage was soon to take place.

How beautifully serene Master Byles Gridley's face was growing ! Clement loved to study its grand lines, which had so much strength and fine humanity blended in them. He was so fascinated by their noble expression that he sometimes seemed to forget himself, and looked at him more like an artist taking his portrait than like an admiring friend. He maintained that Master Gridley had a bigger bump of benevolence and as large a one of cautiousness, as the two people most famous for the size of these organs on the phrenological chart he showed him, and proved it, or nearly proved it, by careful measurements of his head. Master Gridley laughed, and read him a passage on the pseudo-sciences out of his book.

The disposal of Miss Cynthia's bequest was much discussed in the village. Some wished the trustees would use it to lay the foundations of a public library. Others thought it should be applied for the relief of the families of

soldiers who had fallen in the war. Still another set would
take it to build a monument to the memory of those heroes.
The trustees listened with the greatest candor to all these
gratuitous hints. It was, however, suggested, in a well-
written anonymous article which appeared in the village
paper, that it was desirable to follow the general lead of
the testator's apparent preference. The trustees were at
liberty to do as they saw fit ; but, other things being equal,
some educational object should be selected. If there were
any orphan children in the place, it would seem to be very
proper to devote the moderate sum bequeathed to educating
them. The trustees recognized the justice of this suggestion. Why not apply it to the instruction and maintenance
of those two pretty and promising children, virtually orphans, whom the charitable Mrs. Hopkins had cared for so
long without any recompense, and at a cost which would
soon become beyond her means ? The good people of the
neighborhood accepted this as the best solution of the difficulty. It was agreed upon at length by the trustees, that
the Cynthia Badlam Fund for Educational Purposes should
be applied for the benefit of the two foundlings, known as
Isosceles and Helminthia Hopkins.

Master Byles Gridley was greatly exercised about the
two "preposterous names," as he called them, which in a
moment of eccentric impulse he had given to these children
of nature. He ventured to hint as much to Mrs. Hopkins
The good dame was vastly surprised. She thought they
was about as pooty names as anybody had had given 'em in
the village. And they was so handy, spoke short, — Sossy
and Minthy, — she never should know how to call 'em
anything else.

"But my dear Mrs. Hopkins," Master Gridley urged

" if you knew the meaning they have to the ears of scholars, you would see that I did very wrong to apply such absurd names to my little fellow-creatures, and that I am bound to rectify my error. More than that, my dear madam, I mean to consult you as to the new names ; and if we can fix upon proper and pleasing ones, it is my intention to leave a pretty legacy in my will to these interesting children."

" Mr. Gridley," said Mrs. Hopkins, " you 're the best man I ever see, or ever shall see, . . . except my poor dear Ammi. . . . I 'll do jest as you say about that, or about anything else in all this livin' world."

" Well, then, Mrs. Hopkins, what shall be the boy's name ? "

" Byles Gridley Hopkins ! " she answered instantly.

" Good Lord ! " said Mr. Gridley, " think a minute, my dear madam. I will not say one word, — only think a minute, and mention some name that will not suggest quite so many winks and whispers."

She did think something less than a minute, and then said aloud, " Abraham Lincoln Hopkins."

" Fifteen thousand children have been so christened during the past year, on a moderate computation."

" Do think of some name yourself, Mr. Gridley ; I shall like anything that you like. To think of those dear babes having a fund — if that 's the right name — on purpose for 'em, and a promise of a legacy, — I hope they won't get *that* till they 're a hundred year old ! "

" What if we change Isosceles to Theodore, Mrs. Hopkins ? That means *the gift of God*, and the child has been a gift from Heaven, rather than a burden."

Mrs. Hopkins seized her apron, and held it to her eyes. She was weeping. " Theodore ! " she said, — " Theodore

My little brother's name, that I buried when I was only eleven year old. Drownded. The dearest little child that ever you see. I have got his little mug with Theodore on it now. Kep' o' purpose. Our little Sossy shall have it. Theodore P. Hopkins, — sha'n't it be, Mr. Gridley?"

" Well, if you say so ; but why that P., Mrs. Hopkins? Theodore Parker, is it?"

" Does n't P. stand for Pemberton, and is n't Father Pemberton the best man in the world — next to you, Mr. Gridley?"

" Well, well, Mrs. Hopkins, let it be so, if you like ; if you are suited, I am. Now about Helminthia ; there can't be any doubt about what we ought to call her, — surely the friend of orphans should be remembered in naming one of the objects of her charity."

" Cynthia Badlam Fund Hopkins," said the good woman triumphantly, — " is that what you mean?"

" Suppose we leave out one of the names, — four are too many. I think the general opinion will be that Helmintha should unite the names of her two benefactresses, — Cynthia Badlam Hopkins."

" Why, law! Mr. Gridley, is n't that nice? — Minthy and Cynthy, — there ain't but one letter of difference! Poor Cynthy would be pleased if she could know that one of our babes was to be called after her. She was dreadful fond of children."

On one of the sweetest Sundays that ever made Oxbow Village lovely, the Rev. Dr. Eliphalet Pemberton was summoned to officiate at three most interesting ceremonies, — a wedding and two christenings, one of the latter a double one.

18*

The first was celebrated at the house of the Rev. Mr. Stoker, between the Rev. Cyprian Eveleth and Bathsheba, daughter of the first-named clergyman. He could not be present on account of his great infirmity, but the door of his chamber was left open that he might hear the marriage service performed. The old, white-haired minister, assisted, as the papers said, by the bridegroom's father, conducted the ceremony according to the Episcopal form. When he came to those solemn words in which the husband promises fidelity to the wife so long as they both shall live, the nurse, who was watching, near the poor father, saw him bury his face in his pillow, and heard him murmur the words, " God be merciful to me a sinner ! "

The christenings were both to take place at the same service, in the old meeting-house. Colonel Clement Lindsay and Myrtle his wife came in, and stout Nurse Byloe bore their sturdy infant in her arms. A slip of paper was handed to the Reverend Doctor on which these words were written : — " The name is Charles Hazard."

The solemn and touching rite was then performed ; and Nurse Byloe disappeared with the child, its forehead glistening with the dew of its consecration.

Then, hand in hand, like the babes in the wood, marched up the broad aisle — marshalled by Mrs. Hopkins in front, and Mrs. Gifted Hopkins bringing up the rear — the two children hitherto known as Isosceles and Helminthia. They had been well schooled, and, as the mysterious and to them incomprehensible ceremony was enacted, maintained the most stoical aspect of tranquillity. In Mrs. Hopkins's words, " They looked like picters, and behaved like angels.

That evening, Sunday evening as it was, there was a

quiet meeting of some few friends at The Poplars. It was such a great occasion that the Sabbatical rules, never strict about Sunday evening, — which was, strictly speaking, secular time, — were relaxed. Father Pemberton was there, and Master Byles Gridley, of course, and the Rev. Ambrose Eveleth, with his son and his daughter-in-law, Bathsheba, and her mother, now in comfortable health, Aunt Silence and her husband, Doctor Hurlbut and his wife (Olive Eveleth that was), Jacob Penhallow, Esq., Mrs. Hopkins, her son and his wife (Susan Posey that was), the senior deacon of the old church (the admirer of the great Scott), the Editor-in-chief of the " Banner and Oracle," and in the background, Nurse Byloe and the privileged servant, Mistress Kitty Fagan, with a few others whose names we need not mention.

The evening was made pleasant with sacred music, and the fatigues of two long services repaired by such simple refections as would not turn the holy day into a day of labor. A large paper copy of the new edition of Byles Gridley's remarkable work was lying on the table. He never looked so happy, — could anything fill his cup fuller ? In the course of the evening Clement spoke of the many trials through which they had passed in common with vast numbers of their countrymen, and some of those peculiar dangers which Myrtle had had to encounter in the course of a life more eventful, and attended with more risks, perhaps, than most of them imagined. But Myrtle, he said, had always been specially cared for. He wished them to look upon the semblance of that protecting spirit who had been faithful to her in her gravest hours of trial and danger. If they would follow him into one of the esser apartments up stairs they would have an opportu-.ity to do so.

Myrtle wondered a little, but followed with the rest. They all ascended to the little projecting chamber, through the window of which her scarlet jacket caught the eyes of the boys paddling about on the river in those early days when Cyprian Eveleth gave it the name of the Fire-hang-bird's Nest.

The light fell softly but clearly on the dim and faded canvas from which looked the saintly features of the martyred woman, whose continued presence with her descendants was the old family legend. But underneath it Myrtle was surprised to see a small table with some closely covered object upon it. It was a mysterious arrangement, made without any knowledge on her part.

" Now, then, Kitty ! " Mr. Lindsay said.

Kitty Fagan, who had evidently been taught her part, stepped forward, and removed the cloth which concealed the unknown object. It was a lifelike marble bust of Master Byles Gridley.

" And this is what you have been working at so long, — is it, Clement ? " Myrtle said.

" Which is the image of your protector, Myrtle ? " he answered, smiling.

Myrtle Hazard Lindsay walked up to the bust and kissed its marble forehead, saying, " This is the face of my Guardian Angel."

THE END.